THE MYTH OF ARDEN

By Susan Marie Strom

DEDICATION

To all the little ones we loved without ever getting to meet…

Contents

1 The Myth 1

2 The Road to Pent 13

3 An Expansive City 28

4 The New Season 48

5 A Festival 68

6 A Fresh Good-Bye 78

7 The Shores of the River 90

8 The Road Unknown 103

9 A Night on the Town 113

10 Faverly 127

11 On the Road to Paultry 140

12 The Berkiss 153

13 The Isle of DeCorro 164

14 The Other Side of the City 177

15 Paultry 190

16 Ramoth's Return 202

17 A Prison 214

18 Return to Daven 232

19 A Warm Welcome 241

20 Tikii 257

21 An Unwinnable Confrontation 270

22 A Homecoming 279

23 A Calm 292

24 A Ghanrey Welcome 301

25 Nasairre 314

Acknowledgements

I sincerely thank those who helped me along the way, including my dear husband Kevin and children for their support, my knowledgeable friend William Cady for his input, and my mother Susan Wortas for her encouragement.

Those fools and wretched sons of Arden!
Their passions are too great,
and for them they fall like the grain at harvest.
Can they not see the wages of their destiny;
the dangers in the paths they choose?
Soon their lives I'll lay in shatter.
Arden's brothers for Faverly's sisters.

Chapter One: The Myth

The king lay sprawled out on the couch of his private chamber, which was adjacent to the throne room. His left hand rested over his eyes while his right laid by his side playing with the fringe of the blanket underneath him. He simply lay there, quietly pondering the events of that morning. His advisor, a great and noble idiot, had finally come to his senses and obeyed his king: the boy would die, and that pitiful man could not prevent it.

He let out a gentle groan as he rubbed his face, now trying to awaken himself. With a swift motion he swung his legs over the edge of the couch, and for a second, he leaned over with his elbows on his knees, his head spinning, before sitting straight up. The footsteps he heard that had riled him from his rest now paused outside his door.

"Come in you fool!" the king cried out.

The door pressed open, and a young man peeked inside. He was a new servant, fearful to enter the king's presence as most newcomers to the castle were. Hesitantly, he brought his fruit laden tray to the king. Arden was a rather warm and humid place. The fruit was available year-round, and though some might have thought it a treat, the king grumbled loudly at the sight of it; It had become mundane to him.

The server, however, was unaware of the King's displeasure. His whole body seemed bowed over slightly, carrying his offering ahead at arm's length. He placed the dish on the bench next to the king and, without lifting his head or turning around, floated to the door, closing it behind him. The king had to wait but a second till the door opened again, this time without the pageantry as before. Tall and mighty, the king's advisor entered.

"My king, I see the day finds you well," his advisor began.

"Why yes, my dear friend, it does. You have carried out your orders, and with such care! Tell me, how did you manage to conceal yourself?" the king asked.

"My lord, I fear I was not as successful as you had wished," the advisor warned. "I have just returned from the market. Already there are great murmurings among your subjects. They suspect foul play."

"Let them do as they please. What can even the greatest of my people do but speculate?" the king said plainly.

His advisor continued, "The consensus among those I spoke with is that the child died from the fall, or perhaps suffocated when the blankets fell on top of him. A few argue that the babe may have just died, as many infants do, and the nurse watching him was so afraid that she knocked the cradle over to make it look like an accident." The man paused for a moment before he admitted, "Still there are those that suspect it was murder."

"My good man, I fail to see the proof of murder!" the king blurted out, suddenly sitting up.

"Details of this morning, or rumors if you prefer, have spread quickly," the advisor explained. "They say that after the child was removed from the room, the weight of the cradle was so great that three maids together had to lift it back to its place, leaving all of the maids individually blameless of the accident. It is also rumored that the cradle was in no way damaged and that there was, therefore, no reason for it to fall unless a man pushed it. I feel it would be wise to destroy that cradle immediately."

The king thought for just a moment before he said, "I see. I shall have it hacked to pieces so that no man may see the truth behind it. As for the other details, they can be easily explained."

The advisor nodded before continuing, "Then the matter is settled, but another issue presents itself. What of the Sisters? I understand you wanting a son's death, but what threat could those girls present? They are just children."

"I have been thinking upon that myself," the king said as he laid back. It would seem that we ought to limit the stain of infant blood on our hands, yet the Sisters present a degree of danger if they are to produce the next heir to my kingdom."

"My lord, think on this with care," his advisor pled. "The people are torn. They had much hope in your son to unite them. Should they discover the Sisters to be deceased as well, it may cause an uprising. They shall suspect foul play. The countries that sent the girls will be most displeased if they are returned lifeless. For now, none would believe you capable of murdering your son, but if they die too who knows what they will be compelled to believe? It is better to let them live. Tell the people now that you will have another son. Restore their belief in you and keep them dumb at least until the prophecy is a myth and nothing more."

The king paused for a moment, trying to take in all he had heard. He stared down at the floor for a moment before his eyes returned to his advisor. The fool had done him one service in eliminating his heir. Now perhaps he could humor him and keep the girls for a little while.

He straightened up, and in an authoritative voice, he resumed. "Ever since this prophecy was uttered, my men have retained control of that cursed fortress in preparation of this time. I want you to send the girls there. Take them to Faverly as we were told to do. Take the map from my journey and return there. Take with you whatever you think the fortress will need along with ten servants to care for the girls and protect them. Only be careful whom you choose to take. I would not want any more unexpected heirs. In time, in a place so far away, they will be forgotten. Then we will decide."

And so, it was done. The girls were sent away while the king used the anger and confusion caused by his son's death to rally his people behind him. In time, a year or two at most, the memory of the Sisters would fade, and then he could dispatch them. They were just seven little babes: all girls, all born on the same day as the king's son, but each born in a different country. It was foretold that they would be the ancestors together of a single male who would unite the world in peace.

Years of darkness and famine followed that day, yet the king in his high walls was unaffected. Sixteen years passed to be exact before the Myth of Arden once again returned.

● ● ● ● ● ● ●

The king entered his bedroom many years later filled with a fantastic sense of warning. He shrugged his shoulders as if to shake off his feelings as he turned towards his bed and raised his right hand slowly. His fingertips caught the smooth softness of a cord that hung from the ceiling. Gently he pulled it till several young servants entered the room. They occupied themselves with every detail of the king's busy nightly ritual before exiting, closing the door stoutly behind them. The king now lay in his bed, staring into the darkness.

His mind wandered as he thought of the blind man who would entertain him with stories in the evenings and wondered what he must see: blackness, whiteness, red like the look of the sun through closed eyes? His stories were always so vivid as if the man could look into another world. The king had been told again and again by the eternally patient blind man that he saw nothing at all. However, the king had never seen what nothing was, so the form of it was foreign to him. Therefore, if the man had never seen anything how would he know what nothing looked like? He resolved only to inquire again of the man the next evening, for his eyes were growing heavy.

He closed them, but it was so dark that the room remained unchanged. For a minute he fancied that his eyes were still open, but after blinking several times, he became quite sure that his eyes were indeed closed.

He shifted his weight back and forth restlessly, trying to establish a comfortable position before he was able to take in a deep breath and set in. A moment elapsed. The room was completely silent. Again, he shifted between the covers. Yet as he did so he became aware of a noise. The silence was again broken.

"Who was that?" he pondered. A guard, or his wife perhaps? He sat straight up in his bed, his ears straining to listen. Again, there seemed to be no sound. Again, the silence beckoned. His drowsiness overwhelmed his fear. He motioned to lie back down when he thought he heard it again. His heart quickened. His breath grew shallow. It all seemed to be connected; connected to his premonition…

● ● ● ● ● ● ●

"What premonition?" interjected Marcus. His female passenger glared back at him, arms folded, a pursed frown on her lips. She strained to hold this pose as the carriage they were riding in swayed suddenly, forcing her to reach out and catch herself. Marcus tried to hold back a laugh. As he did, she noted the faint wrinkles beginning to form in the corners of his deep brown eyes. He was a handsome man with defined features and dark, tan skin. His hair was black and somewhat long.

"If you are going to keep interrupting me I'll never get through this story," she warned.

"What premonition? I do not remember hearing about one," Marcus insisted. Seeing her glare sharpen, he raised his hands in defeat before motioning her to go on.

Marcus's escorts had explained earlier to his befuddled passenger that under any other circumstances Marcus would not have been so cross. However, he had been traveling almost nonstop for the last four days to arrive at the capital city of Arden, which at that time was called Pent. The reason behind the urgent trip was unknown to all but Marcus, yet his royal position delegated him the luxury of such an expensive excursion unquestioned.

His young, female passenger had been spotted very early that morning as the caravan made way through a small town. Marcus immediately liked her. She had smooth pale skin and long, straight, dark hair. Her eyes were large and a brilliant shade of blue. In exchange for entertainment, Marcus had agreed to let her come along.

As it turned out, Marcus's escorts were being somewhat deceptive about the prince's temperament. In truth, Marcus was always known to be cross.

"As I said before, he had a premonition right before going to bed," the young girl annoyedly insisted.

"Of what, exactly?" Marcus shot back sourly.

"Of sugar, and rainbows! What do you think it was of? You should just know premonitions are always bad," she snapped back.

Marcus paused for a second, seemingly insulted before he gave out a hearty laugh. He hadn't been spoken to like this in some time. He found it almost endearing. This girl was either brave beyond measure or incredibly naive.

"Yes, I guess that is a silly question, please go on," he said with a charming smile.

His passenger smiled back and continued…

● ● ● ● ● ● ●

The king now heard another noise, something closer, louder and in the room! His hand unconsciously reached for the cord to his bell. He searched in the darkness. Where was it? Where had it gone? Where had it been? Within a split second, his hand had touched something else: something warmer than the still air and with solid form.

He gasped, trying to scream but no words could escape his throat. It seemed an eternity of wondering…waiting. Yet slowly there was a light: dim at first but growing steadily from the darkness itself. A form slowly grew out of the light. It was that of a man, nothing more, yet terrifying, nonetheless.

How had he gotten past the guards? Who was he? What did he want? Again the king struggled to speak, but it was to no avail. As the form grew denser, it placed a finger to its lips to show its desire for silence. The king ceased his efforts to speak, for it seemed he no longer could recall how to do so. The form walked about the room, his feet causing faint echoes to multiply in the king's head. The king seemed now almost completely incapacitated by this. He placed his hands over his ears and closed his eyes.

Suddenly able to speak the king boomed, "What do you want from me?" into the stillness that was everywhere but within him. "Why are you here?" he continued.

His words caused the figure to look up towards him smiling. His teeth glowed behind transparent lips! "You have come seeking contentment as all men do, but you do not yet know how to find it or how to keep it," the figure said, lips unmoving.

The king shuttered for it could not be.

The figure went on to say, "Why great king did you not listen to me? I offered you the world, but you would not follow my orders and for what? The Myth lives even if you deny it."

The king then came to himself; a ghost without a body cannot harm you. "But my son," he retorted, "he is dead."

"Ah, but the Myth lives!" the figure boasted.

"Impossible!" replied the king incredulously.

"The future is never absolute. By telling you that which is not certain I was taking a risk. Your actions have changed the course of history for Arden," the figure explained.

"What do you mean? How can a man do that?" the king asked, now looking around for his robe. "Only what was meant to be has transpired."

The form, still smiling, laughed under his breath. "Of course, you are of a small mind. Be content to know that another has been chosen to rule at the time of your death," it said.

"Who?" the king exclaimed.

"Who controls the waves that roll to shore? What use is a fire that burns no more? Where are the flowers before they grow, and when the sun sets where does it go?" the figure replied.

The king stared, baffled. Next, he spoke, "You may think you are clever, but I know where the Sisters are! They..."

"Will be dead by morning?" the spirit interjected. "Not likely. Remember all those preparations you entrusted with your advisor Ramoth? Well, it's not his fault, but what if something, or dare I say, someone, was overlooked? Perhaps one, just one child was accidentally misplaced? Who knows?"

"You are trying to confuse me, but I will not allow it! Ramoth will vouch for himself when I have the time for it, but for now, I must be on my way. Even six dead Sisters is better than all living. Even if one of them is destroyed, the myth will be no more! I am not as afraid of you as you may think. I am the most powerful man alive. And you? You are some transparent fool. Tomorrow at the sun's rise I shall go to the fortress in the Venom Mountains. I will go to Faverly and destroy them all!"

"Go right ahead. Perhaps that is what I desire," the figure said.

"Lies, all lies to distract me from my course!" the king insisted. "Begone! You cannot stop me! My holy men shall rid you from this castle tomorrow! No, this very night!"

With that, the king clumsily pulled the cord next to his bed. Before long a small fleet of servants were in the room trying to make sense of the king's ramblings. The king was soon out of bed, arms flailing. He demanded to see his wife, who soon appeared of her own accord to comfort him. The whole castle was awakened within a matter of an hour as all were needed in the preparations.

The servants ran from this place to that, except for Ramoth himself, who sat behind the meek desk set in the corner of his chamber. His eyes were beginning to blur the words that he could see only by candlelight. In one hand was a response from Cavner, a mining country, confirming the authenticity of some jewels delivered to the castle. In his other was a ring: silver washed in gold.

He turned his attention from the page to the ring, which he rolled between his large fingers making it seem small by comparison. The candlelight reflected off of the tiny filigree wrapped around the band. It was intended, along with a few other small, jeweled pieces, for the wife he never had. His remorse in never spending time apart from his job to find one weighed heavily on him. Yet as before, the ring was soon back in the bottom drawer of his desk as he pulled out the clean sheet of parchment that was needed to send a reply to the country of Cavner.

He started the letter, read over what he had written and then groaned at the sight of it. He seemed unable to think clearly and seeing as this letter had sat unanswered for the last few weeks, he decided to leave the task till morning. He began to prepare for sleep, removing his robes slowly and taking care to place each so that it would not wrinkle.

Before he could finish, a light knock presented itself at the door. Again he groaned as he clumsily returned the articles he had just removed to his shoulders and walked to the door. It was Kayla, the queen.

"Ramoth, the king has gone mad! He speaks rubbish of going to find his sisters and destroy them," she said as she rushed into the room.

"His sisters? You mean the Sisters of Faverly?" Ramoth asked.

"Perhaps that is what he meant," Kayla replied. She seemed distracted by his state of undress.

"Then I must go! I must stop him!" Ramoth said as he turned from her to hasten to the king's chambers. The slightest whimper from the queen's lips was all that was needed to draw him back to her. He froze in his tracks, turning towards her now to see she was holding back tears. "Is something the matter?" he asked tenderly. Slowly he walked back to her and took her hand in his.

She looked pleadingly into his eyes and said, "Please don't go, Ramoth. The king is in such a rush; He asks for only his army. Let him go."

"You expect me to stay when he plans on killing seven innocent girls?" Ramoth asked in surprise.

"I knew you would not be pleased with the idea, but I did not tell you his plans so that you could chase him down!" Kayla scoffed.

"But why then?" Ramoth asked.

"Ramoth, this is our only chance!" Kayla said as she took his hands into her own. "If the king does leave tonight then we have the perfect opportunity to run away together. We can say we are going with him when in reality we are running as far away as we can."

"But Kayla, you speak nonsense! We would surely be caught. Besides, you cannot expect me to throw away the last years I've spent saving them, only to let them go now!" Ramoth said as he motioned to go.

"Oh, you fool," Kayla lamented. "It has been so many years that have now elapsed since you rode off with those infants to Faverly. Why make the time any greater? Simply think on it. What are sixteen years in the breath of your life? Why sacrifice all the years of happiness we could have to make the last worth it?"

Ramoth looked at her tenderly and said, "What joy could I have knowing those girls died because of my selfishness? I was there for all those early years. I watched them grow and learn. If only you could appreciate that! It was the king that kept us apart. He sent me a dozen different places to keep me from returning all these years just so that we could not be together."

"Those little dogs are lucky to have been spared the famine in their fortress all these years and to have lived as well as they have lacking noble blood. Let them die," Kayla said as she turned away from Ramoth.

"Kayla, what has come over you? Why do you hate them so?" Ramoth asked, his large hands leading her back to him.

"It should have been them years ago! Not my little boy, but my husband..." She trailed off for a moment, her eyes searching the floor. "Do you not see all I have given for nothing? My son is dead, and my husband no longer even wishes to look at me. How then can I now lose you too?"

She broke into tears then, falling to the ground at the thought of her only child taken for no reason. Ramoth lifted her and carried her to the bed so she could rest on its edge. He sat next to her, his arm around her. Her tears slowed after a few minutes, and she again looked at him.

"Kayla, it was just a senseless accident. Forget about it," Ramoth tried to assure her.

"Forget?" the queen asked. "It has been so long since you left for Faverly, gone for years trying to make their lives better while I remained, wandering the halls thinking of our love while my husband remains estranged to me. And yet it seems as if no time has passed between us at all. Why can we not have a second chance together?" She searched his eyes, hoping for a response.

"Hush my dear and think not of such things," was Ramoth's reply.

"Why not?" she implored, looking deep into his eyes.

"You know why. The king would have my head for it! Once I was foolish and young. Forgive me for that. Now come, I must go to him and convince him to stay," Ramoth said as he again went to leave.

"Have my words no sway? Stay with me! I need you!" she begged, wrapping herself around his arm so he could not leave.

Ramoth turned back and looked into Kayla's eyes. He whispered to her, "And they need me. The seven of them do weigh out just us two."

"And what if you go and cannot change his mind?" Kayla pled.

Ramoth shrugged and said, "Then I must go with him and try to sway him there."

Kayla looked away and lamented, "Then, either way, we cannot be together?"

"Kayla, either way, you belong to another," Ramoth said as he removed her arms from his.

"That is not how you felt before," Kayla called after him as he left.

"Silence. Be away from here, as I must be away," Ramoth said as he hurried to the king's private chamber."

Chapter Two: The Road to Pent

"Are you hungry?" Marcus interrupted as he removed a small basket from a compartment under his chair. "There is not much, just some leftover fruit and cheese, but the castle is only a few more hours from here so it will go to waste if we do not eat it now." He reached into the parcel and removed an apple. "Here, this is still good." He said as he stood up in the carriage and sat next to the girl. He leaned in close to her with the fruit in front of him. She instinctively leaned away, and for a second, he paused staring into her eyes before smiling jokingly. They both laughed as she took the fruit.

"Thank you. You are most kind," the young girl said before she took a bite.

"It is nothing. At the start of the trip, I had all sorts of wonders. All that is left is this." He trailed off, realizing his subject choice was a little poor. "Well, food is food!" he said chuckling as he took a bite of his apple. "What did you say your name was again?"

"You never asked," the girl pointed out.

"How rude of me, please tell it to me, then," Marcus said between bites.

"Everyone calls me Anny. It is short for Antoinette," the girl explained.

"How wise of you to shorten it!" Marcus teased.

Anny smiled and said, "You know you do surprise me, Marcus. They say you are a great prince..."

"But I don't act like one," Marcus interrupted her. "True, true, it is all my brothers' fault. I was the middle of three brothers. My elder brother was to assume the throne, but he died of a strange illness. My remaining brother was then to assume the throne, but he also fell to an untimely death."

Anny gasped horrified.

Marcus chuckled, reassuringly clarifying, "the death I speak of is a spiritual one! The poor fool lives on, but only for himself. He has taken the luxury to go traipsing off looking for some deep spiritual meaning to life where there isn't any. The older one I mean. No, just the older one. The younger he is dead: yes, dead as dead can be.

"They were so concerned with the crown when they were young, but I wanted nothing to do with it. In fact, since I was ten, I've been wandering these roads in search of real wisdom and adventure!"

"And did you find it?" Anny asked when he had finally stopped.

"Well, a little I suppose before these damn guards tracked me down and brought me back home," Marcus said as he made a rude gesture out the window. "Actually, it was on one of my last trips that I heard this story you speak now, but it has to be years since those times, fifteen maybe twenty."

"You mean you have heard this story before?" Anny said surprised.

Marcus chuckled. "Well of course! Who has not heard the famed story 'The Myth of Arden'! Though no one tells it quite as well as you do. Tell me again where you first heard it."

"My mother told it to me. She was the head cook in a great house," Anny said as she gazed out the window.

"Ah, and whose house was that?" Marcus asked. He had finished his apple and threw the core out the window in front of Anny's gaze.

Anny looked back at him disgruntled and said, "Well it was a great house in the small town near where you found me. I would not be surprised if you had never heard of it."

"I have been from one coast to the other of this silly country. I bet I have heard of the place and probably dined there too," Marcus assured her.

"Well, the village nearby is called Fay Hill," Anny said hesitantly.

14

"Ah, good old Fay Hill! That is just outside of Reed? Am I remembering correctly?" Marcus asked jovially.

"You could not have possibly heard of it!" Anny insisted.

"And why not?" Marcus quipped.

"Because it is so small!" the girl replied while crossing her arms.

"Why I was there just three years ago signing a peace treaty with those fine people, though I do not remember you being there. It is nearer to the border of Paultry in Arden right?" Marcus said with a triumphant smile.

"Yes. I guess it is," Anny conceded.

"See, but what I do not quite understand is why a young and pretty girl such as yourself would be traveling alone from there. Come now, you can tell me," the man said with a wink.

Anny's shoulders slumped, and she went on to explain, "Well, suffice to say all of my family is dead and so I am seeking refuge at the nearest castle. I hear there are jobs available that will provide food and shelter."

"But that is no good," Marcus said firmly. "You would be stuck there the rest of your life! Why not stay at the estate and indenture yourself there? They would treat you much better."

"I have no skills," she said with a sigh as she held out her hands as if to prove that they were worthless.

"But you grew up in a great house. You must have learned something," Marcus pointed out.

"I am sorry I did not," Anny said. "I must be a slow learner."

Marcus slapped his hands together and said, "Well in the least you can tell stories."

"That is the only story I know," Anny confessed sadly.

"But you tell it so well!" Marcus assured her. "Tell you what, you go ahead and take a position at the castle in Pent, which is where we are going. If by the time I must leave the castle for my own, you are not happy I will pay your fees and take you as my own. Once at my castle, you would be treated with the best of care, and I will make certain of it."

Anny looked at him skeptically. She was sure she knew exactly why he would make such an offer, and it had nothing to do with chivalry. "But why would you do that?" she finally mustered the courage to ask.

Marcus turned to her, and for a brief moment as he spoke she felt like a mask had slipped from his face. "Because I know you are lying to me about certain things, and I hope that by being nice you may open up a little to me," he said softly.

"But I am not lying!" she blurted out, her face turning all shades of red.

"If you say so," Marcus said.

"Well, why should I tell you anything anyway?" Anny said, flustered.

Marcus shrugged his shoulders and said, "You are right. You are under no compulsion, but I wish you would trust me a little."

They sat for a moment, the both of them, with arms crossed staring out opposite windows of the carriage.

"He is mocking me," the young girl thought to herself. "Tell me, how famous is this story I tell you?" Anny said, finally breaking the silence.

"I would guess everyone alive knows it or at least everyone who has a common border with Arden, which is everyone," Marcus informed her.

"And who told it to you?" Anny asked.

"I have just heard it my whole life," Marcus said dismissively. "Except, I should say that if you wish to tell it to anyone else, then you ought to get the names right."

"What do you mean?" Anny asked.

"Well it is the king who is called Ramoth," Marcus began. "Ramoth means 'great leader', so you can see it is more of a title than a name. But you do have the queen's name right, which is quite impressive. As for this strange man who you call Ramoth, perhaps he was Cailar as he seems to have the position of head advisor. You know: one who holds no words in the king's presence."

"Well then, shall I finish this great story or would you have me stop seeing as you know it already?" Anny asked dejectedly.

"No, no, go on!" Marcus insisted. "I do wish to see how it ends according to you though you do realize that the king you speak of is one of my best friends but forget that now as this story is entirely fiction."

Anny nodded and agreed, "Yes, it is."

"Then continue, and I will try not to let the name's scrambling get in the way of the story," Marcus said as he leaned back into his seat.

"Well, I left off when Ramoth had gone to see the king then?" Anny tried to recall.

"Yes, yes. Go on," Marcus muttered.

Taking a deep breath, Anny continued...

● ● ● ● ● ● ●

The throne room itself was open to the central courtyard, which allowed billows of starlight to streak the floor. These also found their way into the side chamber, equally unbarred unless heavy doors blocked three separate archways. One of these doors was open, allowing a stream of lamplight to spill across the sections of starlight. Ramoth entered the throne room to find the king standing in his private chamber talking to the general who controlled his army.

"But my lord, I do not understand the urgency in your request. To have a thousand horses by sunrise is impossible. The most I could offer would be fifty," the general explained.

"Fifty? That is not enough!" the king insisted, slamming his hand onto a table.

"Then bend to my expertise and allow me to know where it is we are to attack," the general pled. He waited as the king took a drink.

"Faverly!" the king said as he wiped a drop of wine from his lips, his cup landing with a heavy thud.

"Yes, I know, but I have never heard of this town," the general said impatiently.

"It is not a town!" the king scoffed. "It is a fortress, an old castle built into the southern edge of a craggy mountain. On the east is a field, but on the north side is the steep mountain, which is too sheer to climb down. We will have to guard the door until they starve and let us in."

"How many people are we talking about?" the general inquired.

"There are about fifteen inhabitants there that must be killed as soon as possible," the king explained.

The general thought about it for a moment then asked, "Fifty warriors?"

The king rolled his eyes impatiently. "No, fifteen! Fifteen servants," he carefully enunciated.

Ignoring the insult the general continued, "Then ten horsemen should be more than adequate with five-foot soldiers to be safe. If they are servants, they will open the doors to you."

"But what if they do not?" the king speculated. "We will need force!"

Ramoth paused, waiting for the right moment to interrupt the conversation. He stood patiently as the king rolled around in circles confusing his general with his rambling words and roughly drawn sketches. After much time had passed, he could hold back no more and entered the chamber. The king turned to him for but a moment before returning his attention to his general.

"If we fail it could be the end of Arden," he continued in a foreboding tone. "I will not see one of them escape."

"But my king," interrupted Ramoth, "is it necessary to kill all who are at Faverly? Why kill the servants?"

"I would think it would be quite obvious," the king retorted sharply. "We cannot risk even one of them telling what we did."

"And what exactly is that?" Ramoth accused. "If you are ashamed we might seek alternatives."

"Remember yourself Ramoth," the king warned. "Your tone does not sit well with me. I understood you would be against me going to the fortress to take care of those Sisters as you always have, but the time has now come. I can no longer put my throne in jeopardy over a handful of little girls. We leave tomorrow with or without you. You had your fun and spared them these past years, but the end is now! I can no longer hold my judgment on them. Even you must agree that it is better to kill them than to risk another war with Pacia. Though we would most certainly win, the amount of bloodshed would be great on both sides and for what? A thousand soldiers for seven little brats?"

"My lord, I do not see the threat they present. They are just children! Have you lost your mind that you, the great conqueror of nations, is afraid of a few girls?" Ramoth asked as he paced about the room.

"Silence! I suggest that if you wish to keep your life, you help me find my way to Faverly. Once the girls are disposed of I will decide about the servants, but no promises. Understood?" the king asked. He was glaring at Ramoth with glassy eyes.

Ramoth stopped pacing and looked over to his king. "Your wish is my own, my king. As you command, so shall I obey," he assured him.

"Good. Then get ready," the king said as he motioned for both men to go.

Ramoth turned to leave almost running into a male servant with sweat pouring down his ghost white face.

"My king, forgive my intrusion," the servant begged between heavy breaths, "but there is terrible news from the west quarters!"

"Well speak fool!" the king demanded.

"Your queen: she has been found in a most unpleasant state!" the servant blurted out. Ramoth's eyes widened in disbelief.

"What are you speaking of?" the king demanded.

"I know not the details, my king. I was only told to summon you to her quarters immediately! Please forgive me!" the servant said as he began to back out of the room.

Before the servant could finish, the king had pushed him to the ground and was storming off to the west wing of the castle where his wife's bedroom was located.

Ramoth and the king arrived at the queen's room to find it well lit by the fireplace on the far wall to the doorway. In the corner to the left of this place was a vanity. It had a sizeable silver-backed glass knocked from its brackets and shattered into a thousand pieces across the floor. Each piece sparkled as it caught the light of the fire from the air. On the wall to the right of the fireplace was the queen's bed. Their attention now turned to it, and they could hear the queen's maid weeping.

The king stormed towards her, stopping suddenly only a foot from her realizing the queen was laying in the bed with her head resting on the maid's lap. She seemed sleeping except for many deep scratches on the palms of her hands and feet. The maid was stroking the queen's hair, the tears running down her face.

"What has happened here?" the king shouted. The maid let out a deep wail. "You dog, tell me what has happened to my wife!" he rumbled.

The maid, now frightened, turned her head to him and said, "My king, she came to my room but a few moments ago in a lowly mood. She said she feared to be alone. I brought her back here, and when I saw the mirror smashed, I asked what had come of it. She said she wished to die and had pulled it down to cut herself with it, but it had smashed into fine pieces. It was then I saw all of the small cuts on her hands and feet.

"And did she say what was troubling her?" Ramoth asked.

"No," the maid stumbled, "just that she was very sad. I put her to bed and thought she had fallen asleep. So I went back to my room. However, when I arrived I realized a small vile I keep in my pocket was missing. She had taken

20

it. I ran back here, but she had swallowed the whole thing before I arrived."

"And what was in the vile?" Ramoth asked, now growing more outwardly panicked.

"Te Berry Elixir: I use it to help me sleep. A drop in a pitcher of water is enough for a week, but she drank the entire contents." Again her tears overcame her. "I know for this I must die. Please do not take me to trial!"

She wept now so great that she hardly could take a breath. Ramoth stood in disbelief, his hands numb and his face cold. The king walked to the bed, lifted his wife from the maid's arms and shook her. She was limp, and not a sign of life was still with her.

The king stood still for a moment, looking at her still face in the fire's light. She seemed but asleep, but then he looked at her chest and saw it was still and she drew no breath. He continued to watch while waiting for it to rise, but it did not. He then dropped her to the ground with the care given to a discarded shoe.

"She is dead," he thought to himself before he spoke, "Old woman, you are hardly worth the rope I would need to hang you."

The servant looked up to him with the faintest of hope at his last words as the king left. Ramoth looked at the servant, but she seemed lost in her own world. He decided to take the risk, his last chance, and walked over to the queen. He laid her out on her back and stroked her hair as the old woman had been doing.

"This is my fault," he said to her under his breath. Then to himself, he thought, "I killed her because I would not stay. What is so great about me?" He then fell over her, his head resting on her chest as he cried.

Some guards entered, saying nothing as they came to take the dead queen's body and her maid away. Ramoth did not even hear the maid's cries as she was carried away to her death. He felt too alone.

Now it was customary in those days of Arden that at the death of a family member one did not travel abroad for the sake of morning and remembrance for a certain length of time. Ramoth was overcome but gathered the strength to convince the king he ought not to go so soon to Faverly as it would sully his reputation.

So one more month passed as Ramoth mourned and the king sought comfort where he had always been able to find it, but the king's women were only able to soothe him for those few weeks. Soon he was once again compelled to go, and so Ramoth went with him.

Another month passed as Ramoth tried to find his way back to Faverly. He claimed that his memories of the convoluted forest trails that led there had faded, and it was slow moving with the twenty horsemen and ten foot soldiers the king and his general finally decided upon. There were also the three carriages needed for the king: one for him and two as decoys with five personal guards to the king surrounding each one. Carts, food, and blankets had to be carried, and the slowness of the travel compounded by multiple wrong turns and detours to get more supplies.

However, they did finally arrive, and to the general's relief, the gates were opened to them. They filed into the courtyard and there set up camp inside the fortified walls of Faverly.

None of the guards knew the point of the journey and considered this place just another stop on the way. None could fathom this barely inhabited fortress was their intended target. They remained camped there for the night, resting from the hard journey and leaching off of the fortress's resources…

● ● ● ● ● ● ●

"And how do you know all that?" Marcus taunted. "It is as if you were there."

"Well, maybe I was! Goodness, you are cynical for such a young man," Anny admonished him.

Marcus was about to comment to the fact that had she been there she should be dead right now. Instead, he

22

decided to give her a break. "Come now, do guess my age. You'll never be able to!" he suddenly quipped.

Taken aback Anny said, "What would be the point?"

"Just do it!" Marcus egged her on.

"Fine, you are," she paused, trying to think it through, "thirty-eight."

"Ha! Thirty-three," Marcus boasted. "No one ever gets it right. And how old did you say you were?"

"Seventeen, I think. Maybe eighteen," Anny said after thinking it over for a minute.

"A good age to be! I miss those days," Marcus said gleefully. "Well, actually I do not. I was nineteen when my father finally tracked me down and dragged me back home from my joyous travels."

"Yes, you never fail an opportunity in bringing it up," Anny muttered to herself.

"Well it always bothers me most when I am traveling," Marcus explained. "Take this caravan for example. Ten horsemen are surrounding this one little cart and for what? It just says, 'please, try and attack me!' I would have been better off if they let me go by myself, but my poor father is wary of losing yet another son, and so I must go his way. I could have been to Pent yesterday if I had gone myself. You see there are just as many horsemen as would be needed to storm a fortress!"

The young girl did not so much as crack a smile at his last comment. "And why are you in such a rush? None of your companions seem to know," she said.

"Why should I tell you?" Marcus asked.

"You wish me to trust you? How can you expect that if you are not honest with me?" Anny countered back.

"Please, you could care less what I think of you. You are just curious," Marcus surmised.

"So what if I am?" Anny said with a grin. "If you did not have something to hide you would just tell me."

Marcus rolled his eyes and said, "Fine, I have some unfinished business to attend to."

"Like what?" Anny asked innocently.

Marcus went to say something but stopped himself and said instead, "Oh, border disputes mostly, but now I must be sure to ask him if he has any idea what Te Berry Elixir is. I for one have never heard of it."

"It is the honey of the lower class. You probably have much too refined a taste for it," Anny mused as she wondered who the man was that Marcus was referring to.

"But what if the queen was faking her death? What if it had been a clever plot to make the king think she was dead? Then she and your Ramoth could run off together!" Marcus conjectured happily.

"I am afraid that is not what happened though. If that were true that is what I would have said, but the queen is indeed dead," Anny lamented.

"All the more to give credence to your words should they follow some fact I suppose, but you are wrong about her death for it is just as the king said it was. She died from vanity!" Marcus said as he smiled broadly.

Anny shook her head from side to side as she rolled her eyes. Marcus only laughed, though inside one half of him scolded the other half for being so heartless.

● ● ● ● ● ● ●

Just ten or so miles away from Marcus's carriage in the sprawling city of Pent the king of Arden rolled over for the last time in his burdened sleep. The king, like most of the inhabitants of Pent, had a light tan complexion. His eyes were small and brown, topped by bushy, thick eyebrows. After so many years of decadence, his belly had grown large and round. Unlike others in his court, he liked to have an unkempt beard which was perhaps why he looked much older than he truly was. He rubbed his face, scratching at the hairs as his door opened and Cailar, his chief advisor, arrived with news of the day.

Cailar was, by comparison, much thinner and somewhat gangly in appearance. Though his complexion was like that of the King's his small, squinty eyes were bright blue. He

24

kept a clean-shaven face and was in every other way neatly coiffed with his short hair beginning to grey.

The king tended to sleep very late into the day as matters needing his attention did not usually come to light until noon had shone its course. This was convenient, however, as the king tended to stay up very late. Once asleep, he was known to awaken many times from nightmares and remembrances.

He was presently neither awake nor asleep, but rather somewhere between wandering through dreams as he came to realize Cailar's looming arrival. He groaned inside at the thought and lay for another moment desperately trying to remember what had occupied his mind just the moment before. He heard his door creak open and familiar footsteps made their way into the room. With the window curtains drawn, the footsteps approached the bed.

"Arise, dearest king! The day has come," Cailar said. He seemed uncharacteristically cheerful. Behind him, as there always seemed to be a procession of servants following his command, marched several men ready to prepare the king for his day.

"Another day, how I loathe it," the king replied. "Again I am right back to where I started. What some find comfort in I find only despair. The sun will rise only to set. The stars shine only to fade again. The trees bud and bloom only to return to their frail skeletons once more, devoid of life and color. Again I rise. Again I dress. Again shall I eat, yet again shall I hunger. Again I lie down. Again I rest. Again I tire. What is the point if life is just a constant cycle of birth and death? A play, a dance that is continuous in length, yet seems to double back on itself. If there is a word for life, then it is 'again'."

"We speak of this every morning my king. Have you found no answer that pleases you?" Cailar said as the servants began to ready the room for the king.

"None. What have you to offer today as a possibility?" Ramoth said as he began to pull at his blankets.

"The court jester has said, 'the meaning of life is to laugh,'" Cailar offered.

"And I should take his advice?" Ramoth chuckled half-heartedly.

"Do cheer yourself, my lord," Cailar said. "Marcus shall be here soon."

For the first time, Ramoth's eyes lit up as he said, "My dear friend! How I have awaited his return." The king finally sat up in bed, rubbing his eyes. The servants descended upon him hoping to finish their work before he was fully awake.

"A messenger appeared just a short while ago announcing his imminent arrival," Cailar assured him.

"Good, good," Ramoth said as a servant struggled to comb Ramoth's hair, "and what other news of the country have you brought me?

"None else sir. Nothing new has developed in the last night that concerns the country," Cailar said. Then after hesitating a moment, he continued, "There is one of personal concern that has presented itself."

"And what might that be?" Ramoth asked disinterestedly.

"There is a particular maid who works in the kitchen much as her mother did. She is young and somewhat fair," Cailar began.

"Fair?" Ramoth interrupted.

"Well, she is not as fair as your ladies, but as she belongs to you I would like your blessing to marry her," Cailar said. "You know I am growing in years and she is young."

King Ramoth smirked to himself. "Growing in years indeed!" he thought. The fact that the two were close in age never crossed his mind. Aloud he merely commented, "Tell me, what is her name?"

"Sonia, my lord," Cailar quickly replied.

Ramoth made a face and said, "Sonia? I have never heard of her, but I am sure you two will be happy anyway."

"Thank you, my king!" Cailar said with a bow. "May this gracious act bring many blessings upon your kingdom."

"Now be gone with you. I need to be alone, and you need to be ready for Marcus's arrival," Ramoth gruffly said as he shooed the servants away.

Cailar bowed again and exited. The king by now was dressed and his servants gone. The king left for his breakfast and to handle the affairs of the evening, his mood slightly cheered by the thought that his friend would soon arrive.

Chapter Three: An Expansive City

Meanwhile, Marcus continued to pry into Anny's past as one of his horsemen rode up next to the carriage's window.

"My lord, Prince Marcus!" he began. "We approach Pent. We shall be at the castle's gates shortly!"

"Ah, fine news!" Marcus said, clapping his hands together. "You see, no time at all to go!" He turned his attention to the landscape now passing by the window as the horseman rode on ahead of the caravan. They were traveling through some shallow woods now, but soon these would disappear as the stone walls of the city of Pent grew up.

Pent was tall and crowded. It was by far the largest city in all of Arden having doubled in size again and again in recent years. The promise of work drew in the lowly while the promise of currying the king's favor drew in the wealthy. As such, the new was continually expanding, built sloppily on top of the old giving one the feeling that at any minute any building might collapse onto the narrow streets. There was always the noise of people wandering about and smoke from pipes drifting through the air. This mixed with the aroma of heavily spiced sausage: a delicacy that had become recently popular.

Marcus and Anny entered the city in silence and made way to the castle, which was surrounded by a wall of its own. Taking in the sight of the city turned Anny's stomach. She had expected splendor, but instead it was as if the city were a mold covering the land. The carriage stopped just inside the castle walls.

"I am afraid this is where we end our trip together," Marcus said. "I will truly miss your company."

"But you have not heard the rest of the story," Anny said apologetically.

Marcus assured her, "You can tell it to me when we travel together to Paultry as I know we shall do. If we do not, then I am sure I know how it ends or at least how the king would wish I knew it. Good luck here, Anny. I will be sure to contact you before I leave in a week."

"If you must. Good-bye, Prince Marcus," Anny said as she climbed out of the carriage.

"No, no! Do call me Marcus, everyone else does," Marcus called after her.

"As you wish, my lord Marcus. Good luck with your border disputes," Anny said as she winked at him. She stood in the road watching his carriage roll away and then looked at the castle. It was imposing and thick, made of large blocks of stone. It seemed impressively tall, wide, and impenetrable. She stood at the gate staring. It had not occurred to her till that moment to be afraid, perhaps because she had never envisioned so large a place.

The calm Marcus presented now faded as shrills of fear and frustration filled the young girl staring at the megalith known as the Castle of Pent. She was there in that moment, clinging to the few meager possessions she carried with her staring at the walls.

"I'm so afraid! I cannot do this!" she thought to herself as she felt her feet carrying her towards the castle's entrance. Suddenly she stopped. Her mind raced. It was too late to turn back now, or was it? "I can go anywhere else, do anything else: except this. I cannot do this at all," she thought as she felt her soul shaking. She tightened her grasp on the small package she carried and ceased shaking. Gently she closed her eyes hoping for a moment to regain herself, but they soon snapped open as she feared her own darkness.

Taking as wide a look around as she could without looking out of place she again evaluated her situation. She tried to take in all of the sites: the dozens of people surrounding her, milling about doing as they must. Carts moved in straight lines heading ultimately to various roads just outside the gate's hinged doors. People chattered and clamored, their cries emanated from this direction while laughter drifted from yet another. The stench was incredible. How could these people create such a smell?

Her feet again motioned to move forward, but her entire body resisted this time. She could barely breathe. She had become petrified by fear. A loud crash sounded behind her, and she was suddenly able to spin around to the greetings of two large horses, and the man sitting in the cart pulled behind them.

"Out of the way! Do you want me to run you down?" he shouted. This sudden thrusting of rudeness onto her lap caused Anny to snap out of her daze in a fit of fiery anger.

"Good Sir, I beg your pardon, but I do believe I was here first," she said in as mock a tone as she could muster.

"Well," he retorted, removing his hat as he bowed, "I am quite sorry if I've offended you, madame, but this here is my route and I intend on taking it!" He began to gently shake on the reigns and his horses both started up, forcing his way past her. Anny watched the cart disappear into the crowd. She was so blinded by her rage that she did not notice the cart behind the first pull up to her.

"Can I help you miss?" the man muttered. The obvious sincerity in his voice and the quiet collectiveness of it startled Anny causing her to seek the owner.

"Pardon me?" she said in half disbelief as she turned around.

"I said, 'can I help you'?" the man in the cart said. He was homely but well-built with authority in his posture and voice. The sun glistened off his bald head and deep tan.

Gingerly he reached down and grabbed the young girl's arm, effectively hoisting her onto the cart right next to him in one smooth motion. She stared at him, startled at his forwardness. Immediately she was both taken and suspicious of him. "The name's Jax. It's not my real name mind you, but everyone calls me it none the less so you might as well too."

"Jax?" Anny repeated. Taking a closer look, she noted the man before her was overly tall and muscular with a deep voice to match. He carried himself somewhat awkwardly. He had a round nose and small, flashing brown eyes.

"It comes from my handiness at trials with the ax. My real name's Jack, then it was 'Jack the ax'. Now they just say 'Jax'." Noticing the girl had lost interest sometime before he asked, "And what's your name?"

"My friends all call me..." for a moment she hesitated. "Anny." Jax's smile broadened as he looked at her, yet his eyes seemed somehow to not be focused on her face.

"Heading towards the castle?" Jax asked as the cart began to move. "I figured you must be. I've seen dozens of pretty girls just like you these past couple of years grabbing their bags and expecting an immediate audience with the king. Don't get me wrong or anything, you're mighty well suited for the job, and things have been well this year. What's one more to the king, right?"

"I beg your pardon, but what are you implying?" Anny scoffed.

"You're here to see the king about a job, right?" Jax asked plainly. "In the beginning, the king would have to send out for girls, but lately they just come all by themselves hoping to get some jewels or nice shoes. Maybe get some gold."

Anny's jaw dropped and her face flushed. She stammered, "If you are implying, and I dare say that you are, that I am here to become a member of the king's 'close company' then you are quite mistaken, and I would appreciate you letting me off this cart this very instant!" She grabbed the edge of her seat and turned as if to jump off for the cart was not moving all that quickly.

"Now, now, don't get me wrong!" Jax said, reaching out again for her arm and returning her to her seat. "I only was guessing." He looked at her with apologetic eyes and seeing it was better to ride than to walk to where she knew not she again settled down staring at the road ahead.

"I do not mean to be so rude you understand, but I do not like people that assume so much," she said, trying to mend the situation. Jax smiled and nodded as she spoke, seeming to enjoy so much attention from her. "I am here to get a job as a…cook. My mother was one, and she taught me well. Yes, very, very well!"

"Ah yes, a new cook is always welcomed. I am sorry, Anny. But look, only two kinds of women come to this castle: the ones who want the wealth and fame that only the king could afford to give them and the poor girls in love with a soldier who cannot afford to provide for them yet. They are kept safe here for their efforts till their man is well established and can care for them. The whole staff is just stocked full of them: silly children waiting for the day they can live happily ever after.

The head cook is one such a lady. Her name is Sonia, and she's got a heart of pure gold. She means to marry one of my men, a boy by the name of Paul. If ever two were meant to be together then it is them. Been here going on three years now just waiting for a chance. One more and the two should have enough to leave and get a fair place. So who had the honor of stealing your heart that you would wait that long?"

"There is no one. I simply need to make some money," Anny confessed.

"Well then, you ought to be careful. There are lots of men here who only take what others don't want or haven't claimed. But that's no problem. I'll look after you myself. I may look young, but I'm the head of this castle's guards. If anyone gives you trouble you just come to me, and I'll get them good. I'll be sure to put out the word that you are off limits too. Who knows, maybe you'll meet someone nice. I only remember one other girl coming here like you are. She was married within a month!"

"Really?" Anny scoffed, though to herself she thought that Jax did not look all that young. She suddenly thought of Marcus and then scolded herself as she wondered why she had thought of him at all.

"Honest truth," Jax assured her.

"What's in the cart?" she asked, trying to change the subject.

Jax laughed as he said, "You don't want to know. I've just come from a trial. It was a great one. The man refused to confess till they chopped off both of his feet, hands, and ears!"

"Impossible!" Anny gasped.

"Indeed! Should have just confessed and gone right to the block, but that's not what the crowd likes anyway," Jax explained absentmindedly.

"So what is in the cart then?" timidly Anny asked.

"The man," Jax said grinning.

The cart pulled at last to a large door situated in a small courtyard on the east wall of the castle. Out of it came three men in uniforms who then came running up to them.

"Paul!" Jax cried out in greeting. The man who approached was average height, but muscular. He had thick, short dark hair which matched his tanned complexion. His large, brown eyes twinkled in the sun as he greeted them with a wide smile. "Paul my good man, I want you to meet a friend of mine. This is Anny. I was just telling her about you. Let the men know she is off limits. Meanwhile, get this cart cleaned off. I'll need it in an hour."

"Yes, Sir!" Paul replied. Then leaning in to whisper he asked, "How was it, Jax? Confession or no? You know everyone will want to know."

"No confession till stage three!" Jax gushed. "Absolutely wonderful! Took a good hour I think. And how is Sonia?"

"Sunny's in the kitchen with Megan," Paul said as he motioned towards the door he had just come out of.

"Again?" Jax said as he shook his head.

"Again," Paul said as if it were not something to be believed. "Been there for the last hour crying, but I think Sunny's calmed her down."

Jax jumped from the cart while two soldiers helped Anny down. Soon both were crossing the threshold into the kitchen. The short break in Anny's anxiety ended the moment she laid eyes on the room filled with seemingly familiar items she had seen used in preparing meals. Every corner was crammed with baskets, plates, and foodstuffs. This panic was followed by remorse for her decision only to realize Jax had already made the decision for her. He was behind her still in the doorway. He gave her a nudge, and she stepped further into the hot room. Taking in a deep breath, she turned her attention to the only other occupants: two women sitting at a table presumably used by the servants for meals.

One's face was slightly pale, like that of someone who had been crying but has since found solace. Her paleness was deceiving, multiplied by her bright linens. The woman had very long, blonde hair that curled all the way down her back. Her eyes were blue and her features delicate. She occasionally twisted her fingers such to adjust rings no longer on her hands as if the bare fingers had had rings a long time residing there. Each twist brought a slight moment of panic as she looked down only to remember they had been removed and not lost.

The other woman seemed tired as if she had not slept the night before. She was voluptuous, though she kept her appearance plain with her brown hair pulled tightly back into a long braid. Her hands were small and gentle. Her dark complexion accentuated her rosy cheeks speckled with freckles.

"This here is Anny. She's come looking for a job," Jax said to the tired woman.

"Wonderful! First I have Megan and now someone new? Anny is it? My name is Sonia. This is Megan," she said, waving her hand in the other woman's direction.

Jax looked from Megan to Sonia before smirking. "What happened this time?" he asked, trying to sound as if he did not care though he was suppressing a grin.

"You will never believe it," Sonia said, putting her hands to her forehead trying to rub out the thought.

"Oh really? Well out with it then!" Jax urged her. The previously silent girl rose, the paleness subsiding. She would seem herself again.

"Nothing happened, or at least nothing happened that I cannot fix," Megan insisted.

"Well?" Jax blurted out as he stared at her, his grin now covering almost his entire face.

"Last night," Megan began, "I made the king a very exotic drink. A crate of pineapples came in yesterday, and they were just perfect for it. I took a little of the fruit's juice and a little wine, and before I knew it, I had tasted myself into a bit of a drunken rage."

"And you hit the king?" Jax said half in disbelief.

"No, I just threw a pineapple at his head. I did miss, so I don't see what he is so upset about," Megan corrected him.

"And you are still alive?" Jax said while chuckling.

"I happened to pass out right as the fruit left my hand. It is not like I was aiming for him," Megan said with a shrug. "I am not really sure what possessed me."

"And so he sent you here just to annoy Sonia?" Jax surmised, winking in Sonia's direction.

"I guess so because when I came too here I was with a note saying I can't come back till the king desires it. Sonia here was nice enough to fill in the blanks of the evening for me," Megan said before she paused, rubbing her temples. "My head still hurts. I must have hit the ground pretty hard."

"I don't think it was the floor that gave you that aching head," Jax said with a bit of a laugh as he motioned to leave. Megan smiled at him and waved as he walked back to the courtyard before she turned her attention to Anny who by this time was quite numb.

"Are you alright?" Megan asked as she stepped towards her.

Anny realized her breathing was quite shallow and so she struggled to take in a little more air. The young girl's body was once again shaking and her mind racing as she realized it was not too late to run for it. Alas, there was still a reason for why she had come here. Though the castle may have looked big from the outside here it felt calm and safe. Besides, she had already made so many friends.

"I am fine," Anny finally said. "This castle is just a big place."

"It certainly is!" Megan said as she put her arm around Anny. "How about this: I'll show you around and get you acquainted with where everything is and introduce you around a bit."

"That is a good idea," Sonia said as she pushed the two out of the kitchen. "That will take both of you out of my hands!"

Without another word, Megan took the lead and directed Anny to the kitchen's exit. Sonia looked at Paul once they were gone and gave out a little giggle.

"A pineapple? Yea right!" she said. Paul smiled as he scooped Sonia into his arms. To him, she was perfect, a light in an otherwise dark existence. He often called her 'Sunny' because she was so cheerful but was careful not to say it around her as he knew she was less than fond of the title.

"Oh, my dear, whatever shall I do with you? Day in and out you call to me to be here, and yet I have duties to be attended," Paul said as he rocked her in his arms. She laughed as she pushed him away.

"Charmer," she began, "will you sway me from my mission?"

"And what is this mission of which you speak more fondly than your beloved?" he asked while staring into her eyes. She again responded by pushing him away further, walking instead to the large oven that warmed all the king's meals.

"My mission is to ensure the king receives his meals on time without them being burned," she informed him. She used a cloth to pull open the oven door and then fished the contents out with a long pole. Again she used the cloth to pick it up: a large bowl filled with a stew for the king and his guests' lunch. "I swear all our dear king does is eat and sleep," she said as she poured the food into a serving pot and began to arrange the tray. Three trays in all would be needed: one for the food, one for the dishes, and one for the wine.

Paul watched her for a moment before saying, "Well I can see I am not welcomed here. I will just have to go out to my cold post."

"Cold? It is never cold in Arden. You are looking for sympathy again," Sonia scolded him.

"And do you not pity me, seeing as I must be away from you?" Paul prodded.

"Go, now. If Cailar finds you here…" She was unable to end her sentence for as if the mere mention of his name had summoned him Cailar entered. He too was grinning as Jax had been, yet there was something dark behind it.

"Paul, I do not believe the oven needs you to guard it any longer. I suggest you get off to your post before I am compelled to take disciplinary actions," Cailar said, his expression changing momentarily to one of stern authority. Paul gave a halfhearted bow as he glanced once more at Sonia before leaving.

"Sonia, my dear, is the king's meal ready for him?" he asked. Three servants dressed in ornate robes entered. They were personal assistants to the king and prepared to carry his food to him. Each snatched up one of the carefully arranged trays, and soon they were humming off taking them to the king's private chamber off of the throne room.

"If that is all then I shall need to begin preparations for the king's dinner. Am I to assume he is dining alone tonight or shall Marcus be joining him?" Sonia asked as she turned to a nearby counter, clearing a few dishes away to prepare a spot for her evening's work.

"I believe Ramoth and Marcus shall dine together," Cailar said as he looked around the room. "The other cooks can deal with the staff's meals. Your hands are needed for the king's meals alone until Marcus departs from us. As I told you this morning, I want you to personally tend to their every need."

"Marcus: I do believe he likes fish, is that right?" Sonia thought aloud.

"I cannot say I remember," Cailar muttered back.

Realizing she had spoken aloud Sonia continued, "Then if that is all I will begin preparations immediately."

"I am afraid that is not all, my dear," Cailar said as he walked up behind her, placing his hands on her shoulders while massaging them softly. "You must be tired from such a demanding day and with so many more demands to come. Take my invitation, and I will give you time to rest."

"Leave me alone," Sonia said stiffly as she turned to face him while brushing his arms away from her as she turned. "You know your advances are not welcomed."

"My darling Sonia, I have been speaking to the king. He has given his blessing, which is all that I need to take you as my wife," Cailar explained as he reached out, touching her cheek.

"You dog, you know I would never marry you," she said, pushing his hand away. She went to turn from him, but he grabbed her arm and spun her back around. She again looked at him, yet now she stared him in the eye. "Why do you wish to see me suffer when you know that my heart and soul are for Paul alone?"

Cailar stared right back and stated, "Your heart may be his, but your body belongs to this kingdom. If you wish it back then to marry me is the only way."

"Threats: that is all these are," Sonia snapped back. "Paul has been saving, and soon my debt will be paid off." She was by now yelling and trying to walk away.

"Softly my dear, you know I can make your debt what I wish. Inflate it or make it go away- it is my choice." He now grabbed her waist and pulled her into his arms. He tried to kiss her, but his hold allowed her just enough movement to turn her lips away. Her knees collapsed, and if not for his grip she would have sunk to the floor as her arms tried with little success to again move him away.

"Please, Cailar, let me go. What is it that drives you? You could have any woman here. Why me when you know I long for another?" Sonia pled.

"What can I say of my foolish heart? It is your unavailability that I find most desirable. Forbidden you are, so how can I resist?" Cailar goaded her.

"I do not believe you," Sonia mumbled.

"Then you want to know the truth?" Cailar asked as he continued to hold her.

Sonia by now had stopped fighting only to look up at him with anger flashing behind her eyes.

"The truth, my dear," Cailar insisted, "is that I was foolish enough in the past to allow those I longed for to flee from me. I neglected them, but I will no longer neglect you. You plead and pout saying how you love this soldier, but you are young. You need someone who can provide for you."

"Paul can do that. He is paid well," Sonia said, once again trying to fight herself free. It aggravated her that Cailar seemed to be oblivious to her disgust for him.

"But not well enough. I can get you anything you desire. My estate is large, and my wealth unmatched to most."

"You think I care for your wealth? Paul's love is all I desire," Sonia snidely retorted.

Cailar rolled his eyes and snorted, "Love? You fool! Who are you to speak of love? I have seen a dozen girls just like you. So desperate, you would allow any man to sway your judgment. What you and Paul share is nothing but lust."

"And you pursue me for nobler a cause? You hypocrite, you speak as if you desire me for something other," Sonia blurted out as she finally freed herself from Cailar's grip. A swift slap followed, and Sonia coiled away.

Cailar loomed over her saying, "I have chosen you because I need a young girl to deliver to me the son I need to take over my lands when I depart. Believe me, now it may seem I am cruel. However, when one year by my side has passed, you will have forgotten about Paul. You will remember only my generosity to you. You will be free of your labor and free of the dangers of this castle. I will provide for you and you for me. The sooner you accept it, the better seeing as you have no choice to the contrary in it."

He looked at her for a moment to see if his words had reached her. She was looking at the ground, her hand on her face where he had struck her.

Cailar continued, "I mean only good for you if you agree, but if you should be so daft as to make me your enemy, then my vengeance shall have no end for you or for Paul. Think calmly on it and you will see I offer you more than Paul ever could. If you truly love him you would not make yourself any more of a burden on him then you already have. The date is set for one week from today. If you do not come to the castle's gate at sunrise to leave this place on that day, then my curse is upon you, and you will find no escape."

Sonia now looked at him, anger filling her expression. "If you make me choose, then you shall have a corpse for a wife," she said. Again Cailar responded by hitting her, only this time she fell to the ground.

"You accursed fool!" he screamed. His hand rose as if to strike her a third blow. "I see my words have no sway to you. Sit there on the ground and think of what you are choosing! One week and one week only you have to decide. Is death so welcomed by you that I cannot compete with it?" His hand landed on the nearby table with a heavy thud. "One week and one only!" he yelled as he left the room, his temper raging.

● ● ● ● ● ● ●

Cailar's particularly sour mood so drastically contradicted his earlier high spirits that not one of the servants dared cross him the rest of that day and were rather relieved when he disappeared to the bathhouse to cool off. There he commanded all away for a moment to be alone. One messenger, however, was sent to relay a message as the area became deserted.

The king, meanwhile, was not as pleased with his disappearance for at the arrival of his best friend, Prince Marcus, there was not one man to greet him. Marcus was a fair man though and quickly found his way to the king's chamber.

He patiently sat awaiting the king to notice his presence in one of the many large chairs that furnished the room. The king arrived with half a dozen men all questioning him on different matters for they knew that once he sat down and was served his liquor there would be no more business for that day.

"Sir," one of them pleaded, "I do beseech you to consider the head guard's request for more equipment. Many weapons are too old."

The king raised his arm, and with that, a maid came and served his drink. He took the cup to his lips and with a slight grin said, "I shall consider these matters tomorrow. You are all dismissed." The men then scampered out of the room together following their formal good-byes.

"You have not changed one bit." Marcus began. "Why it is as if I had not been gone a year, but a day."

The king turned around to find his friend rising from his chair to be seated next to his old accomplice. "Why Marcus, it has been too long. How was your trip?" the king asked.

"Very well, we made excellent time. You look tired. Still having trouble sleeping?" Marcus asked as he was served his own cup.

"My sleep is poor at best," Ramoth hesitantly confirmed.

"You must overcome this fear of yours, or it will be the death of you. I know you believe you saw a ghost that day, but that simply cannot be. Maybe there is something else the matter with you," Marcus theorized as he noted the dish of stew cooling on a nearby table.

"But nothing, I did see a ghost, and he wants me, and all of Arden destroyed," Ramoth insisted. He could see his companion eyeing the dish and motioned for it to be brought to them.

"How could a ghost do all that? I mean sure, they can move through walls and not be imprisoned, but then how could they hold a weapon?" Marcus wondered.

"I know not, but that he can and will," Ramoth insisted as he was handed his portion.

"Stubborn in this belief as always. I knew you would not have changed," Marcus huffed as his food was next served. "I mean, even if ghosts are real and they can harm you then how could you ever hope to stop them? So why worry about it, right? Anyway, with that in mind, I have a present for you from a holy man of Ghanrey. He said it is a good luck medallion that will ensure you good rest."

"My faithful friend," the king said as he took the small gold medallion, "I will wear it always."

Marcus grinned at the look of relief in Ramoth's face and said, "Be sure that you do! It will not work if you leave it lying around somewhere! Now let us think unhappy thoughts no more. There is celebrating to be done! I have traveled many a day to be here, and I intend on having a good time."

"And that you shall have," Ramoth assured him. "I am pleased you were able to arrive before the new season. I have a large celebration planned, and I was beginning to worry that you would not arrive in time."

"All the reason for the rush, yet here I am!" Marcus said as he began to eat.

The king again raised his hand, and the maid returned to refill his glass. "And it would not have been so great an occasion without you present," the king said as they raised their glasses in a toast.

● ● ● ● ● ● ●

Megan and Anny wandered the halls that same day for an hour as Megan tried her best to explain each room's function. They arranged for Anny to move into the empty bed in Sonia's room, left by a servant who had recently married. Anny wondered if it was the same servant Jax had spoken of, hoping this was a sign of good luck for her. The pair had visited several more rooms before a servant came running up to Megan telling her the king wished to see her at the bathhouse immediately. Anny agreed to return to the kitchen as Megan ran off smiling for what Anny assumed was her good fortune in being forgiven so soon.

After speaking to the other servants, it became apparent to Anny that Megan's past was shrouded in mystery. It was rumored that she had grown up in a well-off family in a far off land. However, she had failed in finding a suitable husband due to her all too high standards. In the end, she had run away to the castle as every misplaced person seemed to do, just as Anny did.

Once she arrived, she was introduced to Cailar who became secretly enamored with her. Unknown to all but a select few he promised that for a price he would introduce her to the king himself. However, once the price was paid, he found it hard to let her go. On several occasions, he had returned to her and threatened to reveal their past if she did not pay what he felt owed to him. Megan had genuinely fallen in love with the king and his power. She was all too unwilling to allow her secret to end what she had gained.

Despite her protest she, again and again, paid the price, once paid for Cailar's help and now paid for his secrecy for the king was not yet so absorbed in her that she should have more sway than Cailar himself.

It was for that reason alone that she feared to go to the bathhouse though she smiled. It was Cailar's favorite place for the two to meet, and she knew the king would never go there when he had his own private bath well stocked with servants. As she arrived, she listened intently. The entire room was silent, though that was not unusual this time of year as the waters were usually too cool this late in the day for anyone to wish to bathe in them. It was also very dark.

"Where are you?" she called out. There was no answer but her echo. "Curses, where are you? Show yourself!" Her body stiffened as a figure emerged from the shadows. "Cailar?" she questioned.

"Yes, you are alone I presume?" Cailar asked as he stepped closer to her.

"Of course I am. What do you want?" Megan asked impatiently.

"What do you think?" Cailar scoffed.

"I do not have time for this, Cailar," Megan insisted as she looked around suspiciously. "Just tell me what you want, or I am leaving."

"Why my dear, lips such as yours should never have to speak so harshly. Now stop being so difficult. I do believe you know exactly what I want," Cailar persisted.

"I cannot," Megan said as she turned away from him.

"You cannot or you will not?" Cailar asked as he approached her.

"I cannot continue to lie to him like this," Megan pled.

"You speak as if he means something to you or you to him," Cailar grinned. "Well let me inform you that you mean nothing to him. I want you, Megan. I need you. Why dream for what can never be? Be with me or be with no one! Would it be better if he knew? I would gladly tell him that you seduced me, or would you rather tell him yourself?" He then reached out to her and was not surprised to see her resolve melt at the thought of the king knowing the truth about her.

"How long till you leave me alone?" she asked as he took her into his arms.

"Patience my dear, I think our terms may change just a bit. There is a service you could provide me that would be infinitely appreciated. You see, I have just come from informing Sonia that I have the final authorization needed to marry her."

44

Megan immediately pushed him away. "You are going to marry Sonia?" she said in disbelief.

"You did not know? I would have thought you would be happy that there would be someone else to take your place," Cailar said.

"You have been lying to me all along," Sonia pointed out as she went to leave. "To think that I almost believed you did care, but you do not. You think all women are for is pleasure, but you will see our vengeance is a thousand times more effective than your own."

"You misunderstand me, dear," Cailar implored. "I had thought we could come to new terms now that I will no longer need your previous services."

"Like what? You want me to kill someone for you? Is that what your silence costs?" Megan joked sarcastically.

"No, no. Not at all, I just need some information. All I want is for you to keep an eye on Sonia for me. I need to know everything she does and everything she is planning. I would not like my future bride to go missing," Cailar explained.

"You are a fool if you think she would willingly leave Paul for you. Those two were just meant to be together. It is just the way it is!" Megan insisted.

Cailar seemed unfazed and commented, "That remains yet to be seen."

"And if I do that, you will really leave me alone?" Megan asked quietly.

"Yes," Cailar assured her.

"Forever?" Megan again asked.

"And ever," Cailar again assured her. "I would not so much as lay a hand on you ever, ever again. Just return here to me each day and tell me what you have learned. That is all. You cannot say it is an unfair thing to ask."

● ● ● ● ● ● ●

Meanwhile, Sonia sat at the small table reserved for the kitchen staff's meals. Her head rested on her crossed arms, which were draped across the table. She seemed to be weeping softly, but this moment of reflection and loathing was cut short as a hand gently touched her shoulder. She jumped as she spun around to confront whoever it may be. Yet as she came to realize it was Paul her arms sprang away from her sides and wrapped around him.

"My beloved, is there any news?" She whispered.

"Why, yes," Paul said as he sat beside her. "Remember that priest from Vera I told you about? He has returned my letter. He said he would be happy to marry us as he will be in town for the king's festivities. Then we may travel with him back to Vera."

Sonia looked at him surprised and said, "That cannot be so. How could you have found out in time?"

"I sent a letter a month ago, and it arrived the same day as the king's invitation to the festival," Paul explained. "He sent his reply through the king's messenger."

"Then it is true? We can be married at the festival?" Sonia gasped excitedly.

"Yes, of course, if you still want me," Paul said with a laugh. "Not that I would want to stop you if you would like to take Cailar up on his offer."

"Never, never," Sonia said with a sigh. "It is as if fate has intervened."

"Remember, act no differently or Cailar will suspect you plan to leave," Paul said as he looked at her face, slightly blushed from her past tears.

"Do not worry Paul! In a week's time, we will be joined for eternity!" Sonia said, as she again hugged him around his waist.

● ● ● ● ● ● ●

For the first time in almost twenty years, the king slept soundly that night with his new medallion strung around his neck. He was in high spirits, for he planned a feast that would rival all others for the new season to come.

Marcus, however, sat in his room unable to sleep. His thoughts were filled with the girl he had met on the road, the girl named Anny. Only an hour before had Cailar appeared to greet him, begging his forgiveness for his absence. He claimed it was a new maid's arrival that morning that shook his schedule, and he again remembered her: Anny. So she had not been a dream after all.

By no stretch of the imagination did he believe he loved her, though he had spent the day occasionally hoping she would hate the castle's atmosphere and agree to return with him to Paultry.

These thoughts of longing were driven by the realization that she knew too much to not be who he suspected she was. He would have to know the end of her story to be satisfied. He would have to see her again if even for a moment, to satisfy himself.

Chapter Four: The New Season

The young girl raced to the end of the hall, her feet pounding against the old stones that formed it. A sudden pause, as she came to its end, spinning around to see the figure approaching from the darkness.

"Still running from me Cordillina? Why? Your death is inevitable. Why not be brave in your final hour? Why not be true to your fate? Destiny is to be embraced, not run from. It was meant to be that your life should end here and now," it said.

"Who are you?" she cried. The form stopped; its face still in the shadows. It seemed to be waiting for what the girl knew not.

● ● ● ● ● ● ●

Anny awoke to the deep chill of the early Arden morning. Though the days were warm, the nights felt chilly. So it always was in Arden, Sonia would explain, adding that Anny ought never to admit it to Paul.

Though it seemed an eternity had passed, it had been but six days since she had arrived at the castle. All week had been spent preparing for the festival, which was to take place that night. It was the last day of the winter season on the Arden calendar, and so there was a celebration and thankfulness to be carried out in the form of excessive drinking.

Almost a week had past and tonight would be Sonia and Paul's wedding. None of the servants or guards were invited for they feared Cailar would stop the marriage if he knew about it. Only those who would be needed to cover for the two during their absence from the festivities knew. It was too dark in the small bedroom to see Sonia, but

Anny turned her head in her direction and laid there envying her.

The day before Anny heard that Marcus would be leaving the evening after the festival. She had been trying with all her might to forget him, but this severed her last bit of strength as she realized he was going to be gone soon. Since then she had lived in agony thinking about him. The pain at the thought of him leaving was too great, though their time together had been so short. She had spent all week observing him and attempting to find out details about him.

Again she went over the situation in her mind, trying her best to convince herself she was mad for feeling the way she did. She was here for a reason, an entirely different reason. Her plan would be ruined if she left now.

"Marcus is his name," she thought. "I love him, and that seems to be the ultimate problem. I love him, and I have not a chance to be with him. He is smart, handsome and all around non-threatening. I have no chance. I am just a servant, and that is all he will ever see. I am too young. I am not smart enough. I am not experienced enough. So why should he even know how I feel?

"Yet it was not always this way. My logic won until I realized our time was so short and now I think of him and miss him. I think of us in the courtyard, in his carriage, in his life, yet none of it is real. I think of us together, and I tell myself it is not real.

"He must have been with a woman in his life, in his travels or at his court or even now. Some girl he writes to. Who does he secretly desire? Who does he imagine in his arms?

"I am all hopelessness now. Days will pass, and by tomorrow I will have not another reason to see him. I will probably never speak to him again. No more glances as he speaks to his men. No more warmth, just a winter of solemnness. A winter alone and I am so afraid to live the cold summer once more.

"I love him, but that is not enough. He does not love me back, and that is all that matters. I miss him! I will never see him again! He will forget about me. In a month he will have forgotten me, yet I not him.

"I love him, and my heart cries, 'Hopeless! Take your fated path. Love no more. Love your pain more and forget yourself. Forget your yearnings of the flesh and your desires of the heart. Better him to never know and have the faintest remembrance of respect for you then to do something foolish and have him remember that foolish girl!' And that is all I am: a fool.

"What if he is married? What if he has children and a life? What if I am to be alone? What if it all does not matter?

"It does not. Marcus will leave. He will never know. He does not know. So deny it. Forget about it. Deal with the fact you were meant to be alone forever. It is just the way it is.

"And yet, I love him."

Again her logic had brought her right back to where it began. Did she have the courage to take Marcus up on his offer and leave with him? In honesty, she did not believe he even remembered his promise. To do so would also be breaking a promise she had made to herself not long ago.

By now the light from the hall had grown slightly so that the line of the door and the cracks throughout it were visible. The room had only one door, a wash basin, and two beds.

"Sonia?" Anny whispered. Sonia groaned accordingly. "Sonia, are you awake yet?" she again whispered. She had no desire to spend another minute in her cold bed torturing herself. It now seemed better to get up and about so she might be distracted. She had no doubt once Sonia realized today was to be her last day waking up in her bed that she would jump up and be ready to start the morning breakfasts.

"Anny, go back to sleep," Sonia mumbled. "We still have time."

Anny could hear footsteps. "You say that every morning right before Paul comes to yell at us," Anny said, but before she could finish the door flew open, and Paul came stomping clumsily in.

"Get up you cretins! It is far past the time to still be in bed. The other servants must be awoken, the animals fed. Have you no sense of time?" Paul yelled with a laugh as he tried to pull on Sonia's blankets.

Sonia threw her pillow at him as he ran away laughing, though the pillow was caught by the door so that Paul had to run away with the door still ajar. Anny listened to his steps as they quickly grew softer. They reminded her of the pounding feet in her dream.

"Alright, now it is time," Sonia said as she pulled herself from the bed.

"He speaks as if today were any other day," Anny said with a giggle.

"Shh!" Sonia said as she put her finger to her lips with a smile. "Not one word of any of this. Today is a day like any other," she finished with a wink. It seemed the day had begun plainly enough. There were indeed things to be done.

● ● ● ● ● ● ●

Megan rubbed her sleepy eyes as she wandered down the hall to the castle's armory. The previous night had not been kind to the youthful servant. She had not slept at all contemplating for endless hours what Ramoth would do with her while also trying to discover Sonia's plans, if indeed she had any.

Directly after she had spoken with Cailar the week before she had rushed to Sonia's side, and there remained the entire day, but not one word was uttered concerning either Paul or Cailar. And so, seeing as Sonia would not tell her willingly, she tried to form a network of confidants to relay to her whatever they might have discovered.

Jax was the first servant she turned to, being well aware that he would know where Paul was at all times of the day or at least where he was supposed to be. She had met up with him at the armory where he was inspecting new supplies and distributing new weapons. She remembered the encounter as she returned there now: how she had pleaded with him to help her.

The armory was one of her most beloved places to visit beyond the vault that held the precious metals and stones she had come to adore. The room was crowded with blades, swords, and spears piled up along the vast walls, their wooden handles dark with dirt and occasionally blood. Some were foreign, taken from enemy camps after their surrender, while others were worn, the shine lost and the wood splitting. Countless arrows of varying sizes and styles were stacked just to the left of the doorway, some in cases and others tied in bundles. Their bows were stacked beside with spare strings in coiled piles.

The only wall that seemed immune to the crowded disarray was the one to the right of the doorway. Here the adjoining wall was not deep enough due to the placement of the entrance but to support a narrow table's width. All of the generals' ceremonial weapons were kept here in their unmarred state. Beyond this table the occasional ray of light would return from some distant weapon: a shield or a dagger further from the doorway for the room continued indefinitely from the reach of Jax's torch.

Jax was standing by the narrow table, a slew of small daggers before him, just as he had been the week before. There was a bulky man with him sitting at the edge of the table compiling a list for inventory.

"Jax?" she called out as she entered the room slowly. Every time she had done so, a shrill of fearful excitement ran through her. The weapons were a menacing sight, their pointed blades in particular. "Jax," she repeated, "may I speak with you for just a moment?" She was trying to use her most innocent voice without sounding as desperate as she was. She felt like a child standing in the large doorway. Her hand trembled as she rested it on the door.

"Of course," Jax replied, looking up from a dagger, which he placed back on the table. He stood there staring at her with a smile on his face waiting for her to speak. She looked from him to the man beside him and back to him again. "Yes, what is it?" Jax again said in his usual playful voice.

"I was hoping to speak to you privately," she said, looking to the man who by this time had come to realize he was only half welcomed. He rose grumbling and went to the door.

"I will go to the kitchen and get our lunches," he said, giving a not-too-pleased glance at Megan for her interruption. "Maybe I can catch up to Paul and Andrew," he said as he walked out.

"Paul was here?" Megan asked excitedly, hoping maybe Jax had heard something after all.

"Yes, he dropped off several daggers for inspection," Jax replied as he motioned at the pile of weapons on the table. "He did not say a thing about any plans if that is what you meant to ask."

Megan blushed, afraid her desperation was plain for all to see. "Then you are not going to help me? You know Cailar will have my neck if I do not stop this! Do you not want him to leave me alone?"

"And you believe he will leave you alone, after all the lies he has told you? You are grasping at straws here," Jax incredulously replied as he backed a bit away from her. "Even if I did know, which I am not saying I do, but even if I did, I could not in good conscience tell you."

"I thought we were friends, Jax!" Megan said exasperatedly.

Jax was now also blushing and said, "We are, but Sonia and Paul are my friends too. And believe me, I am doing you a much bigger service by not allowing you to stoop to his level. The first day you arrived here I warned you, just as I warn everyone else, not to make deals with people you do not know. And what did you do? You formed a deal with the very worse and now have come running to me. I cannot help you."

"Please, Jax," Megan pled, softening her tone. "How can you be so cruel? I will do anything for you!"

"If I tell you, what good would it do you? Cailar will go back on this deal as soon as he gets bored with Sonia. Besides, you must admit that his silence is not all that important. The king knows, Megan. You have to see that is why you are here and not with him now," Jax conjectured.

Megan turned away from his stare in a flash of shame only to see she had not concealed her actions well. Her eyes caught sight of a sword on a table, and she quickly picked it up as if it were what she had been turning to, rather than him that she had been turning from.

"That is not what I came here for anyway," she said with a bit of nervous laughter in her voice. She unsheathed the sword with considerable effort as it was much heavier than she would have imagined it to be. "This certainly is a pretty piece. Do you know who owns this weapon?" she asked, turning it so that the light from the nearby torch was caught by it.

"Yes," Jax said plainly, taking the sword from her hands. She marveled how easily he was able to maneuver the weighted object. "You see that crest? That is the symbol for Paultry. This sword is from there. And see that initial under it?"

Megan asked, "What does that mean?"

"That is the owner's initial: 'M' for Marcus of Paultry," Jax stated as he inspected the sword. "It does not look like it gets much use."

"So it is our guest's sword," Megan said. "You know I seem to have noticed that our newest arrival cannot take her eyes off of him."

"Anny?" Jax asked, an air of interest in his response.

"Yes, all week I have seen her sulking along the halls, glancing into the king's chamber. At first, I thought it was my dear Ramoth she was after, but I soon realized it was

Marcus who gained her attention." Megan looked intently into Jax's face to see his response.

"I had no idea," Jax said, though he was avoiding looking at her. Megan looked carelessly down at the pile of weapons Jax was inspecting, and it was then that she saw the name "Paul" scratched into the handle of one of the daggers. Her heart leapt, for why she did not know. It was Paul's dagger sitting right beside her. Jax turned his back for only an instant to replace the sword on the table where it was being held till its owner's departure. In that instant, Megan reached out and grabbed the dagger, concealing it behind her back where Jax could not see she had it.

Jax again turned to face her, the sword now put away to his satisfaction. "Do you really think Anny would be so silly as to think Marcus would take her as his wife? It would be quite the scandal," he mentioned casually, still trying to hide his interest.

"I am sure it is nothing but an unfounded desire that will be easily snuffed out should she be given a more appealing offer. You know Jax, I had said I would help you in any way that I could." Jax was now the one to turn away in sudden shame as Megan continued, "I have seen the way you look at Anny. It is not unlike the way she looks at Marcus. But for you, you can offer her so much more than he can."

As Jax continued to avert his gaze, Megan secured the dagger in the folds of her dress so that she might again bring both her arms from behind her back.

"I do not deny that I find Anny to be..." he trailed off, seeming not to know what to say.

"Desirous? Beautiful? She is quite lovely, that is true. She must have come here to find a man who could provide for her. Why should not that man be you?" Megan said as she rubbed Jax's back.

"It is a foolish thing to wish for Megan. I have tried to approach her, but she is not interested in me. I suppose now I know why," Jax said with a shrug.

"No, you have it all wrong, Jax," Megan insisted. "You may think you know what she wants, but I doubt even she knows what she wants: what would be good for her."

"But I could never bring myself to even speak such things to her. She is so young and dumb to the ways of the world. How could I ever approach her as anything more than a friend?" Jax said dismissively.

"Then let me do it! I will convince her to forget Marcus and to accept you with open arms. Do everyone a favor and tell me whatever it is you know about Paul and Sonia and I will help you in return," Megan offered.

"Then you still are chasing this dream of yours to have such information as you know it would loathe me to give should I have it?" Jax sorrowfully replied.

"Jax, your time to find a woman of your own is growing shorter. Sonia will be happier with a man who has wealth and position. Anny will be happier having a man of her own and not some childish dream. And I, well I will be with my beloved as well!"

"You may be right. I have seen many a couple as Sonia and Paul who seemed so perfect together, but their love is weak against the strain of time. What about Paul though? He is a good man," Jax wondered aloud.

"Is it better that we all should suffer just for his sake?" Megan asked. "Jax, no one will know what you have said to me. I will tell Cailar, and he will simply marry Sonia before that time. After all, would it be better they do marry, and Cailar must kill Paul if he wishes to have his bride?"

Jax looked at Megan, his expression one of surprise. "Do you really think Paul's life would be in danger?" Jax asked skeptically.

Megan responded quickly, "Absolutely! Why else would I be trying so hard to protect them?"

"If I tell you, you will guarantee me that Anny will be mine?" he asked, looking into her eyes to be sure she spoke the truth.

"Yes, she will be yours, and we will all be happy. I will even make it my duty to find a nice girl for Paul. First, I have to know..." Megan said with a broad smile.

Again, Jax turned away, and for an instant, Megan thought she saw tears welling in his eyes by the dim torchlight. "You are right that even if they do marry, Cailar will find a way to do away with Paul. For that reason alone will I tell you. Whatever else you choose to do, you choose to do for other reasons." he said, his gaze darting around the room.

"Yes, yes, I understand," Megan said.

Jax took in a deep breath and again looked at her. "They do plan to marry: this very night at midnight in the courtyard. They're leaving town right after."

● ● ● ● ● ● ●

Now concerning Sonia, no one had ever bothered to delve into her past. As far as anyone knew she had lived at the castle her whole life ever since her mother arrived pregnant and outcast with nowhere to go. There had been no end to the speculations as to where this woman had come from. The favored version was that she had been the mistress of a foreign king in a faraway land who had fled when her life became endangered due to her illegitimate heir. Those who had known Sonia's mother said she had been relieved to have a girl and therefore assumed the rumors to be true.

Sonia only remembered a happy childhood, free of conjectured whispers. She was always warmed by the stove, and her mother often gave her food even when there was not enough for the court. No one said anything though. Sonia had become their daughter, and now that she was grown she was still beloved as a daughter by the older servants and as a mother to the young. It was no surprise that Paul loved her. They had known each other since he was ten and arrived with visions of military triumph in his eyes.

Paul had always dreamed of being a general but had only achieved the rank of a royal guard. If not for Sonia he would have abandoned the castle years earlier in search of a position in the roaming ship fleets. At least that is what Anny had gathered to be true. Never having been in love before now, Anny at first could not understand why the two should be so devoted when it cost them both so much. She decided that what made sense, and what she observed to be true, were not related in this place.

In a way she envied them. They were able to follow their hearts freely. Anny feared now that she no longer had one. Her past made that an impossible luxury. If only she had not learned to associate love and friendship with pain and hassle.

Anny thought these things as she arrived at the north wing. She was trying to hurry after having been told to clean one of the many guest rooms for the upcoming party that night. Counting the doors to her left, the young girl stopped at the fifth one. Pushing the door it swung open, reassuring her that she had the correct room as all unoccupied guest rooms were usually kept locked until use.

As she entered, she placed her bucket and mop next to the door and walked to the windows to open them. In the darkness, she did not notice the tall figure creeping up behind her. Her arms seemed weightless, having just put down the heavy pail of water she had been lugging. She raised her gentle hands and pulled back the curtain, flooding the room with light. The figure continued to approach her from behind as she reached for the mop.

Anny had a sudden impulse to sing as she worked. In her mind's eye, the mop was suddenly a handsome stranger asking her to dance at the feast that night. She grabbed the handle of the mop firmly and swung herself around as if they were in a dance, which was when she landed the handle squarely in the stranger's eye. He let out a scream as he grabbed his face, jumping around the room like a child. Startled, Anny let out a shout too and then instinctively started to hit the figure with her mop.

"Stop! Stop! It is me!" he cried out, raising his hands in defeat.

"Marcus?" she exclaimed. "Where did you come from?" For a moment she had been afraid, but now seeing him before her, she decided to be brazen and reached out for him. She rested her hand on his back as he continued to groan, doubled over.

"Oh my," he repeated again and again, "how are you so strong?"

"Well I work a lot and, hey what are you doing here anyway?" she again inquired.

Marcus hobbled over to the bed. When he finally removed his hand from his face, she could see he had a significant, red mark on his cheek.

"Promise you will not hit me?" he blurted out, trying to lighten the mood.

"Well, you surprised me. What in the world are you doing here? Are you trying to give me a stroke or something?" Anny deflected.

"No, no, no! Not at all. Give me a break, would you? I was just waiting here for you. You never told me the end of the story, remember? I mean, I know an end to your story Anny, but you said yours was different."

Anny felt a little disappointment flood her cheeks. Was this really why he had come?

"Okay, it is not just that. Who told you that story anyway?" Marcus continued, seeing he had upset her. "It just has been bothering me. I mean, there is no way you could have known about the king's wife. No one knows that except Ramoth and me."

I flash of fear crossed Anny's face. "I made it up," she insisted.

"Who told you?" he persisted.

"No one did," Anny hissed. How could he be so singular in focus? Could she really mean nothing to him?

"Listen, you may not believe this, but I am on your side here," Marcus explained. "I think I know who told you about the king, but if I say it and am wrong, then you must die because it is confidential. But if you tell me and you are wrong, then there is nothing more to be said, and I will leave this instant. Now tell me, who told you? Please, tell me the truth."

He stared at her pleadingly, and for a moment she was silent, thinking about what he had said and wondering why it mattered at all.

"The man did," Anny blurted out. "The wise man with the unusual powers who foretold the Myth told me."

"That is impossible," Marcus claimed.

Anny continued, "He came to me as a ghost in a dream. I did not believe him until I came to this castle myself. I did not even suspect it was real until you said you had heard the story before. I thought maybe I had heard it when I was little, but your ending is so very different. And if you say that the queen did kill herself, then it was real."

"Okay then tell me what he said to you," Marcus played along.

"He, Barnas, told me the story. He explained to me what had happened, and tried to warn me of what was to come," Anny said.

"Tell me what Barnas said, or I will kill you," Marcus said.

Anny looked at him as if he had just told a bad joke. "I do not believe that," she said as she shook her head from side to side.

"Then tell me because I can protect you. You can return with me to Paultry as we planned, but only if I know what you say is true."

Anny's heart suddenly skipped a beat realizing he had remembered his promise, and she wondered aloud, "What is it you want to know? I have told you everything. It is just a story. Why can't you just let it go at that?"

"You left off when the king arrived at Faverly. What did he do after he arrived?" Marcus asked forcefully.

Anny was surprised. She had thought he was joking before now. Again she paused. In a way, the young girl wanted to tell him, but in another, she did not know if she could trust him with a secret she had promised never to reveal. "Why do you care so much?" she asked again, pulling away from him a bit.

"I only say this because I know who you really are, and I know you will reveal to me what really happened. I told you I journeyed much in my youth. One of the places I went to was that fortress called Faverly. I met the man you speak of and resided there under his training until I was called away by my father. I was there when he made the prediction that foretold the birth of the seven girls. The fact remains that everyone has heard the Myth, but only a handful of people including the king know it to be fact.

"As you know, once the king did away with his heir he went to great lengths to discredit the myth so that no one would believe it anymore. But what happened to the girls, that is what I wish to know. The story goes that the king's men went to Faverly to protect them, but that an army from Pacia attacked and in exchange for the king's life the seven girls gave themselves to the enemy and were killed. In another version they were already gone when Ramoth arrived: slaughtered by a marauding band from Pacia."

"If they are dead, they are dead. What difference does it make now?" Anny asked.

"One of those girls was from Paultry," Marcus said slowly. "I cannot say more than that. Tell me Pacia was responsible, and you are free to go. Tell me what I know to be true, and I will never let you leave my side again."

The last words he said caused Anny's heart to leap into her throat as they played over in her mind. "If you are a student of Barnas, then I know I can trust you," she said cautiously. "You are correct, Pacia had nothing to do with it."

"Then tell me what did. Barnas predicted that seven girls from different countries would be born on the same day as the birth of the king's first son and that they would produce an heir that would rule the entire world peaceably someday. From what I surmise, the king did not want a half-breed for an heir, and so he did away with his son.

That way no legitimate children could be born to the seven girls. But he still had to do away with the girls in case he had another son. Is that not true?"

"You are only partly right," Anny said. She was getting confused.

"Then tell me what did happen. What did the man tell you?" Marcus begged her.

"I cannot imagine the evil that would compel the king to take the life of his own son. I understand the king felt he could have other children, but to destroy life is never honorable: the younger the life, the less honorable it becomes. He desired the girls' deaths as well, but the man I call Ramoth stopped him. I believe the king was not inhibited by fear they would produce an heir, but by vengeance to the man who gave them so much power. Ramoth was different. He was the one to convince that their lives be spared."

"Why would 'Ramoth' care?" Marcus wondered.

"I can only imagine it is because he raised them when they were little. He had spent so many years protecting them and caring for them. I suppose that was his motive. I was never really told. However, I believe that when he saw their lives came at the price of Kayla, his grief clouded his judgment. He as well became led by vengeance, misdirected as it always is."

"So what happened once the men arrived?" Marcus asked anxiously.

"The king and his men stayed for the night. The next night there was a great feast prepared for them," Anny said.

"And you were at that feast. You were there because you were one of the prophesied girls," Marcus said.

"I never said that. I told you it is just a story," Anny maintained as Marcus stared at her.

"But you never fail in your descriptions. The years, the names, the places, how can you know all this?" Marcus pressed.

"I made it up. It is just a story- a foolish dream!" Anny said as she looked away.

"What is your real name?" Marcus said to her in an accusatory tone.

"Antoinette," she replied quickly.

"No, what is it really?" Marcus demanded.

"It is as I have told you. Why do you keep asking? What can I say that would please you?" Anny asked. She was beginning to wonder why she liked him at all.

Marcus grumbled under his breath. "I am losing my touch," he thought to himself. He took in a deep breath, one going from his lips to his toes, and then summoned all the willpower he had to smile rather than yell.

"Alright, your name is Antoinette. Now please, if you will, go on with your story and I will not interrupt. Really, I am just so curious to know how it ends."

This time it was Anny who paused. She could now see how desperate he really was. This made her hesitate briefly. Could she trust him? He knew so much, he must be being honest with her. Maybe for once, she would follow her heart before it was too late. What did she really have to lose anyway? What did he have to gain?

"Very well, Marcus. I will go on now," she said. Marcus simply continued to smile charismatically, motioning with his arms that she ought to go on. "This is how the story goes. The night of the feast, all of the servants were invited at the urging of the king. The king sat at the head of the table with the seven Sisters to his left and right. His general and Ramoth sat to his right, three girls away. The rest of the seats and walls were lined by the men and servants. It was such a large hall that none felt crowded. The food was brought out in large baskets and platters. The harvest had been kind, and so all food was brought except that needed for all to travel back to Pent. You see, the servants at Faverly were under the impression that the king had come so that they may leave and return to their homes now that the Sisters were old enough to be married.

"The feast went on, and many of the servants became drunk. Around midnight the king rose from his chair for one final toast. He raised his glass, and all of his men fell silent. An eerie still crossed the room, and it was not until then that the servants realized something was amiss. The king said 'My dear friends, you have served me well out here in the wilderness. If not for all of your careful attention the girls would not be as well off today as they are. Unfortunately, your services are no longer required past this evening, and this consequentially means that all of you must be eliminated as well. Cheers!'

"There was at first a silence as the servants sat in disbelief, a few even chuckled. However, chaos ensued as the servants tried to flee the fortress. The king's men were swift in detaining all who they saw. The male servants were tied up and taken outside the gates where they were thrown off the cliff. The female servants were first brutalized and then throw to their deaths as well. The sisters were taken to the fields outside the fortress where an apple tree grows. There they were beheaded.

The soldiers remained through the night, gathering up any valuables or food that could be found. At sunrise, they left after having thrown the remaining bodies over the cliff. They returned to Arden, divided the valuables, and went each his separate way. That is how the story ends."

Marcus had been looking at her throughout the story but could see no tears hidden in her eyes.

"I do not understand," he said with his characteristic tone of concern. "If all of the servants were killed, and all of the Sisters as well, then how do you fit into the story?"

"I do not fit in. As I told you, I was not there," Anny stated flatly.

Marcus wondered if she was holding back. It just did not make sense. Even if she had not been there, even if she was not a Sister, then how could she know all of this? Even if by some way unknown the man who had foretold the prophecy had been able to come to her and tell her so much, why did he choose her? What did she have to do with it that she should know?

"You said before that the man who lived in Faverly told you the story and tried to warn you of what was to come. What did he say?" Marcus asked, trying to make it clear in his mind.

"He said that I should not trust the king or his advisor. He did not mention their names: only that they were not to be trusted," she replied.

Marcus grumbled, "But why would he have warned you? You said he did not say the name of the king, so he must have assumed that you would understand which king he meant. Then what is the point of the story? In your version, everyone dies, and the king gets away with it."

"Did not the king get away with it in real life? Things in life do not just end happily, so why should this story be any less true to reality?" Anny quipped before she turned away. Then, looking off into the distance she added, "Or maybe the story is not over yet."

"Anny," he paused and then took her hand, "Okay, it is just a story you heard in a dream, but there is one thing that still bothers me: one thing I just cannot overlook. If that is all true, if you are not indeed a Sister and were not there that night then why would my teacher come to you and tell you all of this? What could he have hoped to accomplish?"

"I cannot say," Anny said.

"You do not know?" Marcus said as he leaned in closer to her. "I do not believe you. Could it be he knew we would meet, that our paths are meant to cross? Is there something important I need to know?"

Anny approached the window. There she laid one hand on its sill as she stared out over the ocean spread out before her. Marcus came to stand beside her and could see almost a smile across her face.

"Tell me, Anny. Tell me I am right. I do not care how you came to be there that night, but tell me the story is true. Just one time admit it."

"It is true Marcus. Now please, never ask me again," she struggled to say.

"Come with me to Paultry. Surely you would not prefer to stay in the castle of the same king who did all these things unless you are plotting revenge," Marcus surmised.

"You really think I would prefer to be your whore then one of the king's faceless servants?" Anny asked.

"I never said that is why I want you to come with me. You may not admit it now, but somehow you are connected to Faverly. That makes you a threat to the king."

"I told you the Sisters are dead. He has nothing to fear then," Anny insisted.

"And all you have to do is tell me your real name, and I will know that is a lie," Marcus said.

She looked at him now and said plainly, "Antoinette is my name. I do not know what it is you wish it were, but that is all I will tell you it is because that is what is the truth."

Marcus could see that she was no longer lost in the moment. She had gone back to her protective shell and would say nothing more concerning the matter, content instead to stare out the large window into the open spaces beyond- leaning a little out, taking in a deep breath of salty air. For a moment Marcus stood next to her to watch.

Anny eventually turned back to him and said, "I would appreciate you keep the story I have told you a secret. Not so much to protect me, though the king would have my life for what I have said, but to protect the memories of the Sisters. It is better for them to be remembered as they are by the people. There is dignity in dying for a cause, even if that cause is a lie."

Marcus shook his head in agreement. "Of course, I will not fail in keeping your secret, but you have yet to tell me if you will come with me or not."

"Maybe. Like you said, why would I want to stay here?" Anny said trying to hide the little excitement she had.

"My carriage leaves tomorrow night. I know these parties run late, and I will more than likely sleep the daylight away. Be waiting for me at dusk where I left you the first day we arrived, and, if it pleases you, I will bring you with me to Paultry. That is unless you would like to come with me now. We could pass the rest of the time together."

"I don't think that would be appropriate," Anny said, her heart breaking slightly that she should turn him down now. "Now if you will leave me, I still have work to do before then."

Marcus made no attempt to outstay his welcome. He turned for the door and did not turn back.

Chapter Five: A Festival

The night's entertainment started early that evening. The day had been spent in breathless anticipation, yet Sonia had managed to arrange things such that there was little left to do once the party got underway. Guests had been arriving since noon, and each required direction as to where they were going and what was to be done with their swords and carriages. King Ramoth had long since made it clear that no weapons were allowed to be brought in by his guests and so the armory was soon flooded by shiny, deadly things that were piled on the same table as Marcus's confiscated contraband. Many guests brought servants along to care for these and their horses while they drank the end of the season away and these newcomers as well required a certain degree of directing.

As Cailar entered the kitchen that evening, it was with a stolen bottle of wine and several glasses. Though he had been yelling much of the day, he was now convinced everything was indeed under control, and he could now take his ease. Looking around with satisfaction he quickly handed a glass, already filled to the brim, to Sonia. She looked at him quizzically and could only assume he hoped to lighten the resolve of his reluctant bride. He returned her glance reassuringly as if he knew what was ahead for their future.

He then filled the remaining glasses and handed them out to those who had been working since sunrise. He proposed a toast, raised his glass, and looked with a hint of anxiousness at Sonia as she sipped as little of the wine as she could without seeming rude. The occasion blessed, Cailar started to leave. Yet something seemed to call him back. Once again he crept up to Sonia.

"Are you prepared for this evening? My carriage will be waiting for us once you are ready," he whispered with great delight.

"My answer to you is still 'no'," she snapped back. Sonia knew Cailar would not strike her in front of so many other servants, so she spoke more forcefully then she might have otherwise.

"Perhaps you misunderstood me earlier. You have no choice in the matter. You will come with me and do as I say." He raised his voice slightly higher then he wished and took a quick glance around to ensure that no one was listening.

"I do not have to do anything I do not wish to. Now leave me alone!" Sonia said, this time turning from him and passing off a tray to another servant.

Cailar seemed like a snake trying to coil himself around Sonia as she fussed over the final plates for the evening. Sonia seemed so calm, yet something Cailar had just said caused her to freeze. She put down the tray and was now looking at him with great concern. Yet a moment later Cailar was gone, and Sonia was again buzzing over the dishes.

● ● ● ● ● ● ●

By the time Cailar arrived at Marcus's side the prince had already finished his first glass of wine and was searching for a pitcher maid to refill it. Cailar walked briskly over, sitting down with a thud.

"Marcus! How are you this evening?" Cailar said as he motioned for a server to bring him a glass and refilled Marcus's.

As his glass was filled, Cailar looked around and grumbled to himself. He had always hated the fact that the king insisted Marcus sit to his right and Cailar just after. It would seem only fitting that he should be allowed to sit to the king's left, but never was this honor given to him and so he tried to act as if he could care less where he had been placed.

"Fine, fine," Marcus replied, "the wine is good today."

"So are the servers. Do you see the maid you requested I arrange that little meeting for you with? She must be something. I would like to see what the fuss is about! She should be filling glasses tonight. Maybe you could point her out to me."

Marcus laughed, "Why I do not believe I have seen her yet." He looked around carefully, and then added, "Maybe she is avoiding me?"

"Think how grand an arrangement I have designed for you! The more you drink, the more she will come to your side! Perhaps you would like me to arrange something for this night as well?" Cailar continued as if Marcus had said nothing about her avoiding him.

"I do not believe I would be up for it as I must be away tomorrow," Marcus lamented.

"This is a poor circumstance indeed. How old have you become? Or is this the first time you have not left the lady begging to return to you?" Cailar teased him. "But still if you are to be traveling that is a good reason to drink none the less!"

Marcus laughed, "Come on now: my reputation will not be sullied so. Though it is true, the trip will go much faster once I am lightened by these delightful spirits."

"Drink then, I say! Once the celebration is beginning to wane, I would say you should get to your room to rest before your departure. I will send a maid to escort you and help you to undress."

"A particular maid of course," Marcus replied. To himself, he thought, "Perhaps Cailar thinks I am joking about Anny running away the last time we met?"

"Of course, whatever you like," Cailar said as he finished the last of his cup. "I will be certain to have someone send her."

Marcus turned to him, giving a weak smile. He raised his glass as in a toast while pointing it towards Cailar's cup.

Cailar nodded back, lifting his glass and giving a salute back.

"You look tired but well," Marcus said after taking a large gulp from his glass. "It must be a relief to have everything underway."

"That it is," Cailar said. His eyes glanced around the room, habitually looking to see that everything was in order. "You know how Ramoth gets before these parties. He is so damn paranoid."

Marcus paused for a moment. "How long have I known you, Cailar? It's been many years."

Cailar laughed. "I do not know; no wait let me think. It has been something like 15 years, 20 years? We have known each other since before the time of the Sisters." He tried to get himself to stop from saying the last part, but it sort of slipped out and hung in the air. Suddenly there was tension everywhere.

"Yes, the Sisters," Marcus said, looking out into the crowd.

"It was a long time ago," Cailar went on. "You know Ramoth does not want us to speak of it anymore."

Marcus nodded. "You are right, of course," he agreed before lifting his glass. "For Arden, for Paultry," he saluted loudly as he again began to drink.

● ● ● ● ● ● ●

Anny had been given the duty of ensuring that no glass went empty and was amazed when she entered the dining hall to see more glasses then she had ever seen in her life. She had lost count that night how many times she had gone to refill her two pitchers.

Tonight was her big chance: the chance to fulfill the promise she had made the year before. She had to decide once and for all what she was going to do: either keep her word and honor, or fall foolishly into Marcus's arms. Her heart pounded thinking about him. She had let her guard slip once that day, and immediately she regretted it. She had been scolding herself trying to stay in control.

She entered the hall once more. She could see at the king's table was Marcus speaking passionately to a man beside him. With every ounce of her soul, her heart cried out to him, "Oh, beloved, if I could but choose both. Though I have no guarantee with you, yet even that must I abandon hope for if I am to fulfill what I have promised to do. That is what I must though. I promised, and that can never be forgotten. Foolish, foolish girl- when will you learn? I must have faith that if it is meant to be then so it shall." Her hands were trembling as she turned away from him.

Instead, she headed to a small table that was crowded with guests. Sometime earlier the king had stopped there to talk to one of them and had since been persuaded to stay. The whole group was laughing and spitting their words out. Though it seemed still early, there were already some visitors who had fallen asleep or passed out where they sat. Others looked quite unwell. She had been eyeing the table for some time, but now was the moment. Now her courage was as best as it could be.

The king was easy enough to identify by the gold around his neck and the crest on his sleeve. He drank from a special cup, which was covered in round, red gems. She slinked in as close to his side as she could get to him and then leaned directly in front of him as she reached her pitcher out to his cup.

"Why what do we have here?" Ramoth slurred out. He reached an arm around her and soon he had buried his face into her bosom.

"My lord, what else is there that I can give you?" Anny replied, laughing along with the crowd.

Ramoth laughed with a grunt, his hands still holding onto her. "I do not recognize you. Are you new? Let me welcome you. Let me show you what Pent can offer." He directed her to sit beside him, and for several hours they were there drinking the night away. Anny sipped her drink, making every effort to put on a good show and smile. Soon enough he would be ready for bed. That would be her chance once they were alone. Yet as the night wore on Ramoth became more and more slurred in speech and behavior. Worse, Marcus eventually appeared to join them. His eyes pierced hers. She knew that look and what it meant. He would not be happy until they were alone.

Before the feast had quite wound down, Marcus had put his head down on the table and fallen asleep right there. Anny looked at the king and wondered if he would be next, but before that could happen, he stood up, reaching his hand out to her. He tucked his arm around her, and the two headed off together towards his private chamber.

They were walking through the main hall when they ran into Megan. Megan was clearly furious, her face was bright red, and her lips were pursed tightly together. She glared at Anny as they passed one another in the busy hall. At first, Anny felt a little guilty, but then a sense of smug pride swelled in her. "Could she really be jealous of me?" she pondered as she walked beside the king. "What a novelty!" She grinned stupidly to herself, but then realized she had to figure out what she was going to do next.

She had never been in the king's private chamber before. Only servants who had been at the castle some time were trusted to serve him, and those servants were usually male. As they entered, they passed two guards who always kept watch.

The room itself had large windows on three sides with floor to ceiling purple drapes. The tops of the windows were arched with small pillars to each side. The center windows had a set of doors that presumably led out to a balcony that would have a grand view of the sea in the daytime. The ceiling was vaulted so that in the dim light the top could not be seen. The center of the room was sunken down with a large, square table at the center. It was low to the ground, with plush cushions surrounding it.

Various treasures lined the walls as well as smaller tables with intricately carved sets of chairs. One of them had some sort of a board game set up on it with a match still in progress. She was a little surprised to see that two fireplaces were flanking the doorway along with a myriad of lamps that gave the room a warm glow.

The table in the middle of the room had a pitcher and glasses waiting for them. Ramoth, as he asked Anny to call him, sat down and began to pour them both drinks. He put one down beside himself for her before enjoying his own. Anny sat down beside him taking the glass and giving it a convincing sip.

She found she had nothing to say at first. It seemed Ramoth was not much for conversation either. For several moments they just sat watching the flames in the fireplaces. Out of the corner of her eye, she looked at him. He seemed tired, and she couldn't help but notice a sorrow behind his eyes. It took her off guard. Quickly she looked away. She could not afford to feel any pity for her enemy.

As she was turned away, she suddenly felt his hand on her shoulder. He was nudging her to turn towards him. He was smiling wide as he came in to kiss her, but she managed to duck away coyly.

"Not so quickly!" she said with a giggle. "You are not relaxed yet." She motioned for him to turn around, but she could see he was unwilling to turn his back to her. She had heard he was cautious. So instead she reached both hands up and ran them through his hair. He groaned and smiled, slowly bending forward so she could rub his shoulders as well.

"No one has given me a massage in so long!" he moaned as his shoulders and head began to drop.

"Really? I find that hard to believe," Anny said. She pressed her fingers deeper into his back and before long he was stretched out on his stomach with his head on her lap.

"Oh, it is not like there are not lots of girls here, but they just come, and we do our thing, and they leave. No one takes the time to really get to know me or anything. You have such strong hands! What is it you do around here? Do you usually work in the fields or something?"

74

Anny had to bite her lip. "No, no I work in the castle cleaning and that sort of thing."

"Well whatever you are doing, keep doing it," he urged her.

Anny continued to rub his back. She was hoping to relax him so she could get his guard down. As she did her eyes were scanning the treasures along the walls for something heavy.

"It must be hard having so many acquaintances but no real close friends. I mean, is it so much to ask for someone to give you a little back rub now and then?" she thought out loud.

"Oh my! Yes, it is!" Ramoth groaned. "Maybe you would understand. I just wish one person understood what pressure you are under when you are in charge of everything! Ouch- yes more to the left! It would be nice if just once in a while someone said 'thank you' or 'what can I do for you?', but instead all I hear all day are requests for more things. What do these people think I am? I am just a man. Some days I just want to be left alone."

"Everyone has days like those, though I guess we common folk have the luxury of being left alone without consequence," Anny sympathized.

Ramoth groaned loudly and then said, "I'm supposed to be perfect. Everything I do has to be just so. How would anyone else deal with that kind of scrutiny? Then they have the nerve to tell me I drink too much? Would not you? I mean, really if it were you with all that responsibility and pressure? No one has any idea what I have to do every day, again and again. If I stopped the whole world would stop with it and then where would everyone be?

"But it is not good enough? It is never good enough! Are any of them that perfect? Oh, no- by no means! Not even close! Yet you ask for a little kindness, and that is too much. One friend, one true friend is all I want, and I have none! One person who understands is all I want, but that is too much to ask. Everyone else has a friend but me. Everyone."

His words dissolved into tears and he buried his face in her lap. Anny was surprised. He wept bitterly for several moments as she held one hand on his back while still stroking his hair with the other. She made hushing sounds, trying to get him to settle. This was indeed not what she had expected. Suddenly the tears stopped, his breathing calmed, and she could hear a faint snoring sound. Ramoth was out cold.

She held her breath for a few moments. Then she carefully lifted Ramoth's head and slipped out from under him. She meant to slide another pillow under his head, but her fingers slipped, and his head hit the cushion she had been sitting on with a light thud. Again she could not breathe thinking he would stir, but he was completely unresponsive.

She tiptoed to a table with a large, silver dish on it: heavy and wide, burdened with deep engravings and thick handles. As she lifted it up for a brief moment, it flashed in the light of the fires revealing her reflection. She could not look herself in the eyes. Her fingers began to tremble as she turned back to the king, the dread object in hand.

This was it: this was the moment she had come all this way for. Finally, the souls of her loved ones could rest knowing she had enacted justice on their killer. Yet the joy she anticipated was not there. The relief she had dreamt of feeling vanished like a mist. She felt only fear and sadness. There was Ramoth himself, a pitiful fool. Was this really justice? It could not bring them back. Nothing could. She looked down at the dish in her hands and into her own eyes in the reflection.

"I will not become what I hate," she told herself. "This all ends here."

She put the dish back onto the table and felt a weight lift from her. It was time to move on, if she could.

● ● ● ● ● ● ●

76

By the light of the stars, Paul felt his way to the courtyard where he was to be wed to his beloved. The priest had already arrived and quietly greeted him. He knew the degree of caution and secrecy Paul had made it clear was required. The two then stood there in silence, waiting for Sonia to arrive. Slowly the stars crept across the sky, yet she never came.

Chapter Six: A Fresh Good-Bye

"I just do not understand where she could be," Anny said as she entered the kitchen the following morning. She had been all over the castle's servant quarters without finding any sign of Sonia. "She never came to our room last night, and I tried to stay up, but I was just too exhausted. Her bag is still there too. She would not have left without it."

"Do not worry about it. Sonia is probably in the bed of one of the guests," Megan said. She alone was in the room, eating leftovers from the night before, still cross and a bit hung over.

"That is a terrible thing to say, Megan! She loves Paul. She would not do that!" Anny scolded her.

Megan smirked at her and offered, "She would if she were drunk."

"I just cannot believe that," Anny said as she threw up her arms in frustration.

"Have you seen Paul at all? Maybe she is with him? They are supposed to be married by now are they not?" Megan said carelessly.

Anny shot her a quick glance. "How do you know that?" she asked.

"Word travels in these places. You do not really think no one else knew but you?" Megan condescendingly remarked.

"I think I will go to the guest quarters after all. The guests will expect breakfast, but there are only the prepared foods served last night. I will just run up with a few things and also look for her," Anny thought aloud as she gathered a tray of food.

"She is probably with Cailar. Take it from me, he can be very persuasive," Megan called after her. As Megan watched her go, for a moment, she wondered if Anny were right about Sonia. It was no matter to her though. Today she was a free woman, and it felt good, at least as good as a pounding headache can feel. Once Marcus left the king would be lonely once more and would be calling for her, suspicions or no concerning her and Cailar. She was certain of that.

● ● ● ● ● ● ●

Anny went directly to check Marcus's room first to assure herself he was still willing to take her with him to Paultry. Having left him alone at the feast, she feared he might be cross with her. Worse, what if news had reached him that she had been alone with Ramoth for a good portion of the night?

Carefully Anny counted the doors again as she wondered if Marcus had had her sent to his room intentionally the day before. Five doors from the left she paused. It was completely silent in the hall. All were still in a drunken sleep.

She pushed the door slightly to peek in. She could feel the air from outside trying to force its way into the cool hallway. The breeze blew in her face, and an all too familiar rotting smell hit her. It was unmistakable, the smell of decay and death. She pushed the door all the way open only to find herself standing in a pool of blood. It was everywhere. At first, she could not find the source, but she soon discovered a figure on the bed covered in a slightly blood smeared sheet. Anny rushed to it, thinking of Sonia.

The young girl discovered the body was on its stomach as she effortlessly threw the sheet off the bed in her adrenalin fueled panic. "It is Marcus!" she thought with a startle. He did not seem to have a mark on him. "Could he have rolled onto a knife in his drunken dreams?" she thought as she struggled to roll him onto his back only to discover this side as well was unmarred. He groaned, and she knew he was going to awaken soon. It took her just a moment more to realize that she had not the victim in her arms, but the attacker.

● ● ● ● ● ● ●

Cailar stood leaning against the wall opposite the bed in the small scantily furnished room that Sonia had lived in ever since her birth. In his left hand, he held a small ring, which he rolled over and over again between his fingers. The bed opposite him was matted straw, and the blankets were thin with wear. Beside that was Anny's bed, and next to a chipped wash basin there was a small parcel of Sonia's things. They were all packed, Cailar would later explain, so that she could be ready to leave in the morning to be his wife.

There were no windows or ornaments. All that remained to testify that a great woman had once lived there was a small circle with lines radiating out of it etched in the wall above the bed she had once slept in. It represented her nickname, Sunny. Paul had called her that all his life up until recently when he saw that it annoyed her so. Feeling all grown up she demanded to be called by her actual name and not some novelty. Even now, as he stared at it, he could hear her saying the words. "Stop saying that," she would say. "My name is Sonia, not Sunny!" But seeing the etching, he knew she must have enjoyed the name even if she pretended to be annoyed.

"When did you find her?" Cailar asked, barely turning his attention from the etching. The guard Andrew was standing in the doorway. He could not lift his head to answer.

"At sunrise," the man whimpered. "That is when I noticed her in the surf. At first, we thought she was just some debris, but as we got closer, we could make out her form. Jax was the one who went down to get her. He identified her once she was on the bank, though it wasn't easy."

"Is that all you found?" Cailar nonchalantly asked.

80

"We found this dagger. It's a guard's dagger. It has a name carved in the handle," Andrew said as he reached into his pocket to retrieve the thing.

"What name?" Cailar asked, this time turning to the man.

"It says 'Paul' clear as day as you can see," the guard said as he held the dagger out. "Sir, as his friend I can assure you…"

"I too thought Paul was fond of this servant girl, Andrew. Perhaps he discovered she had planned to marry me and killed her in his rage," Cailar remorsefully interrupted.

"I cannot say I know anything about what happened," Andrew said as Cailar took the dagger from him, "but we are certain she was murdered. There was no way she could have gotten that dagger put in her like that."

The morning had been hectic for Cailar. There were dozens of noblemen to be attended to and orders for cleaning to be made. Though word had spread that a servant girl was found dead, it hardly concerned the men Cailar saw off. Whoever she was, none of them would be charged even if they admitted to it. Several hours had passed, and the guards who had found her were told to keep their mouths shut until Cailar was available to assess the situation.

"There does not seem to be any additional clues here," Cailar said as he assessed the room. "We must lock Paul up before he has a chance to run. He was foolish to leave his dagger behind, and everyone knows it is a crime against our king for one servant to kill another. We shall set the trial for sunset and have the entire matter settled then."

"As you wish, Cailar," the guard said with a solemn salute. "I have heard that Jax is looking for you. He needs your permission to leave the castle grounds so that he may carry the pyre away from the castle."

"Very well, tell him to meet me in my chamber before he goes to the site," Cailar ordered as he ushered the guard away from the room.

"Yes it shall be done," the guard said in the hall as he bowed and began to go.

Once the guard left the door his shadow was no longer cast across the wall as the light poured in from the hallway. For a moment Cailar returned his gaze to the etching of the sun, staring silently as the silhouette of a woman's small frame drape across the wall replacing the guard's. He spun around to greet its maker, half expecting to see Sonia herself only to find Megan standing in the doorway as the guard had been.

"I assume you have heard the news," he said flatly as he turned once again to the etching.

"I have. News travels fast," she said. "What happened?"

"Apparently Paul killed her in a jealous rage. They found his dagger in her chest. He was on duty that night. He should have had the knife on him the entire night. It is pretty simple."

"That guard said they found her in the sea. Isn't that most interesting? I suppose Paul dumped her there to hide his crime?" Megan suggested.

"Yes, in the water to hide the blood I suppose. No other scene has been found, though on an unrelated matter I have a job for you to complete this morning discreetly," Cailar said turning to her.

"I owe you nothing more, Cailar," Megan explained. "Especially after all I have done."

"Really? Well, consider this sort of the last step to freedom. There is a room you need to go clean, and you must do so quietly," Cailar said as he turned and grabbed Sonia's bag off the floor. He dumped the contents onto the bed and rifled through it before deciding it was nothing important.

"Jax was right about you. You never really stop," Megan muttered under her breath.

Cailar turned to her. She could tell he was quite displeased. Suddenly he grabbed her by the arm and pulled her right up to his face.

82

"What are you doing?" Megan pleaded as she tried to pull away. "You're hurting me!"

"Listen carefully," he whispered, "we had a deal, but obviously I did not get what I wanted out of it, or my bride would not be a bloated corpse right now. Does that make sense to your small brain? If I did not get what I wanted, then neither do you and if you know what is good for you then you will continue to do as I say for as long as I say until I am satisfied. Otherwise, it might be your pretty little head at trial. Does that make sense? Did I speak plainly enough?"

Megan nodded as he released her arm.

"The fifth guest room on the left. Go alone and bring a mop," Cailar said. "Tell no one."

The pounding in her head was so loud she could hardly hear him. Megan quickly scurried from the room with tears down her cheeks. Freedom had seemed so close; How could it have fled so easily? In her haste Megan did not turn back to see a man exit from a nearby room and enter the one Cailar currently stood in.

"What do you think it is she knows?" Marcus asked. After he had awakened to see the room in chaos he had been quick to find Cailar to see if anything were going on in the castle. This prompted Cailar to stop escorting guests to the main gates and to look into the matter of the found body.

"It does not matter what Megan knows or thinks she knows," Cailar assured him firmly. "I will take care of her. She is nothing."

"But what if she does know something? I told you I thought I saw footprints. What if she tells what she saw?" Marcus asked anxiously.

Cailar thought about the footprints for a moment. He knew Megan had seemed surprised about the job he had asked her to do, so then who else might have gone to Marcus's room? Anny's name crossed his mind. Who else could it have been?

Cailar put his hand on Marcus's shoulder reassuringly and said, "She will not say anything when she knows it would mean her own death. Remember, all last night we were together in the king's study looking over land maps. If anyone says different, we will have them hung for testifying falsely against a citizen of higher rank."

"I do not want anyone hurt, Cailar!" Marcus warned.

"And no one will be. Fear is all I need to keep Megan silent. Let her go. I do believe seeing Sonia will sober her to the realities of the consequences if she should speak. As for you, I suggest you ready to go. The sooner, the better if you wish to keep this quiet, my friend," Cailar said as he began to lead Marcus down the hall.

"Just one thing I am unclear on. It is true I do not remember anything that transpired last night, but you have been so good as to tell me that you had Sonia escort me to my room when no one could find Anny. I imagine that is when I lost myself. I must have thought she was Anny, and..." Marcus hesitated for the right word. "And I must have tried to take her. What I do not understand is how that knife ended up in her. How did it get there?"

Cailar seemed lost for a moment but then mused, "I imagine Paul gave it to her to allow her to protect herself. In the struggle, it turned against her. I am sure that will be revealed at trial, which will clear Paul's involvement and with no other suspects, Paul will go free. Though it is possible, he followed you two and attacked her once he saw her in your embrace. That is for the trial to determine."

"And then what will happen?" Marcus asked.

"Sonia is not the first person to die mysteriously at this place. You need not fear anything. I will not allow anyone to be hurt as you request, and I will settle the matter as I see fit," Cailar again assured him.

"I appreciate it, Cailar," Marcus said as they reached the end of the hall. "I cannot have any mark on my name right now, but you are well aware of that. Pent is one thing; Paultry another."

Cailar chuckled, "Yes I could see your brother using this to sway your father into deciding to reinstate him as the heir apparent. How is your father's health? I have heard he is in poor condition."

"Indeed, poor it is, which is why it would be wise that I go and prepare for my departure. Ramoth will expect one last sitting with me before, and I do not wish to disappoint him."

"Farewell, Marcus," Cailar said as he embraced his old friend. "I do hope we see you again under less stressed conditions. You will understand if I do not mention this trivial matter again."

"In that case, it is my last chance to say that I am sorry for your loss. Clearly, I did not know the girl or her relation to you. I'll make this up to you somehow," Marcus vowed. He did not smile as he left Cailar behind. He would have just come out and said that he had killed the girl had he not feared that if Anny knew he was a killer, she would refuse to go with him. No, that was not entirely true. There was his reputation to consider.

Cailar watched as Marcus walked away. "Sonia, Sonia, Sonia..." he thought. "Fare thee well as well. If only you had taken me up on my offer, you would have never been in that room. Instead, we would be together now. Not here in these stalls, but at my estate with all the finest of things. I would but feel sorry for you if you had not brought this upon yourself, but now I fare thee well forever."

● ● ● ● ● ● ●

All servants were usually forbidden to leave the castle grounds, and so it had been decided that Sonia's pyre would be set up in a cart just outside the castle's walls so that they might say their goodbyes before it was taken away. Jax met briefly with Cailar to make the arrangements before he headed off to the site himself. A large group had gathered there as Jax pulled his cart, usually used in trials, up the road near where the pyre was already being constructed.

Good-byes were uttered and flowers set as he jumped off the cart and walked towards the crowd. He saw Megan and waved to her.

"I cannot believe what they say is true," Jax said as he stood next to her.

"I know. To think Paul killed her is laughable. She probably committed suicide to spare herself the agony that only Cailar seems capable of bringing to women," Megan whispered back.

"I guess that makes sense in a way," Jax agreed, "but I saw that knife still in her. It was so deep, too deep for her to have had the power to thrust it without being dead before she got halfway. I think I would know. I have seen enough men die."

"Well, women are stronger, or are you that dumb? She could have fallen on it," Megan suggested dismissively.

"Then how did she get into the moat? Megan, I know what I am talking about here. Someone wanted her dead, but Paul? He had no reason too. There are others with better reasons," he said slowly.

"Men have done stupider things in the name of love," Megan retorted.

"So have women," Jax said plainly. "You still own me that favor. Do not think I have forgotten."

"I did not fathom you had," Megan said as she looked around nervously.

"Anny is here. I saw her. Convince her to come with me when I dispose of the ashes and we are even," Jax said firmly.

"Gladly," Megan agreed with a laugh. "Do me a favor and leave her out in the woods. That one has been trying to get close with Ramoth after all. Can you believe her nerve? Besides, imagine her reaction at the trial."

"I hadn't thought about that," Jax admitted. Maybe she won't go with me then. She'll want to stay."

"Honestly I don't think she knows about it. I'm certainly not going to be the one to tell her," Megan assured him.

86

"Just get her to come with me then, if it is all the same to you," Jax insisted. "I almost feel like I'm doing you a favor again instead of the other way around."

Megan nodded as Jax made his way to the front of the crowd to move the memorial onto his cart with the help of the others. Megan then made her way to Anny's side. She stood looking over her shoulder, which occasionally rose and settled softly in the maid's silent sobs. She had to wait until the pyre had been set on the cart. It was then that some unspoken signal crossed over the servants and they headed each to their awaiting posts. Anny alone stood a little longer.

"Anny?" Megan said as she lightly touched her arm. Anny turned to her and though Megan had been sure she was crying her face showed no flaws. "I do not imagine you are in any hurry to return to the castle's empty hallways."

Anny's gaze returned once again to the cart. "I would be happy never to go back to that place again," she said sharply. "I know I must. I have said my goodbyes, and it hardly seems fit to remain seeing as I knew her so shortly. Yet I feel as if I have known her forever. I'm sure she is in a better place now."

Megan rolled her eyes, but said, "She had that effect on people. Jax said he would take her to the fields off the Candescent River in the Rykuo Forest. That is only an hour's ride from here, and it is the best place. He would probably like it if you went with him."

"I do need to speak with him, but is this the proper time? I suppose I might not have another," she murmured as she finally turned to Megan.

"Yes, you two have much to talk about! I have told you how much Jax is enamored with you. If you go and make a good impression, I am sure he will ask you to marry him. Jax has considerable wealth from battles fought in his youth. I know you have said he is not your type, but let us be honest: Jax can take care of you.

"Men may grow older in appearance, but their minds and bodies remain young in other ways. Think of the great experience he has from his years. He is strong and lively still. You could have many years of happiness together. And do not think it is that he is old, for indeed he is not truly. He only seems that way to you because you are so young yourself. Once you are together and age a bit, you will be glad to have him as your husband. Would it not be nice to have someone for your own? I mean, someone just for you?"

Anny blushed a bit momentarily remembering the night before. She had not had the heart when Megan had brought Jax up earlier in the week to tell Megan she thought Jax homely, so instead she had said he was too old.

"That does not change the fact," Anny countered, "that he takes great pleasure in killing men at trials. I am sure what he does he believes he does so in the name of good, but to kill in revenge is never acceptable."

"How is the trial revenge?" Megan asked a bit confused. "What he does is for his country. Many a time has he confided in me how he feels such pain for his actions, but says nothing less he should lose the respect of the younger guards. Besides, he is so feared by many that you would be well protected by him. He was trained to the highest standard when he was young. I suspect he has lost most of that training from years of idleness, but that does not mean he is not strong. Besides, to prove his gentleness, he wishes you to come simply to pick the place the pyre should be erected. Now to you that may not sound like much, but he is a good man, is he not?"

Anny listened as Megan continued to ramble on, yet her first impression remained with her. She liked him but was utterly unattracted. Besides, all the young girl had been able to think about was Marcus, but how could she go with him knowing that he killed Sonia and would probably kill her the moment they left Pent? If she went with Jax and confided in him, could he be trusted?

Staring at the pyre, she remembered Sonia and knew what she had to do. Perhaps if she went with Jax, she could convince him Marcus was to blame, and then he would let her leave so that she could return to Faverly and live out her days there selling fruits in summer to any nearby towns. How bad could it be? It certainly had to be better than taking her chances with a known murderer, and come a few years she could devise a new plan.

Her thoughts finished, she interrupted Megan's pleas and agreed to go. In her ignorant innocence, it never occurred to her that there was also a degree of danger in allowing herself to go off with Jax into the forest. She just never really believed that Jax was interested in marrying her. Why would anyone want to marry her?

Megan smiled, delighted, as she led Anny to the cart. "Have fun!" she said as Jax hoisted Anny beside him. Megan caught herself a little too late to stop the phrase. "I mean, be safe," she said, a little blushed. Jax softly smiled as he handed Anny a small, lit, glass lantern.

Megan did not move until the cart was far from the walls and growing closer and closer to being out of sight. With a smile, she turned back to the castle. As she walked towards the gates, she could see that Cailar was standing in the shadows of a nearby guard watchtower, observing the cart's departure. Maybe he did care about Sonia after all.

Chapter Seven: The Shores of the River

Jax stared at the sky for one of the few fleeting moments of peace that resounded in that day. The air's gentle warmth magnified the blueness of the afternoon sky. The trip had been unexpected, but he resolved to enjoy what he could from it.

"Such a fine day," he said, trying to avoid a conversation that would bring up the task at hand. After all, he had no intention of dwelling on Sonia's sudden death. Death was common in his occupation, and day by day it touched him less. He was even amazed at times to find himself envious of the men he killed. For them, the struggle between life and death was over, and somehow he found comfort in bringing that inevitable battle to an end.

Out of the corner of his eye, he caught glimpses of Anny as she rode along next to him. She was beautiful, trim, and soft. Her eyes were fixed on the lantern. It seemed a pity that this was the trip he should have to invite her on, not to mention it being the second time they were riding together with a corpse in his cart. She was going to think this was a pattern for him.

He returned his focus to the road ahead, looking intently for where the forest would be parted to their left by the river. The river paralleled the road some distance off. There a flood plain created a lush meadow where he had intended the pyre to go. He again glanced at Anny and thought of her. As he did so, he was glad she could not read his thoughts for if she could, she would have fled from him by now.

"That place looks good," she said, breaking his pattern of thought. "You see over there, where the sun breaks through the treetops, and you can see the rays all fanned out?"

She was pointing into the woods where a large and mighty tree had fallen some distance beyond the road they were traveling. It left behind a large opening in the canopy above. Below, small green shoots pressed upward in hopes of filling the gap in the ceiling. Jax stopped the cart to give the sight a closer look.

"It is a little far," Jax began.

"It is not all that far off, and would you have we put her so close to the trail that all that pass could trample her?" she said, but he smiled in return.

"I think we should wait till we get to the river like I planned. After all, this is not a castle Anny; it is a living place. In a few months, you will not recognize it. The seasons, the winds, everything changes. The road and the river, however, will come close to one another at the same place for a long time to come. Besides, I do not believe you wish that we should set the entire forest ablaze."

She nodded in reluctant agreement, and he started the horses up. On the way back she would tell him about Marcus, but for now, they had to get this done and over with. She watched him as they continued and was struck by the fact that he seemed as emotionless as she.

"Does it not disturb you at all, Jax?" she said.

"Does not what disturb me?" he said, turning his head slightly to look at her while still watching where they were going.

"Here one day she is with us," Anny explained, "and the next she is gone: returned to ashes in such a short period. Yet look around us and in every direction birds sing, the gentle winds wander, and men drink in merriment. To each comes an end. Everything does, all things here cease to be at some point."

"Try not to think on such things, Anny," Jax remarked, "True, we all end, but when we do is not known. Why not enjoy life till then whatever may await us once we pass."

"But how can they all be merry with so much lost to them?" Anny wondered.

"And gained. The sun does set, but it causes us to appreciate the dawn all the more because of it. If not for the dark there would be no knowledge of the stars. Nothing can be all good or all bad. Sonia had a happy life. How can we sorrow should that be all she longed for?" Jax assured her.

The cart jogged to the left causing Anny to fumble with the lamp for a moment.

"It is just that she had so much life ahead of her," she said as she inspected the lantern. She was having trouble getting the lid to rest correctly.

Jax smiled as her lovely fingers wrestled with the lid. "I believe that the only things that are determined from the start are when we are born and when it is we are to die," he offered. "A long life is no better than a short one, and it was just her time even if it would seem otherwise. Even your life could end shortly, so why mourn hers when you never know when it is you may be joining her?"

"You are not really helping me to feel any better," Anny muttered. "If anything I feel worse now."

"I am sorry," Jax said earnestly, "for it was not my intention to cause you any more pain than necessary; However, I did need you to come along."

"Even though you have yet to take my advice?" Anny pointed out.

"Even so, I am glad you decided to come. It should not be that much longer till we get to the place," Jax said with a reassuring nod.

A half-hour more passed before Jax and Anny arrived at the spot where the bank of the Candescent River swelled into the flood plain. There was a large field of grass separating them from the river. The ground was broken by a sandy shore where the curve of the river had carved out a small but deep pool.

"Here we are," Jax said, pointing out towards the river. Anny nodded silently. Jax directed his horses towards the riverbank, stopping nearly parallel to the edge. "Are you ready? Help me out here," he said as he jumped down from the cart. He directed her to arrange the flowers left by the mourners over the pyre as she saw fit. She worked quickly, not wanting to think about what she was doing.

She looked up to see that Jax had taken off his shoes and belt, leaving them a good bit away from the river with his ax beside them. Next, he removed his shirt, an act which caused Anny's face to flush. She could see him reaching to remove his pants as well. Quickly she looked away, but a moment later Jax was climbing into the cart, motioning for her to move onto the front bench of the cart. Apparently he had decided to leave his pants on.

"I think we're ready," he said matter-of-factly. "Hand me the reins."

Anny had wondered how the two of them were to remove a pyre massive enough that many people had lifted it into the cart. Now it became clear. Jax positioned the cart in front of the riverbank and gave out a little whistle. Suddenly the horses began to back up, lowering the cart into the river.

The water quickly rose up, lifting the pyre into the current. Anny had been a bit surprised. She tried to stand to avoid the tide, but it was difficult with the cart moving. Jax was soon drenched and her feet as well. Jax laughed at her, smiling as he joked about the look on her face. He had one arm on the pyre and the other firmly on the reins and cart.

"Okay, Anny. I need you to grab the lantern. Just set a little bit of the straw on fire. Try to get it going low, and it'll spread upwards," he instructed.

"Should not we say something first?" Anny asked, holding the lantern in one hand.

Jax looked at her quizzically. "If that is what they do where you are from then by all means," he said.

"May you be at peace forever," she whispered. The lantern was shaped like a box with a small door on the side and a lid on top. She opened the door then held it close so that some of the straw could catch fire.

"Good, good. Okay then," Jax said.

Anny closed the door on the lantern and returned it to the front of the cart where she had been sitting. Jax held the pyre for another minute and then with a mighty shove he pushed it away from the cart. Again he whistled, and the horses pulled the cart from the water once more. Anny had been holding on tightly to the back of the front bench, but once the cart stopped, they both settled into the back of the cart looking out to the river.

● ● ● ● ● ● ●

Megan's arms burned by the time she had carried the mop, rags, and two pails of water to the north wing of the castle. She placed the buckets down next to the fifth door and reached into her pocket for a small silver key Cailar had given her. As she opened the door, the same heavy stench of decaying blood came to her in even greater force. She pushed her way into the warm room and quickly closed the door behind her.

Her mop forced a puddle to cascade from the wooden bucket as she plunged it into the cool sudsy water. Before long she was mopping dried blood off the old stone. "A print," she thought with a shudder. She could see a partial print of a woman's shoe in the blood. "Must be where Sonia was when he dealt her the final blow," she thought.

She swirled the bubbles and blood across the floor in the river she had now created. Time passed, and before too long the job was done and the bloodied water dumped into the moat below the large windows. "This had better be the last thing he asks of me," she thought. "He will not have the upper hand much longer."

After carefully bundling up the bedclothes so that no blood could be seen on them, she gathered her things and left. It was getting late, and she had to get these final pieces clean. After all, the trial was in just a few hours.

● ● ● ● ● ● ●

Jax laid stretched out in the cart, the sun beating down on his chest. His hands were behind his head, and after a short while, Anny could hear soft snoring. It took her out of the seriousness of the moment as she turned from the burning pyre, which had by now began to smolder, to her companion. He was perfectly at rest here at the very edge of death. What had he seen in his life that this seemed as common as a sunset or as dull as a rainy day?

For a moment she was mad, but then his snoring was interrupted as he sharply snorted and sat up. He smiled as if he had not been sleeping at all, then turned to Anny and pointed out towards the river.

"That's it. It's over now. Nothing more to do," he said. He reached down and brushed at his pants, which seemed to have dried only on the top. "Blast it!" he scoffed as he climbed out of the cart. He wandered over to the pile he had left on the ground earlier and pulled his shirt back on. He waved to Anny to come over as he grabbed the rest of his gear.

"Are we headed back then?" she asked as she walked up to him. Jax turned around to her as he struggled to fasten his belt.

"Not quite," he hesitated. "There is one more thing, but honestly I've been putting it off. I mean, it's not like it is my idea. No, that isn't really important, is it? No excuses, just do what I have to," he said as his hand reached for his ax. He held it out to his side, his grip tightening. "Please, don't make this difficult," he murmured as he reached for the back of her neck.

He was pushing her down to the ground when suddenly his feet went flying over his head, and he landed on his back. He barely saw a flash of her skirt as Anny went running for the woods nearby.

Jax quickly recovered to his feet and gave out a hearty laugh. "Well, that was unexpected! Where in the world did you learn to do that?" he laughed as he chased after her. He hadn't felt his heart racing this fast in years. Anny was swift on her feet to be sure and strong as a mule. As he gave chase his eyes tracked her gracefully leaping through the thick brush of the woods as if she was just another part of the forest. Jax could have just thrown his ax, and it would have been over, but he continued to hesitate. Instead, when he had caught up to her, he tackled her to the ground.

They fell into the underbrush; dead leaves flew up around them. Jax held her firmly from behind as both struggled to catch their breath. Tears started to run down her cheeks though she was fighting not to cry.

"No, no! Don't start that!" Jax said gruffly. He let out several expletives as he rolled her to her back and sat on top of her to pin her down. "You got me good. Where did you learn that? Never mind, I should have expected something. Why couldn't you have just gotten away?"

"How did you know? Jax, just let me go. I swear I'll never return to Pent. No one would have to know," Anny blurted out.

"But I would know. You see that is the problem," he said. He raised his ax above his head and swung it down hard into the trunk of a nearby tree. Anny's face went ashen.

"Look, I know what I am doing. I can make this painless. Why did you run? It could just be over by now," Jax said as he was reaching behind his back. He pulled out his dagger. "Just close your eyes. I swear it won't hurt."

"Have you lost your mind?" Anny balked as Jax held the dagger over her heart.

"Close your eyes!" he yelled. "You don't want me to mess this up, do you?"

"No!" she yelled back, opening her eyes as wide as she could. Again Jax let out a string of expletives as he threw the dagger down into the brush. He grabbed his head like it might fall off otherwise and then sat for a moment, still on top of her, thinking.

A breeze rustled through the still moment carrying with it the smell of dried leaves. It brushed their faces cooling the sweat off their brows. They could hear it traveling through the woods as the sound of fluttering leaves moved past them. It was evening now, and the shadows from the trees fell long to the ground. Finally, Jax looked at Anny, barely placing his hand momentarily on her cheek.

"Anny," he hesitated, "do you, and I mean truly, but do you think you could ever love me or even just like me? Even just tolerate me? I mean, we could run away together. We could both leave Pent behind. But what am I saying? I mean we'd be caught. We'd both be killed. But maybe it would be worth it if I thought…" he trailed off. "Okay, I can tell by your face the answer is 'no'," he laughed.

"I've changed my mind. I choose the dagger!" Anny said, and she closed her eyes and turned her head away.

She puffed out her chest. Again Jax laughed, but looking at her his heart ached. He wanted to reach out and run his worn hand down her neck, but he hesitated knowing she would not respond the way he hoped. Instead, Jax looked to his side, but he had thrown the dagger a bit too far away. He could see a glimpse of the blade. He reached for it, trying hard not to let Anny get away again. It was just too far away. When Jax sat back up, he was surprised to see an arrow sticking out of the tree where his ax was.

In one motion he pulled his ax free and sprung to his feet. Standing behind them a way off was Marcus, bow in hand.

"I missed on purpose!" Marcus yelled out. "I will not miss next time!"

"What luck!" Jax called out. He held his hands out to his side. "Marcus! Marcus, I am so glad to see you! Okay, aim right for my heart!"

"What?" Marcus asked incredulously. "You want me just to shoot you?"

"Yes! Yes! Please, this is perfect! Save Anny! Would it be better if I came closer? No, from where you are it is a clear shot. Come on now!" Jax said, waving his arms towards his chest.

Marcus shrugged then lifted the loaded bow to fire.

"What are you doing?" Jax lamented. "No, no! Not like that! Have you even used one of those before? You are not even holding the arrow on the right side of the bow. You want to kill me, right? Not just maim me?"

"I'm doing the best I can!" Marcus said incredulously.

"Where did you train? Have you ever killed anyone before?" Jax asked.

"Lots of people!" Marcus assured him.

"How many is a lot?" Jax timidly asked.

"Like five!" Marcus called back.

"Five? Five? But you are practically a baby then!" Jax scoffed, disappointed.

"What? They were really big guys; skilled men of battle!" Marcus argued, lowering the bow as he did.

"Okay, you know what, I trust you. It's going to be okay. Just do your best and try not to hit Anny," Jax said as he motioned towards the ground where she had been. What he saw startled him. "Anny? Anny!" he exclaimed. Both men looked around. "Where did she go?"

They looked around for a second before both exclaimed, "The horses!" and began to run back to the field where Jax had left the cart.

"It's still there," Jax called out with relief as he pointed to the cart, which was still where he had left it, but Marcus looked worried.

"My horse is gone," he said dejectedly. Jax immediately punched him in the arm.

"You idiot! She'll get away! She'll get herself killed!" Jax yelled at him. Jax took off for his cart with Marcus following behind.

"Get in! We have to get back to Pent. We have to get to the trial!" Jax said, and the two rode off together. "Did you really miss the first time on purpose?"

● ● ● ● ● ● ●

A thousand thoughts flew through her mind as Anny fled, but the strongest was the sense that she had to get back to Pent. As insane as it might have sounded earlier, having just faced death she knew that if she could do only one last thing, it would be to tell Paul who had killed Sonia. It just did not matter what happened to her now. She had to let Paul know at all costs. She owed him that much.

When she finally arrived at Pent, she was struck by the emptiness of the main street as it was only late evening. The sun was setting, and the sky was a fiery red. All of the commotion she remembered from that first sunny day when she rode through was now replaced by a distant murmur. Every shop was closed and many of the windows dark. It was unsettling, and so she traveled faster.

The wind was starting to pick up now as she approached the main square of the city. The murmur she heard was growing louder. Flickering torches lined the streets. A large gust blew her hair in her face as she made the last turn into the main square, and it was then she could see where everyone was. Before her, the square was filled with citizens.

She had to stop abruptly to avoid running into them, which granted her more than a few dark stares from those before her. However, upon seeing the crests on the reins and saddle of her horse, they quickly lowered their eyes and hurried away. Anny looked around confused for a moment. There was a sense of excitement in the air, but why were all of these people gathered here? A path began to form before her as the people took notice of her. Assuming she was royalty, they parted to let her past.

Slowly she made her way through towards the center of the square. There was a large, raised stage the people were gathering around. Vendors were selling their spicy food. Enormous lamps had been hung from the nearby buildings, their flames burning against the darkening sky. She could hear children laughing and a small group of performers singing. Then she heard someone say the word 'trial'. She dismissed the idea, but then she heard it again: over and over. Could this be one of the trials Jax and Paul had spoken of?

She searched the crowd, and the first person who looked at her she asked, "Who is on trial today?"

It was an older woman who pointed further up the street towards the castle. "One of the guards I believe," she said with a smile.

Anny did not hesitate to hear anything more. It felt like an eternity passed before she made her way around the stage. She followed the main road to the castle, looking for Paul the entire way. The outer gates were still open, and again the seals on the side of her steed allowed her to ride past the few guards posted by the entrance quickly. She rode on to the kitchen entrance hoping it would still be open. When she arrived, none of the other maids were there. She ran through the kitchen into the servants' corridor and headed towards the prison.

She made it as far as the hall outside the entrance to the prison. There she saw a group of men standing outside, among them Paul. His hands were bound with two guards to either side holding onto him. There were two other men as well. One she recognized as Paul's friend Andrew. He stood with his back to her and a small box tucked under his arm. The other, older man she did not recognize. He was dressed in the long, dark coat of the highest officials.

"Paul!" she cried out, and she ran up to him. She did not get far. Andrew instinctively grabbed her as she tried to run past him.

"Anny?" Paul said in disbelief. "What are you doing?"

"Anny?" the man in the coat asked. She turned to him momentarily. He had piercing blue eyes, and his entire face was pale as if he had seen a ghost.

"Paul, I know who killed Sonia," Anny insisted as she pushed Andrew away from her. "It was one of the king's friends."

"No, no Anny! Please do not listen to her, Cailar! She does not know what she is doing," Paul pled to the man in the coat. "Anny please, do not say anything else. Please let what will happen happen!"

Cailar stepped forward now. He grabbed Anny's arm and dragged her away from the others.

100

"Please, Cailar," she began, "I have heard of you! You must tell the king that Paul is innocent."

"Do not say another word!" he snapped at her under his breath, but she would not listen.

"It was Marcus!" she called out to Paul. "I saw the blood! I know it was him!"

Cailar's head fell. The guards all gasped, then looked to Paul who collapsed to his knees.

"No, Anny! Why?" he cried. He continued to sob and mumble, "No…no…run!".

Cailar's grip on her arm tightened. His blue eyes flashed with anger. He leaned as close as he could and into her ear he whispered, "Run! Run as far away as you can. Never return."

He then released her arm, but she just stood there as he slowly walked back to the frozen guards.

"I will not leave you, Paul. I am not going anywhere!" Anny yelled back to the men. "You will be free!"

Cailar stood beside Andrew, his eyes, along with the guards, fixated on her. He mouthed the word "go", but Anny stood firm. She would not leave him. Cailar smacked Andrew's arm with the back of his hand and motioned to the box. From it Andrew reluctantly took out a bloody dagger with the name, 'Paul' scratched into the handle.

"You understand I will have to arrest you?" Cailar said, and he motioned an order to Andrew. Andrew hesitated but a moment before plunging the dagger into Paul's back. Paul fell to the ground, his sobbing abruptly ending: replaced by a gagging sound.

Anny's legs felt numb for a moment. The room began to spin. This could not be, yet there he was bleeding out on the hallway floor. Cailar did not need to warn her again. She saw the guards turning from Paul back to her. This time she fled. Her feet pounded against the stone floors as she fought back tears.

Anny made her way back to the kitchen. She could hear the guards closing in on her. When she opened the door to the courtyard, she ran directly into Jax, who caught her in his arms.

"Anny! What are you doing here?" he scolded. She could not answer, she was crying so uncontrollably.

"Just get her into the cart and let us go!" Marcus said. He mounted his horse as Jax lifted Anny onto his cart. Andrew and the other guards came running out the kitchen door. They did not expect to see Marcus and Jax standing there.

"Stop, this woman is under arrest!" Andrew called out to them.

"You going to stop me?" Jax asked as he reached for his ax. "Didn't think so!" he yelled over his shoulder as he rode off.

"Yeah, the same for me!" Marcus defiantly said as he followed behind.

The guards could hear Jax laughing at Marcus as they rode off. "What a big man!" he exclaimed as they disappeared into the night.

Chapter Eight: The Road Unknown

Jax directed his cart around the main square to avoid the commotion there. They could hear yelling coming from the crowds who were clearly growing restless. Outside the main gates of the city, they were joined by Marcus's caravan which had been directed by the prince earlier to wait for him there. Marcus was relieved to see his carriage and offered to allow Anny to join him. She refused, deciding instead to stay by Jax.

"You should take him up on his offer," Jax said to her once Marcus was gone. "It'll be a long night out here. You might be able to get some rest."

"I do not need to rest," Anny whispered. "Maybe you should leave me here for the guards to find. It might be easier."

Jax shook his head forcefully saying, "Well that wouldn't do. I mean here I just saved your life. I can't just hand you over."

Anny covered her face. She felt like she wanted to cry, but she could not get the tears to come.

"No, no!" Jax grumbled.

Anny lowered her hands, taking in deep breaths. "I am sorry. You are right," she said with a sniffle. They rode behind Marcus in the dark silence.

Jax looked towards her, then punched her gently in the arm. "I'm sorry too; you know for that whole trying to kill you thing," he said.

Anny shrugged her shoulders and laughed. "Thanks," she smiled weakly. "I guess we are even then."

"What were you thinking going back there?" Jax asked.

Anny hesitated before confessing, "I think I know who killed Sonia and I just had to tell Paul."

Jax shook his head, cursing under his breath. "Anny, we all know who killed her. It was Paul."

"Jax, how could you say that?" Anny scolded him.

"That is just how it works," Jax said shrugging off her accusation. "Look, I know you're new to Pent, but whoever gets arrested that is who did it. That's the way it always has been and always will be. It's simple. It's easy."

"But it is not right!" Anny protested. "How is there justice in that?"

"Do you know they found Paul's dagger in her?" he asked as he glanced at her from the corner of his eye. He could barely make out her expression in the dark as she shuttered. "I don't want to think he did it either, but where else could that have come from? You see, there is no reason to think it over more. He did it, and it is terrible. It's like a half-eaten apple. You don't need the whole apple to know it was an apple."

Anny thought about it. She looked ahead at the back of Marcus's carriage. "But I found a lot of blood in one of the guest rooms. It had to be whoever was staying there. Why would Paul be there?"

Jax let out a snicker. "I think the real question is: why would Sonia be there? If you knew that then I think you'd know the answer."

● ● ● ● ● ● ●

Megan fell onto the bed, her long, wavy hair covering her chest as it heaved from her deep breaths. Cailar was already getting up from the bed, wrapping his robe around himself as he walked towards the table in front of the fireplace. He grabbed a pitcher from the table and poured himself a strong drink. Megan watched as Cailar gulped it down. She had never known him to drink, and now he was on his third glass of the night.

"Are you alright?" she hesitated to ask. He had not spoken to her all night. He had just summoned her, and before she knew it, they were back to their old games

104

again. How easy it is to fall back into old routines. "You seem distracted for someone who got what they wanted," she mused.

Cailar laughed, shaking his head and putting down his glass. "What do you know of what I want?" he retorted as he watched the flames of the fire dance.

Megan slipped out of bed and tiptoed up behind him, wrapping her arms around his shoulders. "Just tell me what is bothering you," she whispered.

"You do not have to stay if you have other places to be. He is expecting you after all," Cailar said flatly as he shrugged her off.

Megan went to say something but then thought better of it. Tomorrow would be different, she told herself. Quickly, she pulled her clothes back on and sulked out of the room to her next commitment.

She arrived a different person; the past hour put out of her mind as if it had never happened. Ramoth was in his chambers, both fires blazing and a large table of food laid out before him. It was easier for her when he was drunk, but tonight he was surprisingly lucid.

"What did he tell you?" he asked Megan directly.

"Who?" she retorted incredulously.

"I have not much time. What did Cailar have to tell you today?" Ramoth said firmly.

"He would not speak to me. He seems distressed," Megan hesitantly admitted.

"Were you at the trial today?" he asked directly.

Megan furrowed her brow. "Everyone was," she said as if she were asking.

"Then you know there was no trial. Then you must also know the guard accused of murder never made it to the trial because he was struck down by Cailar's order while some crazy servant accused Marcus of being the murderer," Ramoth said with his eyes trained on her. He could see she was genuinely confused.

"I had heard no such thing, only that Paul had tried to escape and was struck down because of it," Megan assured him, hoping he would break his piercing gaze.

"Something was odd when Cailar reported the incident to me. He would not tell me the servant's name. Every time that came up Cailar became vague. Also, he did not send any guards after them once they fled deciding instead that it could wait until the morning."

"I do not know what these things mean," Megan said dejectedly.

Ramoth seemed to be smirking as he said, "Neither do I, but we are going to find out, are we not? You see, there were other witnesses, and they tell me this servant's name is 'Anny'. Do you know her?"

Megan was surprised. Her face turned flush with anger. "Anny? Do you not remember her? You were with her just after the feast," Megan reminded him, but Ramoth just stared back blankly. "I have spent some time with her, but I do not think she and Cailar are acquainted at all," she continued, realizing Ramoth remembered nothing of the night of the feast.

Ramoth finally smiled as he grabbed his cup and said, "Okay, what else do you know about her? I want to know everything."

● ● ● ● ● ● ●

Anny awoke the next morning when Marcus's carriage hit a bump, almost throwing her from the bench she had fallen asleep on. It was very early in the morning. She'd only slept a few hours on Jax's insistence as the night air had grown very cold. She steadied herself, then saw that Marcus was already awake and staring at her.

Sometimes when you first wake up, time does not exist. You are just floating there, your pure self. That was what it was like: it was only the two of them, and her heart leapt inside seeing him. She wondered for how long he had just been sitting there watching her. Yet the moment passed, memories returned, and her heart broke inside her all over again. The carriage had stopped, and she could hear men talking outside. Just as Marcus went to speak, she bolted from the carriage.

"Wait!" Marcus called after her as he made his way out to Anny. He reached for her but instead ran directly into Jax. In the faint light stood skinny, tall trees that thinned out near the rocky bank of a stream. Marcus's men were unhitching the horses from his carriage to give them a drink. Anny walked past the men along the river bank, stopping to sit on a large, flat rock.

"Let her go," Jax said as he put his arm out for Marcus to steady himself. In his other hand, Jax held the reins to his horses, both of which seemed anxious to get to the stream.

"Sorry, I did not see you there," said Marcus. He motioned towards Anny. "What has gotten into her? I saved her life, and now she is mad at me?"

Jax let out a gruff laugh and put his arm around Marcus. He continued chuckling as he spoke. "Don't let it bother you. She's just confused. You're going to get a laugh out of this. She thinks one of the king's friends murdered her friend! Isn't that cute?"

Jax looked over at Anny as she called out, "I can hear you two!"

Again Jax let out a hearty laugh as he turned to Marcus. "She even told Cailar! That's why those men were chasing her. He is going to want her dead. Isn't that funny? I mean, one of the king's friends?

Jax's voice trailed off, and he stopped chuckling as he slowly turned to look at Marcus. At the same time, Marcus turned to look at him, his eyes wide. For a moment they stared at each other.

"No, no, no!" Marcus began to mouth. He continued to do this as Jax nodded his head frantically "yes".

Before he could slip away, Jax had his large, free hand all the way around Marcus's neck. His horses didn't flinch. This was perhaps not the first time they had seen this. Jax lifted Marcus, pinning him against the carriage while cursing at him. Marcus let out a manly, high pitched squeal which attracted the attention of his men. They drew their weapons, but then each hesitated to strike Jax.

"You! You?" Jax cried as he continued to choke Marcus. Suddenly he released Marcus, who fell to the ground. "You killed Sonia? It doesn't make any sense. Why does she think that?" Jax rambled as he scratched his head. "I mean, look at you!"

Marcus had been motioning to his men to stand down, but he stopped and looked up at Jax indignantly.

"Not this again! I could murder someone if I wanted to!" he insisted as he stood up. "I have killed so many men I cannot even count the total!"

"I'm sorry, did you say something? My ears are still ringing!" Jax huffed.

Marcus puffed out his chest but backed down the moment Jax shifted his weight towards him. The old veteran's face softened, and he smiled once more while looking over towards Anny.

"We have to get her to safety," Jax said in a hushed tone. Anny looked up now at them. She looked angry and started to walk back to them.

"I know, but where do we go?" Marcus whispered back.

Jax looked surprised. "What's wrong with Paultry?"

"I am not going to Paultry," Anny interjected. "I am going on my own from here."

"I can't let you do that!" Jax pled. "You would be easy prey out here."

Marcus quickly agreed, saying, "Jax is right. Besides, splitting up will not change anything. If Cailar has ordered our arrest, then it will be done if his men catch up with us."

"What difference does it make to you?" Anny said, looking at them plainly. "Cailar would not harm you, Marcus, no matter what you have done."

Marcus's gaze dropped to the ground, and he turned away from them.

"You cannot even deny it?" she asked.

"Look at him. There is nothing to deny, my dear. That man's never taken a life," Jax said absolutely. "You can see it in a man's eyes when he has."

Anny thought about it. She so badly wanted for it to be true. "Jax, either way, you know I am the one they are after. I will return to Pent. Then they will leave you alone."

"That would be suicide, Anny," Jax said softly. "I've sworn in my heart to protect you and I will. There has to be some other way."

"There is," Marcus said as he turned around to look them in the eyes. He motioned towards the carriage. Anny and Jax looked at each other shiftily before Jax handed off his horses and climbed in. Marcus sat across from them in his usual spot, but he was only looking at Anny.

"We could go to Faverly," he said flatly.

Jax looked surprised. "Faverly?" he stuttered. "What would you want with that place? It's a place of death."

"It is our only hope," Marcus said as he shook his head. We cannot outrun Cailar's men. They will catch up to us and bring us back to Pent. You two would be put on trial. Instead, we will get on horses and ride ahead. I'll tell my men we are headed for Paultry, but instead, we will take the western path towards Dione. When Cailar's men catch up to my men, they will then try to catch up to us, but they won't succeed. They will reach Paultry only to find we are not there."

"You do not have to go with us," Jax said, "I can protect Anny anywhere we choose to go." He went to slip his arm around Anny, but she elbowed him.

"Have I no say in this?" Anny grumbled.

"Jax, I have to go. If they do find us, there is a chance I could persuade Ramoth to forget the whole thing. Besides, I got you both into it, so I'll get you out of it." Marcus said firmly.

"But why Faverly? Jax wondered aloud. "I could just take Anny far away. You'd never see either of us again. That place is creepy!"

"That is the point though," Anny hesitantly volunteered. "It is not a place that is easy to find or easy to get to. We could hide there while Cailar's men get ahead of us and then head to Paultry. If we run into them there, I believe we have a better chance at finding asylum. Is that the idea, Marcus?"

Marcus nodded, but Jax still looked confused.

"The only way to beat them there is to let them get there first," Marcus quipped.

"I'll do whatever you want, Anny," Jax said finally. "I'm just not sure I remember how to get there. It's been twenty years."

Anny looked surprised, but Marcus spoke reassuringly. "It's been a long time, but I am sure you can manage."

"Oh," Anny said under her breath. "Yes, that would be good then."

● ● ● ● ● ● ●

Soon after stepping out of the carriage Marcus, Anny, and Jax were ready to head out. Marcus did as he had said he would by telling his men he was going on ahead to the next town to lodge there, and that they might catch up to him there. Jax climbed onto one of Marcus's horses, leaving his beloved cart behind. Marcus and Anny rode together on his steed. At first, they went somewhat slowly ahead, but once the caravan was out of sight, they raced to the junction between Paultry and Dione, stopping only once they were sure the caravan could no longer see them. There was a palpable sense of relief as they made their way along the trail which twisted and turned lazily through the forest and up the foothills of the Venom Mountains. They arrived at Daven close to dinner time.

Anny could not have imagined that Daven would be a large city like Pent. Two main roads crossed here, and both were crowded with people. Where the two ways met, at the center of town, was a large square lined with shops and food stalls. She could smell all kinds of spices: cinnamon and grease all combined. People were calling out their wares: each dressed a little differently than she was accustomed to seeing. She found herself unconsciously holding onto Jax a little tighter.

Jax seemed a bit uneasy in the crowd, but Marcus had a huge smile on his face. He was taking in deep breaths enjoying the atmosphere. He pointed down one large road and told her it was the center of the market. There they would be able to get anything else they might need for the trip. For now, he was only interested in getting them some new clothes and then they were off to the inn for the night.

The clothing merchant was a short, thin man with weathered hands. He did not even need to measure the patrons before directing them to the items available in their respective sizes. Anny noted the clothes were worn looser here, with wide sashes around the middles as opposed to the tight, almost corset-like style which she had found to be in fashion in Pent. The colors were a bit brighter too. Her old uniform had been mostly dark grey and white, but the dress she was now handed was dark red with a light blue sash for the middle. Marcus accepted a green shirt with buttons all down the middle. It was indeed more casual than anything she had seen him in up to that point which she supposed was the point in avoiding being noticed. Jax initially refused all attempts to change his appearance, but he did reluctantly tie a bright orange sash around his waist, a move which only caused him to stick out more conspicuously.

Marcus waved Anny out of the store as he reached for his money. When he came out of the store, he had a wide-brimmed, leather hat on his head. He smiled widely, quite pleased with himself. Jax politely noted how stupid Marcus now looked.

Though many large inns were located on the main square, Marcus shunned them all for a much smaller establishment that was off one of the side roads. The traffic was not so noticeable here, though the place looked a little run down. Anny couldn't help but feel a bit anxious as

111

Marcus handed the horses off to the man running the stables next door.

As they entered, there was a small restaurant and bar which occupied the main floor with a set of stairs leading up to the guest rooms. Marcus walked right to the bar and greeted the man there warmly. It was apparent that they knew one another by the way Marcus shook his hand, holding onto it as they spoke.

The bartender, who could not have been much older than Marcus, laughed and pointed up the stairs. Marcus was laughing too while nodding his head jovially. Reaching under the bar, the man retrieved a key which he handed to Marcus while pushing one of the small, lit lanterns resting on the bar towards him. A moment later Marcus returned with the items, motioning to his companions that they should go upstairs.

Chapter Nine: A Night on the Town

They had been given the room just at the top of the stairs so that from the door you could look down and see almost to the front door. The room was larger than expected, with a fireplace to the right and a decent sized bed to the left. Just inside the door was a small table and chairs where Anny placed the parcel of their new clothes.

On the far wall were two large windows with an entirely unspectacular view of the neighboring building. Marcus placed the small lantern on the mantel and threw his hat onto the bed before falling, face first, onto the side near the rear wall. He let out a loud groan, indicating he never wanted to be disturbed and would sleep like this forever.

Anny and Jax might have thought he was joking, but not a moment later they could hear he was snoring. Not wasting any time, Jax excused himself indicating he would be at the bar. Anny's stomach growled thinking of all the food she had seen down in the market, but without any money, she would have to wait for Marcus to wake up.

The young girl was aggravated as she sat down at the small table, her fingers mindlessly pulling at the bundle there. It would not be dark for some time, but she thought it better to build a fire than to sit there smoldering. Anny used the wood piled near the hearth and set it ablaze with the small lantern. The room became cozy as the light from the fire warmed it up.

Anny was about to lie down when the door suddenly opened. Marcus jumped up, a bit startled but happy to see the bartender with a tray of food. Jax was following just behind with a drink still in his hands. Jax placed it down on the table and gave a smile with a little salute as he grabbed the tray of food.

Among the items brought were a bottle of wine and several large bowls of stew along with a substantial baguette. The three ate quickly. The entire time Jax raved about the bar, a feature that surely was the only reason Marcus had selected this place. When they finished all sat admiring the fire, their feet stretched out towards it.

Just as Anny was again thinking of lying down, Marcus announced that they would now be heading to the bathhouse. He grabbed the parcel of clothes and left before either could object. It turned out there was a small bathhouse just across the street from the hotel. Marcus pointed her to the left while he and Jax went to the right, Marcus's new green shirt tucked under his arm. They would meet up at the inn afterward.

As she watched them walk away, her heart sank a little. Though the journey had not been easy, Marcus was at this point the only familiar thing around. She soaked her old clothes in soapy water as she climbed into the public bath. The water was almost scalding and the place practically deserted. It was getting to be late afternoon, a time when most people would be preparing for dinner rather than heading to the bathhouse.

A pair of older women were there with her, chatting from the opposite side of the bath. She could only make out a bit of what they were saying. In reality, her mind was on Marcus. She tried to busy herself, washing out her hair in a meticulous way as to take as long as possible. The last thing she wanted was to arrive at the room before Marcus and be there alone with Jax.

Having scrubbed as much as she could, she climbed out of the tub and wrapped herself in a large towel. She then set about wringing out her old clothes, making sure to get as much of the water out as she could. The dress could dry overnight, but everything else had to be dried right there by the fire which was warming the bath water. After all, she had been too shy at the time to ask that Marcus buy her some new undergarments.

She hung up the clothes and sat nearby running a towel over her hair. There was something beautiful about being clean again. She had not had the chance to clean up since the day before, but even that seemed to be a lifetime ago. When she washed it, she noted that her dress had gotten soiled from her time with Jax when he'd wrestled her to the ground. Though the dirt quickly washed out, she couldn't help but remember him looking at her the way he had.

Would Marcus do the same when she returned to the room? Why even after everything he had done could she not just forget about Marcus? She thought her standards were higher: that there were just some things that a person could do that would make you run away from them. Instead, her heart still pounded at the sight of him, her heart ached to be near him, and she hoped the bath would not remove too much of that familiar smell she had come to love about him.

Was what he had done such a big deal? Could there be a love so pure that it would overlook all those flaws? Surely that would be the most profound, sincerest love imaginable: one where it didn't matter at all what the other did; so unconditional that it bordered on unnatural.

No, she could never shake this feeling of longing for him. It was time to go for it- to let him know she was going to remain by his side forever.

Having burdened herself with these thoughts for long enough, Anny grabbed her clothes and hastily got dressed. Her new clothes were much softer and more comfortable. She wished there was a mirror to see the dress in, but for now, she would have to imagine it looked good.

When she returned to the inn, Marcus and Jax were already there sitting at the bar. Marcus had his new hat resting on the bar and wore his new shirt buttoned up only halfway which was, apparently, the correct style. Both men smiled when they saw her. Marcus motioned back towards the door. They would be going out tonight.

The evening was enjoyable all around. Anny held onto Marcus's arm as if she were his wife. Marcus seemed to tolerate it. Jax meandered behind them like he were their child. Together they came up with an elaborate alibi of how they had met and what their new names would be. It turned out this was all a pointless exercise as not one person asked for their names or cared where they were traveling to or from.

Instead, they enjoyed an anonymous dinner, tucked in the back corner of a crowded room. They were served thick slices of bread covered in gravy. Anny was surprised she was able to finish it quickly, even enjoying some of the fruit offered after the meal. It looked like an apple but was a bit grittier in texture. She decided not to embarrass herself asking what it was. Jax refused to eat it outright. Some small, almond flavored cakes were served last along with more wine. Marcus explained that it was always safer to drink wine exclusively while traveling.

It was dark out when they left, and so they walked along the lamp-lit main streets looking into the shops. Marcus purchased some bags of dried beans for the journey along with a new blanket. They found a nice copper kettle as well to boil water in.

Rather spontaneously, Marcus stopped at a small vendor and grabbed a green and yellow scarf from a display. He twisted it and tied it around Anny's head, grinning in a self-congratulatory way. Scarves were, as he would explain, common where they were headed. She would seem out of place without one covering her head.

● ● ● ● ● ● ●

In the dark corner of the city, the sky above the inn was alight with stars. Though Anny had thought they had traveled much, it had still been nice to stretch their legs. Jax excused himself once more to stop at the bar. Marcus and Anny headed to the room where Marcus dropped the new items by the door, though the blanket he threw on the bed. It had an intricate pattern of bright red and dark green lines. Somehow it cheered the room up.

He sat on the end of the bed and pulled his shoes off, throwing them towards the wall. He leaned back, his feet towards the fire. It had nearly gone out, but Anny quickly had it burning bright again. When she turned to him, he was smiling.

"It's been a long day," he said, "but we make a good team."

Anny blushed. She could hardly breathe as she boldly walked towards him and sat down next to him. She was a little surprised when he shifted a bit away from her. Maybe the entire evening had been an act on his part.

They watched the fire growing before she spoke. "I really enjoyed myself today too, Marcus. For a while there I forgot about everything. Maybe it could always be like this?"

"On the run?" Marcus chuckled, "I am not sure I have the stomach for it. It will be nice to get home for a change."

"What will happen when we finally do get to Paultry?" she barely whispered. She held her breath as he responded.

"I do not know for certain," Marcus said casually. "I am sure you will be safe though."

"That is not what I meant," she began, but her voice was failing her.

Her mind was racing in a dozen directions. She waited to see if he would ask what she meant, but Marcus again remained silent. The silence sliced at her. How much of it could she take?

Her heart was pounding as she stood up. Casually she removed the scarf from her head allowing her long hair to fall down her back. Marcus was still looking at the fire. She reached back and untied her sash, dropping it onto the bed. Even so, Marcus would not look at her, but instead was now scowling as he faced the fireplace. Her heart was racing so fast that she had to move slowly or she might faint. Carefully she pulled her shoulders out of the dress and allowed it to fall to the floor. Still, Marcus would not turn to her. He kept the same stern face.

Anny thought she might cry standing there in her undergarments, her entire body almost exposed. Instead, the young girl reached down and picked the dress up, laying it over the chair before returning to the bed. Marcus had not moved even an inch. She felt he was watching her out of the corner of his eye.

Anny sat beside him, pushing her chest out a bit. She trembled as she wondered what she was doing wrong. The room was spinning slightly, but she had made up her mind: she loved him and was willing to do whatever it took to show him.

Gently she reached her hand out, and as soon as she touched his arm, he pulled away, cursing as he stood up.

"What are you doing?" he blurted out. Anny could not respond. "Do not look at me like that!" he said, pointing at her. "Just stop. Please, you are making all of this so difficult. Why are you making this so difficult?"

The young girl was too frightened to move or respond. He put his hands up to his face and was shaking his head.

"Anny, look I never meant to lead you on. I'm sorry. I thought you knew it was all just part of the fun- part of the game we were playing tonight." He could see she was still unable to respond. "Look, look at me," he said as he again sat down, this time taking her face in his hands. "Look you are beautiful, but it is not that easy. In Paultry it is different than Arden. In Arden, everyone acts like Ramoth. They go around doing whatever feels good. It is not like that in Paultry. We do not just do things because they feel good."

"Why not?" Anny whimpered. "Why not?"

Again he got up cursing. "I am engaged," he blurted out. It was like an arrow had shot straight through Anny's heart when she heard it. Tears began to flow from the depths of her, and the young girl was unable to control them. She didn't hear the rest of what Marcus said, she only remembered it later on. She stood and hastily pulled her dress back on. She then rested on the bed so that her back was to Marcus as she cried as quietly as she could.

Marcus waited a moment hoping she would stop before saying, "I did not want to tell you. I did not think I had to tell you. Anny, please do not be mad at me. It is going to be okay. I will get you to Paultry," Marcus rambled as he sat on the end of the bed. He could tell his words were not working.

"Okay, okay- Anny look. I need to tell you something else, and I do not know if I am telling you something new or something we both know, but it is not just that I have a fiancé back home. I mean, that is important, but there is something else. I did not say it sooner because honestly if Ramoth ever found out, he would kill me, and I mean like literally I would be at trial and be dead."

Anny stopped sobbing as best she could to listen, but the effort was considerable.

"Anny, you can never tell anyone this, but I think you could be my sister," Marcus said as he leaned close to her.

Marcus's assertion was the last thing she expected to hear.

"Marcus," Anny whispered, "that would be impossible."

"Hear me out, okay?" Marcus pled. "When Ramoth first announced the myth every country was to send the girls born on the same day as the king's son. Well you know Paultry is a small country, and my parents thought it would be wise if they sent their child. They had my sister around the time Ramoth's son was born. They handed her off thinking she would become royalty in Arden."

Anny's heart broke hearing this. "Esme?" she whispered.

Marcus's eyes grew wide. "Yes, yes! Esme! Esme!"

Anny sat up to face him, saying, "Marcus, I am so sorry. I am so, so sorry, but I am not Esme. She was killed, just as the others were."

Marcus's affect dropped. He turned away and pounded his fist against the wall. She did not think it was possible for him to cry, yet he soon fell to his knees with his eyes covered, sobbing. She got up from the bed and put her hand on his back. He did not pull away now.

"How do you know this? How do you know? Just tell me, damn it! Ramoth cannot reach us now," he said as he cried. "You knew her? Tell me. I want to know anything."

"I swore I would never say," she insisted, but Marcus stood up and grabbed her by the shoulders. He looked into her eyes with desperation. She felt a shiver go up her spine.

"Please," he said. I spent my whole life trying to get close to the king just so that when Esme was brought to Pent, I could be near her. That monster killed her, did he not? He told me she died protecting him. Him! That coward!"

The young girl's gaze fell to the ground, and she could feel a lump in her throat. Anny had sworn never to tell, yet here was Marcus. Could he be trusted? Feeling his grip tighten, she closed her eyes, and she could smell his musk: that familiar smell she had grown to love. She collapsed forward, and he pulled her into his arms. She could feel his heart pounding against hers.

"Just trust me," he said as he held her.

"Can you not believe me?" she whispered into his ear.

He released her, walking away sharply towards the fire. He turned back, and she could now see all of the sadness had left him and there was only anger in his eyes.

"Anny, you are my friend. I saved your life two times now. I will not fail you. I must know what happened to her. You must know what that is like. You wanted to know what happened to Sonia, right? Even the horrible truth is more comforting than uncertainty."

"And what did happen, Marcus?" Anny snapped. Immediately she regretted it.

"You want to know?" Marcus incredulously retorted. "Fine! Fine, I will tell you the truth, and it is this- I have no idea! None! I was drinking. I was waiting for you! The next thing I know I'm being carried off by a group of women and I am thinking we are about to have a great time, but when I wake up? Bam! There it is- a pool of blood, and there is blood everywhere. Do not look so horrified; I know now that you must have seen it. Do you think I could have done that? Jax was right about one thing, I have never taken a life. Never."

"But it must have been you! Paul would never have done that," Anny insisted.

"And you think I am a better candidate? I am a nobleman, not some paid guard who is trained to kill. Cailar knew what had happened and said he would take care of it. Evidently, he found Paul to be guilty."

Anny wanted to say something, but her head was spinning and throbbing.

"I will have to sleep on it," she finally muttered.

"No, no: you are going to tell me about Faverly!" Marcus demanded.

"Fine," Anny said with a sigh. "I was at Faverly," she admitted. She saw his eyes widen. "I knew your sister. She was a very sweet and loving girl. I am so sorry she is gone. We grew up side-by-side, but I am telling you I was not one of the Sisters."

"Then what were you doing there?" he asked skeptically.

"My mother was the cook there. Her name was Odlin," Anny explained. "I do not think I was supposed to be there."

"Well, no one who could father a child was allowed to be at the fortress, right?" Marcus reminded her.

Anny shrugged as she said, "We never really talked about it. It does not matter except she was always trying to hide me whenever anyone from Pent would come. I was to stay hidden."

"Which is why you survived that night," Marcus said with a sudden realization.

"Exactly, only I did not stay where I was told. I wanted to see the grand party and the king. I knew the Sisters would be all dressed up. I just wanted to take a peek, but what I saw was so horrible."

Anny couldn't help but begin to cry again. Marcus embraced her, holding her tightly against his warm chest while he rubbed her back.

"When we get to Faverly I'll tell you everything I remember about her," Anny whispered into Marcus's ear.

"I would like that," Marcus said. They looked at each other, and then slowly he leaned in and kissed her. Anny felt the whole world melt away. She again reached to remove her dress, but suddenly he pulled away.

Shaking his head, he muttered, "Jax will be back soon." He then climbed into the bed and within moments was snoring.

Anny stood frozen in place for several minutes, but then finally made her way to the bed. She was falling asleep when she heard Jax enter the room. He walked to the end of the bed, stripped off all of his clothes, and fell onto the space between them. She could only be grateful he had fallen asleep on his stomach. The two men then snored all night loudly.

● ● ● ● ● ● ●

Megan had gone early that day to speak to Cailar. As she walked towards the king's private chamber, she was still fuming from what Ramoth had told her about Anny the night before. She peered through the first large archway and could see both Ramoth and Cailar there working. It was a strange sight for her to see them not only together, but also fully dressed in official robes. Cailar was writing something at the central table while Ramoth spoke to another official with his back to them both.

Megan knew better than to enter the room, so she instead waved her hand frantically trying to get Cailar's attention. After a few moments he looked up from his work and saw her, but he refused to meet with her. He looked first to see if Ramoth had noticed her, and when it was clear he had not, he motioned for her to leave.

The rejection made Megan even angrier. After everything she had done, she had thought things would be different. Instead, they were worse. She continued to fume all day until nightfall when she knew Cailar would be in his chamber.

She knocked loudly on the door and then let herself in. Cailar was standing with his back to her, leaning over his desk. He did not turn to her, just motioned to a tray of food on the bed.

"I figured I would see you tonight, so I had extra sent," he stated. "Help yourself. I am just finishing up some business."

Megan could see the tray had some of her favorite foods on it. She was skeptical he had done this on purpose and wondered if they just liked the same things. She shuffled over to the bed and picked up a piece of pineapple.

"Really?" she scoffed.

Now Cailar turned to her. He smiled. "Ramoth is cross with me," he blurted out, matter-of-factly. "He has been trying to act like nothing is the matter, but I am no idiot." He looked at Megan and waited.

"He is mad at you for the same reason I am," Megan said as she threw the pineapple back onto the tray. She could see Cailar was listening. "It was bad enough everything you have done to me up until now, but to know you wanted Sonia instead and now I find out about Anny as well?"

Cailar had been smiling, but when he heard her mention Anny, his affect dropped. "Anny? What about her? What did he say about her?" Cailar demanded.

"I cannot believe you! How many women will it take to please you or is it that you are only interested in the ones Ramoth fancies?"

Cailar grabbed her by her arms and pushed her against the wall. "What did you say?" he cried out.

"That is right. That is right! You awful excuse for a man! Ramoth had his hot, sweaty body all over her. You should be used to having his leftovers by now. Did you know she was two-timing you or do you get a thrill out of it?"

In anger, Cailar threw Megan to the ground. She landed hard on her right arm, but just looked up at him laughing as he paced around the room with his hands on the sides of his head.

"It hurts having someone betray you like that, does it not? How does it feel?" she hissed at him.

Cailar stopped pacing. He looked at Megan with his piercing eyes. "Tell me, has he noticed that Anny is not here anymore?"

Megan laughed. "Of course he has you fool! Besides that, he knows you let her run off! That is right: he knows she is the one who made all those accusations against Marcus." For a moment she almost thought Cailar looked worried. "I guarantee you Ramoth is going to find her and make her pay for it! Finally, you are going to get what you deserve."

Cailar's eyes were now looking off into the distant future. He was looking not at Megan, but right through her. She had wanted him to cry and scream, but he was suddenly calm.

"I have much to do," he said blankly.

Megan looked dumbfounded. "Did you not hear anything I just said?" she snapped, but he did not answer. Instead, he suddenly left the room.

● ● ● ● ● ● ●

Anny felt so foolish she hardly slept that night. When she awoke, she found Marcus had left the room, but Jax was still right next to her. He had rolled onto his back, but luckily Marcus's new hat was placed over him. She sprung from the bed and shuttered a little. She noticed that the supplies for the trip were missing. Her heart began to race: could Marcus have left them here?

She stammered into the hall and down the stairs. Marcus and the bartender both looked up at her startled. They were at the bar, the supplies sitting nearby.

124

"You alright?" Marcus said with a smile. "Is Jax up yet?"

"Why are you laughing? And no, he is not awake yet," Anny said snidely. She was suddenly uncomfortable with how the bartender was smirking at her. "Do you two know each other?"

Marcus was about to answer when they heard Jax coming down the stairs. He was smiling impishly. He gave a little wave to them, but then walked out of the inn.

"Where is he going?" Marcus wondered aloud. "Do you think we should follow him?"

"He is wearing the hat," Anny bemoaned. "We need to burn that hat."

Marcus and Anny gathered the supplies and walked out of the inn. Jax was nowhere to be found. Suddenly Anny remembered the blanket and ran back up to the room to retrieve it. When she returned, Jax was standing next to Marcus with the reins of three donkeys in his hands.

"Aren't they cute?" Jax said to her. Anny smiled and petted the closest one to her on the nose. "I think he likes you."

"Where did these come from?" Marcus asked, unconsciously feeling to make sure his wallet was still attached to his belt.

"I traded the horses!" Jax beamed.

"You traded our horses?" Marcus scoffed. "You idiot! My horse was of high breeding. He was a gift and worth a small fortune!"

"I got two donkeys for him!" Jax admitted proudly. "Now Anny doesn't have to ride with you."

"No, no, this is madness. We are getting my horse back!" Marcus insisted.

"They are kind of cute," Anny volunteered.

Jax was suddenly stern. "Listen, fancy man. Faverly is high up in the mountains. It is a long, steep climb from here, and these donkeys are well suited for it."

"Can you just tell me where my horse is so I can get him back?" Marcus pled, but Jax and Anny were already loading up the donkeys.

"They're a bit slow though so we'd better get moving!" Jax urged Marcus.

Marcus could resist no longer. He climbed onto his donkey, and the three set off.

"Oh yeah, here's your hat," mentioned Jax as he put the hat back on Marcus's head.

Chapter Ten: Faverly

Faverly is a small fortress; an ancient place tucked high into the southeast side of the mountains near the border between Paultry, Daven, and Arden. There is a grassy field to the south and a cliff to the northeast. A stream trickles down the side of the mountain directly behind the fortress, running beneath it and exiting the cliff. For that reason, in the early morning hours as the sun is just rising the place is covered in a strange fog.

There are several trading routes that crisscross the Venom Mountains connecting Dione to its neighbors. However, towards the east two trails converge at a rocky slope. Only once this path is scaled can one gain entrance to Faverly. There, the mountain is steep and some of the ways long, and so it is crucial travelers not get lost. Many a wanderer have forfeited their lives vainly circling the mountains in their travels.

Jax spent the better part of the trip retelling the stories of old. He recalled the valiant battles he fought when invading Pacia, whose warriors were unmatched. Then the warrior spoke of the beautiful, nomadic women of Crewda and their various skills which included spinning wool. Lastly, he spoke of the wonders of Mesu. He claimed they built towers as tall as the sky and ships three times as fast as those of Pent.

At first, Anny listened intently as the stories made the time pass quickly. However, after a few days had passed Jax began repeating himself. With each retelling, the battles became fiercer, the towers taller, and the drink stronger. Anny began to lose interest. Marcus had never been interested in the first place and refused to comment when asked about his adventures. Anny came up with fantastic tales of her life in Fay Hill. Not only had she caught a fish that could talk, but once she was swept up into the sky to dine with a golden falcon.

When they finally came to the rocky slope, Jax paused to tell them how the men from Pent had been stuck here for some time trying to push their carts up the smooth stone. The surface had gotten covered with moss, and the wagons had first to be unloaded. On the other hand, the donkeys had no problem with it, a point that Jax was sure to point out to Marcus.

Past the slope, the trail was narrow and meandered along the tree covered mountainside until it reached the field outside the gate. Jax and Anny paused as Faverly finally stood before them. Marcus continued ahead of them. He seemed eager to get past the gate.

Jax came close to Anny and whispered to her, "I have not forgotten about Sonia. Now that we've made it here, you give the word, and I'll kill him." He then rode on, smiling as always.

Just inside the gates, there was a small, square courtyard framed by the main structure which boasted many doors and passageways. It was made of smooth stones, two stories high, and ran along the east, north, and west of the fortress walls. A roofed balcony covered three sides of the courtyard. Arches supported the gallery with a spiral staircase leading all the way up to the roof.

Just inside the gate, to the left, was a place where the donkeys could be housed. In the center of the courtyard was a well that reached down to the river underneath. Paths crisscrossed the courtyard with overgrown grassy spaces between them. They could hear the sound of rushing water as it fell down the mountainside and also down the cliff somewhere else nearby. Jax looked around confused.

"Everything looks to be in its proper place," he said as he ran his hand over the wooden planks of the gate. "There isn't even a scratch on this door. I don't see signs of blood or anything."

Marcus was sure that by "anything" he meant "corpses", which should have been littering the place. Marcus shot a glance to Anny.

"I'm going to take a look around. You two stay here. If you hear me screaming it's best you run," Jax stated with a wink. He then drew his ax and headed off in the direction of the kitchen to the west.

"Ha!" Marcus exclaimed. "I would protect you!" he said to Anny.

"Certainly," she said, looking around nervously. Once Jax was out of sight Marcus grabbed her arm.

"You know what he is looking for," he whispered. "He was expecting there to have been a great fight here, as was I." Anny turned away from him. He could feel she was trembling. "You told me you were here and you knew Esme. Was it a lie? Was it all just a lie?"

"No!" Anny pled as she turned back to him. Marcus let her go and walked a few feet away with his back to her.

"You had me believe she was beheaded! Why did you lie to me like that?" Marcus growled.

"I told you from the start it was just a story!" Anny continued, "How was I to know she was your sister?"

"Then it was a lie? All of it?" Marcus huffed as he plunked himself down on the stone edging of one of the walkways. "Of all the deceivers, you are the best."

"Marcus, please understand. I do not remember what happened that night," Anny pled as she sat beside him. "We were all here, and then the king and his men came. I was locked away in a secret place, but I could hear the laughter from the feast." Anny covered her ears as she remembered. She started to cry, "I ran out to see, but what I remember must have been a dream because when I awoke, I was back in the secret place. I was back there alone. Everyone was gone. Everything was taken away."

"Another lie to cover the first?" Marcus scoffed. He waited a moment as her tears slowly trailed off. "What of this secret place?" he asked.

"I will show you, Marcus, and then you will believe me. I did not mean to lie about something important to you."

Jax suddenly returned from the west side of the fortress. He glared at Marcus.

"Now what have you done? I leave for a minute, and you have her crying? What is wrong with you?" Jax said as he came up to Anny and put his arm around her. "I was only joking, Anny. I wouldn't let anything harm you. I looked all around, and the place is secure. We can get a good night's sleep for once!"

There was little talking after that. Jax showed his guests to the kitchen where they rested their mats on the floor near the stove. Anny got the fire going while Jax and Marcus fed the donkeys. They ate more beans, as they had done the last several nights, and then fell asleep all together with Anny sandwiched between the two men: Jax with his arm around Anny and Anny with her arm around Marcus.

● ● ● ● ● ● ●

In a fitful sleep Anny could feel her feet pounding against the old stones of a hallway, the sound echoing against the hard walls. It was behind her; It was close behind her.

● ● ● ● ● ● ●

When Anny awoke her heart was racing, and she gasped for air. She looked around and realized that both Jax and Marcus were gone. She looked around in a panic, noticing that the bag of beans was still sitting where she had left it, the cooking pot as well.

The place was quiet in a strange way. Anny was used to the sounds of other people going about their day. The floors between the upper and lower rooms were made of wooden planks that were sturdy but allowed a lot of noise to travel between them. Just above the kitchen was the place that the servant's slept. This time of day there would have been a lot of noise as they were getting ready for the day. The kitchen as well would have been bustling.

Anny stood up and, lost in thought, she wandered over to the stove and for a moment put her hand on it. It had grown cold overnight. She looked around and seeing everything still sitting in its place gave her some comfort, but the silent cold stirred up a deep pain. She longed to hear the familiar sounds once more or to smell breakfast cooking again.

She made her way to the small stables by the gate. She was further relieved to see all three donkeys were still there, and it appeared they had already been tended to. The one that had carried her up the hillside happily greeted her with a series of snorts and whinnies. She rubbed his snout, whispering, "I am glad you are still here."

As she left the stables, she noticed that though the gates were closed, they were not locked. She walked up to the large doors and peeked through a crack between them. She couldn't see Jax or Marcus, but it seemed evident they had gone out for some reason. Maybe they needed more feed for the animals.

Anny figured that whatever the reason, they would likely be hungry when they returned. Perhaps they would even come back with something to eat! So she set to relighting the stove so she could boil more water. But even with that completed, the men had not returned. She was happy in a way. It meant she had some private time to wash up.

Off of the kitchen nearer the west side with the stables was a small room with a large tub in it. The tub drained to the outside, and there was a smaller basin that you could fill with water. It was meant for bathing, though sometimes they would use it to wash large pots. She had to clean it up a bit first, but soon she had the smaller basin filled with some of the hot water from the kitchen. She was happy to undress and dunk her hair into the water.

It felt like she had been scrubbing for some time to get all of the dirt from the trip off, but it also felt good to be home doing her usual routine. She was rinsing the suds off when the door to the kitchen swung open.

Marcus walked in casually, clearly not expecting her to be standing there. He threw his hands out in front of himself and averted his gaze.

"Sorry, sorry! Did not know you were in here," he stammered as he backed out of the room sulking.

Anny had instinctively covered herself as the door had opened, but now she slowly lowered her arms back down hoping Marcus would look at her and stay with her. "It is alright," she said quietly.

Marcus stopped in the doorway, his gaze still at the floor. "Actually I was looking for Jax. You would not happen to know where he went?"

"He is not with you?" Anny asked confused.

"Well, no. When I woke up, he was already gone off somewhere. I have been looking around, but so far I have not found him."

Anny realized she was wasting her time. She grabbed her clothes and began to get dressed. "I think he went outside the gates. Maybe you should go out and see what he is up to."

"Are you sure?" Marcus said, a bit excited. "I mean, if we are alone, this could be the chance we have been waiting for."

Anny stopped tying her sash around her waist to stare at him. Slowly Marcus looked up at her with a sly smile. "You can show me the secret room without him knowing what we are up to."

Anny led Marcus across the courtyard to a hallway on the North side of the fortress. The arched hall ran between the room that was the banquet hall and what was a storage room tucked in the Northeast corner. Halfway down the hall were two large doors that led to the banquet hall. Anny walked to the dark end of the hallway where it seemed to end at a stone wall. She looked at Marcus, hesitating for a moment, but he smiled and nodded to assure her. She thought about asking him to turn his back, but instead, she reached up and pressed one of the stones. There was an audible click as a door appeared in the rocks.

A narrow, curving staircase behind the door led down to a large room under the banquet hall. At first Marcus had to walk cautiously as the hallway and the top of the stairs were very dark; however, the room itself was lit with a diffused light that came through three huge, arched windows. Marcus was surprised. The windows faced into the mountain where there was an underground grotto carved out by the waterfall. Through the windows, he could see a clear, underground lake that the waterfall was flowing into. Light from holes in the cave above reflected off the water and into the room, creating the magnificent glow.

"Amazing," he remarked. "I have never seen anything like this."

"Barnas: this was his study," Anny said as she pointed to the walls which were lined with shelves containing all manner of books and scrolls. "He wrote some of these himself, though others are in languages I do not know."

"Books?" Marcus said.

"You sound disappointed," Anny said as she walked over to a desk.

"Disappointed? No, not at all. I am just thinking how sad it was that you were forced to spend so much time down here with just these books to keep you company. Which one would you say is the most special?"

Anny laughed as she fiddled under the desk. "You mean my favorite? Well, most of them are pretty boring. I did not know what some of them even meant, but I was not down here too often: just when the king's men might be around. That was not very often when I was older."

Marcus heard the sound of a drawer opening and from it, Anny pulled out a book.

"This one was Barnas's favorite, though I cannot read most of it. I thought, well with you being so well educated maybe you could read it to me."

Marcus took the book from her and flipped through the pages.

"I have no idea what it says," he laughed. He studied it for a moment before adding, "What do all these funny symbols mean I wonder."

Anny looked disappointed as she took the book back adding, "I used to wonder the same thing. Maybe it means nothing," she added with a shrug as she replaced the book in its place.

"I guess I have neglected my studies," Marcus joked. "I would much rather have been down in that lake swimming."

Anny walked over to the middle window and pointed out to the grotto. "You can reach that lake if you follow a path behind the fortress. The water is so cold that even on the hottest days of the summer you can go there and breathe in the cool air. It might still be a bit chilly for it but maybe we could go there later."

Marcus walked up close behind her and looked out the window. Anny could feel his warmth on the back of her neck. It gave her a chill which made her jump. She laughed at herself aloud, turning to see Marcus smiling at her.

"It is always a bit chilly down here," she joked before reaching up and unlatching the lock to the window. The large glass swung out, and a stiff, cold breeze blew in.

Marcus stepped back, rubbing his arms.

"That is chilly! You will get yourself sick," he chided. Stepping around her he pulled the window shut again. "Your hair is still wet," he chuckled while smiling and reaching to brush her hair from her face. His hand froze in midair, and his face became stern. He shook his head and walked away from her. "Why do you always look at me like that?"

"What do you mean?" Anny asked innocently. Her heart was beating hard in her chest again.

"You know what I mean. Every time I turn around you are looking at me with that smile. At night I feel you against my back, and honestly, I wish Jax were not here."

"He is not here now," Anny pointed out. Imploringly she looked at him, but his face was sullen, and his eyes fixed on the floor. With a sigh, she turned around. Down below the window the water splashed down the sides of the cave into the pool. She remembered all the hours she had spent standing there, and the loneliness of it overcame her.

She heard Marcus walking back to her, but this time he did not hesitate. He put his arms around her shoulders and pulled her close to him.

"I am sorry. I am so sorry," Marcus whispered into her ear as he began to kiss her neck.

● ● ● ● ● ● ●

The light from the courtyard was blinding as Anny made her way back towards the kitchen. She was humming and dancing along. The heavy weight of the world had lifted, and she knew now that she was never going to be alone again. Marcus was hers now. He would always be hers. Nothing could steal the happiness she felt; it enveloped her and permeated her.

She was surprised to find Jax had returned and was sitting on the edge of the well looking towards the gate with his back to her.

"Where have you been," he asked. He sounded angry, though he was smiling when he turned around.

"Here," Anny stuttered, pointing back towards the hall. "Where were you? We were beginning to wonder when you would be back."

"We? Is Marcus here too because I looked all around and couldn't find either of you."

Anny's face flushed. "I am not sure where he is. I am sure he is close by though."

Jax's eyes focused on her. She felt like he was looking right through her. Suddenly Marcus came out of the doors to the banquet hall. Anny jumped, but Jax did not break his gaze immediately. Instead, he studied her for another moment, then turned to Marcus.

"I found them," he said plainly.

"Who?" Marcus asked though he feared he knew of that which Jax was speaking.

Jax motioned for the two to follow him. They all made their way out through the gates where Jax led them to the cliff along the northeast side of the field. He pointed over the edge. Anny did not move, but Marcus crept up to see that out of the side of the cliff there was a waterfall, presumably draining from the grotto he had seen earlier.

"It is just a waterfall," he said.

Jax then held up to him a piece of dirty rope.

"Does this look familiar?" he asked Marcus. He did not wait for a reply. "Look at that: this type of rope comes from Crewda. Do you see the color and how smoothly braided it is? Rope like this isn't something you'd find in Pacia."

"Where did you find this?" Marcus asked as he turned the piece of rope over.

Jax pointed over the edge saying, "Down there: down at the bottom of this cliff. You see there is still a slip knot in it. This is classic; I mean classic Arden tactics. We did this a hundred times to any village who opposed us during the Noble War. It's quick and it's clean. We did this, Marcus."

"What do you mean, 'We did this'?" Marcus scoffed. "Everyone knows…"

"What if everyone is wrong? Marcus, what if Ramoth did this? What if Pacia had nothing to do with this?"

Marcus looked at Jax sternly. "You should be careful what you say, Jax. A little piece of rope is not going to convince a great many people. You would go to trial for treason."

Jax shouted out an expletive that echoed down the mountain as he rashly threw the bit of rope over the edge. "Do I look like I care anymore? We did this, Marcus. I am sure of it! There is more, down the side of the mountain: scattered all along bits and pieces of the people who were here: the Sisters, Marcus! He did this: he has been lying to us all along to get us to fight his stupid wars."

"Enough!" Marcus yelled back. Then he took a breath and put up his hands pleading, "Even if it were true, just if, what can we do about it? I am not saying it is true but look around. There are just us three. We cannot change what has happened. Getting ourselves killed is lunacy, and you know it. So forget about it."

Jax stared at Marcus intently, his eyes then glancing over at Anny who was silently pleading with him to calm down. Jax's face dropped as his anger gave way. Cursing under his breath, he walked back towards the gates. Marcus turned to Anny, who was now kneeling on the ground looking out toward the cliff. She seemed frozen there.

"It is not true, Anny. You understand, right? It is not true" he said sternly, his gaze fixed on her.

Anny nodded in agreement. She was not sure she wanted to know anymore but felt she must. Quietly Anny arose and followed Jax into the fortress. She found him leading his donkey out of the stable.

"Jax, you cannot just go," Anny pled. He did not acknowledge her as he grabbed his canteens and headed over to the well. "You would be in danger," she pressed.

"I'm not staying here, that's for sure," he griped. Angrily he threw the bucket down into the water cursing, then leaned on the circle of stones as he gazed down into the darkness.

"Please, Jax," she whispered, placing her hand on his back. "I could not fathom the thought of you being hurt. You should come with us."

"I never intended on going to Paultry," he snarled, shrugging her off and staring at her. "You know I could hear you two from right here somehow: all of it: the giggles and groans like a pair of animals. I thought you were someone different. I guess I was wrong. He's a married man, you know. Did you even think about that?"

"He is not!" Anny snapped, then recoiled realizing she should not have said anything at all.

Jax drew the bucket up from the well and finished filling the canteens. "Then when you two get to Paultry maybe you want to ask his wife about that," he shrugged.

Anny stood back as Jax began to saddle his donkey. Marcus then came back in through the gates and joined them, standing beside her. He noticed Jax had already packed his bag.

"He knows about us," Anny whispered to him.

Marcus did not respond but walked over to Jax. "Come with us, Jax. We can all go right now if that is what you want. If you leave, I cannot protect you."

"I don't need your protection," Jax said flatly. He grabbed the reins to his donkey and led it to the gate.

"It's not too late, Anny," he called over his shoulder. "You could come with me."

Anny looked to him and then to Marcus who was walking back to her. He turned her away from Jax and embraced her.

"Go and pack your things," he whispered in her ear. "We will have to leave right away. When they catch him, they will come after us."

Anny was shaking, but being in Marcus's arms made her feel strong. She jumped when she heard the sound of the gates slamming shut. She turned around to see that Jax was gone.

Marcus hurried to the remaining donkeys, preparing their saddles. Anny walked quickly to the kitchen to gather their food rations. Her mind was swimming trying to decide if there was anything at the fortress that she should take with her. She rushed up the stairs to the old servant's quarters and grabbed a few things that were sentimental to her.

At the last minute, the young girl decided to go back to the library for one more thing. When she reached the bottom of the narrow stairs, she was overcome by a sudden sorrow. Returning to the window, Anny gazed out at the pools below.

All of her memories were there before her: of her mother, of the Sisters. She could see them all below playing in the pools in the middle of a hot, summer day.

138

Anny fought the tears not wanting to return to Marcus looking weak. It was death to go and also death to stay. Her love for Marcus was so permeating that life without him seemed impossible. The tightness in her chest begged her to stay. Not a moment of peace had passed since she left, but there was nothing here for her now.

Anny hurried to the desk and quickly pulled open the drawer to retrieve the book kept there. She hoped someone in Paultry could tell her what it said. To her surprise, the book was missing. Her eyes darted around searching the top of the table and the floor. It was gone. Her heart sank, but she told herself there must be an explanation. She must have put it down in the wrong place.

Chapter Eleven: On the Road to Paultry

In the courtyard, Anny meant to confront Marcus, but when she saw him, she quickly lost her nerve. He did not seem to notice that she was upset. He asked if she was ready to go, but was walking the donkeys to the main gate before she could respond.

The trip to Paultry was nerve-wracking. They could no longer stop in towns for fear of being recognized as they made their way down the north-eastern side of the mountains near the border with Mesu. During the day Anny searched ahead hoping to find Jax, and at night she jumped at every noise.

Marcus seemed to grow more distant the closer Paultry grew to them. On the final night, Anny lay beside him wondering why he would not even touch her. At the beginning of the trip he smiled and kissed her as they went along, but by that day he was hardly looking at her.

Anny wondered about the journal but was afraid to ask. She looked at Marcus's bag, but could not decide if the journal was in there. She thought about what Jax had said about Marcus being married as well, but was terrified to ask him. She tried to bring it up in round-about ways, but he would not speak about it. The harder she pressed, the quieter he got to the point that he would only remark on how tired he was.

On the last day, they turned a corner along the trail and before them was an expansive view of the valley were the capital of Paultry sat. The hills here were green and lush, running north to south and covered in sprawling trees with small, bare patches where cows were grazing. A river ran through the valley, splitting the town in half. Arched, stone bridges crisscrossed the river before it drained into the sea to the north. As they got closer, Anny could make out the masts of ships harbored there.

The two made their way along a narrow back trail to a side entrance. There Marcus suddenly jumped off his donkey and told Anny to do the same. She had only a moment to say good-bye to her animal before it was led away by its new owner. She wanted to tell Marcus that she did not want to sell her donkey, but it was too late. They would finish off their journey on foot. As they made way through town Anny wished that she had not packed so many things to take with her.

The capitol was not very large. A stone wall meandered around the town following the curve of the hills. It was broken by arched gates that were all open with no sign that they ever were closed. The buildings inside were circles of stacked stones with thatched roofs.

The streets were busy. Passersby occasionally stopped to glance at them, clearly knowing who Marcus was. Anny smiled to herself, imagining that one day soon they would recognize her as well: not as an outlaw but as their queen.

On a flat bit of land on the west side of the town was Marcus's castle. Compared to the castle in Arden it was small, but it towered above the simple homes around it. Its stone walls were covered in plaster and whitewashed so that the smooth walls glistened in the afternoon sun. Wide stairs led up to the main entrance which was a set of three arched doors. The guards standing there welcomed Marcus and Anny warmly.

● ● ● ● ● ● ●

It was a bit of a shock to the young girl that they were able to walk through the front entrance without any effort. Once inside it became clear why. The doors opened into a social hall which was full of tables and lined with bookcases. There were dozens of small groups of people of all ages dotting the room studying and whispering among themselves. Anny had never seen a library like this.

Marcus did not take the time to explain. He ushered her through to the back of the room where another set of arches made way to a large throne room. The throne was atop a few long steps, like those at the front of the castle. There sat Areal, Marcus's brother.

Areal looked much like Marcus except his face was oval. He had the same shiny, dark black, curly hair, but it came down to his shoulders. His mustache curved over his thin mouth and his round chin sported a constant five o'clock shadow. Anny was sure they had the same eyes. It amazed her in a way how the two brothers could look so much alike, yet only one did she find handsome while the other seemed plain.

Areal was talking to a man beside him when they entered, but it did not take him long to notice Marcus. He greeted him with a laugh, descending from the throne to hug his brother.

"You are back!" he laughed, patting Marcus firmly on the back. "I expected you would be back sooner than later." He glanced over at Anny with a twinkle in his eye, then froze in place as his mouth hung open a bit. He waited for Marcus to introduce her.

"We have a lot to talk about," Marcus said flatly without noticing; "but I need a drink and some food first. I cannot talk on an empty stomach!"

"Well that should not be a problem," Areal absentmindedly said as Marcus began to walk towards a smaller, private room next to the throne room.

Areal smiled at Anny, then motioned for her to follow them, so Anny followed behind with her head down. She wondered why Marcus had not introduced her but reasoned he was just as tired as she. She tried to shrug it off, telling herself that for now, she would have to enjoy the anonymity that would soon disappear when she took her side beside Marcus.

As soon as they entered the room, they heard an exasperated gasp. A statuesque woman with smooth skin and long, dark, wavy hair ran up to Marcus. With tears in

142

her eyes, she embraced Marcus and then began kissing him all over his face. She gave him one last hug before asking him how he was and joked with him about how dirty he looked. She gave Anny only a momentary glance.

"It has been a long trip home, Brinna," Marcus said with a sly grin as he shook his head. The room was a large sitting room with windows along the far wall and a roaring fire to the left. Brinna had been resting there, snacking and reading near the fire.

"You know you missed me," Brinna responded with a wink. She reached out and stroked his grown-out beard playfully. "I like what you are doing here, but you might want to clean this up a bit."

Areal laughed, commenting, "Give him a break. I think he has been through a lot. His companion as well."

With that, the group suddenly turned to Anny, who had been hiding in the doorway still holding all of her bags.

"Brinna, be a dear and see to our guest," Marcus ordered as he led Brinna towards the door. "We are both tired and need a good meal."

Brinna gave Anny a cautious smile as she led her out of the room, turning back momentarily to give Marcus and Areal a little wave good-bye.

As soon as they had gone Marcus walked over and closed the door.

"Marcus, Marcus!" Areal chided. "What have you done?"

Marcus laughed gruffly, looking around the room for anything to eat. He found a plate of cheeses placed near the fireplace and motioned for Areal to join him. He dropped his bags beside the chair Brinna had been sitting in, and the two brothers settled down there.

"It has been a journey, let me tell you," Marcus complained as he shoved cheese into his mouth. "I need a bath, and I need a decent bed."

"I have never known you to be the trouble maker. That is my job!" exclaimed Areal.

"Why are you accusing me of anything?" Marcus joked.

"It might have to do with the men Ramoth sent here," Areal admitted.

"I figured they would be here by now," Marcus said with a shrug.

Areal looked back to the door momentarily before saying, "They tell me that they are interested in a man and woman you were seen with. Is there anything you want to tell your big brother?"

"No, I do not want to tell you any of it, but I will show you something, and it is right here," Marcus said as he reached into his bag and pulled out the book from the study in Faverly.

"What is this?" Areal asked as he took the book from him. His expression immediately dropped as he saw the cover. The prince's hands trembled as he cautiously leafed through the pages.

Marcus grinned, pleased with himself as he asked, "You know what it is? It is from Faverly. I cannot read it, but when I do, I am certain I will find the treasure."

"Faverly?" Areal replied in disbelief. "How in the world did you find your way there? How did you get this?"

"One of my companions showed me the way- the man Ramoth's men are looking for. He went his own way after that, though I suppose our female guest could have gotten me there as well. She claims to have lived there while the Sisters were alive."

Areal looked ashen for a moment. He absentmindedly handed the book back to Marcus as he said, "Could she be one of the Sisters? I thought they were all dead."

Marcus chuckled. "She claims not to be. I swear, everything she said was likely a lie, but in the end, I got what I wanted. I might have even got a little more than I wanted if you know what I mean. Besides, what difference does it make? That myth was all just a bunch of nonsense. This: this book is the real deal! It is the real treasure!" He sat back in his chair with a grin, leafing through the pages.

Areal looked upset for a moment before stating, "You are out of your mind, brother! How many times have I told you that there was never a treasure there? Yet, could she be the last Sister? Marcus, how else would she have been able to get this book to you? Do you know what it would mean if one of the Sisters were alive?"

Marcus rolled his eyes. "The Myth, again? Really, how learned are you? It is there, Areal. I was so close, but you know these lengthy tomes were never my thing. You must know someone who could translate it."

Areal shook his head. "There is no treasure," he repeated sternly. "Not for the likes of you, anyway. Perhaps your companion could have told you what it said?"

Marcus laughed. "I do not think Anny could read it either. She kept calling it a book, but it is something much more than that. See? How could you even entertain the idea she is a Sister? Look at these drawings and funny little symbols. If I could only decipher what they mean! Maybe they are meant to be a map to the treasure!" He paused for a moment as he studied one of the pages. "I cannot even tell you how happy Ramoth will be, and consequently how relieved I will be when I hand her over to him."

Areal quickly became serious, "Then you do intend to turn her over? Why is he so interested in her? Does he suspect she is a Sister? His men would divulge to me nothing."

Marcus shrugged. "There was some drama at Pent, and she was involved. You know how he is. He just cannot let anything go."

"That coming from you," Areal said incredulously.

● ● ● ● ● ● ●

Brinna escorted Anny back through the throne room and then down a short hallway that ran adjacent to the library. There she forced a polite smile as she motioned for Anny to go into one of the rooms. As in the main hall, the doors here were open. Anyone, it seemed, could come here as well.

Forcing an insincere smile back, Anny entered the room to find that it was the kitchen. She was more than a little disappointed. She had been hoping when they arrived to find herself pampered, yet here she was again in the servants' quarters. This could not have been what Marcus had in mind for her.

The kitchen, like everything else, was much smaller than the one at Pent. A large hearth with a crackling fire heated an old iron pot which bubbled and snapped. Many cabinets lined the walls around it. There were two long tables with benches. The end of one was a small, frail figure hunched over a bowl eating slowly. An old woman was sitting at the other end staring at the hearth while looking drawn and tired, though there was a hint of a smile on her face reflected in the wrinkles around her eyes.

As Anny entered Brinna cleared her throat to get the old woman's attention. The old woman looked over to them startled and then waved for both to join her.

"Would you fetch some food for our…guest?" Brinna said, hesitating at the end as if to speak Anny's name would be difficult. Without waiting for a reply, Brinna turned away leaving Anny with the old woman.

Slowly the older woman shook her head while rising from the table and holding her back. "Wonder what has her so upset? Well, never you mind! Take a rest; I've got some stew still hot." The old woman made her way to the hearth where she spooned out some of the stew within the iron pot. She placed it down on the table across from where she had been sitting and motioned with a smile for Anny to sit down. "Well come on and eat up!" she said with a bit of a cackle. "I know I am not the best cook, but it is good enough."

Anny hesitated by the door. "I think there has been some kind of a mistake," she said hesitantly.

"Now there is no need to be ashamed," the woman persisted. "Anyone who is in need is welcome here."

Anny blushed. She looked at the man sitting at the end of the table as she wondered just how unkempt she must look. Reluctantly she put her bags down by the door, sat down, and took a bite. The food looked brown and amorphous but was not bad at all. She found herself for a moment parted from her worries. There was something reminiscent in that meal of simpler days back at Faverly when she might have had a bowl of stew like this in the kitchen with her mother.

"It is really quite good," Anny said to the woman. "You need not be so modest about your skill."

The old woman laughed, pounding her hand on the table. "I have been cooking meals here so long I have come to discover that you cannot please everyone. I have tried, but someone always has something to say."

They continued chatting for several minutes. The man sitting nearby finished his meal and without a word got up and left, giving the old woman a gentle pat on the shoulder as he went. The warmth of the food and fire slowly melted away some of Anny's fears. Things were going to be okay, she thought. This place felt closer to home than Pent ever had. She could be happy here: here beside Marcus.

Still, Anny wondered who Brinna was. After several minutes of small talk, she gathered her courage. "Who was that woman who escorted me here? Was that one of Marcus's sisters?" she casually asked.

The woman laughed. "Marcus has no sisters!" she said, brushing the comment off. "There are, or should I say were, just the three boys."

Anny was surprised, but before she could find out anything more, they were interrupted.

"Are you two talking about me?" a voice from the doorway asked. Anny looked up expecting to see Marcus but instead found Areal. He was smiling warmly which caused his round cheeks to glow red. "Now, Anny was it? Now, Anny, I can tell you Marcus has two brothers, and as I am his favorite he should have already told you much about me!"

"I have plenty of stew left if you are interested," the old woman said as she motioned to get up from the table.

Areal put his hand on her back, gently pushing her back down into her seat. "I am a grown boy now, Gigi! I can get my own stew if I want!"

The two went back and forth before Areal relented, accepting a bowl before sitting next to Anny. He quickly ate the entire portion in just a few heaping bites, leaning back afterward with his hands over his belly with a satisfied grin on his face.

"Is not Gigi the best?" he boasted.

"All right, that is enough out of you!" Gigi chastised. "Are you sure that is enough food for you?"

Areal patted his stomach and gave out a loud burp. "I was just with Marcus having a snack, so this will do for now," he assured her.

"Is he back? Well, then I am surprised by Brinna being so down. What has she to be sad about? All she talked about was him coming back."

Anny suddenly felt very uncomfortable again, but she hoped Areal and Gigi would not notice as they were caught up in their conversation.

"Did she seem down?" Areal said, acting surprised. "Maybe she was just overwhelmed. You know he looks a bit untidy after traveling so long." He looked at Anny shaking his head as if she would understand, but seeing the look on her face he blushed and quickly looked away. "Not that you look untidy!" he stammered. "I meant only that he looked untidy!"

"So is that where you came from? Traveling with Marcus?" Gigi interjected. "Explains why I have never seen you around here before. Are you going to be staying here a while then or will you be heading home again soon?"

"I plan to stay," Anny affirmed. She noticed Areal looked serious all of a sudden. She could not help but remember what Jax had said to her just before he left. 'You had better ask his wife about that' or something to that effect. She felt like she had said something wrong. Maybe she was foolish not to see it, but then maybe Brinna was Areal's wife?

"Gigi," Areal said. "Would you do me a favor?"

Gigi shrugged her shoulders. "What now?" she moaned happily.

"Would you bring some more cheese to Brinna? Now that you mention it I do think she could use a little something to cheer her up and Marcus and I ate all of her snacks."

Gigi nodded. "Naughty boys! I would have brought you your own!" she scolded.

The old woman walked over to the counter, grabbing Areal's dirty bowl as she went. She shuffled around for a minute before leaving with a new plate of food. Anny kept her eyes on her bowl slowly eating the bit that she had left. She felt like Areal was looking right at her. She wanted to make a good impression on him but feared that opportunity was past.

Areal quietly waited until Gigi had left. "I traveled a lot in my youth," he began softly, suddenly smiling again. "Marcus tells me you two traveled from Faverly."

"Marcus told you that?" Anny asked cautiously, a bit surprised.

"Have you spent much time there? It is not an easy place to find," he casually continued.

Anny did not look at him. She shook her head from side to side. "No, not really."

"Then you never did meet Barnas?" he asked, checking to see how she responded.

"Do you really have no sisters, none at all?" she asked back, suddenly turning towards him.

Areal was surprised. "None," he said back.

"Not any at all?" she persisted.

"Why do you think I have a sister, or..." his thought trailed off, "Is this about Brinna? Did Marcus tell you she was his sister or something? I suddenly feel like I am reliving last year all over again! No, she is his wife! If he told you otherwise, it was to deceive you."

Anny felt her heart drop as if it had broken into many small pieces. She fought back tears as Areal continued talking, the events of the last weeks rolling through her mind.

"Well, I should maybe not say wife, technically they are betrothed, but that is merely because Marcus cannot marry until our father's passing. Once he is officially coronated the wedding can take place, but that is a formality: maybe not worth mentioning," he babbled on.

He stopped and looked at the young girl. Her face was hung low, and she was shaking. "Anny, I can see the way you look at Marcus. I do not wish to be hurtful, but our time is limited. I am sorry if he lied to you, but trust me I am trying to help. Listen, I need to know if you are really from Faverly. Please trust me: could you be one of the Sisters?"

Anny did not respond, and so Areal continued. "Anny, please I know this is a lot to take in, and I am sure my stupid brother has lied to you a lot, so you have no reason to trust me. I am sure he told you that you would be safe here, but you are not. Ramoth sent men here. They arrived just a few days ago. Anny, they will arrest you if Marcus hands you over. He has no real power to stop them either. Paultry might have a king, but he is just a figurehead. Our father holds no real power, and neither do us boys. Ramoth is in charge here, and we have sworn to do as he commands. If he should order you to be handed over, we are both required to do so or risk our lives. To disobey would be foolish unless we had a very compelling reason to refuse…"

"You are right," Anny interrupted matter-of-factly. "I do not trust you, and you do not know what Marcus and I share. He will protect me. I am sure of it."

She stood up and grabbed her things before storming out of the kitchen and heading back towards the lounge to find Marcus. She heard Areal call out to her, but it was too late. Standing there in the throne room was Anthony. She froze for a moment in disbelief, then motioned to flee back to the kitchen.

Before she could turn to go, Anthony ceased her arm and grinned at her. "Please do not be so quick to leave. I am so happy to be graced by your presence finally! I was getting tired of waiting." he said smugly.

Anthony had with him one other guard who followed behind as she was dragged out of the throne room and through the library towards the large arched doorway. She screamed desperately for Marcus to come to save her. Patrons looked up from the commotion, some even crying out in distress.

At the bottom of the grand stairs, there was a carriage with two saddled horses prepared to go. Anthony ripped her bags from her and shoved her into the carriage with the other guard, who took the opportunity to tie her hands together. She continued to cry out as Anthony dumped the contents of her bags. Everything she held precious scattered across the floor. Some items, including a small, white, stone box that had been her mother's, shattered into tiny pieces.

Satisfied it was nothing but junk, Anthony turned his attention to the top of the stairs. There stood Marcus. Behind him was Brinna. Her face was puffy as tears were streaming down her cheeks. Gigi was with her, holding her as if she might fall to the floor otherwise.

Areal was there too. He was throwing his arms in the air, yelling at Marcus. Marcus did not flinch. He rose his arm, indicating that Areal should be silent. He then smiled at Anthony, waiting for the guard to approach him so that he might shake his hand. The two men spoke cordially for a moment and then Marcus waved him farewell.

All this Anny saw through the tears running down her cheeks as she fell silent. Her whole body became numb, and she was unable for a long time to think. She did not see the look of triumph on Anthony's face as he entered the carriage. She did not see the calm Marcus displayed as he walked back into the castle. She could not see the conflicted tears that Brinna shed, nor did she see Gigi struggle to the bottom of the stairs to put the broken items carefully back into Anny's bags. Least of all could she see the stern gaze in Areal's eyes as he watched her carriage disappear along the cobbled street.

Chapter Twelve: The Berkiss

Something about the carriage that carried Anthony and Anny through the city of Paultry reminded her of the one that she and Marcus had ridden in. It made the whole experience all the more bitter as images of Marcus sitting across from her flashed before her eyes. Instead, there was the face of Anthony, arrogant and prideful. She would have given anything to go back: to skip all of her time at Pent and return to Paultry with Marcus right when he had offered. Would things have turned out differently if she had?

To think in such a way was pointless now. No matter how much she wished, she could never go back. She looked out the window and was surprised to see the arched stone railings of one of the bridges that cut over the river. She wondered if Anthony knew the way back to the mountain road, yet at the end of the bridge they turned left, away from the mountains to the south and towards the bay to the north.

"The captain will be surprised!" the other guard said to Anthony with a hint of nervousness in his voice. He was an average built man with wavy locks of blond hair. He smelled of fermented drink and his hands, though resting on his lap, occasionally tensed up- pulling on his trousers as he spoke. He was looking at Anny out of the corner of his dark eyes. He spoke of her as if he knew her, though there were so many guards at the castle she was hard pressed to remember him in particular.

Anthony chuckled, "It would make this all worth it just to see the look on his face." He then ran off a series of expletives describing the captain's character.

His friend chuckled back. "Is he still insisting that we continue on to Breka? It is a good thing you did not let him go on without us! I had not wanted to think of what Ramoth might do if we failed, but now there might even be a nice reward in it for you. Maybe even a promotion with the new opening."

Anthony glared at him like a man who was about to strike, yet before he could take action, the man continued, "I mean with Jax being gone is all. Do not look at me like that! You know I would never have meant that."

It was then that Anny suddenly recalled who the other guard was. She believed his name was Jordan. He was sometimes with Anthony when he would come down to the kitchen looking for Paul. Outside the castle, he looked like a stranger, but she could place him now. He was friendly enough, but something about him had made her uneasy: like he was afraid of her though he hardly knew her.

The carriage slowed, and their seats jostled as they made their way down the pier. "That would be enough!" Anthony called to the carriage driver. They stopped, and the men jumped out. Anthony thanked the driver and his aid as Jordan helped Anny from the carriage. She had not noticed when she was forced into the carriage that the drivers were dressed as the guards of Paultry. For some reason, this slight sliced at her. Not only had Marcus handed her over, but he had provided their ride to the pier. What reason would he have to do that? Could he not have just handed her over and not aided them further?

Jordan noticed the sudden change in her demeanor. "Easy there," he said to her. "They have no quarrel with you. They are just doing their job. That is all any of us are doing."

The guard grabbed her by the elbow and began to lead her down the pier. Anny looked back and could see that Anthony was still talking with the drivers.

"I remember you now. You are Jordan, right?" She whispered to him. She waited for a moment, but he did not answer. "I remember you at Pent, how you always followed Anthony around and would tag along with him and Paul. How can you say you are just following orders? Do you think this is what Paul would want? Would he not want justice?"

Jordan looked uncomfortable. He was shaking his head from side to side as they continued down the pier. "Look, Anny, I barely know you. When Anthony asked me to come along on this mission, I told him I had no idea who you even were. He had to remind me. But what I do know is that you were not the one who held one of your best friends in your arms as he bled to death from a wound you inflicted. That fine man back there was. You want to call that, 'just following orders'? Do you even have a concept of what it means to live for something besides yourself? I would guess not.

"Paul understood that: he understood so well he was comforting Andrew as he lay there dying. Did you know that? Of course not! You do not know because you were already running away like a coward protecting yourself. Each of us took a vow to carry out the law. That purpose is greater than any one of us. You act like we are just blindly following orders. No, no if there was ever a better example of honor and integrity between two men then what happened to Paul then I do not know of it.

"You see despite what you might think I do not decide if you live or die. Anthony does not decide either. That was up to you when you decided to do what you did. Now Ramoth may choose to do as he likes and to that end, he might choose justice or perhaps show mercy. Do you hope he orders Anthony to rip every finger from your perfect, little hands before you die because that would be justice?" Jordan stopped walking and looked at her. "Tell me now, is it really justice you are looking for?"

Anthony had caught up to them in time to hear the end of what Jordan was saying. When Jordan had finished Anthony forced a smile and patted his friend on the shoulder. "You are a good man, my friend," he said.

Anny thought it strange to see Anthony smile particularly given the subject. It did not last, however, as his smile faded back into his familiar scowl as he turned to her. He was about to say something to her when he was interrupted.

Walking down a gangplank from the nearest vessel was a short, stocky man with a matching short, stocky demeanor. His name was Guy Alistarr, captain of the Berkiss. For over ten years he had commanded the Berkiss as it traveled the coastal trade route from Pent to Breka, which is in Mesu. It was one of Ramoth's prized sailing vessels having been obtained from the most excellent shipbuilders of Mesu upon their defeat in the Noble War.

It stood out as being a bit larger than the other boats in the dock with each plank in the hull spanning over 60 meters in length. It boasted flowers ornately carved into the railings along the bulwarks that blended into a twist of vines down the stern. The figurehead was none other than a carving of Ramoth himself.

It seemed a little out of place, and indeed the shipbuilder had intended something else to be there. Upon learning that his vessel was to be gifted to Ramoth and the original figurehead replaced he renamed it "The Berkiss" which translated from the ancient tongue of Mesu meant "great man". Ramoth was pleased with this, not realizing that when two words were put together, the translation would be understood to mean, "man-great" or, more simply, "conceited".

For many years it functioned as a patrol ship, but over time it began carrying along trade goods until finally it was converted entirely to a cargo ship. Typically this time of year it could make the trip from Pent to Breka in a matter of weeks with the return being faster due to the tides. However, Ramoth had made it clear to the captain that he was to take Anthony to Paultry in the fastest time possible.

This disruption to his engrained schedule coupled with sailing through the night had enraged Alistarr, but he had to acquiesce to the order. He waved at the men and smiled sarcastically as he approached.

"Well, look here!" he gushed. "Would this be Anny? Here I thought we were chasing a mirage at sea. Does this

156

mean we can carry along to Breka, or are you going in search of the other one too?"

Anthony rolled his eyes. "No, the prince himself informed me that he does not know the whereabouts of the other fugitive, but it is no matter. I can assure you Ramoth will be happy to reimburse you for your losses having secured this one alone. Therefore, we must return immediately to Pent as we had planned."

"Great!" Alistarr said through clenched teeth. "Great, great, great!" he repeated. "We can depart in an hour. I have to prepare the ship.

"I had thought those preparations would be completed by now," Anthony replied. "What have you been doing this last hour? I told you to prepare the ship the minute I left!"

Alistarr looked as if he was going to say something nasty back, but he managed to hold his tongue and again forced a smile. "We have been working as quickly as we can. You want a safe voyage, no? A broken ship does not sail very fast indeed. If you are ready to go then please, return to your bunk, get settled, and we will be heading along shortly. Might I suggest you put our 'guest' into my stateroom?"

"She can stay with us," Anthony retorted. He grabbed Anny's arm and began to direct her up the gangplank.

"I understand you feel it your duty to keep her in your custody but understand that I cannot be held responsible for anything that might happen to her. You understand do you not? For her safety, my stateroom would be an elegant solution," Alistarr called to him from the pier.

"I will keep her in my sight. You have nothing to fear," Anthony called back to him.

Once aboard Anthony led her to a set of stairs near the stern that led below deck. The bay of the Berkiss had two rows of bunks down the middle with the edges reserved for cargo. However, since they had not stopped often, there was very little cargo on board. Anthony walked between the rows of beds to the last one on the right. He motioned for Anny to sit, and so she sat on the lower bunk.

Jordan sat across from her on the neighboring cot in the row.

"That captain sure is something," Jordan said as he took off his boots.

"That he is," Anthony agreed. "I am sure you heard the captain," Anthony said addressing Anny.

The young girl looked up when she realized he was talking to her. She shrugged her shoulders, not sure to what the guard was referring.

Anthony leaned down so that he was very close to her face before he continued, "What he said was that if you leave my side, his crew might try to take advantage of you. So do not get any bright ideas of running off."

● ● ● ● ● ● ●

"Is that worse than what you intend to do to me?" Anny asked.

Anthony shrugged his shoulders and motioned towards the stairs. "You want to add to your misery then be my guest."

"You want me to take the first watch?" Jordan interrupted.

Anthony shook his head. "No, you rest. I could not sleep right now if I wanted to. I will let you know when I am ready."

Jordan nodded, then pulled himself up to the top bunk and stretched out. Before the ship had left port, he had nodded off. Anthony sat down at the end of the bed below Anthony's, looking hostilely towards Anny with glassed over eyes. The boat rocked gently from side to side. Time slowed to a crawl.

● ● ● ● ● ● ●

The night was long and relatively quiet. Anny slept fitfully. She had never been on a boat before, and though she enjoyed the sound of the waves hitting the hull, she felt a bit nauseous. Men came and went from the cargo bay, taking shift manning the boat as they sailed through the night. She could hear their boots stomping on the deck above and the occasional burst of laughter. Her wrists ached. She could not help but try to free her hands from the ropes, but each attempt failed: leaving behind red marks.

She began to wonder what would happen to her when she reached Pent. Would she be sent to trial as Jordan had suggested? Why else would Ramoth have sent for her? Was it possible he suspected her ties to Faverly? Twice she convinced herself that she should run and throw herself overboard, but she could not bring herself to do it. Though it was the most logical action, there was still that shred of hope that Marcus would come and save her. She knew there was another way as well; that if she confessed to her crime, she might be spared the trial and hung instead. It seemed an odd hope to have.

Dawn finally broke, and as the morning rays reached the bay, she felt relieved that a new day had come. The rest that had eluded her all night came, and she slept peacefully for a short while.

● ● ● ● ● ● ●

"Here, take this," Anthony said to her while he kicked the side of her bed to startle her from her sleep. He thrust a small paper package into her hands. Inside was a little roll and a piece of dried fish.

"What is it?" she asked as she took a small bite.

"Breakfast," Anthony said through a full mouth, "and lunch, so make it last."

She noticed Jordan was gone and that a little better than half the crew were still in bed either eating or sleeping. She looked around for the captain before remembering he had his own stateroom. The two had just about finished when Jordan appeared with two cups of wine. Anthony took a large gulp from one, then handed it to Anny. She refused at first, but he assured her it was all they had to drink at the moment. Both men laughed at the look on her face as she took a sip.

"It is a bit strong for breakfast," Anny said, handing the cup back.

"I am just messing with you!" Jordan said, handing her the other cup with watered down wine in it.

Still chuckling, Anthony laid back down. He closed his eyes and waved his arm at Jordan. "Take our guest to the 'facilities'," he commanded in a very stern tone.

"Why me?" Jordan pled, but Anthony was ignoring him. "Alright, come on then," he said to Anny dejected.

They made way to the deck. In the morning light, the ocean sparkled around them. She was surprised they were traveling so far from shore. Jordan led her to the back of the ship. Around a corner, there was a small alcove that faced the stern of the vessel. There was a pot, and there was the ocean.

Jordan's face was bright red now, even to the tips of his ears. He just pointed and nodded, "I think you know what to do," he stammered.

The smell was overwhelming, even in the open air. "Are you not going to turn around?" Anny asked.

"What if you jump overboard? If I lose you Anthony will be more than a little cross with me," Jordan objected.

"My hands are tied together. How would I even begin to swim to shore? We are at least 15 kilometers from there!" Anny pointed out.

Jordan reluctantly turned around. "If you jump I am not going after you!" he warned.

"What about my hands, will you not untie me? How am I supposed to do this with my hands tied?" Anny barked.

"Figure it out!" he snapped back. "I do not know what you need to do so how can I help?"

Though it was difficult, Anny managed to do what she needed. She tapped Jordan on the shoulder so he knew he could turn around. He jumped a little.

"All done?" he asked.

"Yep," she replied.

160

When he turned around his face was slightly less red, but he was looking at her again like the way he had when they were in Pent. Again, she felt uncomfortable.

"Is something wrong?" she asked. "Anthony will be expecting us."

Jordan took a deep breath. "Anny I do not know what will happen when we get to Pent, but we do have this time right now. If this is the end for you then maybe we should be spending this time wisely."

"What?" Anny stammered. She tried to back away from him, but there was little space to do so without returning to the wretched stench behind her. Instead, her foot slipped, and she let out a yelp as she tumbled into Jordan's arms.

"Shh! You will draw attention!" Jordan whispered as he helped her get back on her feet. "Just think about it and if you agree then later wink at me and I will find a place for us to be alone."

Jordan kissed the back of her hand: pressing his lips there a long time, then turned away to return her to Anthony. After dropping her off, he held his finger up to his lips and winked at her before returning to the deck.

Anthony noticed the beguiled look on her face. "What was that all about?" Anthony chuckled. "Did you fall into the pot? I could hear you yell from here."

Anny thought to tell him what Jordan had said to her but then realized that if left alone Jordan might be her way of escape.

"Nothing happened. I just slipped," the young girl said. Her face blushed.

"Is Jordan coming on to you?" Anthony asked frankly. "I knew it was better he did not come along but when he heard what I had been commissioned to do he practically begged me! The fool I am for letting him. It is like having two prisoners to guard now. Oh, don't flatter yourself. He's just desperate: it's pathetic."

● ● ● ● ● ● ●

From then on Anthony would not let Anny out of his sight. A few times Jordan tried to catch her attention when Anthony was not looking, but each time she pretended not to see him or held her eyes open so that he could not misconstrue a mere blink for a signal of lewd intention. More than once Anthony asked her what was wrong with her face and suggested she accompany him to the deck for some fresh air.

It was one such occasion after they had been at sea for almost a week, in which she found herself standing by his side watching the little waves from the wake of the ship as they crash together behind the Berkiss. She would always remember that day, as the sun set the sky alight before giving way to the stars.

It was something frightening and fantastic to see the stars over the dark ocean. Below and above was this dark void ready to pull you in. Against the darkness were these tiny spots of light that seemed so proud until an unseen cloud brushed their courage away. She felt like she was once again part of their greatness: as if she had been a part of it before but had since been separated from it. It was all meant to be together, yet by the light of dawn, it would be sundered once again.

"You know," Anthony said as he looked up, "when I was little I would look at these same stars. I had a name for each of them, not that I can recall them all now. I remember wondering if the stars were happy because they were so bright, but then I reasoned that they might not be able to see their own light. They are all the way up there, just casting light into the darkness. Now, how can you see the light unless there is something that catches it and sends it back to you? If there is nothing to catch it, will you believe there is only darkness?

"Yet, think of those who catch the light of others, are they not the happy ones? Do they not see the light that is coming at them and snatch it all up for themselves? They have no light of their own, yet they reason the light is theirs. How foolish, for once the light ends what will they

162

have? So it is that those who are sad may one day be the happiest when they trust the light they cannot see, yet those happy now once cut off from it will be forever in the darkness."

Anny looked up at the little points of light. She tried to see if they were happy or sad.

"So then," she asked, "are you the light or the darkness?"

Anthony chuckled, "In the daytime does it matter?"

Chapter Thirteen: The Isle of DeCorro

After they had been at sea many days, the ship came to rest off the shore of the Isle of DeCorro. Named after its founder and benefactor, it boasted a long boardwalk with many piers. Onshore, there were only a few streets with houses crowded around them. On the corner of the main drag was a large bar which doubled as a hotel of sorts. The remaining buildings off the main road were mostly places of trade and barter. Beyond the town were dense, uninhabited jungles.

The isle sat almost directly between Crewda and Ballast. It was considered neutral territory for the two countries before the war and so to that day still had little in the way of security. It hosted a black market that benefited Pent so that Ramoth's usual guards were not present. Rather each man was expected to take care of himself.

When he learned they planned to stop, Anthony was livid. Captain Alistarr reminded him that he need not get off the ship, yet his men needed a rest.

Anny did not know of this plan until she awoke from a deep sleep. She had been dreaming once again that she heard the sound of feet pounding on the stones of a long hallway. The young girl almost fell out of bed, her heart pounding to the same beat as in her dream. She was surprised to find that for the first time since they had departed Paultry the ship was entirely dark and quiet. In the stillness, she could make out that most of the beds were full and the ship did not seem to have its usual rocking motion.

She held her breath as she climbed slowly out of the bunk. Every little move seemed to make a noise. Anthony stirred, but then turned away from her. She bit down hard on her lower lip as she tip-toed to the deck of the ship. The night air was damp and all of the stars shown overhead.

There was a light breeze and just enough light to make way to the railings. Taking in a deep breath, she made her way slowly across the deck. She looked out to sea expecting to see land, but all she could see were a few lights off far in the distance.

"Have you been to DeCorro before?" she heard a voice say from behind her. She spun around and could make out the figure of the captain. "We are not that close, but you might make it if you are a good swimmer," he remarked as he leaned on the railing next to her, looking out towards the town. "We are going to moor there tomorrow so maybe it would be better if you waited."

Her affect dropped. She felt silly for thinking she would be able to walk off the ship. She twisted her arms just so, causing the ropes around her wrists to cut deeper into her skin. She winced but tried to remain quiet as if Anthony would awaken at the slightest noise. Alistarr noticed and motioned for her to place her hands into his. She lifted her arms, and he pulled a sharp blade from his belt. Carefully he cut the ropes off her wrists and tossed the frayed cords overboard.

She rolled her shoulders and stretched her arms to her sides. "Thanks," she whispered.

"Now do not try to throw me overboard! I am a great deal heavier than I look!" Alistarr joked. He pointed to DeCorro, changing the subject by saying, "You can find all kinds of things in DeCorro. I know I do not look it, but I have six daughters. That is six mind you, not a single boy and the two youngest are still at home. They are about your age. You would not believe the list of things they give me every time I leave port. 'I need a bracelet daddy!' and 'See those hats with the feathers? I need one!'. This will be the first time I have been here that I have no idea what to bring them. What would you suggest? I did not have a chance to see them before I was shipped out again, and I have to bring something."

"I am not sure what is fashionable in Arden," Anny admitted. "A few girls had these tiny pinky rings. They were so delicate with intricate filigree. I think they are becoming popular, but you are meant to wear more than one."

"More than one?" the captain gasped. "Well, I have to buy them in lots of six so let us hope one is enough." Alistarr chuckled to himself, then looked at her as if he wanted to give her advice but had then thought better of it. "Get back to your bunk. It will be light soon."

The young girl looked longingly towards the tiny lights in the distance one more time, then nodded and turned to go.

"No, wait, young lady," he said after her. She turned back to him. "Life can be unfair. Sometimes we mourn that fact, and other times we celebrate it. I am going to do my best to talk some sense into Ramoth, but there is only so much a guy like me can do. You understand?"

Anny now realized how light it was becoming. As the captain spoke, she looked deep into his eyes. They were dark black and hidden behind a thick, wrinkled brow. For a moment he had forgotten to be the captain and was looking at her like a father would. His sharp tone softened, yet behind his words, there was the distinct hint of fear. Was he afraid for her, or was it something else?

Suddenly she was angry again. She wondered why no one would help her, yet at the same time, she understood that to ask for help was like handing them a death sentence. Was there no one willing to take her place? Had she done something so vile, or was it she who was vile? What was it about her that was intrinsically detestable? Her anger stirred, and she forced it into herself. How could one so worthless expect anything else?

Still looking him in the eyes, she said plainly, "I understand." She hoped it would ease him, but his pain seemed only to intensify.

Just as she was about to leave they both heard a loud thud come from below deck. Anny jumped and stepped away from the noise towards Alistarr. A moment passed, and then the sound of feet heavily clubbing along the heavy

166

plank floor was followed by the same sound rushing along the stairs. Anthony came flying up onto the deck. He looked around wildly, then seeing the captain and Anny standing there his look of bewilderment vanished into one of pure anger.

"What are you doing?" he screeched at them. He snatched Anny's arm and, upon seeing that she was no longer bound, shot an incredulous look at Alistarr. "Are you trying to stop her or are you helping her along?" he snapped, lacing in expletives as he looked around for more rope.

"Dare you to speak to me like that on my ship?" Alistarr warned as he wagged his finger at him. "People ought to be treated with more dignity than that!"

Anthony was still looking around when he replied. "Really? And why is that? You are a servant of Ramoth the same as I. So then why are you so proud? We have our orders. Am I the only one to be faithful to them? Where do you keep the rope?"

"What part of this did I ask for?" Alistarr shot back. He then walked away, muttering to himself.

As soon as he was gone Anthony released Anny's arm and collapsed down onto a nearby crate. He wiped his brow with the back of his hand and was trying to catch his breath.

"Thinks he knows everything!" he grumbled. "He acts like I asked for all of this!" He took in a few more deep breaths, then looked up at Anny. "I thought I told you to stay put? What if something had happened to you?"

The young girl looked at him, unsure what to say. "What difference would it make? You want me dead, so what difference if I drown?"

"Okay, I will tell you the difference. You see if I return now without you do you know what Ramoth would do to me? Not just me but Jordan, the captain, maybe even the entire crew would be executed! Maybe that does not matter to you. Clearly, you do not think that is your problem, or maybe the thought pleases you, but I would like to get out of this whole thing alive if at all possible."

Out of the corner of his eye, something near the back of the crate caught his eye, and Anthony stopped to reach for it. Having found a suitable piece of rope, he cut off a section and tied her wrists back together again. Unapologetically he tightened the cords as far as they would go.

Suddenly, they both heard a loud thud come from below deck. Again, a moment passed, and then the sound of feet heavily clubbing along the heavy plank floor was followed by the same sound rushing along the stairs. Jordan appears at the top of the stairs looking pale as a ghost. He looked around wildly, then seeing Anny and Anthony rushed over to them. Anthony rolled his eyes.

"Some help you are!" he yelled at his fellow guard. "Why were you sleeping? How much did you drink last night?"

"No more than usual!" Jordan stammered. The color was slowly returning to his face.

"Get her out of my sight for a bit. I need a break." Anthony said as he pushed Anny towards Jordan. He then walked away towards the stern of the ship. Jordan looked at Anny, then smiled and gave her a little wink.

"Seriously, forget about it already!" Anthony called back over his shoulder.

● ● ● ● ● ● ●

The crew all slept in that morning, but once enough men were up Alistarr ordered the ship to be brought into port. Jordan and Anny sat down in the cargo bay dejectedly watching the others depart for shore. They could smell sweet, greasy air coming from above and the sound of music playing far away. Jordan lamented Anthony's choice, pointing out that there were many varieties of drink available on shore. One, in particular, made from pineapples, piqued Anny's amusement.

168

Just as all hope seemed lost, Anthony appeared and told them to come along. He'd changed his mind and decided he could not spend another minute on the ship. He looked Anny in the eyes and told her she had better cooperate. She nodded in the affirmative, meaning it at the time as she was excited to get to leave the ship. Jordan also affirmed that he would not let Anny out of his sight. He gave Anthony a proud salute and then ran ahead of them up the stairs to the deck.

As they walked to the gangplank, Anny saw Alistarr leaning against the door of his stateroom, grinning. Anthony shot him a dirty look as they walked past.

"Enjoy the city!" Alistarr called after them.

The central pier had many shops with open stalls offering all kinds of wares. There were clothes, shoes, and foods Anny had never seen before. One booth was filled with carved boxes and statues. Another stall had cages full of small birds that she mistook as pets, but quickly realized were actually a local delicacy.

The bar at the corner of the pier and the main road was, however, the big attraction for the crew of the Berkiss. As they entered, they found that most of the men were already there, singing loudly and drinking. The middle of the room had several rows of tables and benches. To the right was a stage where musicians were banging on drums and strumming lutes. A man was playing the flute while ladies who were barely dressed danced around him.

Jordan grinned and found them a table in the front corner where he could see the dancers a little too well. Anthony blushed, choosing to sit with his back to the noise but with a good view of the ocean. Anny sat in the corner, boxed in on either side by the men.

Across the room from the stage, she could see a large bar with barmaids bustling drinks and snacks around. When a server came, she was excited to hear the men ordering food to go with the libations, but when they did not order anything for her, she remembered they had not brought her along out of charity.

She sat and watched all of the commotion as her companions ate and laughed. She was surprised when Anthony offered her a piece of his meal. He had additionally ordered a single drink, which he was nursing slowly. Jordan, however, polished off many drinks while assuring Anthony that he was fine and could handle it.

Anny noticed that to the right and left of the far wall were two doorways. The one closest to the bar must have led to the kitchen, for the barmaids made their way in and out at leisure. The other door was used less frequently at first, yet as the evening went on, she noticed more and more men disappearing behind it.

They were there many hours before Jordan noticed the door. "What do you think is back there?" he asked Anthony. Since the door was a ways behind him, Anthony had to turn around to look.

"Beats me," Anthony said with a shrug. "We had better get going soon. It is getting late."

A moment later one of the dancers approached their table. She eyed Anny suspiciously, then whispered something into Anthony's ear. The sound of the music made it so that Anny could not hear it, but Anthony smirked before shaking his head no and politely declining. Undeterred, the woman went to Jordan and whispered into his ear. The guard's face blushed, and he immediately jumped up from the table.

"Jordan, no!" Anthony said firmly, but his friend was already leaving the table.

"It will just be a minute!" Jordan said gleefully. "We can go as soon as I get back!"

● ● ● ● ● ● ●

Anthony and Anny were too embarrassed to look at each other. They sat in silence, suddenly very interested in the beat of the music and the clouds floating over the sea. They waited half an hour. Then another hour went by. Periodically Anthony would assure his company that it would be just another minute. Then he began to threaten to go find Jordan. Finally, he threatened to leave without him. Slowly the sun had set, and the pier was now very dark. Some of the men from the Berkiss had already returned to the ship while others were sleeping on the tables or playing cards together.

Anthony shifted nervously in his chair. "It has been too long. It is not safe to still be here," he asserted. He looked at her and grumbled, "Where is he?"

Just then a woman let out a bloodcurdling scream from behind the door. Anny could hear what sounded like a scuffle and then Jordan calling out in terror. Anthony leapt from his chair, his hand on his weapon, and slammed the door open.

On the other side Anthony found a large room full of smoke. Pastel-colored cushions surrounded small, round tables laden with glasses. There in the middle of the room near one of the tables was Jordan, stretched out lifeless. There was a large bloodstain across his chest and a woman, also covered in blood, was knelt over him striking him.

Anthony rushed to his friend's side, pushing the woman away as he lifted Jordan's head on his lap. "Jordan! Jordan! What happened?" he begged as he shook his friend.

"He owes me money! That good-for-nothing!" the woman said, pointing at Jordan. "That was my best wine!"

"Wine?" Anthony hissed. "You are worried about wine at a time like this?"

Jordan stirred.

"My friend! Can you speak? Tell me what happened and I will avenge you! Where are you hurt?" Anthony pled. Anthony put his face close to his friend's. "Please, I am listening," he whispered.

Jordan slowly forced his eyes open.

"More..." Jordan whispered.

"More what?" Anthony begged.

"More wine," Jordan said.

Anthony ripped Jordan's shirt open to find there was no mortal wound. He smelled his hands. Wine? It was wine!

Without thinking, Anthony slapped Jordan across the face. "You drunk idiot!" Anthony cursed, half angry and half relieved. He quickly paid the woman for her wares, then picked his friend up and dragged him back into the bar.

"He is fine," Anthony called out to Anny as they walked into the room. "Fine, but an idiot."

He hoped she would be relieved, but Anny was not even there. Anthony dropped Jordan to the floor and bolted out to the pier.

● ● ● ● ● ● ●

Anny had begun to run before she had even thought about it. Some part of her brain just took over, and she found herself flying down the main drag. It was challenging to see having just come out of the brightly lit bar, but she ran into the dark with her arms stretched out before her.

Anny did not know how much time she would have before Anthony would catch on that she was gone, and so she ducked into a small alley to catch her breath. She was afraid if she just ran straight down the main road he would spot her.

The young girl inched her way down the dark lane but found it was a dead end. There was a door there, but when she knocked no one answered. She wondered if she had done the right thing. Should she try to return to the ship? Alistarr might be willing to hide her until she could escape. She did not want to risk his life though. She wanted to get out of town and into the jungle. From there maybe she could escape. Perhaps she could stow away on another ship.

"They are closed," a man's voice from behind her said.

She had thought she was alone, but out of the shadows, a figure appeared. She could barely make out that his clothes and hair were unkempt. He smelled like he had been out in the streets for a while. "All of these businesses are closed for the day. No one else will be around for hours."

"Please do not hurt me," Anny begged.

The man surprised her and chuckled. "Why would I want to do that? You think just because I am currently homeless that I am some kind of a threat? Geeze, well that is the last time I try to help someone out. Look, I am just telling you that you might try coming back another time, like during the day."

Anny felt foolish. She thought maybe she ought to apologize. The man approached her and reached out for her arm.

"Why are you tied up like this?" he asked, but then the man's face contorted, and blood spat out his mouth. He fell to her feet and began grabbing her heels.

Anny covered her mouth to stifle the scream as she tried to back away from him, but he was holding onto her tightly, crying out to her and whimpering. Anny was crying now too, begging him to let go. She was torn between pushing him away and trying to help, but there was no escape. Anthony was standing behind him with blood dripping from his hands.

Anthony reached down and wiped the blood from his dagger onto the man's cloak. He then grabbed the young girl's arm and pulled her away. She looked back at the man, but he was now barely moving. Anthony dragged Anny through the main street towards the pier. The commotion had not attracted any attention in the late hour. Only the bar they had been in still had lights streaming from the windows.

They ran past the lights, stopping just as they reached the edge of the pier. Only the light of the stars above lit the rest of the way. Anny was finding it hard to breathe. She could see the stars and hear the water, but she could not move forward with certainty.

Anny closed her eyes and forced in a few deep breaths. When she opened her eyes again, they had adjusted to the darkness, and she could see Anthony was panting too. She had never seen a man like this. His eyes were flashing despite the darkness. His chest heaved high, and his breath bellowed out in a deep, steady rhythm. His long hair had come undone and had fallen around his eyes which were trained in the direction of their ship.

Looking at him her heart fluttered. Despite everything up to that point a little voice inside wondered if maybe he was the one she had been longing for. Despite the mistakes and all the regrets what part of her still held out hope in this utterly hopeless situation? Her hands began to shake, and a deep coldness filled her.

Anthony was still holding her arm tightly. As she shook his focus shifted to her. He glanced at her quizzically, looking her up and down. His grip on her arm tightened, and he pulled her into him. Desperate, she melted into his arms, his eyes staring into hers.

She had only a moment to look deep into his eyes, but that was all she needed. The next moment, he raised his arm and struck her across the face. She crumpled away, the pain being almost a pleasant distraction. He flew into a rage, hitting her again and again, the whole time cursing at her.

He cried out over and over, "Why did you do that?" and "He is dead! He is dead!"

Now she understood the look in his eyes. She heard Jax's voice mocking, "Have you never killed anyone before?" Without warning, he kicked her in the ribs. She felt a pop, and a sharp pain ran down her back.

She grabbed her side and pushed on her rib to ease the pain. She looked up to see a light coming towards them. It was Jordan.

He called out to Anthony, perplexed, grabbing him and pulling him away from her. In the commotion he chastised him, reminding him that Ramoth had made him promise not to hurt her before the trial. Now Anny plainly understood why he had been so protective of her. He was looking out for himself.

By the light of Jordan's lamp, she saw Anthony was splattered in blood. She looked down at her dress and saw much of the blood had rubbed off on her as well. All at once it struck her: the man was dead. There he had been dying at her feet, but she was too wrapped up in getting away to see it. How deep had the wound been? Was this her fault?

Anthony quickly led them back to the Berkiss, afraid anyone else might see them. They would have to leave as soon as possible. Anny and Anthony went below deck. Jordan roused Captain Alistarr, and after hearing from Anthony what had happened, he agreed Anny would need to be confined the remainder of the trip. This time Anthony did not object when the captain led her away to his quarters.

● ● ● ● ● ● ●

"You're lucky to be alive," the captain said as he closed the door to his room behind them. It was a simple room with a small bed and table. He lowered the flame on his lamp and hung it from a hook near the door. "Not in the mood to talk? That's fine. I need you to understand that the moment you stepped foot back on this ship you became my problem."

He studied Anny's face. She was looking away from him at the table. "You know Anthony could have killed you if he wanted to. What were you thinking?" He waited a moment for her to reply before he continued, "This whole thing is not to be spoken of again. There was no man; there was no confrontation. We were never even here. You will stay put, and you will obey every order given to you, is that fair?"

Satisfied, Alistarr grabbed the lamp and left the room without waiting for a reply.

Anny sat perfectly still in the dark for some time. Her body ached, and her mind felt disconnected. Her side still hurt if she did not press on her rib. She had to take short, shallow breaths to keep the pain down. She began to feel tired, and so she laid down. In the stillness she could hear outside the door there was a bit of activity as the ship was being readied to leave. Some time passed, and all was quiet again. She could hear the sound of the water striking the boat, and though the room seemed to be rocking gently from side to side, she was not sure they had left the harbor.

She closed her eyes, hoping to sleep. She tried to tell herself that she was safe for now, but for how long? Though she tried desperately to keep the image from her mind, she could not help but see the man's amorphous silhouette again and again.

Was Anthony right? Was that man dead because of her? Had she plunged the knife into him? Did that mean that Anthony was not guilty? Though he had done the deed, did he not do so thinking he was saving her? What of the man himself? Should he have even been there? What had his life been like that he should be there? Was he homeless? Destitute? Does desperation justify that which is immoral? Did that same desperation justify what they had done to him? Had it been moral for her to run in the first place?

Where was that man now, and where would she be in a few days when the trial ended? No, not her body, naturally, for that was most certainly to be destroyed. She thought of her inner something: the thing that made her who she was. Would that also be destroyed? What was this thing made of that it might be? She tried to remember things from so long ago that she doubted now they had ever been real.

There was no one in all of Arden who knew or who she had ever heard ask about such things. Death was natural and unpredictable, yet here was the unpredictable becoming certain, and in the stillness, she found neither rest nor resolve. Her mind raced, the night dragged on and just as it seemed the first light of dawn was finally breaking she drifted off to sleep.

Chapter Fourteen: The Other Side of the City

The sun was hanging low in the sky as the Berkiss approached Pent. Alistarr looked out to the city, the masonry of the castle was glowing orange in the setting sun. It was a tradition of his to stand there in that spot when they arrived home. He liked to reflect on the trip and mentally prepare for his homecoming, but today was different. Pent had never seemed so ugly to him, nor the sight of the castle so grizzly.

As they drew closer, he noted several ships in the harbor that were foreign to him. He struggled to make out where they might be from, though each seemed to be from a different place. Perhaps he was imagining things. His thoughts were interrupted by steps approaching from behind.

"Finally, and not a moment too soon! I tire of being at sea. I will never forsake the comfort of solid earth under my feet again!" Anthony said as he rested himself on the railing beside Alistarr.

Alistarr did not shift his focus. "A fine mood you are in, and a fine prize awaits you I am sure. Let us hope the warm earth comforts you as you seem to be short on friends these days. As for me, I will take the sea." He paused to look smugly at Anthony, but it seemed the young guard was not paying him any attention. "Do you want me to get her? I mean, I would like just a moment to make sure she is ready."

Anthony shrugged. "What difference does it make? With all of your finagling what is one more delay? Please, do what makes you happy. Just know I will be watching."

Watch he did as the ship made into port, finally coming to rest in its usual mooring. The crew cheered and sang songs as they tied the ship to the dock and began to disembark.

• • • • • • •

"Why do you run? It is inevitable. Inevitable. It is nothing to fear. Nothing to fear..." the voice echoed. Again she heard the sound of feet pounding on a stone floor. The steps grew louder and closer together until Anny woke with a start from her dream.

Alistarr was sitting at the end of her bed. She was surprised to see him and wondered if his entering the room had not been what aroused her. For the last several days he had only come on occasion to bring her food and water. He had never stayed, but now his face was drawn. She looked around, and things did feel different. It took her a moment to realize the boat was no longer moving.

"We have arrived at Pent, Anny," he said in a hushed tone. "I will have to hand you back over to Anthony now."

Tears welled in her eyes, and she broke down crying. The two strangers held onto one another as Alistarr tried to comfort her.

"I am so sorry," he kept repeating again and again as he hushed her.

"There must be something you can do," Anny pled. "There must be something."

"You would be willing to risk his family's life?" Anthony scoffed from the door. Anny looked around Alistarr to see that Anthony had let himself into the room. "He might try, but he cannot protect you and would be foolish to do so. Now let us go."

Anny cast her eyes to the floor. She knew he was right. She hugged Alistarr before leaving him on the bed to turn herself over to Anthony. He immediately tied her hands back together. "Why are you limping?" he grumbled. "Do try to look presentable. Nothing more pitiful than someone who refuses to stand up straight."

As they left the ship, Anny found herself disoriented. The sun was so low in the sky that she was not sure if the sun were rising or setting. The young girl searched for Jordan, but he was nowhere to be found, nor did Anthony mention him. On the pier, she took one last look up at the ship, but Alistarr was not there to see her off either. She was alone.

Now from the harbor, it was a short walk up the cliffs to the harbor gate which separated the town from the port below. This part of town was built up against the cliffs where a short wall ran along a path wide enough for carts to make their way from town to the shore. This path ran west to east, ending at the outer wall of the castle where a side gate was located. Once inside the walls, it was another short walk to the inner gate where the servant's quarters were.

Anthony entered the castle this way as it was a shorter trek than if they were to try to go to the castle's main gate. They had been walking in silence until they entered the inner gate. Here was the small courtyard she remembered standing in with Jax so long ago. Anthony paused and looked around. "Where is everyone?" he muttered. "I have only seen a few guards I do not even recognize."

Anny wondered what he meant. There had been many people at the pier, but here in the courtyard things were usually quiet when the sun was low morning or evening. Could it be his conscience playing tricks on him?

They walked through the kitchen and down the servant's passage to the main hall. There Anthony greeted some guards he knew who informed him that Ramoth was in his private chamber. One of them led the way while chatting with Anthony about where he had been.

"Good luck to you!" the guard said as they stood outside the door to Ramoth's chamber. "Our leader has been cross for some time. The older guards say they have not seen a light under him like this in a decade."

Anthony shifted nervously before remarking, "Well I have good news, so what have I to fear, right?"

"Right?" the guard said with uncertainty.

The door was opened for them, and their presence announced to Ramoth. He was sitting near where Anny had left him sleeping, drink in hand, his arm around Megan. Behind him, the doors to the balcony were open, though the drapes were drawn so that they fluttered in the cool air. Ramoth jumped from his seat at the sight of Anthony, extending his arm to greet him.

"Anthony! Finally, a man around here I can trust! I was expecting you after having spotted the Berkiss from my balcony. This must be Anny!" Ramoth rambled as he looked the young girl up and down. "Here I thought we had never met, but you seem familiar. Perhaps we met in passing."

Anthony had been holding onto Anny's arm tightly ever since they had left the Berkiss, but now Ramoth tugged her away.

"You may go, Anthony," he said firmly.

Anthony wavered, hesitating to ask, "Sir, if I may, I request that when this criminal is brought to trial that you would see fit to allow me to run the proceedings."

"That will not be necessary," Ramoth said as he dragged Anny away from him. "I will handle this personally. There will be no trial."

"No trial!" Anthony blurted out, but he could not help himself.

Ramoth turned to him, his cavalier smile gone. "I said, 'you may go'."

Anthony stood a moment longer then left quietly.

"Bah!" Ramoth cursed as he forced Anny down onto the couch that was beside him. He took his spot as before, taking a deep drink by habit. He then leaned over to Megan, whispering into her ear. She nodded and left the room, closing the door behind her.

"You look like you have seen better days," Ramoth quipped. "So why not let me help you? There is only one man in all these lands who can save you, and you are looking at him. You heard what I just said. I do not wish to

180

send you to trial. In return, I ask that you tell me the truth, okay? Why did Cailar let you go?

Anny was a bit taken aback. She knew she had to choose her words wisely.

"What do you mean?" she asked hesitantly.

Seeing the king's expression told her this was not the right approach.

"When you hurled those vicious and unlawful attacks against one of my dearest friends, why did Cailar just let you go?" Ramoth angrily retorted, slamming his hand down on the table in front of them.

"I did not think he did," Anny thought aloud.

"Well, he did!" Ramoth blathered. "Maybe I should ask this another way, what is the connection between you two? Why did he protect you? What have you done for him?"

"Nothing!" Anny said desperately. "Nothing at all. I do not even know him."

"You mean the entire time you have been a maid here he never asked a favor of you? Anything? Even something that at the time seemed inconsequential?"

Anny did not know what to say. She was too terrified to speak.

"You need to tell the truth," a voice from the balcony said calmly. He had been standing outside just out of sight. His voice had been enough though: Anny immediately knew that it was Marcus.

"Yes, listen to your friend," Ramoth said. "He asked I spare you and in return, you would have information. So far you have been less than forthcoming. Out with it!"

Marcus looked directly at Anny. He nodded softly. "Tell him," Marcus said. "Tell him who you really are and then we leave here together. This can all be over: a terrible misunderstanding."

Tears of relief flooded her eyes. Why had he put her through this? Did he need for her to prove her love? She turned to Ramoth and confidently asserted, "I am from Faverly."

The room fell silent. Ramoth looked sternly at Marcus, disbelief in his eyes. Then he looked back at the young girl, and from the very depths of his stomach he let out a hearty laugh. Tears were rolling down his cheeks as he struggled to breathe. "Marcus, Marcus! You told me what a hoot she was in bed, but you failed to mention she was a complete fool!"

Anny glared at him but was almost immediately distracted by the sound of Marcus laughing as well.

"Why is this so funny?" she demanded. She stood up and walked over to Marcus. "You believe me, do you not? Do you not believe after everything I showed you? How can you deny it?"

Marcus calmed himself enough to reply. "Because, Anny, all those girls were killed! Remember how Jax even found the rope? You know how hard it was for me to pretend like I had no idea what he was talking about? We planned the whole thing, Anny! We made sure everyone was dead!"

"No, it cannot be. You were not involved," the young girl said in disbelief as she backed away from him.

"I have your proof right here," Marcus said as he walked to the table that sat near the doors to the balcony. There was a bag on it, and he dumped the contents out in front of her. Seven gold bands clanged to the table. "These bands were permanently affixed around each girl's neck. Seven bands here, count them! How do you think we got them off? We did not break the bands to do it!"

He continued to giggle as Anny approached the table. She looked down at the bands and began to shake. Mindlessly she reached out and touched them, counting them out one by one.

"See, Ramoth?" Marcus continued. "I told you that you had nothing to worry about. This girl is crazy. She thinks she is a Faverly Sister, but the problem with that is she is alive! That must be why Cailar tried to spare her. Maybe the princess wants to try one of the bands on herself?" Marcus picked up one of the bands as he spoke, then thrust it into her hands. "For you my lady," he said with a bow. Anny sunk away.

●●●●●●●

Anthony's feet stomped down the main hall as he left Ramoth's chamber. Besides rage, he felt that intense hunger and thirst such as one feels when after a long voyage you are home once more. He replayed in his mind over and over Ramoth's words. He tried to devise an argument that would have changed the king's mind. He turned down the passage to the servant's quarters. He paused to pound his fist on the wall. His rage intensified and his face grew red. He did not hear the footsteps behind him. He only felt the sharp pain in his back, and then there was darkness.

●●●●●●●

Anny stumbled out to the balcony in a daze. Her breathing was heavy: labored by her injured ribs. Her eyes welled. She looked out over the ocean which was red with the setting of the sun. Below, the Berkiss sat in the harbor looking as peaceful as it ever had. She looked straight down but saw only jagged rocks exposed periodically by the crashing waves of the sea. She imagined herself running and jumping out into the water, but she was so high up that even in her dream she crashed down on the rocks to her death.

Marcus watched her intently from the room. He was trying to remember what she had looked like that first day he had seen her versus the disheveled mess he saw now. Ramoth walked up to him and placed his hand on his friend's back.

"I am glad you are here, Marcus," the king said matter-of-factly. "Now, more than ever, I will need people around me that I can trust. Together we can deal with this unpleasantness before us. One way or the other I will soon enough know if Cailar can be trusted."

"You two have been through so much," Marcus replied absentmindedly, "will you forgive him if he is honest with you? I know, in the past, you two had other things between you, but I had thought all that was through with. I mean, you seemed appeased with this last killing, though I guess Anny is a new betrayal."

Ramoth thought about it for a minute. "What Cailar did to me all those years ago is not soon forgotten, but I thought he had learned his lesson when I ordered him to strike his son dead. And you are right; when I had you kill that servant girl, I felt like we were even. Now this 'Myth' resurrects itself again. I can never be rid of it?" Ramoth walked back to the fire, staring intently at the flames. "Perhaps he is keeping it alive? Where is she?" Ramoth grumbled.

The door suddenly opened as Megan returned, this time with Cailar.

"Ah, finally! The man of the hour!" Ramoth mocked. "Would you like a drink my dear, old friend?"

Cailar looked at him soberly. "Where is she?" he demanded.

Ramoth straightened up, "I thought it would be a nice surprise for you, but here you knew what I was up to?" He glared at Megan. "Did you ruin the surprise? It seems the three of us hold no secrets, save one. Why did you let this criminal escape, Cailar?" he demanded as he pointed to the balcony.

"Are we really in the business of chasing down frightened children? Look at her! What threat to you is she?" Cailar yelled back at him.

"So you admit that you intentionally let her go?" Ramoth scoffed incredulously. "In a way, I am pleased that you are being forthcoming with me. Maybe I have made this out to be more than it is. It need not be an issue at all. Let us agree it is just a misunderstanding, one that I have corrected."

184

Ramoth walked up to Cailar, and from his waist, he removed his dagger. He held it out in front of him with the handle pointed towards Cailar.

"I just had this made. It is a thing of wonder: the jewels and the metal. It is flawless in its construction, and with it, I will put an end to the Myth once and for all."

Cailar's brow furrowed. "The myth?" he asked. "What are you talking about?"

"Ah!" Ramoth exclaimed, "There you see I thought we had agreed to be open about all this. Trust, my friend, trust is what makes life possible. With it, we rule kingdoms, and without it we destroy them."

Cailar looked first at Ramoth, and then to Anny. "You want me to execute her? Is that it? What would that prove?"

Ramoth smiled. "No, nothing like that! You see, I have already made up my mind about you. I know all I need to know."

Ramoth then turned to Megan, who had been standing by Cailar's side.

"I want you to execute her," he ordered as he handed Megan the knife.

Megan took the dagger, then looked at Ramoth imploringly. "You would risk our child?" she whispered to him.

"A king must trust his queen, my love. Prove to me where your loyalty lies." Ramoth said to her.

Megan looked from him to the dagger, then slowly started to walk to the balcony. Anny was standing with her back to them, but now she turned around in time to see Megan approaching with the weapon.

"Megan, no!" Anny pled as she lifted her hands in self-defense. "Marcus, please!"

Megan was shaking as she held the dagger with both hands over her head. She was about to strike when Cailar called out to her, stopping her.

"Megan, no!" he called. "No, I beg of you. Do not harm her."

Ramoth shook his head. "So it is true. You are conspiring behind my back. I had thought we had ended all this a year ago, but even death does not stop your betrayal." Ramoth sat down in his chair, somberly looking at the ground.

"We already know your secret, Cailar! Anny told me everything!" Marcus interjected. "You had best tell the truth. When did Anny tell you she was one of the Faverly Sisters?"

Cailar looked out at Anny. It was like she was miles away. He wanted nothing more than to run to her, but that time had long past. He shook his head dejectedly and made his plea.

"Please, Ramoth, let her go. She is innocent in all of this," he said motioning to Anny. "She knows nothing. Let her go. We both have enough innocent blood on our hands."

"Do we?" Ramoth scoffed. He turned his hands over in front of him. "What is one more stain?"

"Please, Ramoth. Let her go, and I will go to trial and confess to anything you wish. You can have me publicly humiliated. Just please let her go."

Ramoth looked up to him, his eyebrow raised. "Why would you do that for this criminal? Even you could not believe her lies!"

Cailar turned to Anny. "Anny... No that is not right. It is because Cordillina is my daughter."

"You have a daughter?" Megan gasped. She looked at Anny with disgust. Then she placed her hand on her stomach. "No, no this cannot be."

Anny fell back against the railing of the balcony. "I never knew my father," she whispered.

Cailar sat beside Ramoth and spoke to him, "Ramoth, you know why at the time I had to keep her hidden from you. After what befell my son and your wrath. I am sorry! I am so sorry I ever touched Kayla! Nonetheless, I had to try to keep Cordillina safe. Her mother stayed away from here at Faverly so I could keep an eye on them away from you.

If you thought I loved the Sisters, it was only a father trying to protect his daughter."

Ramoth continued to look at the ground, shaking his head.

Cailar pled, "I thought she was dead. I would have sworn last year I saw their bodies with my own two eyes. If I had just known." His stopped long enough to look up at Anny. "It had been so long since her mother let me see her. If I had just known before all of this happened, but by the time I figured it out it was too late."

"Enough!" Ramoth demanded. "You let her escape. You let a criminal escape! There is no excuse for that! An old friend or not, your daughter or not, a king must seek justice and fulfill the law. Again and again, you have betrayed me! I have tried to fulfill this burden. What is left for me to take from you?"

"I have offered you my life," Cailar begged. "What more can I offer?"

Ramoth looked at him, "What joy is there for me to take your life? No, that is temporary suffering while mine will be never-ending. Her life; You will watch as I end her life. Perhaps then my wrath against you will be satisfied as you live out your days without her. Megan, kill her!"

Megan's hesitation melted away, and in a burst of anger, she began stabbing at Anny. Weak from her injuries, Anny struggled back against her but felt herself falling back.

Cailar jumped to help her, but Ramoth grabbed hold of him, and the two men fell to the ground.

"Illina! Illina!" Cailar cried out, "Marcus help her!"

Marcus had been standing there, dumbstruck. But now he drew his sword. Ramoth managed to roll on top of Cailar and pinned him to the ground.

"I want you to see this!" he told Cailar as he pushed his face towards where the girls were fighting. "Go, help Megan!" he called out to Marcus.

Marcus nodded. He looked out the doors of the balcony at the two women. Just then, the sun dipped below the horizon, and the sky turned dark. Raising his sword, Marcus instead struck Ramoth in the back. Ramoth let out a yell as he collapsed to the ground, pinning Cailar below him.

Their faces were almost touching as Cailar watched the struggle lift from Ramoth's eyes. As the king took his last breath, he seemed for the first time to be at peace.

In a panic, Cailar pushed Ramoth's corpse off and rushed to the balcony. Megan had heard Ramoth's scream and had turned just in time to see Marcus pulling his sword out of her lover's back. For a moment time froze but then seeing Cailar's approach she channeled her grief to force Ramoth's dagger through Anny's chest.

Anny grabbed the handle as the two women fell back onto the railing. Blood poured out of the wound as her head grew lighter. She grabbed Megan to keep from collapsing, but it was no use. Megan was too weak, and they both went toppling over the railing.

Cailar sprinted to catch them, but he was too far away. He reached them in time to see their bodies, bloody and mangled tossed by the surf below.

He fell to his knees, his hand landing in the wet blood on the stone floor. He held his hand up and thought of what he had said before.

"Illina. Illina, how can I lose you again?" he thought.

So overwhelmed by grief was he that he did not hear the pounding at the door or the creak it made as it opened. He did not hear Marcus approach. He barely felt Marcus's sword pierce his heavy heart. He did not notice the men who entered the room who then greeted Marcus warmly. The men signaled to the ships in the harbor, and out of them poured more of Marcus's army.

Marcus stood, triumphant for a moment. He took the signet ring off of Ramoth's hand. He took Ramoth's cup, and together he and his men toasted to his health.

● ● ● ● ● ● ●

One year later, Marcus stood on the same balcony in his finest robes. He was admiring his ring as it glinted in the late evening rays. He was still gleefully drinking out of Ramoth's old jeweled cup.

He heard a pounding on the door and jumped, half expecting an army to come rushing in. He had to look down at the pier to assure himself all was well. There were his ships. There were his men. The Berkiss was not there but should return in another week with supplies from the other side of the continent.

Brinna opened the door. She was herself dressed in her most beautiful gown of royal blue with yellow lace trim. It barely could cover the bump on her belly. She smiled when she saw him. "There you are! Our guests are waiting! What is taking you so long?" she asked.

Marcus laughed. "Just enjoying the evening air!" he fibbed.

"What is that in your hand? You are not still using that gross, unwashed cup are you?" she grimaced.

"No!" Marcus insisted.

"Give it to me! Let me see!" she said as she tried to snatch it from him.

But he refused, instead, hurling the cup out to sea before she could get ahold of it.

"That is very mature of you!" she goaded. "Now come on!"

The two left, side by side. The cup sank into the sea never to be seen again.

Chapter Fifteen: Paultry

A sudden gust of wind caused the branches of the tree overhead to sway wildly. Julia grimaced, clutching the book in her right hand tightly as she reached out to steady herself on a neighboring bow. She was perched on her favorite spot: a branch halfway up the tree that faced the town. From here she could see into the yards of neighboring businesses and homes. Small buds were surrounding her, only now beginning to bloom in the spring sun. In a few weeks the leaves would fill in, and it would be the perfect place to hide away from everyone. For now, it was barely dried out enough from the winter rains for her to enjoy the bit of sunshine the day afforded.

Her skirt fluttered, then fell to rest as the breeze died down. The girl brushed her long, dark hair from her eyes. She lifted her book in front of her, but she was not looking at it. Instead, she gazed over the top into the yard of the blacksmith. His apprentice would be arriving soon, and she longed for just a glance.

"Julia?" a voice yelled from below. "Julia!? What are you doing up there again? Julia, I've been looking everywhere for you. Your father is looking for you!"

Julia jerked the book up and pretended to be reading it intently.

"Julia?" Bess moaned.

They had been friends since they were little, but with the recent passing of her parents Bess had taken on the role of Julia's servant. They were both still trying to adjust to this new arrangement.

"I will climb up there and drag you down myself if you make me! Your father is going to let me go if you do not listen!" Bess insisted.

"Oh, do not be absurd!" Julia called down. "You are practically family!"

"That is easy for you to say!" Bess retorted.

"Just one more chapter!" Julia insisted.

Julia lowered the book just enough to catch a glimpse of the man she had been waiting for as he walked into the shop. Her heart leapt inside her chest, but just as quickly it was over.

"Julia!" Bess pled, "I have better things to be doing!"

"Fine!" Julia mumbled.

She closed her book and held it up, motioning for Bess to catch it. Bess's face turned red as she held out her hands. Bess closed her eyes tight as Julia carelessly flung the book down to her. The book landed safely in Bess's hands, and with that, she let out a sigh of relief. Next Julia flung herself from the tree, landing hard near her friend.

"I wish you wouldn't do that!" Bess scolded.

"I am fine," Julia whispered under her breath as she rotated her ankle to make sure it was still in its place. "Where is my father?"

"He is in the lounge," Bess said. She then held up Julia's book. "I'll be sure to put this back in the library where it belongs!"

"No, no leave it in my room," Julia instructed as she motioned that they should go. "I am not quite done with it yet."

● ● ● ● ● ● ●

Julia and Bess walked together into the castle and through the library. They made their way through the throne room and to the lounge just off it.

Julia looked at Bess quizzically. "Are you not going to drop that book off in my room?" she asked.

Bess shrugged her shoulders and smiled wryly. "Oh, yeah. I'll be on my way," she assured her.

Rather than leave Bess just stood there, grinning stupidly. Julia rolled her eyes and let herself into the lounge.

"What was it you wanted, father?" she asked as she entered the room.

Inside she found Areal sitting beside the fire with two other men.

"Julia! Where in the world had you run off to?" Areal scolded her.

"She was hiding in the tree again!" Bess shouted from the door.

"I think I can handle things from here, Bess," Julia hissed.

As Julia turned back and headed over to her father the two men with him got up and approached them. One she was unsure she had ever met but the other she recognized immediately.

"David!" she gushed. She wrapped her arms around him, and the two hugged each other. "I did not think you would be coming this spring at all! I have missed you!"

"Well," David stammered. "I wanted to bring Johnathan along and last spring he was unable to travel due to his apprenticeship.

"Johnathan?" Julia parroted in disbelief.

She reached out to hug the other man, but she could hardly believe he was the same boy who had left for Pent two years before. He was now a good bit taller than her with thick curls of blond hair and a deep tan. He was very muscular, even compared to her cousin David, who though about the same height as Johnathan was not quite as well build or as tan. David had the same dark, curly hair as his uncle Areal with the smile to match.

"It is good to see you, Julia," Johnathan said softly. He always spoke softly around her, and his eyes were often cast to the ground when he spoke.

"Bess, do be a dear and get us some lunch," Areal called out.

192

"Yes, sir!" Bess called back, hesitating at the door for a moment longer before she left.

"Well this explains the 'better things' Bess said she had to do," Julia scoffed. "I am sure you know she missed you, Johnathan."

Johnathan smiled shyly. He seemed nervous as he went to bite his thumbnail. Realizing this was a bit rude, he rested his hand on the ax which he always carried on his belt. It had been his father's when he was a guard at Paultry. Julia had known them both her entire life, but when Johnathan's father passed Johnathan had moved to Pent with David to take on an apprenticeship.

"How is your apprenticeship going?" Areal asked as he turned to the group. "By the look of you, they have you out chopping wood every day!"

"Something like that," Johnathan grinned. "Every time I mess up Francis makes me go out and find more wood. He says it is to build character, but I suspect he just needs the wood."

Johnathan laughed, then as it happened to then occur to him he reached into his pocket and pulled out a small, carved bird. He held it out to Julia.

"You made this?" she remarked as she took it from him. It was carved so delicately that she thought she could make out each feather along the bird's wings. "That is impressive."

She went to hand it back, but Johnathan put up his hands saying, "No, no! It is for you. I made it for you," he said, pushing it back to her.

Julia looked down at the little thing and thanked him. Areal was watching the three intently, but now he scoffed and headed out of the room.

"I had better let you guys have some time to get reacquainted. Besides, my dear little brother has sent me a lengthy letter here," Areal quipped as he waved the letter over his head and left the room.

David let out a sigh of relief once the door closed behind Areal, chuckling, "Whew! I do not know why uncle makes me so nervous. He is nothing like my father. Maybe if he were a bit sterner, I would feel more at ease."

The three sat down on the couches by the fire while Julia put the little carved bird on a low table that sat between them. David and Johnathan sat across from her, David leaning in while Johnathan leaned back.

"How is she holding up, by the way?" David whispered, motioning towards the door.

"She has been acting a little weird. I cannot say that I blame her. I do not know if I should talk to her about it or not. She seems fine most of the time, so I hate to bring it up and ruin her day. I do not even know what to say," Julia whispered, fearing Bess might still be lurking nearby.

David nodded. "We tried to say something when we first saw her, but it was so awkward. We knew something was wrong when we had not seen her father, but we had no idea."

"What happened to them, I mean to her parents?" Johnathan interjected.

"They just got sick," Julia shrugged sadly. "Her father had returned from a long journey. A day after he came down with a fever and a few days later he was gone, and her mother had the same symptoms. She passed away a week later. They say there were at least three other men from the Berkiss who came down with the same symptoms, but they all survived. Her mother made her come here to stay with us until her father recovered: probably saved her life."

"That is too bad," David said somberly. "Do you remember when he would let us all play on the ship? You would be ordering us around. Ha! We would dream of sailing away forever. It seems like yesterday he was promoted to captain. He was so proud and made us all call him 'Captain Jordan', except Bess refused and called him 'Daddy Captain'."

"Well she is a bit younger than us 'old folk'," Johnathan joked.

"You should be careful talking like that! A real 'old folk' might hear you and get mad!" Julia joked.

"You mean like your father?" Johnathan quipped. "I am serious though! That was like ten years ago already. Doesn't that make you feel ancient?"

Julia thought about it for a moment. "Well maybe a little," she hesitantly admitted.

The old friends bantered on for a bit before Bess arrived with their lunch. David and Johnathan jumped up to help her, still unaccustomed to the change in her station.

"It seems so strange for you to be serving us!" David jested as they all sat down to eat.

"I don't mind at all," Bess blushed as she handed a drink to Johnathan. "As long as we are all together it is not so bad. I mean, it could be worse."

An uncomfortable silence fell over the room. David and Johnathan looked at each other, urging the other to say something.

"Johnathan and David are sorry to have heard of your parents' passing," Julia interjected. The two boys looked relieved.

"Oh," Bess's face turned red as she turned away from them. "It is not something worth talking about. I mean, not something I want to dwell on."

Again, the room fell into an awkward silence.

"Johnathan brought you a present!" Julia remarked as she handed the carved bird to Bess. Bess's eyes lit up when she saw it.

"This is amazing! It is really for me?" Bess gushed as she held the bird tightly.

"Of course," Johnathan said, though he was scowling at Julia. "Not that it is perfect; Francis keeps criticizing me on my handiwork. He says I am only suited for baser chores."

"But it is lovely!" Bess assured him as she held it to her chest. "I will cherish it forever!"

By now David was feverishly shoving his food into his mouth, wanting desperately to flee from the table.

"We had better get going! Eat faster!" David urged them. "If we do not hurry, we will miss high tide."

Julia and Bess looked at him. "Are we missing something?" Julia joked.

"I just have been looking forward to getting to the beach like the old days," David informed her.

"It'll be too cold," Johnathan chimed in, crumbs falling down his chest.

"Can we go?" Bess asked Julia.

Julia chuckled, "Well if Prince David says so then I guess we are. He outranks me!"

The four finished their lunch and then headed out to the beach by the north harbor. As they left Areal saw them. He waved, scolding them for leaving behind such a mess. He called out to Julia that he wanted to speak to her when she returned, but only Bess heard him.

● ● ● ● ● ● ●

The water was cool and choppy at the harbor. The afternoon sun sparkled on the tiny waves as they lapped futilely to shore. The sand was moist making it hard to find a dry place to sit down. The wind still gusted on occasion disrupting the top of the waves.

David and Johnathan wasted no time in stripping down to their undergarments and jumping into the frigid water. They wrested and splashed in the deeper water, trying to see who could outdo the other. Bess stood in the shallow waves with her skirt hiked up around her waist. She was laughing at her friends as they started to turn blue.

Julia sat nearby on a rock draped in the boy's clothes. She would never admit she found it amusing to see them attempting to drown one another. She was even a little irked at herself for eyeing Johnathan so closely.

Two years before, just after his father had died, Johnathan had poured his heart out to her. Unfortunately, she did not feel the same. Even then she was in love with another, with Lucien. The look of pain in Johnathan's eyes

196

then had been almost too much to bear so that when he decided to go away with David for the summer, she had been relieved. She was sure he would find someone else. Yet here he was, looking at her the same way. His eyes were piercing her soul as if no time had gone by at all, but since she did not feel the same way it made her uncomfortable.

Of all places, she and Lucien had met at the market. She had been reaching for a piece of fruit, and he bumped into her while on his way to his apprenticeship. Here was this rude, smelly individual who seemed to have no idea who she was. They bantered back and forth before deciding to share the fruit. She thought nothing more of it, but then the next week he intentionally bumped into her again, this time insisting they take a walk along the beach though it would make him late to work.

As it would turn out he was the son of a local farmer who had recently arranged for him to begin working in town with the blacksmith. Though a fantastic opportunity, he felt like he was ill-suited for the work: something that might have added to his agitation that day they met. Further, it was clear that his father and the blacksmith were pressing him into a marriage with the blacksmith's daughter.

Julia was familiar with the blacksmith's daughter, Eva. She was a lovely creature: soft-spoken and charming though a bit plain. Why he should be complaining was beyond her given Lucien was the antithesis of beauty. His eyes seemed to be not quite the same size, and his skin was oddly blushed.

Despite all that, it soon became apparent to her that the boy had more ambition than he was letting on. Having been betrothed to David for as long as she could remember, Julia sympathized with him. Lucien bonded with her, day after day over their mutual lousy luck. She found herself falling for him. Suddenly his face was beautiful to her and his smell inviting. This went on for a long time. Then six months prior things got out of hand. What was just a passing flirtation began to cross the line so that the two found any excuse to be alone together.

This sort of thing was frowned upon, as you can imagine, by both their families. Areal demanded Julia leave the boy alone until he could speak with Marcus about her long-standing betrothal. He was confident he could make it go away, and that given a choice Lucien's parents would accept a proposal of marriage to Julia.

However her uncle Marcus had yet to reply. When she saw David and the letter he had given her father she was sure it was about the betrothal. She had wanted to ask David about it but thought better of it as she did not want to have to explain who Lucien was.

Julia was a bit anxious to get back to the castle to speak with her father about it, though as her thoughts wandered to memories forbidden who else should approach but Lucien himself! She looked away in disbelief, then back in joy as he was walking straight towards her.

"Lucien!" Julia called out as she waved to him.

The remark caught Bess's ear. She turned back to see Lucien was now sitting next to Julia, whispering into her ear. Bess could not have been happier. Once Julia and Lucien were married, she was certain Johnathan would give up on Julia.

"You look funny. Have you been talking to my father by any chance?" Julia kidded. She tried to look into his eyes to gauge his response, but he was looking down at the ground.

"Something like that," he said breathlessly. He reached out and squeezed her hand saying, "Julia I have to tell you something. I am to wed Eva tonight."

Julia jumped up from the rock without even thinking. Her hands covered her face as she gasped.

"What are you talking about?" she stammered. "Why? I mean, what about us?"

Lucien hesitated for a moment before finally looking at her. "Julia, Ramoth just came to the blacksmith's shop. He demanded to see me and ordered me to marry Eva. He said it was that or death. He then offered a substantial dowry for her."

Julia slapped Lucien hard across the face. The sound echoed over the water, catching David and Johnathan's attention.

"You foolish, filthy, beast of a man! I would choose death before giving up on our love! Yet one threat from my uncle and you throw it away?" she yelled at him.

"Julia, we can still see each other. The marriage would mean nothing!" Lucien pled.

"Are you a fool? I will not be your mistress!" Julia shouted back.

"What is going on here?" Johnathan demanded. He was now standing, practically naked and dripping wet, behind Julia. "Is this guy giving you trouble?"

"I didn't realize your friends were here," Lucien said as he motioned to leave. Before he left, he turned back to say, "I question the love from anyone who would rather see me dead than apart from them."

Julia waited until he had walked away before she began punching herself in the legs, yelling obscenities. Johnathan reached out to her, but she jumped up and stormed off towards the castle.

"What was that all about?" David asked as he wrestled to get his dry clothes over his wet skin. "We should go after her."

"I'll know where to find her," Bess assured them. "That is a shame. She must be heartbroken."

"Who was that?" David asked as they started to walk back to the castle.

"Lucien," Johnathan replied. "Oh, I guess you wouldn't know who he is. He's a local farm boy. I didn't realize he and Julia knew each other."

"They have been close for a while now," Bess volunteered. "But you know since Julia is 'betrothed' to you David she had to keep her distance."

David and Johnathan both winced at the remark.

"I had not realized she had met someone," David said as he looked at Johnathan who was equally troubled.

"Oh, you know how we young people are!" Bess joked, taking their arms as they walked. "She'll get over it. I mean, she is a princess. She has responsibilities. Not like me…"

● ● ● ● ● ● ●

Julia planned to hide in her tree, but before she could get to the back of the castle, her father stopped her.

"Julia? What is the matter?" he asked as he tried to comfort her. "Stop trying to get away from me! What has gotten into you?"

"What did the letter say?" she blurted out. "What did it say?"

"Julia, we should talk about this when you are calm. What have you heard? What happened?"

"I just saw Lucien. Do not make that face! He came up to me and told me he is to marry Eva. Is that true? Has uncle done this?" Julia blurted out.

Areal shook his head from side to side. "We need to talk," he said as he wrapped his arm around her shoulder and walked her to her room.

Julia's quarters were simple: a bed and an oversized window. She had a large chest for clothes and several books stacked on the end of her bed. Areal had to move the clutter to sit down beside Julia. Jammed into the corner as almost an afterthought was Bess's bed where she had been staying since she moved to the castle.

"Listen, you know we have been waiting for my brother to let us know about letting you out of the betrothal," Areal said as he put his arm around his daughter. "Well the letter that David brought did speak of it, and unfortunately he is completely against it."

Julia was not sure she could be more heartbroken than she already was but with this news, her heart sunk even lower. Her lips pressed into a firm scowl.

"The letter said he would be arriving here shortly to escort you back to Pent," Areal continued. "He wishes the marriage to be immediate. I thought we would have a little time to talk this through, but he arrived here just a few moments before you. He and your aunt are readying themselves for supper."

"I will not go!" Julia insisted. "This is my home."

Areal pulled Julia against his chest.

"Well now, do not lose hope!" he assured her. "You know as well as I that David and Aunt Brinna have worked miracles in convincing him not to be so unreasonable before. I am sure they will convince him again tonight!"

"It will be too late! Lucien…" Julia began.

"Have faith in him too, darling!" Areal interrupted. "If he truly loves you he will not go through with the wedding."

Julia wanted to believe him but felt utterly hopeless.

Areal lifted his daughter's chin so that he could look her in the eyes as he said, "My darling, I promise you I will do everything in my power to stop this. Just give me a little time. Let me handle my brother. You wait and see!"

Chapter Sixteen: Ramoth's Return

David was surprised when they arrived at the castle to see his father and mother.

"We were supposed to arrive a week after you," his mother explained apologetically, "but you know your father and how he hates to travel!"

David laughed nervously. "Yes, well we did take our time as there seemed to be no need to rush. What are you two doing here?"

"Son," Marcus said gruffly, "I do not need to tell you that at your age it is better to be married than not. Now your mother and I, we had to wait. That is the custom of Paultry, but not of Arden. I do not want you to have to squelch your natural urges!"

"What are you talking about, and please stop," David pled.

Marcus continued, undaunted, "You and Julia have been betrothed since your birth! I think it is long overdue that we proceed with the nuptials."

"Father, with all due respect, and as I have stated before, I do not love Julia that way! She is my cousin!"

"I have been asking that he listen to us," David's mother interrupted. "You can hardly expect him to marry someone so closely related when you were not forced into such an arrangement."

"So I am to be Ramoth everywhere but in my own house? I have made up my mind!" Marcus abruptly shouted.

Brinna and David were caught off guard by this. They both paused to look at one another. Brinna walked over and gave David a reassuring hug not realizing his clothes were damp. David was surprised she did not let him go but held onto him for a while longer.

"It will be okay," she whispered in his ear. "Maybe when we are all in Pent he will calm down, you know?"

David forced himself to smile, but he was still not convinced. His father was not even looking at him anymore, but instead had his gaze square on the drink in his hand.

"You may force us to marry," David finally spoke, "but to expect a child is lunacy. I could never..."

David broke off, the thought causing the room to spin momentarily. Marcus shook his head. For a moment his warm smile returned.

"My son, there are certain realities I had hope to shield you from, but it seems you leave me no choice. Your betrothed has been consorting with the locals and with one boy in particular. Your uncle had the gall to ask that she be released from her obligations over it! I have seen how you have struggled to maintain your commitment and honor in this matter. I have watched as you have turned away one woman after the next. Again and again, you have acted nobly. Well, as for your cousin clearly we cannot say the same.

"Why are you telling me this?" David asked. "Is it vital I know her business?'

"An heir to the throne is critical to Arden and Paltry," Marcus continued. "Believe me, I wish there was another way but if we wish to maintain our hold we must cement our allegiances, and we must do it before the only heir to the throne of Paltry has some illegitimate offspring! I do not care how you feel about it. We all have to stop thinking about ourselves and think about our people. They need an heir: the best they can get. You can give them that security. After that, I do not care what either of you does."

● ● ● ● ● ● ●

David crept sheepishly back to his room. His head was throbbing from having the same argument over and over again. He had thought maybe after all this time he would see Julia in a different light, but there was the same girl he had always known and cherished as a dear cousin. How could he betray her like this? He retired to his quarters where he found Johnathan. He had already changed into dry clothes and was waiting for his friend.

"What are your folks doing here?" Johnathan asked when David gave him the news. "You look upset."

"My father is going to not only force me to marry Julia, but he expects an heir as well!" David scoffed as he tried to wrestle his damp clothes off.

"Woah," Johnathan said. "I mean though it isn't entirely unexpected."

David was wrestling to get a dry shirt over his head as he grumbled, "It is crazy! In Paultry the son does not marry until his father dies. Then we could all be happy! Now all of a sudden that is over! All because she could not control herself."

"Who could not control themselves?" Johnathan asked, his curiosity piqued.

"Julia!" David agitatedly scoffed. "He told me she is sleeping with a local: probably that guy we saw at the beach."

"Lucien? Are you sure?" Johnathan asked.

"It was strongly implied!" David assured him as he fastened his dry pants.

Johnathan lowered his head contemplatively.

"Oh, what is it to you?" David snapped. "You go around ogling her knowing full well that we are engaged!"

"You don't even like her that way!" Johnathan snapped back. "Now you care?"

"Well if she is to be my wife I do!" David insisted.

Johnathan got up to leave, but David stopped him.

"Where are you going? Are you going to pour your heart out to her again? Pathetic!" David badgered him.

Johnathan took a step back and raised his hands in front of him apologetically as he said, "Listen, friend, we are both in no condition to do this right now."

"Do you fantasize about her," David continued, "when we are all together? Right under my nose, you disrespect me?"

Johnathan shook his head sadly saying, "You are fighting things that have nothing to do with me. She made it clear how she felt about me, and I respected that. Are you going to do the same?"

David did not hesitate. He pushed his friend away with a sharp jab. Johnathan went down hard, hitting the back of his head on the hearth of the fireplace as he fell. David tried to wake him up, but he could not.

● ● ● ● ● ● ● ●

After looking for some time, Bess found Julia perched in her tree, book in hand.

"Where have you been? I looked everywhere!" Bess called up to her friend.

"I had to speak to my father," Julia said coolly.

"You are waiting for him to leave the blacksmith shop, aren't you?" Bess surmised.

Julia rolled her eyes saying, "Well what if I am?"

Bess rolled her eyes back at Julia. She watched her for a moment before saying, "You want me to wander over there and see if he is still there? It's likely he has already gone home to get ready."

"Ready? Ready for what?" Julia said innocently.

"Oh, come off it! We all heard what he said to you!" Bess confessed.

"I do not know what you are talking about," Julia said keeping up the charade.

Bess sighed, sitting down at the bottom of the tree. She was looking down at the grass as she asked, "Are you really going to be marrying David soon? You know he is a catch if you would give him a chance."

"You would like that!" Julia sarcastically laughed, "Imagine David and me and then you and Johnathan. It would make for a lovely day!"

"I would like that!" Bess confessed. She was trying to get Julia to smile again but to no avail.

"I suppose this is all my fault anyway, for being so naïve..." Julia began, but then she stopped.

"What is it?" Bess asked, quickly standing back up.

"I just saw him. Lucien really is leaving early," Julia said with disappointment.

Bess could see the pain in her friend's face. She replied, "I am sorry, Julia. We should go inside and have ourselves a treat! I can try that cookie recipe again and maybe this time it will work!"

Julia covered her face and took in a deep breath. She motioned to toss her book, and Bess caught it just before it hit the ground. Next came Julia, but she did not speak to her friend. Instead, the young girl ran to the front of the castle and waited on the steps to see Lucien go by. She waited some time, but he never came.

"He must have gone another way," Bess said. "Can you blame him?"

● ● ● ● ● ● ●

Julia felt mixed emotions about going to dinner that evening. On the one hand, she was devastated and ready to run to Lucien to stop him. On the other, she wondered what good it was to stop a man unwilling to stop himself. She looked up at every noise expecting him to come bursting into the room to tell her that he loved her still and would defy Ramoth. Around every corner, she expected to see him, yet he was not there.

She entered the castle's private dining hall and was happy to see that her Aunt Brinna was already there waiting for her. Since she had never known her mother, she looked up to her aunt as a substitute.

Brinna suffered very much from homesickness. She had felt happy in the little castle in Paultry and was hesitant to leave for Pent when Marcus assumed the throne. She tried to be supportive, but she preferred a somewhat more secluded lifestyle. The queen begged Marcus to consider spending a bit more time in Paultry during the summers, but he was always particularly anxious when away from Pent. Marcus had on many occasions snarkily assured his wife that she was welcome to stay behind if that suited her.

The two greeted each other with a warm hug.

"It is so good to see you again!" Brinna sang as she squeezed her niece.

"It is good to see you too!" Julia said as she hugged her back. "Why are your clothes damp?"

"Oh," Brinna said, her face turning flush. "Never you mind! You know how these things are! Come sit next to me so we can chat a bit before the boys get here."

Julia took her place next to her aunt. She rarely ate in the formal dining space. It had a long table that was a touch too big for the room so that getting around when everyone was seated was a chore in and of itself. The fireplace was also a bit oversized so that when everyone gathered, they often had to let the fire go out to keep the room a comfortable temperature.

Now, however, with the fire burning and the two seated it was very inviting. The two wished no one else would show up to eat.

"So how have your studies come along? Are you still interested in learning all those ancient languages?" Brinna excitedly asked her.

Julia shook her head as she laughed. "Well, you know my father. He keeps trying to get me to learn them, but it is so boring! I much prefer to read the classics: you know, tales of heroes who triumph in places far away from here."

"Here is not so bad!" Brinna said. "Some days it is all I can do to not think about wanting to be back here."

"Will you be staying long?" Julia hesitated to ask.

Brinna reached out and squeezed her hand, saying, "At least a week or two! I have been looking forward to being here. Bess is supposed to make me my favorite meal, but she did not sound too confident she could do it.

Julia's face looked concerned. "Things have just not been the same since Gigi passed. I learned from her what I could. Maybe I should be in the kitchen helping Bess!" she offered.

"Oh, no! Do not go! We can still cook together another time. If she really cannot get the spices right, we will have to make some of Gigi's famous potatoes ourselves!" Brinna assured her.

"That is a deal!" Julia said with a smile. "You just have to get the pan so hot; I think it makes Bess nervous. It is an unusual thing to do, I think. You know my father even tried to show us how it is done? What are we going to do?"

It suddenly struck Julia hard that soon she would no longer be here to put up with Bess's bad cooking, or to watch as her father tried to help. Her father and Bess would both likely be staying here, while she would be sent away. 'What are we going to do?' She was going to be doing nothing: nothing but leaving. The tears came up to her eyes with one sneaking out before she could stop it. Brinna quickly jumped up out of her seat and gave her another moist hug.

She whispered into her ear, "It is going to be okay, Julia. I swear we will never let him hurt you."

● ● ● ● ● ● ●

On his way to supper, Areal ran into his brother. Marcus was just outside the door to the dining hall.

"Spying now are we?" Areal said with a wink. "Come on! You are becoming paranoid like your predecessor! Do you not recall how in this very place we would make fun of him? We would fill our glasses and laugh at how one so powerful could feel so powerless. Yet here we are."

"It is good to see you too," Marcus sarcastically replied. The two brothers greeted one another with an embrace before Marcus continued, "Things do look a bit different when you are the one sitting on the throne. Have you seen David? I went by his room, but he was not there."

"I have no idea. Maybe he is already inside?" Areal offered.

Areal motioned to open the door, but Marcus stopped him.

"No, I was listening, and he is not in there. It is just Brinna and Julia," Marcus said flatly.

"I am sure he will be along soon," Areal said, then as if the thought had just occurred to him he said, "It is a fine position you have put him in: all of us. He might need a little time to get his head straight."

"Now you are going to start with me too?" Marcus grumbled. "It is a humbling thing to be here. No one remembers who I am, just who I was. Well, I am Ramoth now. I have obligations. You are all taking advantage of my love for you!"

"Is that what it is, or do you know that what you are asking of the kids is too much? Remember how our father raised us?" Areal pointed out.

Marcus looked at him crossly and said, "Do not you go bringing father up. That is not fair!"

"Need I remind you how much you loved Brinna and to what lengths he went to make it happen," Areal reminisced. "Why would you deprive David of that?"

Marcus shook his head. His smile had faded as he looked at his brother solemnly saying, "This is going to sound crazy, I understand, but you remember The Myth?"

Areal's brow furrowed. "Yes, naturally. What of it? Not that you ever took it seriously. You want to beat me over the head with it again?"

"No, no but could you blame me? While you were traipsing around the country I studied every book in that library: every topic you can imagine yet there was nothing there about that gibberish you were spouting when you got back from Faverly: absolutely nothing to suggest there were powers at work that could not be seen or measured.

"Yet, since I have been at Pent, I have been having these strange dreams. Do you remember my predecessor would complain of such things as well? I hear a voice, and it is taunting me. I wonder if it could be Barnas, but that cannot be! He died long ago, yet that is what my predecessor swore he dreamt of as well. You have studied such things. Is that even possible?"

Areal thought about it for a moment before admitting, "I know very little about it. I tried studying that book you brought back from Faverly, but it was written in such riddles I could never make sense of it. It was like someone who had gone mad tried to write down their thoughts. Yet, Barnas was quite reasonable. You know I thought at first the book was written by Barnas as I had seen him with it, but now I am questioning that. It is written in the language of Mesu and Barnas was not from there as far as I could tell. What has this voice been saying to you?"

Marcus grimaced, "It is in a language I do not understand, but then I will catch a few words here or there between the weeping and wails. They are things like 'sorry' and 'be silent'. The night before your letter arrived I had the clearest dream so far. There a figure was standing with his back to me. It was saying over and over again, 'calamity'.

"That is not much to go on. If only you had kept up with your studies me might know what is trying to be said," Areal scolded.

"Yes, yes, now is the perfect time for a lecture. I am working on it!" Marcus scoffed.

"Now that you mention it though," Areal interrupted, "when I visited Faverly all those years ago, before your predecessor visited there and The Myth was spoken, before all that he had already many followers. I spent some time together with them, but they were all a bit eccentric.

"There was one woman in particular though who always wore a veil. She would whisper things to Barnas, and he would sometimes repeat them to me. She spoke once through him of a great calamity that would befall the world if steps were not taken to avoid it. When asked what those steps would be she ran from me very upset. I guess I have been known to have that effect on women! Well, obviously I did not take it seriously at the time, but could there be a connection? I mean between her and your dreams? Maybe what Barnas told your predecessor was part of that plan she spoke of?"

"I thought Barnas was the sage? Why would he be acquiescing to some strange woman?" Marcus scoffed.

"I thought so too, but given what you have said and my trying to interpret that book, maybe he was just a figurehead: a puppet if you will. He might be trying to warn us against taking the plan any further," Areal surmised.

"How could he? He is dead, right?" Areal wondered aloud.

Areal shrugged. "This kind of sorcery is a strange thing I am unaccustomed to. If they were dabbling in things that they should never have been then perhaps his mind was disturbed so that when he was murdered an echo of himself continued to haunt his murder."

Marcus rolled his eyes. "How is that even possible? By what mechanism does a man's mind escape his body to go on then and speak without lips? That is insanity! Why am I even asking you these things when you have always been so fanciful?"

"When we were both young, we spoke of such things, but you would not believe me," Areal started. "Now even with your own experiences, you are willing to dismiss them to believe only in what you can taste and feel? What of it then? If you are willing to dismiss your ears when they hear this man scream, then dismiss all of your faculties. Perhaps even now you are dreaming! What then can ever be known unless we trust what our bodies tell us? You should not dismiss this just because you cannot explain it."

Marcus scowled. He hesitated to speak for a moment before whispering, "Brother, if these voices are to be believed, then it is imperative that Julia and David marry."

"What does that have to do with it?" Areal retorted.

"The only way to avoid the calamity would be to fulfill The Myth, right? Just as my predecessor was to have his son marry those women and their offspring to mix, so am I to have my son marry his close relative."

"What?" Areal said as he scratched his head.

"The pairings in The Myth were always between cousins! If David is the closest thing we have to the son of Ramoth, then Julia is the closest thing we have to one of the Sisters. It is worth a shot, right?" Marcus triumphantly insisted.

"Is that why you are doing all of this?" Areal said in disbelief. "What if fulfilling The Myth is what would bring about the calamity?"

"No, no! Dear brother," Marcus said as he put his arm around him, "think about it! Barnas screams out to us because we did not follow through with the plan. If avoiding calamity was his goal then would he not let things be? Hey, we will never know if we do not try! Am I right?"

Areal thought about it for a moment, picking up a small, silver key he kept around his neck and twirling it between his fingers as was his custom when he was nervous. After a brief reflection, he agreed that he would have to think about it. Marcus continued to hold his arm around him as he opened the door to the dining hall. There was Julia. She looked upset. He had promised to protect her, but what of The Myth? Could what Marcus suggested be true? Given her birth, perhaps it was.

● ● ● ● ● ● ●

When Johnathan awoke his head was throbbing, and he found himself locked in one of the small cells in the basement of the castle. The rooms were rarely occupied with some of the neighboring cells being used for storage. One had nothing but cheese locked inside. A guard was posted nearby. Johnathan had to appreciate their dedication to dairy security.

● ● ● ● ● ● ●

Meanwhile, David found a quiet corner to gather his thoughts. After Johnathan had fallen, David had run to his father, who upon hearing the source of their quarrel became enraged. He promised his son he would take care of the matter and that he should ready himself for dinner.

So David sat on a small bench in the garden near Julia's favorite tree. His heart was pounding against his chest, and it was everything he could do to calm himself. The prince felt betrayed on all sides, and as the sun was now setting, he wondered what the right thing to do would be.

Off in the distance, he could hear bells clanging. A flock of disturbed birds passed by cawing loudly. The wind picked up, and he felt a chill go down his back. He wished Julia was there. He hoped they could talk like they had before all of this nonsense began. He wondered what her feelings were, but also knew it likely did not matter.

Chapter Seventeen: A Prison

Supper was well underway by the time David made his way to the dining hall. The smell of familiar food and the brush of warm air in the room brought him back into the moment. Julia was sitting with his parents and her father. She looked bored but perked up when she saw him.

"There you are!" she said with a touch of relief. "We saved a plate for you, but, oh, where is Johnathan?"

David sat beside her. It was obvious he was angry. At first, it made her happy as she hoped he was as unhappy about this arrangement as she was, but then she was a little irked that her future groom was not a little more pleased with the thought of marrying her.

"It is not proper that Johnathan should be here this evening," Marcus said before David could reply. "We have family matters to discuss."

"What else is there to discuss?" Julia snapped back. "We could talk about your insufferably small, easily bruised ego but that is hardly a pleasant conversation for any mix of company."

Areal began choking on his food. Brinna jumped up to see if he was okay, but he motioned for her to sit down as he reached for a drink. David gently touched Julia's arm.

"It is okay, Julia. Do not go getting yourself in trouble," he whispered to her.

"I will not be quiet!" Julia continued, "In fact, I will be the most miserable person you can imagine until you all get the idea out of your heads that I can be controlled like this!"

"You have done a fine job raising her," Marcus grumbled to Areal. Areal was still catching his breath.

"Now, Julia we must remain respectful," Brinna implored.

"I will show respect when I get it!" Julia yelled, pounding her hands on the table for emphasis. "Just look at you with that snide little smirk of yours!" she remarked as she pointed towards her uncle. "People like you think you can do whatever you want to whomever you want without repercussion. It is sickening!"

"Who is greater than Ramoth?" Marcus questioned. "There is no authority above me, child. You will come to understand this one way or another."

● ● ● ● ● ● ●

Johnathan heard a commotion approaching. He jumped up from the bench in his cell and watched as two of Marcus's guards forced Julia into the cell next to him. She was still slapping and cursing at the men as they closed the door to her cell behind them. She was yelling obscenities and punching the walls so that at first she did not notice him. When she did, she froze in place and stared at him quizzically.

"This is a fine place to meet!" Johnathan joked quietly. "Let me guess- you did not finish your supper?"

Julia shook her head 'no' in disgust. "What are you doing here? Did David do this?"

"Well technically it was Ramoth who did it. I mean, David was nowhere to be seen when I woke up, but I am pretty sure those are Ramoth's men guarding the door. David's alright?"

Julia nodded the affirmative as she looked at the guards. They were standing at the doorway looking out into the hall. She had never paid any attention to the men previously. They had always been a fixture around her uncle; all be it usually quiet ones. She wondered if she ought to have noticed sooner just how many had accompanied Ramoth on this visit to Paultry.

"What do you mean 'woke up'. Were you taking a nap or something?" Julia whispered as she continued to watch the men.

Johnathan looked over at them and taking her lead whispered back, "Well I am not certain what happened. David and I were arguing, I think, though I do not remember the whole thing well. The next thing I know I am down here and I have the worst headache you can imagine."

Julia pointed to the back of her head then motioned for him to turn around. When Johnathan did, she gasped.

"The whole back of your head is bloody. Did you fall or did something strike you?" she whispered to him as she shuttered.

Johnathan shrugged his shoulders. "I have no idea, but it is David we're talking about. I probably just slipped or something."

"You should be resting in bed, not stuck down here," Julia scoffed. She was rubbing one of her arms trying to get her stomach to settle back down. "Besides, why would they lock you up for slipping and cracking your head open?"

"What did you do? Come on, you can tell me!" Johnathan egged her on.

"I just got in a fight with my uncle. He is an insufferable person to deal with; Nasty and condescending: you would think that all knowledge was his, yet a dimmer person never breathed."

Johnathan chuckled. "I am sure David will have us out of here soon," Johnathan said, sitting back down in his cell.

"I would have said so too but he was there when the guards grabbed me, and he did not say a word. I think he was almost happy about it! What has gotten into him?" Julia wondered aloud.

Again, Johnathan shrugged. He sat down with his back to her, leaning against the bars between them.

"This is likely my fault," he began with a sigh. "We were arguing about you right before I woke up here. That much I remember. David was livid with me because of how I felt…and still feel about you.

"I mean, it is no secret, right? Only, I'd thought if I went away maybe I'd forget or maybe I'd come back good

216

enough. It is unfortunate none of that happened. Still, I never should have let my feelings come between all of us. David is right; I should have backed down. I should never have said anything, to begin with. I mean, even without him I am so far from what you deserve.

He felt the warmth of her hand on his shoulder. He put his hand over hers. "You are different, Julia. Different from anyone I've ever known. I want you to be happy, and I know I can't be that person for you. Whatever you choose to do I'll support you. I'll fight for you, just to see you smile again."

Her hand squeezed his shoulder causing him to turn to her. He saw that tears were running down her cheeks. She reached her free hand through the bars, resting it on his cheek, and looked into his eyes. She wondered why she had never been able to see him before now. Without thinking, she pressed her face between the bars and pulled him in for a kiss, but Johnathan pulled away when they heard someone coming down the hall towards them.

"I am here for Julia," they heard a familiar voice say before Bess appeared at the door. She was waving Marcus's signet ring in the guards' faces and smiling coyly up until the point that she looked over at Johnathan and Julia. Then, her jaw dropped, and she let out a scream.

"Johnathan?" she streaked. "Johnathan, what are you doing down here? What has happened?"

Julia composed herself quickly. "My uncle is just flexing his muscles, Bess. I am sure if you take me to my father I can clear this up."

Bess looked dejected. "I was only sent for you, Julia. I didn't realize you were even here," she explained to Johnathan.

He smiled at her warmly. "It is okay! Just get Julia out of here and then you can worry about me."

One of the guards left his post by the door to open Julia's cell. He grabbed her arm and began to walk with her to the hall. Julia tried to catch Johnathan's eye to tell him somehow that she would be back, but he was still trying to assure Bess that everything was fine.

Johnathan was smiling at her, pressing her hands into his reassuringly. It was as if Julia did not exist at all to him. She wondered if he was moving on and was conflicted: both relieved and upset. Yet even this feeling was washed out by a flood of embarrassment. What had she been thinking trying to kiss him?

Just as Julia and the guard made it to the door, Bess called after them, "No, no! I can take her to her father! You need not bother!"

Bess hurried to her friend's side and motioned to lead her away.

"Stop right there! I have orders to stay with her. I will not let her out of my sight until told to do so," the guard insisted.

Julia rolled her eyes. She remembered this guard. His name was Bran, and he was known to dote on Marcus to curry his favor. She was going to tell Bess that it was okay, but when she looked at her friend, she could see she was a bit more nervous than usual. Bess affirmed this by looking her right in the eyes and not so subtly winking at her.

The trio awkwardly made their way up the basement stairs, Bess and Bran both insisting on keeping ahold of Julia's arms, to the hall that led between the kitchen and the throne room. Bess guided them down the hall, insisting Marcus was in the lounge.

As they were walking past the library, Julia imagined punching Bran in the nose and running for the front door. She could see herself bursting through it into the night, and vanishing down the north path towards Lucian's farm. Julia could see the way through the woods to their secret meeting spot by the river where they had spent so many nights just holding onto one another. She wondered if he was there now waiting for her like he would have been if all of this was not happening.

Should she risk it or was she a fool for even thinking about it? If he loved her would he not come running out

218

from behind the throne, ambushing Bran to rescue her? Instead, her knight in shining armor was Bess, for whatever that was worth.

They entered the lounge and found David sitting by the fire, staring into it. He did not break his gaze as they came.

"Thank you, Bess. I will take back my father's ring now," he said flatly. Bess handed it to him and then returned to Julia's side.

"Where is your father?" Bran asked impatiently.

"He will be here shortly. You can leave Julia in my care until he arrives," David said, waving his arm towards the door. Seeing Bran hesitate he turned to him with a stern glare. "Is there anything else? If not I suggest you attend to other matters."

Bran indignantly walked to the door, trying to keep his pride intact. After the door had closed behind him, Bess squealed and hugged Julia.

"That was great! Now, what do we do? How are we going to get Johnathan out?" Bess gushed.

David smiled, his stern face melting a bit by her enthusiasm. "I need you to go be a lookout for me, Bess. Go sit at the top of the stairs to the basement. Be sure you are not seen but report back to me if you hear anything."

"What is your plan?" Bess asked excitedly.

"I need to speak to Julia first," he said. "In the meantime keep an ear on Johnathan, so we know he is okay."

Bess looked disappointed, but she quickly hurried from the room.

"What is this all about?" Julia demanded after Bess was gone. "Does she know you are the one who put Johnathan down there in the first place?"

David shook his head. She could see just mentioning Johnathan's name was enough to anger him.

"We need to talk about us right now, not anyone else," David sternly remarked. He was looking at her out of the corner of his eye.

Julia furrowed her brow as she tried to read his face. She sat down in the chair beside him. He was rolling the signet ring between his fingers. She waited for him to speak, but when he did not, she tried to break the silence.

"I am guessing your father is not coming?" she mused. "That would be preferable as I am not sure I care to hear more of what he has to say."

"My father is asleep upstairs. Your favorite aunt got this for me," he said as he held the ring out in front of him. "I told her I needed to talk to you alone. There are things we need to discuss."

"What is there to talk about? I thought we were in agreement already. Have you changed your mind about our engagement?"

David sighed. His gaze fell to the floor as he said, "Julia, you know I love you as my cousin, and you love me as well in the same regard, but if you are to be my wife we have to start to think of one another in a different light, and it is very much starting to look that way. My father is insistent to the point that even my mother cannot persuade him. It just has to be accepted, and I think we can work it out. Both of us have to be willing to make an effort."

"It is not that simple, David." Julia mocked.

"Because of Lucian? Your father has, unfortunately, told us all about the two of you. Honestly, I would love to be spared additional details. At this point what does it matter?" David said with a shrug.

"Because he is married? How kind of your father to spare him, right? I suppose I am to be grateful? You two had no right to interfere!" Julia lashed out at him.

David's face flushed red for a moment, the color traveling all the way to his ears. He held his tongue as to choose his words wisely, for what he first wanted to say would have angered her.

Taking a deep breath, he said, "I am sure you are angry, but believe me if the tables were reversed my father would have sent my lover away in an instant, likely even killed her. It is not like the opportunities did not present themselves over and over, yet I held myself back because we were engaged. True, neither of us seriously expected to end up married, but I knew it was a possibility and I did not wish to hurt anyone: them or you.

"Do you now see that I had a vow with you, and I decided long ago that I would honor it up and until the time that our engagement ended. If you are hurting now, you have only yourself to blame for your lack of discipline."

Julia pounded her fist on the table.

"You cannot control who you love!" she snapped back at him.

"Yes you can," David stated. "Love is a choice, Julia. It is an action. You can choose to love someone by acting in a loving way. Genuine love is not a feeling that comes one day to vanish the next, but a commitment to act even when those feelings fade. Tell me, did Lucian truly love you? To what do his actions speak? Look to them and not his idle words. Forget your feelings as well, but look at how you have acted this entire time. Would you say you have been loving: pounding on tables and screaming at all of us? If this is the outcome of your feelings, then you can keep them. That is not love; it is something dark and ugly. It is love turned on its head; corrupted to selfishness."

Julia sat quietly for a moment. She certainly did not feel loved by Lucian at all anymore. It was quite the opposite.

"Julia," David whispered, taking her hand. "Julia, I would love you just as I always have if we are married or not. I need to know that going forward you would at least try to make this work: that you would rededicate yourself and control your actions so that they are loving. If we both do that, then this can work. We can do what is the right thing even if it is not what we would wish for ourselves. I mean, is that not part of our calling to be selfless for the good of our people? Perhaps in that my father is correct. In that, we might find true happiness in fulfilling our purpose."

Julia's eyes grew red and puffy; her lips pursed tightly.

"But David, I still love him," she insisted. "You do not just forget that kind of love."

David let go of her hand and rolled his eyes. "I wish I could get through to you. You or my father. You are not ready to get married to anyone."

"As charming as your cold approach to the matter is, given you have never been in love as I have might I suggest that your platitudes might not stand up to reality?" Julia sneered.

"And yours do?" he chuckled. "Where is Lucian, Julia? Where is he right now? He does not love you. Why can you not see that? One-sided love is no love at all. True love only exists where two individuals share it. If you are the only one committed to this foolishness, then I would suggest it is nothing but a fantasy."

Julia wanted to slam her hand on the table, but she knew he would say something about how "unloving" she was being. Instead, she stormed out of the room.

● ● ● ● ● ● ●

Bess remained vigilant by the stairs until Julia came trudging by. She walked right past her, barely even noticing that she was there. Bess could hear as the princess stomped down the stairs into the basement. Then the familiar clank of a cell door slamming shut echoed up the stairway.

David followed shortly behind, but having come just in time to hear the sound of her cell closing, he shrugged his shoulders and shook his head.

"Some people would rather live in their own cell than take help from others," he said to Bess. "You might as well get some rest. I will see you in the morning."

David left Bess by the stairs. She was hesitant to leave her friends, but it was now well into the night, and there seemed to be little else she could do. Timidly Bess returned to her room. She tried to sleep, but she could hear people arguing nearby.

• • • • • • •

The slam from her cell door woke up the guards and
Johnathan, who had all fallen into restless slumber.
Johnathan looked sleepily at her, surprised she had
returned.

"I don't think you know how 'escaping' works," he
joked. "I wasn't expecting you'd be back."

Julia was looking over at Bran. He was smirking at her,
happy to see her in her proper place.

"Well I was expecting to have it out with my uncle, but
when I got to the lounge it was just David. Can you believe
he started lecturing me about love and commitment? The
gall of him!"

"Well, you are his future wife after all. He probably
was hoping to smooth things out between you and his dad,"
Johnathan suggested as he settled back down.

"He ought to be on my side, not driveling on and on
about things he knows nothing about!" Julia insisted.
Looking around she realized the cell was a bit dirty and she
hesitated to sit down on her bench.

"Nothing about what?" Johnathan asked politely. His
eyes were closed as if he were about to drift back off to
sleep.

"About love! About what it is like to fall madly in love!
What else could I do but what I did?" Julia said as she
paced her cell.

"You didn't say that to him, did you?" Johnathan asked
as he again sat up from the bench.

"Say what? About him having no clue? Of course, I
did! If I had not gotten so cross I would have had a lot more
to say as well!" Julia boasted.

"Oh, Julia. Julia, I love you but what about Ellason?
Aren't you forgetting about her?" Johnathan asked, now
looking directly at her through the bars.

"No. Who in the world is Ellason?" Julia asked.

"He never told you?" Johnathan said, surprised.

"Out with it! Who is she?" Julia impatiently insisted.

Johnathan looked embarrassed. "I thought you would know. Maybe he doesn't want me to say anything."

Julia smirked wryly. "Are you telling me this whole time David has had a secret lover of his own? The nerve of him!"

"No, no! Julia, you misunderstand," Johnathan insisted. He looked over at the guards who had settled back down. Leaning closer to her cell he whispered, "Fine I will tell you. Listen, back when we were all like fourteen or so, do you remember David started taking lessons with the guards? He was learning swordplay, that sort of thing."

"Not particularly. I thought David hated weapons of any kind. A poor quality indeed for a future king I would say," Julia commented.

"Okay, well when he was about fourteen he was taking lessons," Johnathan continued a little irked, "His mentor, Gregory, had a daughter."

"Ellason?" Julia surmised.

"Yes, Ellason," Johnathan confirmed. "She was helping them out with the lessons. It turned out she knew a lot about swordplay from her father, and he would have them spar a bit, you know just practice with sticks."

"And they fell in love, is that it?" Julia asked disinterestedly.

Johnathan shook his head and said, "Well no, not exactly. They became friends. Like they became really, really close friends. I think David might have grown to love her, but he did not want to ruin the friendship by going there, you know what I mean? Besides, he was engaged to you, so he kept things cordial and light between them. But then one night Ellason confesses that she is in love with him. She said she couldn't take living a lie anymore, and she wanted to know if there was any chance he felt the same way. He lied and told her he didn't. That was the last he ever saw of her."

Julia seemed unimpressed. "Pity. My uncle sent her away, did he not? What was the point in that? I mean at fourteen who knows anything about love?"

Johnathan's face went pale. "She killed herself, Julia. When David told her there was never going to be anything between them, she threw herself on a sword. Her father found her the next day. According to David, Gregory wouldn't even talk to him, and shortly thereafter left town."

"That sounds more like someone who was obsessed than someone in love," Julia retorted coolly, but inside she was shaken.

"He still blames himself for it, I think," Johnathan continued. "So maybe you could go easy on him."

"Still his friend after all of this I see. Men always stick together," Julia lamented to herself as she watched Johnathan doze off.

● ● ● ● ● ● ●

David left Bess and returned to the room that he and Johnathan had been sharing. He was supposed to meet his mother there to return the ring, but instead, he found his father waiting for him. Marcus looked at David squarely. He reached out his empty hand while waiting for him to say something.

"I am sorry, father," David said as he handed him the ring. "I thought I could talk some sense into my cousin. It seems the two of you get your stubbornness from the same place."

"I am not stubborn!" Marcus instinctively retorted. "What am I to do with the two of you? Marcus muttered as he shoved his ring back on his finger.

"I truly am sorry, father," David uttered, the frustration in his voice evident. "I believed if I could speak to Julia alone, I could convince her that going along with our engagement was in the best interest of our country."

Marcus perked up, a smile growing across his face. "My boy!" he exclaimed as he leapt up to hug him. "You have the makings of a true Ramoth, boy!"

"I did not say that I was happy about it," David continued. "Yet what has my happiness to do with it?"

Marcus put his arm around David, saying, "With honor comes happiness, my boy! The weak seek out an easy path, but a wise man takes the difficult path that will lead to a rich reward. I am relieved, and I imagine I will not have any more trouble from you. I have already spoken to your mother about this, and we make way for Pent in the morning."

David looked startled. "Tomorrow?" he repeated back.

"Yes, tomorrow. Is there something wrong with your ears? Tomorrow!" Marcus said, drawing out his last pronouncement of "tomorrow".

"Have you not only just arrived? You should rest before attempting the return," David pled.

"Listen, son. We need to get Julia away from Paultry immediately. Her attitude will change when she sees Pent." Marcus said. "She has never seen the big city and thus is rebelling against something she does not even understand. When we get her to Pent, and Julia sees all there is she will forget about Paultry. Besides, I plan a little stop along the way so that the trip is not too exhausting!"

"What about Johnathan?" David asked, looking at his father.

"Seriously? Do you seriously want someone who tried to hit you traveling with us? That is just not a good idea. I already spoke to my brother, and he agreed to keep an eye on him here for a while," Marcus explained.

"So then Uncle knows that we are leaving in the morning?" David thought out loud. "I am surprised he is okay with this."

"Naturally! And might I add he agrees that a change of scenery might dampen these outbursts from your cousin. It was practically his idea! So you see there is nothing you need to worry about. I will see you in the morning bright and early. We will be leaving just before dawn."

With that, Marcus said good night. David was relieved in a way not to have to face Johnathan right away. His parents were under the impression that Johnathan had attacked him first, a point that he allowed them to believe.

226

Suddenly leaving sounded quite good, yet as the young prince tried to sleep, David could only think of his friend. Results by any means might have been his father's belief, but he feared it was becoming his as well.

● ● ● ● ● ● ●

Julia was startled from a shallow sleep by the sound of her cell opening. Standing outside the door was David. It took a moment for her eyes to be able to focus on what she was seeing. He was holding a lamp and beckoning her to come out of her cell. She hesitated, sitting up to stare him down.

David pled with her, waving his arm faster and faster while pointing from her towards the hallway. Julia grinned, folding her arms and legs defiantly in front of her. Bran suddenly appeared from the shadows, grabbed her by the arms and dragged her down the hall. She yelled out in protest, waking up Johnathan.

Johnathan shot up panicked, letting out a loud snort as he awoke. He muttered a few incomprehensible things before realizing that it was just he and David. "Oh, It's you," he said, rubbing his eyes. "Where is that guy taking Julia?"

David looked at his old friend somberly. "Johnathan, we are leaving for Pent."

"Now?" Johnathan stuttered back. "Your dad isn't wasting any time, I guess. Look if this is because of what I did, then I want you to know I'm sorry old friend. I mean, if I roughed you up it was an awful thing to do. I hope you are okay. You know we're still friends."

David's shoulder's slumped in relief. "No, it is I who should be apologizing. It is all just as much my fault," he uttered.

Johnathan reached out to him, and the two men hugged through the bars.

"It's just a tight spot your father has put you in. We've been through worse, right? We'll get through this as well!"

Johnathan said. He waited a moment, expecting David to open his cell. "I'm guessing I'm staying here then?" Johnathan asked with a nervous laugh. "I mean unless there is going to be a trial?"

"Goodness, nothing like that! My uncle is going to take good care of you until you are well enough to travel back to Pent. That is if you would like to finish your apprenticeship there," David assured him, looking around to realize Bran had taken the keys to the cells with him.

Johnathan now seemed relieved, but at the thought of returning to Pent, he merely shrugged his shoulders.

"What is the point? Maybe it is better for you two if I disappear," he suggested.

"You know we would both hate that!" David laughed. "Besides, who will Julia have left to complain to about me?"

Johnathan laughed, gave his friend one last hug and told him he had better be on his way.

"Well tell your uncle to hurry up and get me out of here!" he added.

"Bran took the keys. I will have to send him back," David explained as he waved goodbye.

"Until next time then. I'll keep an eye on things here for Julia. You can tell her that. Tell her she can count on me to keep her father in line!" Johnathan joked as his friend disappeared down the hall; However, once David was gone a chill set into Johnathan's bones as he had never felt before.

● ● ● ● ● ● ●

The sky was beginning to lighten when David stepped out the front doors and down the stairs to the carriage that awaited them. His father and Julia were already there. Bran held the door for him. Julia was uncontrollably sobbing while Marcus sat disinterested across from her.

David looked around. "Where is Uncle? Is he not going to see us off?"

Marcus moaned, waving at Bran to hurry up and close the door to the carriage. As soon as he did, they began to move.

"How should I know? I knocked on his door, but he never answered," Marcus said gruffly.

"It is not right that she does not get to say good-bye," David insisted. "We cannot just leave!"

"If we do not leave now, we will not make it to the next village in time," Marcus retorted. "Why are you angry at me? If he had not been drinking last night, he might have been able to get up! Am I responsible for him?"

David had looked back to see that several of the guards were lagging behind.

"They are not ready to go yet either? And where is mother? Why the rush?" David asked.

"They will catch up," Marcus assured him. "Will you please stop crying, Julia? I am sure you will see your father again shortly."

● ● ● ● ● ● ●

Areal awoke at his usual time when his servants came to attend to him. He washed, dressed, and ate a simple breakfast per usual. He then went to Julia's room to see if she was up yet. To his surprise, he found Bess, still in her clothes from the day before sleeping on top of her blankets.

He startled her awake, asking if she knew where Julia had gone off to. He wondered if she had run away in the night to see Lucien, but Bess assured him she was likely still in the basement.

His face flushed with anger. At the end of supper the night before, his brother had assured him that Julia would be returned to her room for the night. He wanted to give his brother a proper tongue lashing but decided rather to rescue his daughter before any further harm might come to her.

Had Julia been there still she would have heard him yelling obscenities long before he reached the basement hallway. Instead, when he entered the room, he found Bran kneeling over Johnathan: his lifeless body face down on the floor. Areal wrestled the guard away from him, but it was too late. The cord around Johnathan's neck had done its deed.

"What have you done? What have you done?" the king screamed. He grabbed Bran and threw him against the wall. "Where is Julia?" he demanded.

Bran laughed, "Where'd you think?" Bran smugly replied.

Areal's face turned ashen. All of the light drained from his eyes. He began to beat Bran over the head, pouring out on him all the anger he felt towards his brother until he saw blood running from Bran's face. The guard fell to the ground where Areal stabbed him with his own dagger until Areal was assured he was gone. He then ran back to Johnathan, shaking him, but it was no use.

"I am sorry, old friend," he thought as he looked around. He found an old bag that he tied over Johnathan's face. He did the same to Bran, pulling off Bran's guard jacket and putting it onto Johnathan. The king then hurried up the stairs where he met up with Brinna. She shrieked as he almost ran into her, begging to know where David was. It did not take the two of them long to realize what had happened.

"What has gotten into him?" Brinna lamented. "Why is he doing this? It is not like Marcus to behave this way!"

Areal took her hands and placed his bloodied signet ring into them. "Brinna, take this. I have to go. You are in charge until I return. Close all the gates: all of them. Let no ships in or out. And get rid of all of the guards from Arden! All of them! Throw them out and lock the gates behind them. Your people are counting on you. You are queen until my return."

He began to walk away but turned back suddenly. "Oh, and send someone down to clean up the basement. Not you or Bess, just someone with a strong stomach. Two of Marcus's guards are down there. Dispose of them quietly."

"But where are you going? Brinna called after him. "When will you be back?"

She did not get a reply. Moments later Areal was on his best horse racing towards the side gate.

Chapter Eighteen: Return to Daven

After traveling for three days, Julia was exhausted. For the first few hours of the journey, she cried until she could not force the tears out anymore. Then she slept as best she could. Even when Julia was not sleepy, she would just lay there with her eyes closed hoping her uncle and cousin would say something that she could use against them later. However, they never spoke of her. If they spoke at all, it was about hunting or fishing. At one point they talked for almost an hour about a musical troupe she had never heard of.

She knew they would have to stop eventually, and that opportunity came when they arrived at Daven. Marcus was still fond of the bathhouses that operated there. In fact, he had been known to make many special trips to Daven in the years that he had been Ramoth.

His choice in hospitable dwellings had improved with the wealth that he now possessed. No longer was he crammed into a dingy room off the main drag. Now he stayed in the nicest inn. The staff there were always happy to see him and quickly prepared rooms for him and his guests.

Julia was a little surprised to be given a room with David. Though she protested that it was not proper, Marcus assured her it was "close enough". She had to wonder what plans he had for himself if he was willing to allow her out of his sight.

Four guards were assigned to chaperone them. Julia was more than anxious to get out of their shared room and explore the city. She found her legs were a bit wobbly from the trip and her belly ached for anything other than more of the rations she had been given.

David was surprised by her enthusiasm. For the first time since the trip began he thought he saw a bit of light behind her eyes, though her lips were pressed into her typical and ever-present scowl. Though he had only accompanied his father to Daven a few times before, he knew of a small establishment that had some of his favorite foods. There would be spiced lamb and rice, something a little foreign to Arden but typical of the northern regions like Mesu. He hoped she would enjoy herself: maybe even relax a bit and begin to take in the wonders of Arden.

They set out down the main drag, guards in tow: two leading the way with two behind. Julia was surprised to see the streets were full of all sorts of different people from many stations in life, yet all paused and slightly bowed as David walked by. She had never seen David like this. She thought him meek, yet here he walked with his chest pumped out and a big grin on his face. The young women, in particular, gasped, swooned, and basically made spectacles of themselves.

David took particular pleasure in this, waving back to them then turning to Julia with a shrug, shaking his head back and forth in mock humility. What could he do? The young princess wondered if he was trying to prove a point with this grand procession through the town, but what was impressed on her the most was how transforming a bit of recognition is to a person.

They'd almost reached the dining establishment when the guard standing behind Julia collapsed to the ground. It happened so fast that she thought he must have tripped, but as she turned to her left to help him up the guard who had been beside him went tumbling down as well to her right.

As she reached for the fallen guard, she felt David grab her around her waist. He pulled her forward as the guards who had been in front of them turned with weapons drawn. They were readying to attack whatever was behind her, but before she could even turn around to see she heard the awful clanking thud of their bodies hitting the ground.

She could hear people screaming and sensed the rustling of feet as the people around her pushed to flee the crowded street. David's weight was moving her forward, but abruptly he stopped and released her just as he went flying backward. He yelled something out to her, but his voice cut out as she heard the crashing of wood against the hard, stone street.

Instinctively Julia tried to run, but someone grabbed her from behind and threw her over their shoulder. She pounded her fist on their back demanding to be let go, but they took off running with her down the street. She struggled to lift her head to see if David was okay. All she could see were several bodies among the chaos lying lifeless on the ground.

The figure that had grabbed her ran for about a minute, ducking down one dark alley and then another. Julia was screaming for help, but the streets were much narrower here and were practically deserted. Her voice seemed to echo off the barren walls.

Suddenly the two stopped, and she heard the grating noise of rusting hinges. Again, Julia struggled to look up. To her surprise, they were now outside the city fleeing across a small patch of open grass. She could see the city walls disappearing as trees began to obscure her view. Her arms gave out, and she doubled over. Blood began to rush to her head. She struggled to get a deep breath.

The whole world was spinning, but after a short time, she was no longer moving. She felt herself being put down. When she opened her eyes, she could make out a figure with the full strength of the sun shining over its shoulder looming over her. She began swinging her arms at it, but each punch that landed hardly seemed to have any effect.

"It's me, it's me!" he pled as he grabbed her arms to stop her from punching him.

Julia's eyes struggled to adjust to the light. She could barely make out the man's face, but she recognized his voice.

"Johnathan?" she whispered.

The figure nodded. "I've come to rescue you!" he boasted.

"Johnathan!" Julia said with relief. She threw her arms around him, and he squeezed her back. "What just happened? Who was attacking us? We need to go back! We need to go back for David!" she blurted out all at once.

"I'm not going back! I'm rescuing you from that man, you silly thing! Why would I go back? I'm not going back! You and I are free now! We're going to get out of here and never look back," Johnathan insisted. He leaned in to kiss her, but she pulled away.

"What are you saying?" Julia asked. "David did not hurt me. We were being attacked. You must have seen them."

"Them? Julia, I rescued you from David," Johnathan explained as he took her hands. "I got rid of those men who were keeping us apart, but they can't hurt you anymore. Not so long as I am around. Julia, something remarkable has happened!"

Julia shook her head in disbelief. "How hard did you hit your head?"

"Julia, what I am about to say, well it will seem shocking, but you must know." He paused and took in a deep breath. "Julia, David had me murdered."

"But Johnathan, look you are alive," Julia stated, wondering if she was missing the point.

Johnathan seemed excited as he explained, "I know! I know! I was in my cell where you left me, and then David spoke to me, but he didn't let me out. He just left me there, and I thought that was odd, but then Bran, you remember him, well of course you do; Bran came into my cell, and he choked me to death! I can still recall the feel of the rope and how there was this pressure in my head. Julia, I woke up and I was in this dark place with a light, but there was also a door, and I opened it, and at the end, there was this old lady, and I punched her right in the face! I escaped death! I punched her in the face, and I ran!"

Julia looked at him for a moment, before reaching up and pulling back the collar of his shirt. She looked at his neck carefully.

"There are no marks here. Your neck is fine," she said timidly. She hesitated to try to turn his head, but to her surprise when she did, she found no sign of injury.

"I'm perfectly fine!" he said, beating his chest. "I'm even better than fine! See how I bested those guards? I've got strength like you would not believe! I can even feel you, Julia."

"Feel me?" she asked, but immediately regretted it.

"As soon as I was out of that dark place, I could feel you. I ran out into the daylight, and I could sense your presence. I felt your sadness and despair. I followed it right down the sheer mountain cliffs into town. Julia, we are meant for one another. Do you not feel it as well? Do you not sense my love, my fear, my presence?"

Julia looked at her old friend: his eyes were flashing in the sunlight, his breathing was heavy, and his heart racing. He pulled her tighter into his arms and kissed her while pushing her against a tree. She was struggling back, but he was unmovable.

"I will make you understand," he said. "There is so much more. There is…"

His voice began to slur, and his eyes were suddenly glassy. He shook his head from side to side, then slowly crumpled to the forest floor. Standing behind him was a short, wrinkly little man Julia had never seen before. He was holding a blow gun in his hand.

"He is going to wake up very soon and very angry. We go now," he said as he motioned for Julia to follow him.

● ● ● ● ● ● ●

Marcus looked at David and then to the guard's body on the floor before him. "It would seem you are lucky to be alive," he said. "My best men…you are my best men?" he yelled at the remaining guards.

They were all badly injured, David still limping from where his hip had hit the ground.

"I want to know who did this. Who did this?" Marcus snapped at them.

David looked pale. "It was Johnathan, father. I saw him with my own eyes. He acted alone. Julia must be with him."

"Johnathan? How is that even possible?" Marcus boomed. "We left him back in Paultry! You know what, I do not care. Find him. Search the town and the roads: just find them! I want his body here before tomorrow!"

● ● ● ● ● ● ●

The little man led Julia through the woods to a small path. There he had tied up a pair of donkeys. One of the animals greeted her as if they were old friends. He loaded her onto it while taking the other for himself. He drove them as hard as he could along the path until they reached the edge of a river where the forest became thick, and the road began to meander.

"I know these routes better than anyone!" he assured her. "We're safe now. Very safe."

"How can you be so sure?" Julia asked. She kept looking behind them.

"This forest is like a thousand mirrors," he said with a plain face. "If you do not know where you are going, you might travel in circles, but if you do know you can get there very fast. The mirrors, they will protect you. They will disguise your presence from Johnathan."

"Has everyone here hit their heads or something?" Julia whispered to herself. "So now that we are safe, we can head back to Paultry, right? I mean, you do intend on returning me home?"

The man shook his head. "No, no. Paultry is not safe for you. That man will easily find you there! I take you to your father. He is waiting for us near the top of the mountain."

Julia laughed without thinking.

The man chuckled back. "I could take you back to your uncle or to that man if you prefer," he laughed.

"On second thought, weird place in the forest it is!" she agreed.

● ● ● ● ● ● ●

It was still daylight when Johnathan awoke. His head was pounding, and his arm hurt. He looked frantically around, seeing that Julia was gone. He could no longer sense her. He worried some harm had come to her, but more so his anger burned that she had left.

Then David appeared in his mind's eye. Had he followed them and taken Julia? His anger doubled at the thought of Julia in David's arms. She could not be nearby, or he would sense her.

He walked back towards town, finding a man just entering by the gate he had fled from. He pulled him from his horse by his neck and stole his purse off his body. He then jumped onto the horse and headed out towards Pent.

● ● ● ● ● ● ●

"We have gone this way already, have we not?" Julia asked.

Shortly after entering the dense woods the young girl had become hopelessly disoriented. Her guide did not seem concerned.

"This is a short cut," he explained. "Sometimes you have to go back to move forward."

"Right," Julia said. "I do not think I caught your name."

"You did not ask," the man said. "Funny given you were willing to travel with me! I must have an honest face!"

"Well my name is Julia," she said.

"I know!" the man sang. "And I am... just here to get you to your father."

238

"It is nice to meet you 'just here to get you to your father'," Julia quipped.

The man laughed. "You are spunky! Your father told me so."

"Are you really taking me to my father?" Julia asked.

"Your parent, yes! You ask too many questions," he said with a huff.

"Sorry, I am just trying to make conversation. This is all a bit weird, do you not think?" Julia said as she looked around the unfamiliar surroundings.

"Life is weird. When it is not weird, then that is weird," the man offered.

"Great," Julia sighed.

● ● ● ● ● ● ●

Night came, and Julia and the stranger were forced to camp for the night. He fell asleep almost immediately and snored very loudly. Julia looked up at the stars: they seemed so different here. She wondered what she was doing, but also what Johnathan had been talking about. Suddenly she worried what would happen to him if David found him, but then again, she did not even know if David was okay.

Just as she was settling down the man gave out a shrill scream. Julia jumped to her feet, ready to defend herself, but there was no one around. The man was sitting up, breathing heavily. Julia asked him if he was okay, but he assured her it had just been a bad dream.

● ● ● ● ● ● ●

Early in the morning before the sun had fully risen, Julia and the man set out again. They had been traveling up steep dirt paths, but here the trail seemed to be curving along the mountain. Suddenly the trees parted, and there was a large field with a small castle with four corner towers and a large, wooden gate. The early morning light bounced off the white bricks, giving them an orange-red glow. A small waterfall cascaded down from the cliffs above, disappearing behind the structure. To her right was a magnificent view of the valley beyond. She remembered what Johnathan had said about waking up in a castle.

The gate opened for them, and her father came running out to greet them. Julia hugged him tightly, both of them crying in relief. Areal turned to the old man and thanked him. He nodded, humbly leading the donkeys into the fortress.

"I am so relieved you are okay!" Areal said as he led her inside.

"I cannot believe you are really here! What is this place?" Julia asked. "We are not in Paultry."

"This is Faverly; it is part of Dione sort of in between Arden and Paultry," Areal explained as he locked the gate behind them.

They entered the courtyard where the old man was tending to the donkeys. Julia was surprised to find a woman a bit younger than her father standing timidly in the center of the square. She had a rather large bruise on her face but was smiling warmly at Julia. She motioned to greet Julia with a hug but instead pulled her arms back and awkwardly pointed towards a door to her right.

"I have some food for you," she blurted out.

Chapter Nineteen: A Warm Welcome

Julia felt like she had not eaten in a week. The food was amazing, seasoned like she would have expected back home: a stew with root vegetables and a touch too much salt. No one spoke, but that hardly bothered Julia as she felt she could not get the food down fast enough. The old man did not seem bothered to talk as well as he heaped another helping of the stew into his bowl.

When she finally stopped to breathe, Julia saw the woman was looking at her intently, not directly as to make it obvious, but more so out of the corner of her eye.

"I am Julia!" the young girl exclaimed, holding out her hand in greeting.

Julia did not want to make the same mistake she had made with the old man. The woman took her hand and shook it. She had an unusually strong grip, and her hands were very warm.

"It is nice to meet you," the woman replied, her eyes darting back and forth anxiously between Areal and Julia as she said it.

Julia was beginning to lose confidence in her social skills. "So, Faverly was it? That name sounds familiar, but I cannot recall where I might have heard it," Julia casually remarked.

The woman smiled and nodded.

"Umm, so how do you two know each other?" Julia continued as she motioned to her father.

Areal cleared his throat nervously. Just as he went to speak the old man stood up, putting up his hand asking him to stop. He then excused himself, leaving Areal with the woman and Julia. There was an awkward silence as Julia waited for her father to say something.

"You see, Julia," Areal began, "Umm, well this is Cordillina, but I call her Anny."

Julia looked at him quizzically for a moment as she sounded out the names in her head before remarking under her breath, "Odd shortening but I guess I can see it." Then loudly she added, "Nice to meet you! So do you prefer I call you Anny or Cordillia? That name sounds so familiar too. Like I read it somewhere."

"I see you have kept her up on her studies," Anny whispered to Areal.

"The girl reads what she wants to! I cannot make her do anything," Areal protested.

"Where was it that I heard it? Oh, never mind! What difference does it make? I can call you Cordillia, right?" Julia continued. "So how do you two know each other?"

"Cordillina and I have known each other a long time, Julia" Areal carefully explained. "Since before you were born in fact!"

"Hmm, you know now that I think of it did not uncle once mention someone named Anny?" Julia asked. "Or was it 'Anne'? I am so bad with names!"

"I did know Marcus as well," Anny volunteered. "But it was a long, long time ago. I have not seen him in years. In fact, he is the reason Areal and I met."

Julia grimaced. "At least something pleasant came out of your meeting my uncle. I am sure my father has told you that we do not get along."

Scolding, Areal replied to her, "Julia! It is not well to speak of your uncle in such a manner!"

"Really, father? He had me kidnapped! I knew you would rescue me though. I just kept telling myself that at any moment you were going to be there. I did not expect all of this," she said as she motioned to the room. "Where are we again exactly?"

"Faverly," Areal said matter-of-factly.

"Okay, I know but what are you guys doing here? What is this place?" Julia asked. "When will I be able to go back home?"

242

Areal sighed, "My darling, there are many things we need to explain to you: things I have been keeping from you."

"Like what?" Julia asked. She was beginning to feel a knot in her stomach.

"Julia," Anny said, "This place is a special place. There are forces at work here that do not seem to exist fully outside of here."

Julia rolled her eyes. "Yes, I have heard a lot of that lately."

"Do not be so dismissive," Areal said to her. "I suppose I have done you a great disservice by allowing you to believe as your peers do, but here it is possible to go against the natural order of things. I did not want you to be aware of it, because it can be so dangerous. Now, now I see I should not have been afraid of teaching you the truth. You will have to hear it all now anyway, and it will be harder than if you had known something of it before."

"Is this the same nonsense Johnathan was telling me about?" Julia snidely remarked. "You all sound ridiculous."

"You met up with Johnathan?" Areal asked, the blood draining from his face. He reached out and put his hand on top of hers.

Julia pulled her hand out from under his. "Yes, and he was going on and on like a mad man about a castle and a woman he punched in the face. That is not to mention the bit about being murdered but now being alive. I think there is something in the water here making you all crazy." When she stopped speaking, she noticed that both Anny and her father looked upset.

"Julia, I do not know where to begin, but here it goes: Johnathan was not lying," Anny said. She pointed to her face, "He was here, and he did strike me. He caught me off guard. I did not expect that he was able to pass through the gateway."

"Here we go again," Julia said. "Gateways? People magically teleporting about? Enough of this nonsense! Tell me plainly what is going on. I will not believe any more of these lies!"

"She is not lying!" Areal insisted. "Anny, and now Johnathan, have the ability to travel back from death. Each time they do so, they return to this place and gain powers that are not natural to this world."

"Are you crazy?" Julia asked. She looked down at her empty plate. She wondered how long she had before whatever was in it drove her mad as well.

"I am telling you the truth," Areal said as he pounded his fist on the table. "I saw his dead body myself! Bran strangled him to death in his cell! Did he mention that? He then came back to life here, just as Anny has before. He returned and escaped before Anny could stop him."

"I am just grateful that you were not hurt, Julia," Anny said in just above a whisper. She was holding her head in her hands staring at the table.

"He was here then?" Julia asked.

Anny nodded in the affirmative. "He knocked me unconscious and then ran away. I assumed he was seeking you out. You are very special, Julia. I am sure that just as I have always been able to sense you, he can as well."

Julia looked from Anny to her father. "He did mention something about being able to sense me. I have no idea what that means."

"The power that resides here is in you, Julia," Anny said. "It lives in me, it lives in Johnathan, and it lives in you as well. It is ours to control if we can learn how. Johnathan can sense that power. It draws you two together just like water pulls itself from two droplets into one." Anny reached out her hand, taking Julia's. "It draws us together as well," Anny said.

For a moment Julia could feel something she had never felt before. It was like the energy inside her was being pulled out of her towards Anny. She could suddenly feel Anny's energy as well: an enormous, endlessly deep well. Julia quickly pulled her hand away. She stood up, slamming her hands on the table as she did.

244

"What a load of nonsense!" she yelled as she stormed out of the room.

● ● ● ● ● ● ●

Julia drew the cool, open air of the courtyard deep into her lungs. She looked up to the sky, longing for some sense of normalcy, thinking that maybe if she reached her hands up, she could magically teleport back to Paultry: back to her tree. She and Bess would laugh in the noon sunshine about how silly this dream had been.

That is where the old man saw Julia. He was perched up on the roof of the building, looking down into the courtyard. He saw her standing there with her eyes closed and her arms stretched out over her head.

"What are you doing?" he called down to her.

Julia's eyes popped open, and she saw the little man staring down at her.

"If you want to get up here you have to take the stairs!" he called down to her. He pointed to the tower that was in the back-right corner of the courtyard. "The stairs!" he repeated.

Julia made way up the narrow, curving staircase to the roof of the castle. It did not look safe to cross over the roof to get to where the man was sitting, but she surmised that if he could make it then so could she. She carefully inched her way to him, sitting down beside him. From here they could look out over the valley below.

"That is quite a drop-off!" Julia exclaimed. "I should not have looked down."

"Wiser words were never said," the old man agreed. "Look out, not down. Look out, and it is beautiful. Look down, and it is terrifying."

"Looking up is not too fun either. It makes you feel like you are falling," Julia said, her gaze out over the valley. "I think I can see Pent from here."

"Yes, that is Pent all the way out to your right. You can barely see a little bit of it. You cannot see Paultry because of the mountain, but it is that way," he said as he pointed to her left. "Daven is over there at the bottom of the mountain," he said, pointing down and to his right. "And you are right here."

"I just want to go home now," Julia said, looking back in the direction he had indicated.

"But you are here now," he pointed out, "and where you are is where you are meant to be."

Julia wanted to cry, but it was not her style to do so. She bit down hard on the inside of her lip to keep the tears back. Paultry seemed an indefinable distance away.

The old man sat with her a moment before saying, "My name is Toshi."

"You liar!" Julia retorted back. "Your name is 'your father sent me to get you'."

"No, I clearly said 'just here to get you to your father', but you can call me Toshi for short."

"You seem to know your way around here, Toshi. Have you been living here long? It seems like a strange place to want to live."

"I have been here with Anny for many years. My grandparents brought me here from my homeland. They were to help Anny translate books that can be found here. When they passed on, I continued to help her. She cannot leave this place, so I have learned many ways to get down the mountain for supplies. Sometimes I bring her sweets. She has a sweet tooth. I tell her, 'do not eat this all tonight! It took me many days to go get it!' But she cannot help herself! They will be gone, and I will say, 'show me one. There must be one more left!' but there never are."

Julia smiled. "Why can she not leave?"

Toshi looked at her, then back to the valley. "There are many reasons. For one, she cannot control her power away from this place."

"Right," Julia said skeptically. "What is the other reason?"

"If Marcus knew she was alive he would put her to death."

Julia sat up a bit straighter. "So, she and my uncle do not get along so well?"

"When I went to go get you, she said to me, 'tell her nothing' so I tell you nothing. Yet here they have had the chance to talk to you, and they have bungled it. So I will tell you everything. Part of the truth is still a lie. Only the full truth can have any impact."

"Sure, right. What happened between my uncle and her?"

"From what I understand the two of them were a couple. This was back before Marcus became Ramoth. Anny was very much in love with him: the kind of love a young person has for another if you know what I mean."

Julia thought of Lucien but said nothing and tried to keep a straight face.

"Well, maybe you don't know what I mean. You might be too young. Anyway, Anny thought they were going to end up together, but when Marcus had the chance to protect her, he instead used the opportunity to secure his place as Ramoth. He stabbed his predecessor right through! Anny was killed in the process. She fell over a railing or something."

Julia tried to remember the story of how her uncle had become Ramoth. The story seemed to have changed over the years, but it did involve some kind of epic sword fight in a room off the throne room. She could only really remember the image of her uncle standing over his predecessor's body with a red jeweled cup in hand, toasting his victory.

"Obviously she survived. She is down there eating stew with my father," Julia pointed out. "Is it not more reasonable to assume she somehow survived the fall?"

Toshi shrugged. "In my land, there are stories of people who can cheat death. We call them 'Huhus' or 'awakened ones'. Their essence is linked to a particular place. It is said that if they are killed, they return to that place unharmed. Those are the stories of my ancestors. Now Anny has returned, and Johnathan returned as well."

"That is absurd!" Julia said.

She was getting agitated, but then it occurred to her that from where they were if Johnathan had somehow been teleported to that place it would explain how he had been able to catch up to her and David. She looked over at Toshi. He was calmly looking out towards Pent, which looked like a speck from where they were.

"So, Anny wakes up back here and cannot leave without my uncle realizing that she was alive? If she cannot be killed, then why bother?" Julia asked.

"When Anny woke up, she was not alone. On the other side, she saw someone: a woman named Megan. They had fallen together. She could see Megan and something more. Inside Megan was another essence: a baby. There was a baby inside Anny as well. She dragged herself and Megan back through the portal to save them all."

"Johnathan?" Julia thought to herself. "Is Johnathan Anny's son or something? Is that why he was able to come back? Wait, what am I even thinking? The stew! Why did I eat the stew?!"

"A man named Jax was here when they crossed through the gateway," Toshi continued. "He had come to this place looking for Anny. When she explained what had happened, he realized that the children would be in great danger if Marcus knew about them. You see the son of Megan, his father was Cailar, but Megan had been the mistress of the Ramoth before your uncle. You can see how people might think he was the true heir to Arden."

"You mean Johnathan, do you not?" Julia hesitated to ask. She desperately tried to recall what Jax had looked like to see if there had been a resemblance or not.

"Yes, Johnathan. Jax agreed to adopt him as his own to keep his identity safe."

"What happened to Megan? Is she still here?" Julia asked.

"She killed herself," Toshi said sadly. "From what I understand she was very distraught after the death of Ramoth. When she died and did not return, we thought it was because only Anny had the power to go through the gateway, but now I wonder if one has to want to return. Johnathan was able to return, but how? We know so little about it. His essence must have been tied to this place at some point."

Toshi seemed lost in thought for a moment. Julia waited for a bit for him to continue, but his mind seemed to be someplace else.

"That is very sad," Julia finally said. Her heart was racing. Her skin felt clammy. "What about Anny's child? Did her child make it?"

Toshi nodded, then turned to her. "Julia, you must have suspected it by now. You are Anny's daughter."

"That cannot be," Julia insisted. "My mother's name was Rosemary. She was a commoner who died giving birth to me. My father erected a monument in the town square to her!" Suddenly she froze. "Wait…my father…" she broke off.

"Yeah, about that," Toshi said, "That would make Marcus your father."

"My uncle? My loser, pig-headed, self-absorbed uncle?" Julia stammered.

"Yes, that one," Toshi agreed. "You know, the current ruler of all of Arden. There was a really good reason your father did not want you to marry David."

"Oh no. Oh no, no, no!" Julia said. "I mean, I thought this could not get any creepier."

"You see now why Anny had to stay here. If Marcus knew she was alive, he might also have suspected who you were. It is no coincidence that you two are so alike."

"I am nothing like my uncle-father-whatever!" Julia scoffed, standing up to leave. "I mean, my uncle? This is all too much! It makes a nice story, but people do not come back once they are dead. I should never have drunk the water here!"

Toshi smiled. "You are stubborn like him!"

"Stop it!" Julia angrily replied. "I am going to go back down this stupid mountain and find my way home."

"Your mother is going to be so mad at me," Toshi lamented.

"Why? Because you told me this fairy tale? What am I saying? You mean that weird old lady because she cannot be my mother!"

"No, she is going to be mad at me because of this," Toshi grinned.

"Because of what?"

"Because of this!"

Toshi grabbed her ankle with one hand and tripped her.

● ● ● ● ● ● ●

Time seemed to slow as the roughness of the roof slid under Julia's hands. She sensed her feet going over the edge and then the feeling of falling. She could not tell which way was up or down. Suddenly her body was hitting tree branches, and then there was a pain like she had never known before. Her entire body crumpled, but in an instant, it was over.

She was now standing in a dark hall or cave. Julia could not tell. Was there even solid ground under her feet? She looked down, and her hands were transparent with a pale blue light pulsing through her veins. Around her were others with their own light in every color of the rainbow scattered so far away they twinkled like stars. She wondered what the lights meant. Some were bright, and some were dim, but all around her, the light felt warm. It felt like a soft love she had never known before. There was nothing but peace and calm.

Before the young girl was an opening full of light that the others were all spiraling towards. Julia thought of what Johnathan had said and turned around. To her surprise, there was a door: a large, green, square door with a gold handle. She pushed it open and felt herself falling through.

When her eyes opened, she was in a strange room. She was shaking. Her hands felt cold. The ground felt cold. She stood up, and she felt surprisingly stable. The room was completely dark aside from light pouring through three windows behind her. She could make out what seemed to be shelves with books, and a large table was to her right.

She turned to the windows and looked out. They overlooked a grotto with an underground lake that was aglow from light cascading down from holes in the cave's ceiling. She felt like she had been here before. Then she heard the sounds of footsteps echoing down a corridor. There was a sound of something heavy scraping against rock, and then footsteps coming closer. She turned to her right, and there were Anny and her father. They were both crying and grabbed ahold of her. Toshi was standing behind them. He looked like he was in trouble.

"I knew you would be alright," Toshi muttered. "And it was the quickest way to convince you."

Anny and Areal looked at him with daggers in their eyes.

"Remember I saved her from Johnathan!" Toshi said with a grin. "Now is probably a really good time to tell you all about that!"

●　●　●　●　●　●　●

After recovering for a few days, David was beginning to have his full strength back. His father had not left his side as he waited for his men to find Johnathan and Julia. David was starting to get a bit stir crazy having been confined to his quarters for so long.

Marcus sulked, annoyed that the search had gone so poorly. As the guards spread out from Daven, they informed Marcus's other squads stationed around the area. None had returned word of any sightings.

"If they have gone into the woods, we will likely never find them," David conjectured.

"Can you imagine your cousin roughing it in the woods? She would be complaining the entire time about wanting to return to Paultry." In a high-pitched mock tone, he said, "'I want to go home.' 'Oh, this is far too moist!'

'You call that a tent?'". He stopped to laugh. "Now that I think on it maybe we should let him keep her."

David was grinning. "Have we heard back from Paultry?" he asked.

"Not yet," Marcus grumbled. "Maybe by tomorrow but it is likely it would take a bit more time. It is good to see you up and about. You have some good color in your face again."

"I am worried about Julia, father. I should be out there looking for her," David said as he stood up from the bed and walked over to one of the windows in the room.

"I will not have you out risking your neck!" Marcus declared. "Once they have been located, they will be brought to us. All we need do is wait."

There was a sudden and frantic knocking on the door. Marcus yelled for whoever it was to enter. A haggard man stumbled into the room. He was wearing the uniform of a palace guard.

"What news have you?" Marcus asked excitedly.

The guard hesitated. "I have traveled from Pent, your highness. Sir, the city is under attack!"

"What?" Marcus said in disbelief. "What of my generals who were tasked with protecting the city in my absence?"

"Sir, a man broke through the main gates in the middle of the night. He lit fire to the city and killed any guard who dared to stop him. Many of your citizens fled, but those who sought refuge in the castle were cornered there and are being held captive. I alone was allowed to leave so that I might deliver this message. The man, he called himself Johnathan, has demanded that Princess Julia be handed over to him or he will kill the remaining subjects."

"Seriously?" Marcus cried. "What lunacy is this that one man takes down my entire army?"

"He is likely telling the truth, father. I felt his strength myself. We must stop him." David whispered into his father's ear.

Marcus looked at his son dumbfounded. "You think he is acting alone? That is just what he would have you believe! Traitors: there is likely a whole band of them, and we will root them out! How many men are still in this city?"

The lone guard shrugged, looking to David.

"I believe there were at least twenty at last count," David guessed.

Marcus called for four of them to be brought to him. "We shall show them how we deal with traitors!" Marcus gushed.

Ramoth ordered two of them to travel to Paultry to deliver a message to his brother requesting he send reinforcements to Pent. The others he sent ahead to Pent to report back what they saw. The remaining guards he split in half, ordering some to stay to protect Daven while the others were to accompany him to Pent. As they loaded into their carriage, David seemed worried.

"What is the matter, my boy?" Marcus asked. "We will soon have this all settled."

"But, father, and forgive me for saying this but, if Julia is not with Johnathan then, where is she?"

Marcus paused and thought about it. "I had not considered that."

"Further, if we are to hand her over, but we do not have her, then how will we convince Johnathan to allow our people to go free?" David wondered.

"When I think of it, nothing would make me happier right now then to hand that bratty cousin of yours over to Johnathan. I mean, imagine the look on her face! It would be well worth it!" Marcus said with a lingering smile. "But we do not need her to get him out of there. We shall use brute force to do it."

"Perhaps we might send word along with your couriers that Julia's help is needed at Pent? If she knew what was happening it might smoke her out of wherever she is staying," David suggested. He watched as his father's face lit up.

"Why, yes! I was just about to suggest such a thing!" Marcus said. He cleared his throat then ushered one of the guards over. "Have the couriers to Paultry left yet? I need to speak to them and a few other men. I have a decree which must reach every corner of Arden!"

● ● ● ● ● ● ●

Julia sat in the courtyard leafing through one of the books her mother had out on a table. It was written in a language she barely could understand. Suddenly her father's wish that she study ancient languages seemed to make more sense. However, Julia had neglected such pursuits for other, more pleasurable ones.

She could hear footsteps approaching and knew it was her mother. When Anny appeared, she looked rather timid. The swelling in her face had mostly gone down, revealing soft features underneath.

"I cannot understand any of this," Julia admitted apologetically. "Foreign language was never my strong suit."

Anny looked over her shoulder at the book. Effortlessly she read off a few lines, then translated, "Tension causes distortion. A gentle hand yields the best result. True strength reveals itself in restraint."

"What does that even mean?" Julia asked. She was getting agitated. Of all the questions she wanted answered she knew the most pressing ones would not be found in any of these tomes.

"I think it is about basket weaving," Anny said as she tried to look at the cover. Then seeing Julia's face, she added, "I can feel your frustration. I know you are angry with me."

"You do not need magic to figure that out," Julia snapped back as she threw the book aside.

"Under your anger is pain. I have caused you pain," Anny continued.

Julia turned from her and said, "That should be obvious as well." She paused for a long time. "How could you just let me go like that? If you loved me, then why send me away?"

Anny covered her face, taking in a deep breath. "I always wondered if this day would come," she said softly as she lowered her hands. "I told myself that you would never know and that this curse would end with me, yet here you are. How can an imperfect being give account for their actions? Would you have been happy here, cloistered away with no friends? I feared I would not be enough for you. It broke my heart to send you away, but I knew that in Paultry you would have a simple and happy life. What could I offer you?"

Julia turned around. Her face was stern. "You could have offered me your love. What else does a daughter want from her mother?"

"But what I did I did out of love," Anny pled. "Oh, Julia, I know it would be impossible for you to understand, but the love I had for you as my child was a thousand times greater than any other love I had known before. If it were not for that love, I would have kept you here, selfishly to be with me. There is a love that does not seek its own fulfillment, but what is best for the object of that affection."

Julia scoffed, turning away again. "You never even visited me! Are you telling me you were so afraid of my 'father' that you could not even come to visit?"

"I would have liked that, but I cannot control the power within me when I leave this place. I had tried to go, but again and again, it overwhelmed me. It was not like I did not think of you every day. Julia, I could sense you. Though you were physically far our love ties us together. Love can bind beyond the physical realm. Even in death, I could feel your love for me, and mine for you. Where everything else ended, that continued, and no matter what happens it can never be broken."

Anny reached out to Julia, but Julia walked away. Anny sat down at the table, her head in her hands as tears fell to the ground. She wished Julia could understand how much she loved her, but in a way was relieved that she did not.

Chapter Twenty: Tikii

Julia managed to avoid her mother for the rest of that day by following Toshi around, helping out where she could but mostly convincing him to goof off as much as possible. He started to teach her how to play a game named Tikii that involved dropping sticks with characters marked on them and then having to match the characters. If you could not make a match, your opponent was allowed to move one of their pegs on a wooden cube that had holes drilled in paths around it. As the cube was rolled new each game and could only be turned to a side without pegs already on it once the game started, there was a bit of luck involved. Toshi claimed it was popular in Mesu where he was something of a champion, yet three games in she was beating him easily. Was he letting her win?

The next morning, however, she found Toshi had left for Fay Hill to gather more supplies. She was not surprised. Her father had tried to prepare her the night before for the inevitable time when he would have to return to Paultry without her. He promised he would visit and that Toshi could take messages back and forth between them: a service he had been providing her mother for many years. Still, knowing Toshi would return with the supplies her father would need for his journey home made her feel more alone than she already felt. Suddenly she was wondering if a marriage to David, as fake as it would be, would be better than remaining in exile.

Just thinking about it was depressing. Julia looked over at the game she and Toshi had been playing and wondered if she could play it by herself. Then she remembered the library she had seen in the secret room. Her mother had been bringing volumes up for her to study, but all of them had been about the ancient language of Mesu.

One, in particular, she recognized as a small volume her father had her transcribe over a summer long past. Upon realizing where it had ended up, she regretted that she had done such a poor job. There were undoubtedly many errors her mother was not aware of. In at least one instance Anny had mistaken a doodle she mindlessly drew in the margin as having some significance to the text. Julia wondered though if there might not be something that was a little more scandalous down there as well.

The castle was quiet now with no one to notice what she was up to; so Julia crept over to the doorway and hastened down the stairs. She was halfway down when she felt a blast of cold coming from the room and the audible sound of water splashing against something: not unlike the noise a heavy rain makes when it pounds down on a roof.

Julia hesitated for a moment, but curiosity got the best of her. She continued, stopping at the door to the room and peaking in. There was no one there, but the splashing sound was coming from the windows. She walked over to them to see what was making the noises.

The center window was open and a rope ladder was hanging out it. Far below her in the cavern, she could make out the silhouette of a person kneeling on the rocky shore of the underground lake. The water was choppy: splashing every which way. Julia thought she felt the ground beneath her shaking. As she stood there, it got stronger. The windows began to rattle, and water shot up randomly: striking the ceiling of the cave. Her instinct was to step back, but she found the whole thing fascinating.

The rumbling subsided, and the crashing water began to turn into water spouts. Five of them danced around the lake in harmony before joining into one. This spout pulled from the lake so much water Julia could see things on the bottom that were not visible otherwise: markings glowing from the lake floor. She wondered what they meant as she hurried over to the table to grab a piece of parchment to scribble some of the designs down on but instead, she found a book resting open on the table.

To her surprise, the book had the same symbols drawn on the pages. They began to illuminate as if they were on fire. The water spout outside the window was soon glowing too: half of it water and the other fire.

Julia grabbed the book, then returned to the window where she stood with her mouth open. She had a sudden and irresistible urge to reach out the window and try to touch the water spout. Her hand, as if acting on its own, reached out towards the window. Then just as quickly as it appeared the entire spout collapsed back into the lake. The symbols disappeared, and the water was perfectly placid.

Julia stepped back from the window, clutching the book. She wondered if her mother had seen her as she hastened to stuff the book down her blouse. She tiptoed quickly to the stairs, taking them two at a time until she reached the top where she bumped forcefully into Areal. He caught her just as she went bounding backward, the two steadying themselves for a moment before speaking.

"What are you doing?" he demanded kindly.

"What do you mean 'what are you doing'? What are you doing?" she snapped back as she led him away from the stairs.

"Was not that you making all of that commotion? The whole place was shaking," Areal said as he tried to look behind her.

"Me?" Julia said incredulously. "You would blame me when there is a crazy, I-can-not-be-killed, I-shoot-fire-from-my-limbs lady walking around?"

"So it was your mother?" Areal surmised.

"Yes, it was my mo…." She stopped herself from saying it. "Cordellia. It was Cordellia."

"How rude! I thought I raised you better!" Areal lamented.

Julia rolled her eyes, "I am not calling her mother!"

As she spoke the floor shook beneath them. Areal grabbed the sides of his head and grimaced as if he were in trouble.

"Did you have something to do with all this?" Julia inquired. "She is down there throwing a fit."

Areal motioned for her to follow him further away from the stairway so that they would not be seen should Anny return shortly. He was fiddling nervously with the small, silver key fastened around his neck.

In a hushed tone, Areal confessed, "We had a bit of a fight."

"That is hardly surprising," Julia stated flatly. "How can you not fight with someone like her?"

"What do you mean by that?" Areal asked, suddenly a bit defensive.

"Never mind. We have just not been getting along as either of us might have imagined. You know I always wondered what my mother was like. I would visit her 'grave'. I would talk to her. I always felt like she was not that far away. I wonder now what all of that means."

Areal gave Julia a hug. "I must apologize for the deception, my darling. You will always be mine. That can never change. I am proud of you. I always have been. I always will be."

Julia squeezed him back. She thought he felt a little thinner than usual. Was the cooking here to his liking? She took a step back, holding his hands as she asked him, "Am I the reason you two are fighting?"

Areal chuckled. "A little. Does that please you?"

"A little," she confessed.

"Well do not let it worry you. I just made the horrible mistake of suggesting that Anny might have made more of an effort to visit. I mean, your uncle visits Paultry so infrequently. It would have been nice had you two had some time together."

Julia nodded, "Maybe, but I am not sure anything would have prepared me for all this."

"Well, she just lost it. She threw a pot at me and stormed off," Areal continued. "I suppose I should have known better. Living up here all alone has made her a bit reclusive and out of touch. She is trying though. I should not have pushed her. It is not like this has been easy on her either."

Julia thought about it for a moment, but then just shrugged it off. "She is a bit old to be making excuses for," she said aloud, but inside Julia was wondering what hope she had of ever returning to Paultry if she were to display the same powers as her mother. Were they really uncontrollable?

Areal was shaking his head as he confessed, "I feel awful about this whole situation, Julia. It was never my intention that you end up isolated out here as well. The thought of leaving you here breaks my heart, as does the idea of putting you in danger should you accompany me back home. I wish I understood all of this better. I have been acquiring books, studying what I can, and yet I cannot make sense of it. Should there have been something more I could have done?

"Even having seen all I have seen I still question it. It is so beyond what we know in our quiet little town. I read of stories of people like her from long past, and I want to believe that there is some merit to it. Yet my faith flags, and I wonder just what it is we are dealing with. I feel I must take her word for it, I mean what she is experiencing, yet even with the proof in front of me why such doubt? What is it that holds one back from accepting it?"

Julia smirked. "You have never trained me to believe anything without proof. What else in life demands devotion devoid of evidence?"

She gleamed with pride to herself for a moment before remembering waking up in the chamber after falling from the roof. It was simple enough to find a way to dismiss everything else she had seen as being caused by some manner of trick or delusion, yet returning from death: what explanation in the normal realm of things was there for that? Her father's conundrum was now hers as well.

"Yet given proof why do we still question it? What amount of proof would be enough?" Julia wondered aloud.

Areal continued to shake his head solemnly. "There is no amount of proof sufficient for one who does not want to believe. Perhaps that is the rub. Julia, I do not want to believe it. I want you back home with me again, like it used to be."

Julia felt the same, but for lack of words, she just held her father as they sat quietly in the broken sunlight of the courtyard.

"Do me a favor, would you?" Areal whispered. "Please, in the future just call her 'Anny'."

● ● ● ● ● ● ●

David and Marcus stood outside the gates of Pent. They had been completely smashed in, and the streets were deserted.

"What did the scouts report back?" David asked as he marveled at the devastation.

"They never returned," his father replied. "I am really, really glad right now that I left your mother at Paultry."

"What?" David said. "You told me she wanted to stay."

"That is what I meant," Marcus said. "Obviously."

"So, what is the plan?" David asked.

"Well, we could try to lure him out," Marcus said as he began to look around. "We just need to find someone we can make to look like your cousin. Clearly, I am out."

The two men looked around, seeing only the burly guards who had accompanied them remained.

"It might be wise to wait for the reinforcements from Paultry," David said.

● ● ● ● ● ● ●

The next morning Julia found herself unable to concentrate on her studies. She leafed through the books, but her mind was on Toshi. Julia wished he would be back already, but knew he was unlikely to return until the next day.

It was dreary and raining outside, so Julia had brought her study materials to the kitchen. The book on weaving had gotten wet from being carelessly left out in the courtyard. Julia had tried to prop it up near the stove to dry out. Her mind wandered as she watched the fire in the stove crackling.

"How goes your studies?" a voice asked over her shoulder.

Julia jumped in her chair, grabbing her chest as she scowled at her mother.

"I did not hear you come in!" Julia explained. She looked intently at her book rather than looking at Anny. On closer inspection, the page was upside-down.

"Oh," Anny exclaimed. "I am sorry. I did not mean to startle you. Would you rather I leave?"

"You can do whatever you want," Julia said nonchalantly. "I am just studying as you wish."

Anny sat down across from her. With the north winds bringing rain, the kitchen was one of the warmer and dryer places in Faverly. She caught a peak of what Julia was looking at.

"Did I give you that book?" she asked.

"Of course. How else would I have it?" Julia murmured.

"It just looks so boring," Anny said. "I had not remembered it being so dull."

Julia just shrugged without saying anything. They sat in silence for a bit before Anny got up and began to boil some water. "I will make us tea," Anny said as she took two cups off the shelves. "Toshi is bringing more tomorrow so we can drink what is left."

"You do not expect him until tomorrow then?" Julia asked disappointedly.

"I would wager he will be back tomorrow evening. He always takes a bit longer getting back. You know, going down the slope is easy. It is coming back up that is a bit of a climb. Besides, just between you and me, I think he gets a bit lost."

This made Julia smile. "I knew it!" she chuckled.

"While we wait why not play Tikii with me?" Anny suggested.

"You know how to play?" Julia challenged.

"Of course! I taught Toshi everything his grandparents taught me." Anny said.

Julia raced from the kitchen to retrieve the game. When she returned, she found Anny had already prepared the tea for them. The books were now thrown off to the side of the table.

"Wow, how did you make the tea so fast?" Julia asked as she set the game down. "I was only gone a moment."

"Oh, you learn a few tricks as you get older," Anny chuckled.

"Like how to win this game?" Julia wondered aloud. "Did this game belong to Toshi's grandparents then? Touching it I almost feel I know them. What were they like?" Julia inquired. "Were they very old?"

"I suppose you could say that, though if I say they were old will you think I am old?" Anny laughed. "They must have been in their seventies or eighties when they came here. They were the only ones Jax could find who could remember how to read the old language."

"You mean of Mesu?" Julia said as she moved her peg ahead a space.

Anny nodded in the affirmative. "Yes, but Toshi was just a young man then. His parents had passed, and his grandparents wanted to pass on their knowledge to both of us."

"And now onto me, I suppose?" Julia lamented. "But Toshi seems much older than that. Is he not in his eighties?"

Anny laughed out loud, holding her stomach as she did so. "Eighty? No! Oh dear, I am glad he is not here to hear you say that! No, he is in his sixties." Her mother replied. "He is not that much older than me. How old do you think I am? No, do not say. Do not say it!"

"Oh," Julia exclaimed. "I had no idea! I would have thought him a lot older. Maybe it is the way his forehead is wrinkled?"

Instinctively Anny reached up and started to rub her forehead trying to feel if there were sufficiently deep lines to age her.

"Well never mind," Anny continued, trying to change the subject. "I promise not to say anything to him. He is vain enough as it is. There is no need to demoralize him. Age is not everything, and he is rather wise for his age. Maybe that is what it is."

"He is wise," Julia agreed. "You two must know each other pretty well being here as long as you have."

"It has been many years. For a while, I was here alone. A man named Jax, oh, but I guess you must have known him, anyway he would bring me volumes from Paultry that your father had procured, but I could not translate the books by myself. That is when Jax went to Mesu to find anyone who could read what was written in that book you have there." Anny pointed to the book that Julia had been trying to read.

"It is written in a dead language," Anny said, referring to the book. "Toshi's grandparents were some of the few people we could find. They lived in a remote fishing village that bordered the seas north of Mesu. There are not a lot of visitors that far north! They could read it, but most of what they said made so little sense. I have to believe it is written in riddles."

"Where did this book come from? Is it significant?" Julia asked innocently. In fact, it was the book she had stolen from the library with the symbols she had seen in the lake bottom of the grotto.

"The man who used to live here wrote it," Anny explained. "At least that is what I thought. He was always carrying it around and reading from it. Your father was saying something to me the other day about him being a phony and someone else being the true mystic. I am not sure I followed what he said, but that man was the one who originally foretold 'The Myth'."

"You mean the myth that the former Ramoth made popular? I will confess that it was not part of my studies. It sounded like a lot of malarkey, but my father in hearing this spent considerable time yesterday filling me in on the details."

Anny smiled. "It sounded like 'malarkey' to a lot of people. There were very few who heard it and believed, but the man underestimated Ramoth. You see, the man, Barnas, Barnas believed some of the things that were written in that book."

"What part?" Julia asked, looking at the book suspiciously.

"The book conjectures every person contains within them certain 'pieces'. If the pieces do not work together, then the person does not exhibit special powers. However, it might be possible to basically breed such characteristics, if you know what you are doing," Anny said as she leafed through the book.

"This passage here," Anny said as she pointed to one of the pages, "it says that certain pieces are likely tied to the date of one's birth: that on certain days the pieces would be one way and they would vary on others. Other pieces were related to your parents."

"I see," Julia said as she took the book. "Thus, why you would want to gather people born on the same day and try to produce offspring from them. Was that the idea behind the Faverly Sisters?"

"Only it did not work, or more likely I should say it was never given a chance to work. Who knows what might have happened?" Anny mused as she closed the book.

"But it did work," Julia said as she looked Anny in the eyes. "The question is, how did you get your powers? Was it an accident? Did it have something to do with you being raised here? If so, then why did the other girls not display the same abilities?

Anny blushed, but then said, "Well the others were brought here as infants. My mother fell pregnant with me while she lived here. You see my mother was one of Barnas's followers. She met my father when he accompanied Ramoth here. Apparently, they hit it off, and I believe one or the other then convinced Ramoth that the children should be raised here."

"It is becoming harder and harder to tell who was using who in this story," Julia lamented.

"My mother once said, 'Charity is nice, but greed will do.' Anny said as she sipped her tea.

"What an idiot," Julia let slip.

Anny raised her eyebrow then said, "Why do you not tell me what you really think? Now I am afraid to know now what you think of me!"

"I do not mean to be rude," Julia apologized, "but that sort of thinking cost your mother her life. It cost them all their lives. They should never have made a deal with Ramoth."

"I suppose they all underestimated him," Anny said. She went to elaborate but then thinking better of it dismissively stated, "I had never really thought about it."

"That is an understatement," Julia said.

Julia could see she had upset Anny who was looking down into her cup with a contemplative stare.

"This game is so hard," the young princess remarked, trying to change the subject.

"Not every game is meant to be won. Some are meant to be lost with grace," Anny replied.

Julia thought about it, then asked, "What was your mother like?"

"She was beautiful: just like you," Anny gushed, her smile returning. "Odlin was her name. I cannot tell you how much you remind me of her. She had the same hair color and eyes. She was a kind person. She did not speak much, but she did everything she could to make me feel like I was just as important as the other girls. You know they were treated like royalty? Sometimes I felt like I was the outsider. It was a strange thing to feel so lonely surrounded by so many 'friends'."

"Is that why you sent me away? You did not want me to feel that kind of loneliness?" Julia wondered. "But then you took it all upon yourself. You did not have to do that. You could have reached out to us. I would have loved to have visited!"

Anny smiled a sad smile. "I guess I have wasted a lot of time being afraid. It is just, in this book it also speaks of a calamity that will end the world."

"What?" Julia exclaimed frightened. Suddenly she did not want to touch the book anymore.

"I guess I might be wrong, but when I first awoke after coming for the second time through the gateway, I could not control myself. I was so angry that I ran into the woods and fire just shot out of me. I thought that if I let myself go, I might burn the entire world. It was then I realized that there was a connection between emotions and my abilities. If I could not control my emotions, then I would not be able to stop from hurting people. What if you were there when that happened? What if I was startled? It might even be an accident. I could not take that risk.

"I thought of ending my life to avoid it: the calamity, but then I thought of you, and I could not do it. I could not leave you to face the calamity alone if there was a chance instead that I could prevent it. There is a passage about it here towards the end that I have never been able to figure out. Maybe you and I together can figure it out. Together we might be able to save everyone."

Julia hesitated, but then asked, "What does the passage say?"

Anny grimaced, leafing through the pages until she found it. Reading it aloud it said,

268

Time is at your fingertips. The future sets the past.
Do not enter the forbidden gate.
In seeking to end, it is begun.
Eternal Mortal. Meet fate to your back.
In surrender is victory.

"Well that clears things up," Julia scoffed, glancing down at their game to discover that her mother was two moves away from beating her.

Chapter Twenty-One: An Unwinnable Confrontation

Julia woke in the courtyard from an unplanned nap to find the sun was already getting low in the sky. The air in the mountains was still chilly this time of year as evening came, so she pulled a blanket around her tightly as she sat there waking up. The young girl wondered if in a month's time when summer would be in full swing, if it would still be as chilly, or if the cool air would at least taper off. She enjoyed this brief moment of peace aware that they were becoming few and far between.

She heard Toshi calling from outside the gate. Eagerly she went to let him in. She had been waiting for him knowing this was the time her mother said he would return. He had promised Julia some of her mother's favorite sweets whenever he had more, and she was certain he would have them with him. When she opened the door, she thought he looked a bit pale.

"You are back, but, oh, what is the matter?" Julia said as she took the reins of his donkey from him.

"Matter?" Toshi replied. "Why nothing is the matter!" he insisted with a forced smile. He reached into the pack and pulled out a small parcel. "Here, take these and hide them from your mother. I suggest you eat them all before she finds out that you have them."

Julia scooped up the package and headed off to the roof of the castle where she and Toshi had sat before. As she went bounding off, Areal emerged from the kitchen.

"Toshi! Welcome back!" he greeted him. "Do you need any help unloading the supplies?"

Toshi handed him a few parcels, then motioned silently towards the kitchen. Areal raised his eyebrows quizzically but obediently followed Toshi into the kitchen.

"We are being awfully secretive about cheese, are we not? Not that I do not appreciate where you are coming from!" Areal chided as he put the parcels down on the table.

"Where is Anny?" Toshi asked as he looked around.

"I am not sure," Areal admitted.

Toshi motioned for Areal to come closer. He leaned in to whisper into his ear, "When I was down in Fay Hill I heard rumors that Pent is under attack."

"Well this is poor news indeed," Areal said. "Now that we have ample supplies should I head back to Paultry at once? I might be needed there."

Toshi looked around as if they might be heard. "There is more: your brother, Marcus, has ordered a decree that Julia is to return to Pent at once. I hear that the city is under siege by a large band of traitors who will kill every last citizen if she is not handed over."

"A 'large band of traitors'? You mean Johnathan?" Areal asked. "Or is this a ploy to get ahold of Julia?"

"It is likely both," Toshi said. "What are we going to do? Should I tell them? If Julia knows she will put herself in grave danger."

"And Anny alongside her," Areal assured him. "No, I will head out to Paultry at once and ready my best fleet! I am sure we can best him."

"No, no!" Toshi insisted, but Areal was already leaving.

Areal pulled open the kitchen door grandly, and Anny and Julia came tumbling into the room.

"Too late," Toshi lamented.

"I have to go to Pent at once!" Julia exclaimed as she dusted herself off. "I know I can get through to him!"

Anny shook her head. "No, Julia! We cannot take the risk that he would harm you."

"How can he?" Julia retorted. "I am invincible like him!"

"I do not think that is the kind of harm your mother means," Toshi volunteered. "We know so little at this point.

If he were to…well…'join' with you there is no telling what could happen."

"It could be the end of the world!" Anny insisted.

"Not this again!" Areal said. "Everything to you people is the end of the world! I have been hearing about the end of the world my whole life now! It is not going to happen before the world actually ends itself from want of waiting. I am a king! I will take care of it!"

"Oh, like I have not heard that before!" Anny retorted. The mockingly she continued, "'I am the king. Oh, look at me! I can do anything all by myself!' For once will you accept help? I think Toshi and I can handle this!"

"You cannot even leave the grounds old lady," Toshi said, motioning for Anny to sit down. "Do I look like I want to die? So why not we all just forget about this? We can have a nice piece of cheese and forget that I ever said anything."

Toshi began handing out slices of cheese until they were all sitting around the table suspiciously eying one another in silence.

● ● ● ● ● ● ●

The following morning David returned alone to the broken gates of Pent. Having spoken to his father he had lost all hope of reinforcements arriving in time. So David decided that it was time to make his stand. His people were suffering, and he would not stand idly by.

David was proudly disguised as Julia: donning an oversized blue dress. He covered his hair with a cloak and hid beneath it his sword before mustering his courage and stepping foot into the broken city. The smell of burnt wood and rotting flesh assaulted his nose. He wondered if his beloved home would ever be the same as he walked by boarded up, silent buildings.

He moved carefully through the city past the main square to the gates of the castle. They were barred tight, but even from here he could hear people crying out in pain. He feared they were starving to death. He went to pound on the door but then realized that if he did so, he would alarm Johnathan. Instead, he tried gently rapping, calling out softly, "Johnathan, I have come as you asked."

He kept this up for an hour, banging louder and louder as he grew desperate for the door to open. Finally, he gave up. He sat with his back to the door and lowered his head between his knees. He was a broken man who had wholly and miserably failed his people. Their screams echoed through his mind. He sat there for several minutes trying to collect himself.

"No!" he finally cried out. "No, it will not end this way!"

The young prince leapt to his feet, throwing off his cloak as he drew his sword. He pounded loudly on the door and yelled, "It is David! Open the door, you coward!"

But nothing happened. Still, the door remained closed. The prince lowered his head in defeat, but just as he did the doors swung open. They opened with such force that they knocked him clear of the walkway. He looked up to see Johnathan racing past him towards the main square.

Moments later distraught citizens came streaming out of the castle, cheering David's name. They lifted David onto their shoulders as they celebrated. He was relieved that they were now safe, yet he wondered where Johnathan was going. As long as Johnathan lived, he was a threat to them.

The crowd carried David towards the square. There, people were beginning to come out of hiding. As David was dropped into the center of town, the people there pointed to the main gate saying the 'mad man' had gone that way.

David hoped if he rode fast enough he might catch up to Johnathan. He ran to where he had left his horse, only to find the horse was missing. David cursed at himself, knowing Johnathan must have taken it. Now he would have to locate another animal and quickly.

He doubled back into town. As he asked around frantically people again began to cheer from the ramparts saying, "Look! Paultry's fleet has arrived!".

David stumbled up to the top of the rampart in disbelief. He looked out over the sea and saw the full fleet of Paultry entering the harbor. On the flagship's deck, he could barely make out what appeared to be his mother waving to the cheering crowds.

"Seriously?" he called out.

• • • • • • •

Down at the harbor, the fleet brought much-needed supplies as well as men to secure the main gate. Brinna was surprised to see her son's choice in wardrobe.

"What is all this?" Brinna said chuckling as she wrapped her arms around him. "Are you in disguise or something?"

"I do not have the time to talk about this now, mother," David pled. "I need a horse. You must have one."

"Oh, I have a whole bunch!" his mother said, motioning to one of her generals to bring one off the ship.

"You will need to secure the city. I have to go after Johnathan," David explained.

"Johnathan? Is he the leader of the pirates?" Brinna asked excitedly. "Oh, but you cannot go! You are needed here!"

"Pirates? What pirates?" David wondered aloud.

His mother did not respond as she seemed to be looking around.

"Where is your father? Are he and your uncle together by any chance? I was hoping your uncle was with you," Brinna continued.

"He is not back at Paultry?" David asked. "If he is not there, then who did you leave in charge of Paultry?"

• • • • • • •

Bess looked down from the throne at her people. They went about the library, mostly ignoring her. She wondered where the key that unlocked the cell with the cheese in it was.

● ● ● ● ● ● ●

After so many days without knowing where she was, Johnathan could at last sense Julia's presence again. He rode away from Pent, being able to only think of being rejoined with her. It was as if his entire body ached for her. He had no need of food, water, or sleep. He just needed her.

He rode David's horse until it gave out. Then he ran along the road until he was able to find another. He went all that day and into the night, the whole time feeling like she was beckoning him nearer.

The stars lit the midnight sky, casting an ethereal glow across the farmer's fields. This was a rural place he had never been to that was close to the foot of the Venom Mountains, but he knew she was near here. He walked through one field, and then another.

As he approached the edge of the woods, he heard a voice call out to him, "Johnathan, I am here!"

Through a bit of thick underbrush he struggled, but then the trees parted to reveal a large lake with a waterfall flowing into it hidden in the middle of the wooded area. Floating above the water was a cloaked figure. There was no doubt in his mind it was his beloved Julia. She reached out her delicate hand.

"Come to me my love," she said. "We shall be joined as one."

Johnathan stopped just at the edge of the water. "Come here, Julia. I am right here," he pled.

"Come to me," it beckoned.

Johnathan hesitated. Suddenly he was unsure.

"Julia?" he asked as he stepped to the edge of the water.

The figure waited no longer. Throwing off the cloak and floating above the still waters was Anny.

"Keeper of death!" Johnathan exclaimed. "I bested you once and will do it again! What have you done with my love?"

"She is my love, you poor boy. I will not hand her over to you!" Anny said.

The woman raised her arms, and the water of the lake reached up and began to pull Johnathan down.

He struggled, laughing as he called out, "Yes! Yes, kill me again and I will only come back stronger!"

Johnathan slashed at the current with his ax as it pulled him towards the middle of the lake, but the weapon could do no damage. The water began creeping up around his chest, pulling him down as well. Anny looked down into the water as he sunk beneath the surface. For a moment watching him struggle pity overcame her. The feelings of love that Julia had for her friend overwhelmed her. Johnathan felt her grasp weakening. His head shot up out of the water gasping for breath.

Tears welled in Anny's eyes. Her precious daughter: there was nothing she would not do for her. There was nothing greater she could offer.

That morning, as she was leaving Julia had caught her and Toshi by the gate. Toshi used his blow dart to knock Julia out before agreeing to keep Julia safe until it was all over. Anny remembered how beautiful Julia had looked. She sent her one last thought: 'I love you'.

Anny took two of Toshi's blow darts from her pocket. She aimed for Johnathan and watched as the dart flew out of the gun and into his flailing arm. Johnathan did not seem to notice it. He was struggling still, but now his movements were growing slower.

Anny then took the other dart and stabbed herself in the arm. As the drug took effect, she sunk into the water in front of Johnathan. He saw her as they looked eye to eye. She wrapped her arms around him, and they closed their eyes as they both drifted into eternal slumber.

● ● ● ● ● ● ●

There was a persistent chill in the air at Faverly that night. A stiff breeze blew followed by an ominous silence. The sky was cloudy, and the courtyard grew suddenly dark as the stars hid behind the clouds.

Toshi sat straight up, looking over to Julia and Areal. After Julia had been knocked out, he had tied her up to ensure she would not run after Anny. Areal was tied along with her.

The father and daughter sensed what Toshi did as well. Julia had felt her mother's anxiety building all day. She tried to urge her to return, but it felt like nothing was getting through to Anny. Then there was peace: a calm, deep, empty peace.

Tears began to fall from Julia's eyes. She knew her mother was not coming back. She felt Johnathan was also gone. Only a faint sense of her love for them remained: a small, ever-present dagger in her heart: a wound that would never stop bleeding, but she cherished the pain as a reminder of the love she had for them.

"You have to let us go!" Areal pled. "Anny needs us! I just know it!"

Toshi nodded, then jumped up to let them free. Areal looked to the stairway that led down to the study as Toshi untied the ropes, expecting Johnathan to come running up to them.

"I will go and see," Toshi said. "I will call if I need help."

Areal protested, but Toshi was already running to the doorway with their only lantern before Areal could stand up. Areal held Julia as she cried.

Toshi walked carefully down the stairs. When he made it into the room, he called out to Anny, but she was not there. The room was empty except for something laying on the floor where Anny should have been. He reached down and carefully picked it up. It was his blowgun. He remembered her taking it that morning just before Julia had found them.

Anny had said to him, "I need this, and I need you to stay here. Please, this is hard enough. Do not look at me like that! This is something I have to do, Toshi. I cannot let her get hurt. You know this is the only way to stop him. Please look after her. It will be alright. I promise I will return this to you."

He could not help but cry as he held the blowgun to his chest. In all of these years, it had never occurred to him that he might have to learn to live without his friend. He hesitated to walk up the stairs, but he knew the others were waiting.

As soon as Areal saw him he knew. Julia, Toshi, and Areal held onto one another and wept until the sun came up. Julia looked up to the sky and wondered how it could be that the sun still rose. How did it have the strength to keep shining?

● ● ● ● ● ● ●

When next Anny awoke, she was standing in the other realm in the dark place between life and death. Johnathan was by her side. He saw her and motioned to go back through the door, but she took his hand. She shook her head side to side and pointed instead to the light.

Johnathan thought it strange: through her hand he could feel the love he had for Julia. Inside his heart, the young man could feel it as strongly as ever. He looked at the door, and a strange thought echoed through his mind,

"In surrender is victory."

Chapter Twenty-Two: A Homecoming

Still shaking, Julia made way to the bedroom. Her father and Toshi were close behind. They all collapsed exhausted into their beds and slept for a few fitful hours.

When she later awoke Julia found both the men in the kitchen drinking tea and trying to finish off the last of the stew that Anny had prepared before she left. Julia quietly joined them, though the food seemed to stick in her throat. The game she and her mother had been playing was still on the table.

Areal reached out and squeezed her hand. Smiling reassuringly, he said, "Did you get any rest?"

"A little," Julia mumbled. "The whole place seems so different without her here; It is like all of the air has been sucked out of it. It is too quiet."

Toshi chuckled. "She had a way of filling a room," he reminisced.

Toshi reached into his pocket and pulled out a small ruby ring. The square cut stone shimmered dully in the afternoon light.

"I found this in the study this morning. It was your grandmother's. Anny used to say it reminded her of her. The first time she awoke down there, it was on her finger though she did not know how it got there. Maybe it can remind you of Anny."

Julia took the ring. She remembered seeing her mother wearing it, though she had never asked about it. She slipped it onto her right hand. It was comforting somehow to have something of her mother's.

"Father," Julia said after a moment's reflection, "now that Anny is gone there is no reason for me to remain here. I think we should all return to Paultry now."

Areal grimaced. "What about your engagement? Not to mention that now that you have passed through the portal you might begin to exhibit the same strange powers your mother did."

"Julia is right," Toshi interrupted. "She should be fine away from here unless she passes through the gateway another time. Paultry will be safer for her. With the chaos Johnathan started, it is likely more people will come looking around. Marcus himself might even return if he links what happened to The Myth."

Areal looked distressed. "If my brother finds her he will take her back to Pent," he conjectured.

"Well, I cannot stay here!" Julia insisted. "Mother wasted her entire life here. For what? We are no closer to finding out the truth than when we began."

"That is a fair point," Toshi interrupted. "Besides, I do not wish to remain here any longer. I will teach Julia what I know, and then I will return to my homeland. Being here without Anny, like Julia said, is depressing!"

Areal did not look pleased. He tried to think of another place she might be safe. Before he could think of anything, Julia spoke.

"Father," she said, "If Toshi would let me then I wish to travel with him to Mesu."

Areal went to object, but then stopped himself. He looked at her and realized her mind was made up.

"Would she be safe there?" Areal asked Toshi.

Toshi had gotten up from the table to wash out his bowl. He stood by the stove with his arms crossed and a big grin on his face. He let out a little grunt as he slapped his hands together.

"Why did I not think of it?" Toshi replied. "Listen, in the bedroom, I think I can find it if you give me a moment, there is a cloak that was often worn by Anny's mother, your Grandmother Odlin! She wore it whenever strangers were coming here, or so Anny told me. I think a lot of the women here wore something similar. Even I used to wear it sometimes when I would go to Paultry. You remember?" he asked as he motioned to Areal.

Areal nodded hesitantly, rolling his eyes at the memory.

"Well then," Toshi continued. "For all your brother knows Julia is dead. You can say she died or that you must assume as much, cover her up, and masquerade her as my wife!"

"That is ridiculous!" Julia lamented. "They would know as soon as I opened my mouth that it was me."

"Not if you only speak in my language!" Toshi suggested. He then danced around the room speaking in his native tongue before explaining, "You will be sure to learn quickly that way! After I am sure you have learned enough we will go to Mesu. You can forget about the cloak then. Likely no one would recognize you out there."

"I guess it is no worse an idea than leaving you here," Areal said to Julia. "Assuming your mind is made up about going."

Julia nodded then thought to herself, "If they discover me I can just jump off a cliff again! Then I would be right back here anyway!" Immediately she scolded herself. "That is not something to be cavalier about! Besides, what about mother? Is that why she did not return, or did she choose to stay over there?"

Images of her mother struggling with Johnathan as she dragged him into the other world flashed before her eyes. She imagined her mother pounding on the door, but it would no longer open for her, or perhaps she had blocked his way. Could she still be there trying to hold the door shut? Did she need her? Was she okay? Julia flinched, but Toshi and Areal were too caught up in the moment to notice. She became aware that as she was lost in thought, her father had still been talking.

"…which is why you should wait until the spring comes round again to make the journey. But what am I bothering with this for now? Once we are home, it will be easier to decide. It is too upsetting here." Areal was saying.

"There is much to do, but there is also no rushing the matter," Toshi assured him. He was still standing by the stove. "I will need a bit of time to sort out what to bring and what to leave behind."

Toshi's face lit up as if he had remembered some forgotten thing. He left the kitchen with a purposeful stride. Areal looked at his daughter once more.

"Are you sure you are sure?" he asked.

● ● ● ● ● ● ●

Toshi and Julia tore apart the servant's bedroom where they had been staying looking for Julia's grandmother's cloak. When Toshi found it in the bottom of a chest, Julia was surprised to see that it was not a cloak, but a complete outfit. The dress was black with a high waist and delicate lace cap sleeves. The matching cowl had a hood with the same lace detail around the edges. Julia could wrap the cowl around her head so that the lace obscured her face while her eyes were hidden under the hood. Imagining Toshi running through the streets of Paultry wearing it explained her father's earlier reaction.

"It suits you," Toshi said with an impish grin.

"Thanks," Julia sarcastically replied as she took the hood off. "I feel like it will be hard to blend in wearing something like this in Paultry."

"I did it!" Toshi joked. "So can you!" he assured her, then absentmindedly he added, "Some gloves went with it, but they were ruined. We might look for another pair."

"I think it is fine without gloves. What happened to them?" Julia asked.

Toshi did not answer. He just shook his head and waved her out of the room.

● ● ● ● ● ● ●

A few days later the weather cleared. By now Toshi had loaded the donkeys with books and supplies for the trip. He had a bag of his belongings as well as a few mementos. The rest he left as it was, cleaning the kitchen for the last time and putting the fire in the stove out.

As anxious as he had been to go, now that all things were ready he hesitated. His emotions overcame him as he looked around the familiar surroundings. He could remember so many evenings spent reading in the courtyard, sitting on the roof, and walking the paths around the fortress. He wondered how quickly the place would fall into disrepair. At the same time, he wanted to leave some things behind just in case of, or rather for, Julia's inevitable return.

Julia was watching Toshi from the bedroom. She had just finished dressing in her grandmother's clothes, though she still had the cowl down her back. Her father dropped the dress she had been wearing into the cedar chest that the cloak had been in.

"Are you sure you want to leave it here?" he asked sadly. "Is this not one of your favorites?"

"There hardly seems room to carry it," Julia said, turning from the window. "Besides, I might need it. What if I come back?"

Areal shook his head, closing the chest with a loud thud. "I hope that never happens," he said as he walked over to her. He wrapped his arms around her and kissed her forehead. Seeing the dark gown stirred some distant memory he could not place his finger on. He hoped that the ruse would fool his brother and everyone else for that matter.

"Well I hope you slept well because it is going to be a long day," Areal said as he gathered the last of their things.

"I tried, but Toshi was having another nightmare," Julia said as she followed him out of the room.

"He seems to have those a lot," Areal lamented.

When Toshi saw Julia and Areal emerge from the bedroom, he put on a brave face and urged them to hurry up and load the last of their things onto the donkeys. As they left he closed the gate, but had no way of locking it from the outside other than to brace a few rocks against it. It was plain that leaving the place as such made him uncomfortable as if it was now a tomb to the memory of Anny.

Putting that aside he led his companions down the side of the mountain to Fay Hill. This took most of the day into the late evening, but when they arrived there was a family happy to greet them and host them for the night.

As it turned out Toshi regularly stayed with this family when he visited the town. The father owned the confection shop that made the treats Anny had so adored. His wife and two small children lived in a room above the store near the entrance to the small town. Toshi had befriended them when, years earlier, he had agreed to help the man with his deliveries to the nearby estates.

So whenever he was in town, he stayed with them. They were happy to meet his traveling companions and most anxious to hear about his "wife". Because of this, Julia was forced to sit in silence as Toshi explained to them that she was a terrible cook, had a habit of knocking things over, and was horribly afraid of sparrows. She did find that she was picking up Toshi's language very quickly. She soon learned how to say, "I hate you" and "Shut up".

Wearing the hood proved more challenging than Julia had expected. When dinner was served, she did her best to keep her head down, though she desperately wanted to take the hood off and thoroughly enjoy the meal. She began to understand why her mother chose freedom in exile to this.

Tea was served with the sweets after dinner. The hood became invaluable as hidden tears rolled down Julia's cheeks. The others did not know, but on the day Toshi had brought some to her she had gone up to the roof to hide there from her mother so she could eat them in peace. When she got there, her mother was waiting for her, knowing she would have the sweets with her. Anny demanded that Julia share, and then as Toshi had warned she quickly ate almost all of them. She had been perturbed at the time, but now the memory warmed her heart.

In the morning they gathered a few last supplies from the town before heading off. They knew it would take several days, and that there would be nights spent under the stars. On the second day, Toshi noted that Julia had become a bit quiet.

"What is it that has gotten you to finally close your mouth?" Toshi jested as they walked along. With the donkeys having as much to carry as they did there was only room for one of them to be riding at a time with it being Areal's turn to have a rare and much-needed rest.

Julia shrugged. "I guess there were just so many things that I wanted to ask Anny, but I did not. I thought we would have all of this time. It stretched out endlessly before me so that I did not seize the time that we had."

"Like what?" Toshi asked. "I studied with her. I could be of help. Unless this is some woman thing!"

"Oh, goodness no!" Julia assured him. "Nothing like that!"

"Well out with it then," Toshi insisted.

Julia hesitated for a moment, trying to come up with the right words. Finally, she said, "It is just that, my mother seemed preoccupied with this 'calamity'."

Toshi nodded in agreement. "Yes? What of it?" he prodded.

"She spent so much of her attention and focus on it that I wonder if she did not miss the bigger picture. I mean, think about it: she and I were both in a place that neither of us can explain. We came back from the other side of death."

"Yeah?" Toshi said, unsure where she was going with all of this.

"Does it not make you wonder what that place was? It is as if there is this entire world that we are unaware of, yet we live our lives in this little bubble thinking that what we see around us is all that there is. Even given a glimpse of the other side my mother still chose to focus her attention on things over here: I mean saving the world and protecting me, but to what end? What if all of this does not matter?

What if ultimately it is what is on the other side that matters? What if all of her focus and study was wasted on the wrong things?"

"I can see this is important to you," Toshi said, "and I see your point. If we are to save everyone, then what are we saving them from? What exactly is it that is on the other side of death?"

"Precisely," Julia agreed, "If we do not know what that was, then how can we know that what we are doing here is the right thing? How can one know what is right?"

"In my country, it is a little different than here. Here everyone does not think about death at all. They go about like it will never happen to them, and when it does strike close, they ignore it. In my country, we believe that when you go over to the other place, you just come back again to here: like what makes you gets rearranged and returns anew."

"Like melting down old pots or something to forge them into something new?" Julia analogized. "I do not know. It felt more permanent than all that. I mean, I was still me, but there was something more. This strange presence surrounded me. It was like the purest love one can imagine. It was personal too, not just this vague feeling but as if I had awoken from a dream to remember that there was my great love next to me: one I had been seeking all this time yet there he was right beside me and I had somehow in my dream forgotten. I felt he was waiting in the light for me to return to him. At the time it was like I knew him intimately, but now that I am back the memory has faded quickly. Who or what was that?"

Toshi shrugged, "Why would you forget something that important? Maybe it was then that you were dreaming?"

Julia was troubled by it even more so by the lack of answers Toshi could supply. What was it she had experienced? Why was it now so hard to recall that love that made every other love she had ever felt seem inconsequential?

286

●　●　●　●　●　●　●

Days passed as the three traveled, not stopping until dusk when they would set down camp for the night. It was difficult with nothing between the towns, but there were a few places travelers gathered to rest for the night so that some might keep watch. They were lucky one night to run into such a group headed in the opposite direction as them.

"We headed to Paultry, but when we arrived in town the gates were locked shut, and no one was being admitted," one of the travelers explained. "So here we are headed back with empty hands and stomachs."

"What is it you are selling?" Areal asked. It seemed none of the travelers recognized him.

"Selling?" the man said in surprise, "Oh! No, no we are not merchants. We are musicians! So I suppose you could say we sell love and hope and shenanigans!"

"By what name do you go?" Areal asked intrigued.

"You do not know?" the man jested. "We are the 'Tula Brothers'. This is my brother Jay, my other brother Roy and my other-other brother Guy. And I am Bob! I am the leader and the most talented." At this remark Bob's brothers laughed, each insisting that it was he who was the true talent of the group.

Julia laughed when she heard the name. "I have heard of them! They are quite famous in Pent," she whispered to Toshi, who in turn informed Areal.

"You have played for the great Ramoth?" Areal said as he acted impressed. "Why then, but we are simple travelers yet might we impress on you to astound us with your craft?"

The troupe whispered between themselves before agreeing they should be paid in supper. For that evening the brothers played many songs as Toshi and Julia danced around the campfire.

The first they boasted was the most popular, and after that, the rest would have to do. On Areal's suggestion, they made up a silly song about a king who loved cheese more than silver. Eventually, they all settled down to sleep, Julia still humming one of the tunes to herself. She would often do that from that day forward, particularly on the lonely days to come.

• • • • • • •

Deep in the night, something startled Julia awake. She could not fathom what it had been: an owl or an acorn falling from a tree? She looked around, but everyone was asleep save her father who was sitting near the campfire tending to it. She wondered if he could not sleep or if he was trying to keep an eye out for everyone, yet he did not seem his usual jovial self. His rounded cheeks were pale, and his shoulders slumped. He was toying with the small key that was still around his neck.

It worried her to see him like this. She wondered if her leaving would be too much for him, or if there was something else on his mind. Either way, she would not disturb him. Moments of quiet to reflect were few and far between for him.

• • • • • • •

In the morning the entire group headed out to Paultry. Areal had convinced the Tula Brothers to return, guaranteeing them that as a close friend of the royal house he would assure their entrance into the city. They would not arrive until it was close to dusk, but the familiar sight of the tiny village nestled into the valley at the foot of the hills made Julia's heart leap with joy.

At the main gate the guards initially stopped them, but to the Tula Brothers' amazement when the guards saw Areal, they quickly allowed the group to enter. An impromptu celebration broke out in the town square as the citizens came out of their dwellings to cheer the return of their king. The Tula Brothers played their music, and everyone was dancing and singing.

While the celebration continued, Areal marched into the castle triumphant with Julia and Toshi. He was excited to tell Brinna that he was back, but when Areal entered the throne room, all he found was Bess. She was surrounded by a group of three men who were rubbing her shoulders and offering her raisins. Areal cleared his throat to get her attention. She seemed annoyed by the interruption, but upon seeing who was standing before her, she quickly changed her demeanor: slumping her shoulders and lowering her head.

"What in the world is going on here?" Areal insisted.

The servants scattered, leaving Bess to explain. "It is not what it looks like!" she insisted. Seeing all of the food scattered about she added, "I did not touch your cheese while you were gone. You can check and see that it is all still there!"

"That is because I have the key to the cell!" Areal snapped back, patting his chest where the small, silver key rested.

Timidly Bess walked over to Areal and returned his signet ring before explaining, "I'll be returning this now. Brinna left me in charge, but we are happy you have returned."

"She left?" Areal said astounded. "Where did she go? Who gave her permission?"

Bess had just noticed Toshi and the mysteriously cloaked woman standing by the doorway. She was distracted by them for a moment before looking back to Areal.

Ignoring his question, she asked, "Where is Julia? Didn't you go to bring her back? Is she safe? We heard that Pent..."

"There is no easy way to say this, Bess, but Julia is dead. Robbers killed her." Areal said. "I had been on my way to save her when I saw it happen. You know how dangerous those roads can be. I guess she was trying to return here on her own."

Bess crumpled into Areal's arms and began to cry. Julia motioned to comfort her, but Toshi grabbed her arm and stopped her, shaking his head at her. Areal hugged Bess, trying to calm her down.

"It is just so unfair!" Bess lamented. "You see, Queen Brinna received a letter from Ramoth explaining that Pent was under attack and that your fleet should be sent at once."

"And...?" Areal anxiously asked.

"And so she gathered your fleet and left immediately," Bess sobbed. "Did she make it in time? Are the others okay?"

Areal shook his head. "I never made it to Pent. I returned once I knew Julia's fate. I am certain though that Pent is no longer in danger. I mean, no I am certain as one of Ramoth's men told me everything is fine. The fleet ought to return soon."

"That is small relief now," Bess sniffled.

"What was she thinking? I am glad that Pent is safe, but I told Brinna not to let anyone in or out," Areal grumbled to no one in particular.

"Oh, I guess I should have explained it better," Bess continued, "The queen said that if she sent the fleet and was able to free Pent that the first thing she would do once she was certain that everyone was okay would be to demand that Ramoth, in turn, fulfill his debt to her.

"You see in the letter, it said in it that Ramoth would be indebted to you if you helped him. Queen Brinna said that Ramoth made that promise a lot, but no one ever collected on it for fear of displeasing him, but that he could not deny her. Not that it matters if she demanded the engagement be called off if Julia is gone."

"The engagement is off?" Julia exclaimed.

The princess ripped her hood off and ran to hug her friend, but Bess in seeing her screeched a loud, shrill scream before turning pale and dropping to the floor. She fell quickly so that Areal failed to catch her, and she hit the ground in such a way that the whole castle seemed to shake.

Areal scowled at Julia, but he was also trying not to laugh. Tears of relief rolled down his cheeks as he tried to get Bess off the floor.

Chapter Twenty-Three: A Calm

The Tula Brothers remained in Paultry for several months after their arrival. Julia enjoyed going to their shows in the evenings after she and Toshi finished her studies for the day. The young woman continued to wear her grandmother's hooded gown, though she no longer needed to hide her face. Instead, she was able to be out in the light, laughing and enjoying the familiar sights and smells she had longed for.

Occasionally she ran into Lucian and his new bride, but he acted as if they did not know one another. In a way this was true. She felt different on the inside. Her priorities were slowly changing, and she was beginning to see the world almost as if it were an illusion while the other side she had witnessed became reality. All the little things that had been so important before faded away and only the things she had been able to hold onto on the other side, relationships she nurtured with those she loved, seemed important.

It was late fall when Paultry's fleet returned from Pent. Julia was unaware of it until she came out of her bedroom and heard crowds cheering in the streets. She ran outside to see what the commotion was only to be greeted by the sight of the sailors parading through the streets, cheering and carrying with them treasures offered as gifts by her uncle.

She hurried to find her father so that he might meet up with them as they gathered in the main square outside of the castle. There he welcomed them back, applauded their brave efforts, and ordered the day to be a holiday. Julia took this to mean that for today her studies were on hold. Before Toshi could stop her, she ran into the crowds to find something fun to do.

She ended up sitting in the square watching the crowds dance to the Tula Brothers' music which she had come to love. It was blustery that morning, with the winds scattering newly fallen leaves over the dancers. She pulled her cowl tightly around her arms and sat on the edge of a flower box. She had bought herself a fresh pastry from the bakery and slowly nibbled it while tapping her foot to the music.

She was keeping an eye out for Bess hoping that she would join her, but as she scanned the crowd a man from across the square caught her eye. Her breathing stopped, and her heart leapt into her throat. She wanted to run away but was choking on her breakfast. The man approached her and wrapped his arms around her.

"David?" she muttered, "What are you doing here?"

He continued to hold her while whispering, "I thought you were dead. It is so good to see you."

"It is good to see you too," Julia uttered, though she was afraid he was about to throw her over his shoulder and drag her from town.

"How did you escape?" David asked once he finally let her go. "I mean, the last time we were together you were being dragged away by Johnathan. I am so sorry that I could not save you. We were looking everywhere for you."

David's countenance fell remembering their time in Daven. Julia reached out and squeezed his hand.

"I think you got the worst of it," she assured him. "For a while there I was worried you were dead."

"But how did you get away? Were you hurt?" David inquired anxiously. "When we did not receive word from your father that you were okay, I feared the worst! My mother assured me that you were probably fine, that your father was likely keeping you to himself considering what had happened, but I feared the worst."

"I was worried about you too, but when we heard nothing, I thought you must be alright," Julia explained as they sat down on the edge of the stone flower box where Julia had been sitting.

"I still cannot figure out what happened. Why was Johnathan able to do those things he did? Why? Why would he turn on me like that? How did you get away?" David asked, looking out into the crowd. It was clear that the returning sailors knew who he was and often nodded in respect to him in passing while the others in the town paid him no mind.

"A man named Toshi saved me," Julia explained. "He saw Johnathan carrying me through the streets, and he knocked him unconscious. He took me away to his home in the woods where no one would find us."

"Wow," David exclaimed. "That sounds pretty intense. He must be a skilled fighter."

Julia chuckled. "He had a blow gun," she thought to herself, but aloud she said, "Oh yes, he is powerful and wise. He kept me safe in his little cottage until we heard that it was safe for me to return to my father. He had been looking for me you know."

David's brow furrowed. He reached over and took the rest of Julia's pastry, eating it in one bite.

"Yes, my mother told me that he took off looking for the both of us," David said after swallowing the dessert. "I guess he was not happy with the arrangement after all. Do you know what happened to Johnathan? I keep receiving reports that he is dead, but each story is a little different. Some say a group of bear hunters took him down, while others said he was attacked by a bear or a mountain lion or something. How was anything able to stop him?"

Julia feigned ignorance. "I have no idea. Toshi had just heard that he had been killed. That is all I know. Maybe he had been on some drug or something, and when it wore off, he was defeated."

"I would like to meet this 'Toshi' fellow and thank him in person," David said after thinking about Julia's idea for a few moments. "Perhaps he could tell us more. Where can I find him?"

"He is here," Julia confessed, "though he is a bit reclusive. You should let me talk to him to let him know you are coming."

"That is hardly necessary!" David insisted. "I just want to ask him if he knows anything about what happened."

"How about we all have dinner tonight?" Julia suggested. "I can make sure he is there."

"You two have become close, have you not? Is that why you are keeping him from me? I am sure you guessed that our engagement is officially off," David said as he did a little dance in his seat to show her he was happy the engagement was over. "You do not have to hide your feelings," he continued with a wink.

Julia's face turned red from embarrassment. Though David was joking with her, she got the impression there was a deep sadness behind his jesting.

"No, no it is nothing like that," Julia insisted. "He has become something of a mentor to me. What about you? Have you met anyone special?"

David's face became serious again, "No, I have been so busy with repairing Pent I have not had much time for anything else. It is so strange: when I was engaged to you it seemed that there were all these women throwing themselves at me, but as soon as the engagement was off they disappeared. It is funny how that works."

"Johnathan told me about the girl, the one who…" Julia hesitated to say.

David nodded. "Did he?" he murmured.

"I am sorry for the things that I said to you when we were here in Paultry," Julia said. "I had no idea what you had been through. My pain so blinded me that I could not imagine the same pain lived in others."

"It seems to be more common than we think," David agreed, "but do not feel as if you need to apologize. The whole situation was not our faults. Tell me, did Johnathan tell you anything else while you were together? Did he tell you why he was so angry with me?"

Julia turned away from David. His sadness was palpable. She did not want to lie to him, but she also was not sure how to comfort him.

"He did not say anything to me," she lied, "but he was acting so irrationally we can only deduce that something caused a madness in him that was not logical. The Johnathan we knew and adored loved us back, David. Of that I am certain."

● ● ● ● ● ● ●

That night Julia arranged for everyone: Areal, Brinna, David, Toshi, Bess, and herself, to have dinner together. Toshi at first refused, stating he would not share a meal with anyone like David, but at Julia's insistence, he relented.

After having spent most of the day celebrating Julia was excited to have a warm place to rest for a while. Her uncle's presence had marred the previous meal they had shared. Tonight he was happily absent: attending to the affairs of Pent as Brinna would explain. So the evening was relaxed and cheerful.

At his mother's urging, David recounted the tale of how he had "saved" Pent. He went on to explain that because of this the citizens had wanted to make him king, much to his father's chagrin. However, David knew he still had a bit more to learn. David believed getting rid of him for a while was part of the reason his father had suggested that he and Brinna return with the fleet to Paultry for a while.

Toshi was cold to David at first, but once he heard of how he had tried to protect Julia, he began to warm up to him. By the end of the evening, he was marveling them all with tales of Mesu and his time there before he had become a hermit in the woods. When asked about Johnathan he followed Julia's lead and claimed he did not know what had happened.

As Julia listened, she wanted to tell David that she planned on traveling to Mesu soon, but he already seemed so burdened by the recent loss of Johnathan that she did not think it wise to worry him further. She was not even sure how long she would be gone. She hoped it would be only a few months or maybe a year at most, but she had no way of knowing how long it would take to acquire the knowledge that she needed.

David remained with them a week before he and Brinna boarded their vessel back to Pent. The Tula Brothers would be traveling with them. They were particularly excited to return to their fan base in Pent and had offered by way of fare to play for the royal family during the trip.

Julia waited on the pier until their ship was out of sight. She wondered if she would ever see David again. Though she had been frightened when he first arrived, things seemed to have returned to what they were between them before Marcus had interfered. Now she wished her cousin, no, her brother would find someone who would love him more than she did.

The weather was becoming increasingly chilly. Areal implored Toshi to wait until the spring to make the trip to Mesu, but Toshi insisted that there was no more time to waste. The day after David left, Julia and Toshi boarded her father's fastest vessel on its way to the capital city of Mesu, which was called Ghanrey.

Three days into the trip they made a smooth voyage to Breka which was west of Paultry. They harbored there one night and then followed the coast for another three days. On the seventh day of their trip, they reached the mouth of the Chay River, which led directly to Ghanrey. The journey up the river lasted about a week and took them further south. The water here was crystal clear so that you could see all the way to the bottom of the riverbed.

On the last day of the journey, the Chay River expanded to a crystal-clear lake called Lake Boda. To the west was Chay Falls, where the Chay and Char rivers joined just as they came tumbling over a cliff made of pure white limestone. Between the two rivers on the edge of the cliff sat Ghanrey.

As Julia would find out, the waters of the Chay River were considered sacred though those of the Char were not, because the Chay River had its origins in the Venom Mountains, as where the Char came from lakes to the west. In hearing this, Julia could not help but remember the grotto at Faverly with the water and the strange, glowing symbols. She remembered there had been a waterfall there too, but it seemed to drain into a lake at the base of the mountain according to what her mother told her.

Toshi and Julia left the crew of the ship onboard while they scaled a steep set of stairs that were carved into the side of the cliff to the right of the falls. These led to an ornate bridge that allowed them to cross the Char River and enter the city.

The city itself had many channels carved into the streets and walkways that carried the water of the rivers into the heart of the town. It was the citizen's way of bringing good fortune. They explained that there was something magical about the mixture of the sacred with the ordinary that made the location special.

All of the women were dressed as Julia was in long gowns with matching hooded cowls of black, brown and navy. The buildings were made of white limestone with green roofs. That was because the roofs were made of copper that had rusted in the moist air. In the center of town, the waters that filled the channels pooled to create a fountain.

Toshi insisted Julia dip her toes into the channel for good luck. It seemed a bit silly, but she did it anyway. She could not understand how they could think the water itself was special. Without her mother, the water would do nothing extraordinary. Besides, she had been able to feel a strange energy from Anny just as she could sense from Johnathan, yet the water made her feel nothing. It was just water to her.

Satisfied that they were properly blessed, Toshi found a small shop and sat down to eat lunch. He ate so fervently that he did not seem to have time to breathe between bites.

He ate until his stomach poked out, and when Julia tried to speak to him, he raised his hand to her indicating she should stop. He ate all of his food and then began to eat Julia's as well. She had to slap his hand to keep him from taking her last portion.

"I am never going back," he said after pushing his plates away and sitting back in his chair. "No never. I can never go back to eating that slop you call food."

Julia laughed. She had to agree the food here was better: covered in seasoning and fried in cast iron skillets rather than being boiled. The young woman wondered if the fresh mountain stream water made a difference. It was interesting to see Toshi enjoying his familiar surroundings while she seemed so out of place. Julia suddenly appreciated what Paultry must have felt like to him.

"We need to speak to the king," Toshi said. "We will need his help if we are to be allowed travel to Nasairre."

"Nasairre?" Julia asked surprised. "I thought we would be studying here."

"Yes, well I fibbed a bit. I was afraid your father would not let us travel that far. Ghanrey might be the capital, but it is not the most sacred place of the Huhus. To get to the most ancient of texts, we would have to travel to Nasairre, and the only way to get there is with the aid of the king. Only his ships are allowed to dock there."

"Now you tell me?" Julia scoffed. "What of my father's vessel?"

"I already told them to return in a few years!" Toshi boasted.

Julia's stared at him in shock before saying, "You did what?"

"I am only trying to make this as easy on you as possible!" Toshi said as he got up from the table and began to walk away. "Surely you must have known this would be a long and cumbersome journey, but to get to the truth, there is no other way!"

As angry as she was, Julia had no choice but to follow Toshi to the south side of the city where the castle for the king rested near the edge of the cliffs.

.

Chapter Twenty-Four: A Ghanrey Welcome

They waited for hours before they were granted an audience, despite Toshi mentioning several times that Julia was a princess from Paultry. Once an audience was granted, they were ushered into the king's private chamber. It was full of a strange smoke that rose from tiny metal dishes with bits of incense burning in them. Long, ornate tapestries covered the walls in red and gold colored thread broken by tall, square windows that gave a grand view of Lake Boda beyond. A figure rose and greeted them warmly

Julia was genuinely surprised to meet the handsome ruler, Durhan. He was not much older than herself and a good foot taller with smooth, soft skin and eyes so dark that when she looked into them, she thought that she was looking into the night sky. He moved gracefully, like royalty ought, yet smiled so warmly that she was put at ease as if they had known each other for many years.

"Welcome to Ghanrey, Princess Julia of Paultry!" he said to her in her language as he took her hand. "It is my pleasure to meet you."

"The pleasure is mine," Julia said back in his dialect.

Durhan was impressed and commented with a chuckle, "You speak our language! Well, that is a relief. I know only a little of what is spoken on the other side of the mountains."

"This is Toshi," Julia explained as she motioned to her traveling companion. "He is from your land and has been teaching me your ways. I am still learning."

Durhan smiled at her, and the two just stood with goofy smiles on their faces before Toshi interjected.

"It is a pleasure to make your acquaintance, King Durhan. When last I was here your father was still on the throne."

Durhan shook his head from side to side, "Oh, no, no. My father is still the ruler here. I am just filling in for him as he is away on a hunting expedition. This time of year, the deer begin to migrate south close to here. He will return in a week or so. In the meantime, I have the pleasure of hosting my distinguished guests! Julia, would you be willing to accompany me to dinner tonight?"

"That would be most appreciated," Julia gushed. She smiled at Toshi, but he was grimacing. "Toshi will join us, of course," she added.

"Naturally!" Durhan replied as he motioned to a small seating area.

The three sat down, and moments later servants began carrying in dishes the likes of which Julia had never seen before. There were large, coral pink fish with pointy, sharp teeth grilled whole and tiny bowls with a brown sauce to dip the meat in. There were vegetables as well to dunk into the sauce and a white dessert pudding that Julia had never seen. When she erroneously tried the fish with the pudding, both men held their laughter until after she had tasted it.

Toshi's mood had sharply improved with the prince's invitation to dinner, and they both seemed to enjoy having to show Julia what proper etiquette looked like. Toshi decided to wait until after his belly was once again full to bring up Nasairre.

"Does your father go hunting often?" Julia was asking as Toshi stuffed the last bit of his pudding into his mouth.

Durhan nodded, "I would say so: in the spring and fall when the deer are migrating. There are woods far north of here where they spend the summer. My father must know every trail they like to follow because he comes back with many deer. It will make for an enjoyable winter! Does your father hunt?"

"Oh, no! Never," Julia chuckled. "He will go fishing sometimes, but I think it is just an excuse to go out on the water for the day. He never brings anything back."

"I would like to learn to hunt like my father, but as I am the oldest, I must remain here. I have a younger brother who goes with him. The stories they tell! I wish I could be a part of them. You must understand what that is like."

Julia nodded, "Yes, it can be quite the burden, but there are benefits too I suppose."

"Yes indeed," the prince asserted, "yet here your father has let you travel all the way out here! What is the purpose of your travels? Not that I am unhappy that you have decided to come. Tell me what your desire is, and I will do anything to make you smile, sweet Julia."

"We have come seeking your permission to travel to Nasairre," Toshi interjected before Julia could speak.

"Nasairre?" Durhan asked, "Why would you wish to travel there?"

Toshi tried to sound casual about it as he explained, "We are seeking whatever knowledge we can of the Huhus. We have already done what we can from Paultry. Without your help, we can go no further."

Durhan looked distressed. "That place is forbidden," he reasoned aloud. "I am not certain that I can give such permission in my father's absence. Then again, if we wait until he returns, he might refuse your request. Why are you studying the Huhus?"

Durhan directed his last question at Julia.

"Well," she hesitated, "I believe the Huhus had knowledge of some strange activities that have been occurring in Arden. There are things that we cannot explain, nor have our resources offered anything in the way of an explanation."

"What sort of strange things?" Durhan asked, genuinely intrigued.

"Unusual storms," Toshi said, "earthquakes…that sort of thing."

Durhan nodded, "I can see why that would be concerning, but I will have to think on this matter before I can give you a reply. You two will be staying with us tonight? I insist! In the morning I will give you my answer."

●●●●●●●

Julia and Toshi reluctantly agreed and were shown to separate rooms in the castle. It was becoming late in the evening, and Julia was exhausted. She dropped her bag by the door and tumbled into the bed fully dressed. She was dozing off when there was a knock on her door. It was Durhan.

"I am so sorry to disturb you," he said upon seeing her sleepy expression.

"It is alright, really," Julia insisted. "I was just resting my eyes! Would you like to come in?"

"No, I am afraid given the circumstances that would not be appropriate. I was hoping you might join me this evening."

Julia agreed and began to follow him down the hall.

"You see," Durhan continued, "this time of evening I like to go out on my boat onto the lake, but there is seldom anyone to go with. Would you keep me company?"

"I would be happy to," Julia said.

The two made way down the hall and eventually were descending a steep set of stone stairs just outside the castle walls that ended in an alcove underneath the city. There Durhan's ship was moored. It was big enough for four people to sail in it but small enough that Durhan could comfortably sail it himself. He directed the boat to the middle of the lake before lowering the sail. He was sitting across from her, and for a little while he merely pointed out the various buildings they could see from the boat. She was able to quickly identify the tall windows that were part of the king's private chamber.

"It is really lovely here," Julia said as she gazed up at the city. She noted her father's ship was indeed gone from the pier where they had left it.

"It truly is," Durhan said, though he was looking at her. "The sun will be setting soon. You do not want to miss it. Once it goes down, we can count the stars together."

Julia tried not to react, but her lips crept into a smile. "Do you treat all of your guests like this?" she kidded him.

"All of them," Durhan insisted. "It is only polite even if it makes some of them uncomfortable. Now let me ask you something. What are you really doing here?"

Julia shrugged. "What do you mean? We are looking for passage to Nasairre."

"Yes, but why? What business does a beautiful young lady have with that place?" Durhan asked as he leaned in to hear her response.

"As Toshi said, we are just looking for some answers," Julia remarked.

"I have a feeling Toshi is not being completely honest with me," Durhan confessed. He grinned at Julia's surprised expression before continuing, "He might be a skilled talker, but you wear your thoughts for all to see. I saw how you reacted when he told me that there had been earthquakes and storms near your home. Why else would I have to steal you away so that we might have a quiet moment alone to chat about it?"

"Is that the only reason?" Julia asked.

"It is not even the best reason," Durhan assured her, "but if you are to be my wife, we have to be honest with one another."

"Wife?" Julia blurted out. She was surprised and happy all at the same time, but suddenly she was unsure she was hearing him right.

Ignoring her comment entirely Durhan continued, "Why are you really headed to Nasairre? It is not a friendly place. I would be worried about you."

"What is there to be worried about?" Julia asked. "Is it that dangerous?"

"What exactly has Toshi told you about the place?" Durhan asked.

"Almost nothing, I guess. Just that the Huhus studied there and that is where we will likely find the best materials to study."

Durhan raised an eyebrow before commenting, "He did not mention 'Tu Vertan'? How would you say, 'Death's Gate'?"

"Death's Gate?" Julia gasped.

"Yes, the Huhus believed it was possible to create beings that could never die. They were far advanced from where even we are now. They tried to manipulate first the elements around them and then eventually life itself. They built Tu Vertan and claimed that by it one could travel to the other side of death and then back again. One by one they entered the gate until all were gone, but none ever returned.

"We could not destroy the gate for fear that the innocent might come back, and so instead a patrol was put in place. The Guards of Nasairre protect that place from anyone who would try to enter that gateway and from anything that might come back out. Anyone who steps foot on that island without permission is put to death. Even those given permission are not always allowed to return from that place. It is not something pleasant to think about, but if its secrets were to be understood, you can imagine how dangerous that could be. Mesu has many enemies."

"*Do not enter the forbidden gate,*" Julia thought to herself. To Durhan, she said, "I am surprised Toshi did not mention these things. I will have to speak to him about it. Maybe he does not know."

"Please do," Durhan urged her, "because if you find that it is not a trip worth taking, I would hope that you would consider staying here with me instead."

Julia was not sure what to say. She looked away from Durhan up into the night sky. The brightest of stars were beginning to shine.

"I can sense it in you, Julia," Durhan confessed after they had sat in silence looking up to the sky for some time. "Oh, I am sure you will deny it, though your face betrays you. My family came to power because we could feel the essence of others, and now I sense in you the energy that was spoken of in the legends of the Huhus. They claimed

306

that within everyone was the capacity, but that our essence was so tied to our bodies that only death could release it. For those who came back, the essence was not bound as tightly so that it could escape the body and perform what we might consider unnatural things.

"I imagine that is why Toshi wishes to take you there. Perhaps he senses it too. I have never thought it something to fear, but there are those who fear it and would attempt to snuff it out. Still, you do not have to go. I will permit you simply because you ask it, but please do not go. Stay here with me. I feel a connection to you that I cannot explain. We could have a happy life here."

Julia smiled at Durhan and assured him that she would think of it. Then she sat beside him with his arm around her and together they tried to count the stars.

●●●●●●●

The following morning after getting herself presentable Julia went in search of Toshi. She knew where to find him. He was once again stuffing his face in the king's chamber.

"Look at what Durhan has presented to us!" Toshi said between bites as he pointed to the table.

There were small cakes and hot cups of tea. It appeared Toshi had consumed the majority of it in her absence. Julia sat down and grabbed the last bit of cake before pouring herself a cup of tea.

"Durhan has been a most gracious host. I quite like him," Julia remarked before sipping her tea.

"He has a good palate for sure! I have not had 'yakay' since I was a boy, "Toshi said pointing at the cake. "You see all those layers? There is cream between each one. I have no idea how they do it. Delicious!"

"You are getting fat," Julia pointed out.

Toshi laughed as he grabbed his stomach and said, "No I am not! This is just what a healthy belly looks like! Besides, I will need my energy if we are to travel further.

Have you heard from Durhan yet? Have we his permission?"

"We do, but there are things we need to talk about first," Julia said, putting her tea down.

Toshi was eyeing her cake. She quickly took a bite before he could steal it from her.

"What sort of things do we need to talk about?" Toshi asked, clearly disappointed that there was no more cake.

"Wow, this is good," Julia said as she savored the bite. For a moment the cake made her forget what they had been talking about, but then she looked at Toshi and said, "Why did you never tell me about Tu Vertan?"

"Tu Vertan?" Toshi said, "I have never heard of that."

"Oh, come now!" Julia scoffed, "You know about the Huhus but not about their greatest 'achievement'?"

"Oh, that Tu Vertan! It slipped my mind. You know us old people!" Toshi said. "I better get packed up! It is getting late!"

"You stop right there!" Julia said, banging her fist on the table. "Sit back down and talk to me or we are not going anywhere. That is better. Now tell me, why did you not tell me about the 'Death Gate'?"

"In my defense, it was called "Tu Grasa" when I was a boy: the 'Life Gate'," Toshi said with a nervous grin.

Julia did not look impressed. She stared at him until he continued and whenever he hesitated, she glared at him until he went on.

"All right," he said sullenly, "I will tell you. I mean, I always intended to tell you, but I thought it better to wait until we got to Nasairre. You see, when I was a boy, there was a renewed interest in the Huhus. A man whose name no one speaks started a cult. They took over Nasairre and began to study the gateway. He believed that he could end Ramoth's advance.

"You see, by that time Ramoth had already taken Pacia to our south and was using their warriors to threaten Dione to our east. Our king, Durhan's grandfather, King Leeman had gathered all of our bravest and was heading towards the southern border in anticipation of an attack which left Nasairre vulnerable. It is located far out to the north in the sea. When the man and his cult attacked, they took the guards prisoner.

"I guess those men were not enough because in the night they would attack ports and kidnap anyone they could. Those who escaped told us that they were using the prisoners as experiments: throwing them into Tu Vertan. They wanted so desperately for the Huhus to return, but no one ever came back. In their desperation, the cult members began sacrificing themselves, but they were not able to return either.

"Eventually their leader was captured in a small fishing village trying to kidnap more people. Before he was executed, I begged him to tell me what had happened to my parents, but he just laughed at me. I was a young boy then, powerless to do anything. We went to Nasairre looking for those who had been taken, but they were not there.

"I have dreamed of my parents every night since they went missing. I hear them calling out to me, begging me to end their lives. Wherever they are, it is not life or death. It is something far worse."

"I am so sorry," Julia said. "I had no idea."

"I thought if I could bring you to Tu Vertan you might be able to tell me if you could sense them there," Toshi admitted. "If there is a chance for me to save them, then I am going in there, and I will bring them back."

"That is madness, Toshi!" Julia protested. "If the others did not return than neither will you. It is obvious that there is only one person who could go in there with any hope of coming back."

"I could never ask you to do that," Toshi lamented. "I am an old man. I am willing to go."

"No, I will not let you. Toshi, I cannot be killed. Remember?" Julia said as she reached out to him.

"I know, an 'Eternal Mortal', right?" Toshi scoffed.

Julia hesitated for a moment, his words spinning in her head.

"*In seeking to end it is begun,*" she said. "What if we have this all backward? What if the calamity that we are trying to end has already begun, but it is not something happening here: it is happening in the other realm? By trying to end death, they merely trapped themselves into some space where there is neither life nor death. They would be trapped there forever. If this is the calamity, the text warns of then you must agree only I can stop it. It is my duty."

Toshi shook his head frowning, "We should take this one step at a time. Let us first go to the gate and see. If you cannot sense the others on the other side, then I will not let you enter. We will destroy the gate once and for all."

Julia agreed, realizing that she might have to work on being a more effective deceiver.

● ● ● ● ● ● ●

Durhan was distressed when Julia gave him the news. "How can this be?" he said as he took both her hands. "The boat, the stars, my beautiful eyes! Have none of these things convinced you to stay?"

Julia smiled while looking into his 'beautiful eyes'. "Believe me," she said, "nothing could make me happier, but I must do this."

Durhan scoffed and said, "You are too much like me: always acquiescing to responsibility. Very well then, if I cannot convince you to stay, then I will have to go with you. That way I can be certain no harm comes to you."

"You cannot leave the capitol now!" Julia insisted. To herself, she thought, "Not without Bess around."

"We will just have to wait until my father returns in a few days," Durhan said with a grin. "In the meantime, I can show you the city. I promise it would be just as a courtesy. I am not trying to change your mind! Recall that I do this for all of my guests!"

And tour the city they did. For several days Durhan took Julia to his favorite places, ending each night with a trip in his boat out on the lake to count the stars. Each day felt like a gift as they did not know precisely when Durhan's father would return. He bought her little gifts, one a box made out of the stone that the town was famous for.

When the king did return, Julia was a bit disappointed. She had been hoping for one more day, but now nothing was stopping her from traveling to Nasairre. Early the morning after his return Durhan had one of his ships prepared to go. She and Toshi boarded just before it set sail down the Chay River towards the sea.

● ● ● ● ● ● ●

The trip down the river was much faster than it had been trying to travel upstream. The crew worked diligently navigating them towards the coast, and from there the ship headed due north out into open water. Julia had never been this far out to sea before. She had enjoyed watching the waves splash beneath them in the clear river water, but here the ocean was dark as if it would swallow you whole.

Durhan sensed her unease and tried to comfort her. He wrapped his arm around her as she sat on the deck of the ship looking out over the bow. "What are you thinking about?" he asked as he pulled a blanket he had brought over them. The wind was chilly this time of year and the further north they traveled the colder it became.

"I was just wondering how I am going to convince Toshi and you to allow me to do what I have to do," she said. "You know, you never asked me what I plan to do once we arrive in Nasairre."

"There is no need to," Durhan said flatly. "I trust you. I love you. What else do I need to know? When this is all over, I expect we will sail out to Larmond, and I will treat you to the delicacies there."

"You are taking this hospitality thing much too far," Julia joked.

"Yes, well if I might be serious for a moment there is something I meant to ask you. I was going to wait until this matter was settled, but I find I cannot hold myself back any longer."

"Alright?" Julia said, wondering why he was suddenly acting nervous.

"Julia, from the moment I met you I did sense something special about you. You are a princess, and I am a prince. Your country and mine have always had cordial relations. You are beautiful, and I am beautiful. It would seem we could make something of this. I know I have joked about it a bit in the past, but in all seriousness, I would like you to consider marrying me."

"'Marrying'?" Julia parroted back. "What does that word mean?"

"Oh, well you become my wife and I your husband? Does that explain it?"

Julia was not entirely shocked, but not prepared for him to say what he had either.

"What if I say 'no'?" she asked.

"I would be devastated, of course!" Durhan said, holding her even tighter.

"Well then, I guess I would have no choice but to accept, assuming our fathers agreed, naturally," Julia said with a smile.

"I am sure we can convince them," Durhan said as he leaned in and kissed her.

● ● ● ● ● ● ●

Toshi was fast asleep below deck when Julia crept up next to him. It was early the next morning. Most of the crew was already busily tending to the ship above them. She was eyeing his bag. She reached out to open it, but before she could get to it Toshi's hand snapped up and grabbed her by the wrist.

"What are you doing?" he asked. "My ears are old, but you are clumsy."

Julia grumbled, "You know what I want. Toshi, we are going to have to talk about this before we get to Nasairre."

Toshi turned away from her in the bed and mumbled, "When we get to Nasairre I will give you anything that you need. Until then I keep everything with me, you understand? I am not making the same mistake twice."

"Toshi, I cannot do this alone," Julia insisted. "Listen to me; you know this is the only way that I can bring them back. I want you to promise me you will do it."

"I promised before, but now that you are being sneaky I wonder if I should make you promise you will not doubt me again!" Toshi said.

"I promise! I do! Why do you not trust me?" Julia said as she smiled at him.

"You are a bad liar, little one," Toshi said as he went back to sleep.

Chapter Twenty-Five: Nasairre

After traveling another day, they spotted Nasairre in the distance. The crew raised the royal banner so that the guards on the island would not attempt to harm them. The island was small with only one pier to moor at. There were two guards keeping watch on the dock and two more holed up in a tower that overlooked the ocean.

In seeing the prince, the guards put down their weapons and greeted them. Julia wondered if she ought to have covered her face as she stepped off the boat. The men were looking at her like they had not seen a woman in a long time.

"Prince Durhan!" one of the guards exclaimed. "What brings you out to this wretched place?"

"It is dreary," Durhan noted. "Ah, but before business let me introduce you to Julia, my betrothed."

Toshi was so caught off guard that he almost fell off the pier.

"Oh, and that is Toshi. We have come to see Tu Vertan," Durhan continued.

The men looked uneasily from one to the other. "We are glad that you are here," the guard replied. "We have been hearing strange noises coming from that gate the last few days. It is like someone is knocking on the other side. We are all concerned but prepared to face whatever might come out."

"Well there is your answer," Julia said to Toshi. "I have been able to sense a great power too as we approached. There is no question now what must be done."

Toshi's face had gone pale. He did not speak, he only nodded.

"Take us to Tu Vertan," Julia ordered.

Dark clouds had been swirling overhead for days, but now the winds began to howl as the group made their way up to the top of the peak at the center of the island. From there one could see the ocean stretching out for miles in all directions. Far below there was the pier and their ship. Close to that, she could see the small camp where the guards lived.

The gate was located in the center of a flat rocky clearing on the top of the peak. There was a stone archway covered in glowing symbols. A heavy wooden door was secured inside of the arch. One could see both sides of the door, but only one side had a handle. Julia was surprised that the door looked nothing like the one she remembered from Faverly.

Julia walked up to the gate and ran her fingers over the glowing symbols. They looked like the ones she had seen in the grotto, but they were different somehow. She pulled her mother's book out of her bag to compare what she saw to the drawings.

"This symbol is upside down," she thought aloud, "or are mine drawn backward?"

"What do you see?" Toshi asked. He had been following behind her a short distance.

"I am just comparing these symbols to the ones in the book," she remarked.

"What symbols?" Toshi asked, coming a bit closer.

"These ones," Julia said as she pointed to the arch and dropped the book back into her bag. She soon realized that only she could see them.

"Alright, Toshi," Julia said firmly. "You said you would give me what I needed when it was time. It is time."

"What are you two whispering about?" Durhan asked. He came up to them and looked at the arch as he said, "It just looks like a normal door to me."

Toshi handed Julia what she asked for. She slipped it into her pocket, then Julia turned to Durhan.

"Durhan, what I am about to do I have to do, or I would not be the person you love," she explained.

"Come again?" Durhan asked.

"I am going through that door," Julia said. "No, do not say anything! I will be safe. I know of another way: another door that leads out of whatever darkness is in there. I will rescue the others. I will lead them out of that dark place and to safety. I need you to destroy this gate as soon as I am through. Take the arch apart and smash every last stone to pebbles. Burn the door. That is the only way to end this. Then you can all be free of this place. Burn the pier or smash it before you go. Then meet me at Faverly. I will be waiting there for you."

Durhan searched her eyes, then looked skeptically at Toshi who nodded back reassuringly. Durhan nodded slowly back.

With that, Durhan said to Julia, "I will do as you ask. Whatever you say, my love."

"I love you too, Durhan," Julia said. She kissed him once more, then waved to Toshi and called out, "I will see you later! Make sure everything is done as I asked of you!"

Toshi nodded, then watched as Julia turned and opened the door. Though there was nothing to see, she vanished into thin air as she passed through the archway. A gust of wind slammed the door shut behind her. After the door closed the winds suddenly calmed, the clouds vanished, and the ocean became perfectly still.

● ● ● ● ● ● ●

As soon as Julia had passed through the archway, the entire space went dark. She turned around and reached out for the door to close it, but it was gone. Nothing could be seen, but voices could be heard not far away. Julia looked down, but she did not see the light from within herself that she had witnessed after falling from the roof at Faverly. Nor did she sense the loving presence. No, it was quite the opposite. The place dripped of the fear and despair as one feels when they know they have betrayed that perfect love and will never know it again.

316

"Hello?" she called out. "Hello, who is crying?" She inched towards the sound as she reached out into the darkness.

"Who is there?" one voice replied.

"Am I hearing things?" said another.

More voices could be heard, crying and whimpering.

"I hear you, but I cannot find you," Julia called out.

"What a strange accent," a voice whispered. "I do not think we ought to trust it."

"What choice do we have? Where is it coming from?" another voice asked.

Julia's foot finally hit something solid.

"Ouch! Look where you are going! Are we not miserable enough?" it yelled at her.

"Are we going to go through that old bit again? Oh, woe to me!" another voice mocked.

"It is better than nothing. Stop complaining!" the voice replied.

Julia stopped moving and begged, "Oh I am sorry! I am so sorry! I cannot see anything."

"Neither can I!" admitted one voice.

"Nor me!" echoed another.

"All you would be able to see are a bunch of idiots," one sarcastically uttered.

"Oh, shut up!" a voice responded.

"No, you shut up!" the sarcastic one spit back.

"Who said that?" yet another interrupted.

Julia tried to wait for them to stop, but she feared they never would.

Finally, she said, "My name is Julia. I have come to rescue you!"

"Oh, not that old bit again!" a voice mocked.

"You just said that," a voice whispered.

"Well I am tired of this game," the voice replied.

"Then come up with a new one," someone else suggested.

Julia looked around. Wherever they were, it was pitch black. She looked down at her arms, then began to feel around for her pocket. She reached in, and the item inside pricked her finger.

"Ouch!" she thought. "Well, I guess that will do."

Julia waited a moment, then the pain began. It radiated up her arm and down into her chest so that she fell to her knees and struggled to breathe. Julia gasped for air; then her arms began to glow again. Now when she looked down, she could see her pale blue inner light. The pain stopped, and she stood up. The doorway to Faverly was before her.

"This way!" she called out. "Come to me; I know the way out!"

The others began to murmur, then shout as they ran to her.

"I can see it!" one called out.

"Look, I can see it too!" another chimed in.

"Move towards it! Quickly!" said yet another.

"We have waited for so long!" another voice joined in.

She was afraid they might knock her over, so before they could, she pulled open the door and stood off to the side. She then watched as one by one the figures ran through the doorway. The space became silent. The young woman felt a chill run down her spine as she wondered if she was completely alone.

"Anny? Johnathan?" she called out desperately, but there was no response. "Mom?" she tried, but they were not there.

"Is anyone here?" she called out again, but she was sure now that the place was empty and the prisoners free.

Julia sighed in relief. Tears of joy ran down her face as she passed through the gate back to Faverly.

● ● ● ● ● ● ●

When Julia awoke, she was back in the study above the grotto. To her surprise, no one else was there. Her joy quickly faded to panic as she ran up the stairs into the courtyard. She threw open the door and felt the crisp sunlight of a fall's evening. She called out to anyone who might hear.

She recognized the courtyard, but it did not look the same. She could not exactly tell what was different. She checked the kitchen and found some of the pots she remembered were still there, but not nearly as many. The fire was smoldering as if it had been used recently.

She went up to the servant's bedroom and began looking for the dress she had left behind. It was not there. Additionally, many of the beds that had lined the room were missing.

"Where has everything gone?" she wondered. "Where is everyone?"

She heard a noise from the courtyard. With trepidation, she inched towards a window and looked out. She saw a group of men standing in the yard. They had on long robes and were conversing happily with one another.

Suddenly the oddness of the courtyard struck her. "That tree..." she thought. "That tree in the corner is so small. It is just a sapling. It is like it has grown younger."

Then she could hear her mother saying, "*Time is at your fingertips.*"

"Is that how they did it? Is that how they cheated death: by manipulating time? When I passed away in that place...have I gone back how many years?" Julia wondered to herself.

Julia fell to her knees, shaking as she looked down at her grandmother's dress and felt the bump in her pocket where Toshi's dart still rested with a bit of her blood on the poisoned end. She reached into her bag and pulled out the book her mother said belonged to Barnas. She flipped through the pages, confirming to herself that it was unchanged.

In a flash, images of Toshi and Durhan arriving at Faverly only to discover she was not there crossed her mind. She could see the pain in her father's eyes as he learned she was gone. She wondered how David would react.

She wondered what year it was as she hugged the book to her chest. Was her father even alive? Certainly, Durhan might not be. If she journeyed beyond Faverly in search of them might she inadvertently change the future forever?

"The future sets the past," she thought to herself.

She wanted to cry, but this was not the time for it. She waited by the window until the men had gone to the kitchen, then she pulled her hood over her face and ran to the front gate. She was getting the door open when one of the robed men came by.

"Oh my, you startled me!" he said. Seeing the woman standing by the open door he smiled and called out, "We have a visitor! Please, you are welcome to stay. Do not be alarmed. We are very friendly." Julia turned around just as the man said, "My name is Barnas. I am pleased to meet you."

Julia put out her hand and shook his. She hesitated, but his smile put her at ease. She carefully lowered her hood and said, "I am Odlin…"

Made in the USA
Las Vegas, NV
26 September 2021